SWEET PRINCE

The Passion of Hamlet

SWEET PRINCE

THE PASSION OF HAMLET

A NOVEL BY

DOUGLAS BRODE

American Literature Series, v. 2

FAP BOOKS

FLORIDA ACADEMIC PRESS, INC.

Gainesville and London

for
Tyler Reese Brode,
my grandson.

Published in the United States of America by Florida Academic
Press, Gainesville, Fl., May 2004

Library of Congress Catalogue Number:
2004102291

Cover art, Ophelia by Millais © Tate Gallery,
London, by permission. Cover prepared by Gordon Woolf

Copyright © 2004
by
Florida Academic Press
ISBN 1-890357-10-3

INTRODUCTION:
ONCE UPON A TIME
. . . IN DENMARK

As more than one critic has pointed out over the intervening centuries since the Bard wrote what is arguably his greatest play, Shakespeare's *Hamlet* proved so rich in theme, character, poetry and philosophy that each successive generation could believe itself to be mirrored in the work and, more significant still, its title character. Not surprisingly, during the recently expired 20th Century, Hamlet was interpreted for the post-Nietzsche generation as a pioneer Existentialist, a young man in search of truth as to the nature of reality, the original seeker after an answer to our ultimate question: Does anything mean anything, or is life merely, as Hemingway would put it, a dirty biological trick?

During the nineteenth century, however, most serious interpretations had been of a philosophically *romantic* nature, once Goethe decreed that the true tragedy of Hamlet was in providing "a great action laid upon a soul unfit for it." For a hundred years thereafter, audiences were treated to onstage renderings of a 'soft' Hamlet, eventually resulting in the questioning of Hamlet's masculinity.

In other, simpler words: Was Hamlet 'gay'?

Certainly, the tagging of Hamlet as a 'sweet prince' by longtime companion Horatio might lead to just such a conclusion. One cannot imagine Banquo speaking of Macbeth in such terms! Others, however, have offered a far more remarkable alternative. While admitting Hamlet's 'softness,' the American scribe Edward Vining in 1881 provided a devastating answer in his tome, *The Mystery of 'Hamlet'* (Lippincott, Philadelphia), an all-but-forgotten book that was, in its time, swiftly dismissed (however unfairly) by intellectuals and academics as obvious quackery masquerading in the guise of serious criticism. Nonetheless, his ideas were hotly discussed during that century's waning years. Nearly three decades later, Vining's 'outrageous' concept was revived by the Berlin-based writer-director Sven Gade for his epic work *The Dream of Vengeance*, generally considered the most impressive silent cinema treatment of Shakespeare.

As to my novel *Sweet Prince*, I set out to provide what hopefully would be a work that directly addressed today's readers with fresh fuel to the old fire that Vining set a match to and Gade later fanned. The book will, hopefully, serve as one more variation on the legend that Shakespeare provided the definitive version of, yet which existed in popular culture both after and before he created the greatest single play of all time. Also, I consciously hoped to create, for post-millennial readers, an apotheosis of all the differing interpretations of what Hamlet might be thought to 'mean,' as well as earlier archetypes which the Bard drew upon, consciously or not, collected together for the first time in a work which, in attitude, is informed by Shakespeare's play.

His sources included a previous Elizabethan era play on the Hamlet legend. Thomas Kyd, he of the blood-and-thunder brand of dramaturgy, had offered up a *Hamlet* of little style or substance. This, Shakespeare doubtless saw, sensing he could vastly improve upon Kyd's primitive rendering. We do not know whether Will—who, as always, wrote his plays under extreme pressure to provide Burbage with some new work—actually read any of the varied sources preceding Kyd's version, most recently a volume of gory short stories published (in 1608) in London by Thomas Pavier, including one called *Hamblet*.

Pavier had played free and loose with the narrative versions that already existed, adding and deleting as he so chose while adapting story elements discovered in *Histoires Tragiques* by François de Belleforest (Paris, 1570). That Gallic mythmaker likewise felt no compunction to be true to previous versions while reshaping the story as he saw fit. In both these books, the tale has a tragic ending only because that's what their own readers preferred. Such was not the case in *Historica Danica* (circa 1189), a combination of history and legend (no one then felt it necessity to keep the two separate) penned by Saxo Grammaticus. This is the first known volume to set down in print a tale which had already existed, for more than 150 years, as part of the oral tradition in northern Europe. In Saxo, the character known as "Amlethus of Elsinore" (and elsewhere in Danish lore is referred to as Amuleth) effectively achieves revenge against his uncle and lives, if not happily ever after, then at least a full, rich, long life as ruler of Sjalland.

I set out to write an historical romance, less influenced by Shakespeare than true to Denmark in the eleventh century as historians now believe it to have existed. My descriptions of every day life, political turmoil, references to Norse mythology and the existing mindset of that time are presented after years of research, offering an historically accurate portrait of northern Europe at that moment in time when Amlethus/Amuleth/Hamlet actually lived. This is something that Shakespeare did not concern himself with, creating what the critic Maynard Mack once rightly described as a unique literary world—its brilliance as drama aside, one that has little if anything to do with historic Denmark. On the other hand, I believe it to be a necessity to accept that the tale of Hamlet has long since passed from history into myth, now serving as a kind of darkly romantic fairytale for grown-ups. For that reason, I chose to include a number of the key anachronisms (the existence of Kronborg castle at such an early date, the presence of portraiture in the at-best embryonic stage of western art, etc.) that Shakespeare introduced. This can only result in one more fantasy derived from history—perhaps a valid description of *all* historical drama and narrative.

This was, in fact, a time of transition. The Renaissance that had begun more than a century earlier in Europe's southern climes slowly worked its way northward. All indications from Denmark's earliest scribes suggest that the man we now know as Hamlet was to Denmark what Arthur had been to England some five hundred years earlier: the first 'modern' prince, the one who brought both civilization and Christianity to a pagan land. Owing to its early origins, Arthur is forever shrouded in myth and legend. Hamlet, half a millennium less removed from us, can more possibly be restored to his historic reality.

Finally, a word as to the dialogue. During my initial attempt to pen *Sweet Prince*, I opted for the normal approach of writing those words my characters (for, indeed, they are now—if only momentarily—*my* characters) would speak. It did not take me long to realize this wouldn't work. No matter how hungry I was to reach back beyond Shakespeare and come to grips with an earlier 'truth' about that melancholy Danish prince, I faltered at every attempt to write a speech knowing, like any other humble author, that I would not, could not come close to creating a single line of dialogue that could compare to what Gentle Will had provided. If I continued in that line, I would compete with Shakespeare and, of course, fail miserably. Either I had to scuttle the project (which I didn't wish to do) or find some other approach.

Eventually, I happened on the concept of living out a writer's dream—collaborating over the centuries with my inspiration. My approach was to comb every one of Shakespeare's plays, sonnets, and longer poems for lines that might serve my purpose. All descriptions of place, action, and character are my own; every 'spoken' line is Shakespeare, slightly altered where necessary for dramatic context. My 'aesthetic' included a desire to avoid, whenever possible, lines that actually appear in *Hamlet,* for that would lead to something of a low order: a paraphrase of the play, combining a Monarch Notes study-guide for unprepared students with the paperback "novelization" of some original screenplay.

Rather, this had to be an historical novel that, to borrow from the Bard, would come to praise Shakespeare, not to bury him. This explains why only seven lines from the play *Hamlet* appear in these pages, the bits of dialogue I could not complete the work without. Do not look for any of the famous monologues, though. No "to be or not to be" speech here, nor are legendary lines lifted from other plays, for that would have led to something garish on the order of a "Shakespeare's Greatest Hits" CD. Ninety percent of the dialogue is composed of lesser-known lines that fit my purpose. On those rare occasions when a famous phrase is used, my objective was to include it in an entirely new, different, hopefully humorous context, an ironic reference which would keep my novel modern in spirit by deconstructing the experience of reading it even as you do precisely that.

For however successful I may or may not be at presenting my own take on Hamlet, it seemed only fair to myself and my reader to occasionally remind both of the master craftsman whose intellect and imagination served as the starting point for this book, and indeed most of the culture—high, middle-brow, and popular—of the past four centuries.

Douglas Brode
03/08/2003

BOOK ONE

A DREAM
OF PASSION

1.

Shortly before dawn on a wind-nipped day during the waning hours of what in time would come to be referred to as The Dark Ages, the great action which opens our tale unfolded. Its precise date? Long lost in the mists of time, wherein fact and myth intermingle owing to gross inaccuracy on the part of that era's scribes. Yet we can say, and with some certainty, that this momentous event occurred near, perhaps directly at, the mid-point of the 11th Century.

Whatever the specific calendar date may have been, minutes before the sun began its daily climb to the sky, pursued as Denmark's elders believed by the rabid wolf Skoll, an advance party of Fortinbras' ten-thousand man army abruptly moved out of a red-orange autumnal forest two miles south of Kronborg's high walls. The Norwegians had, until that moment, kept hidden behind a natural fence of thick underbrush lining the beech tree woode. Following a wave of their king's leather-gloved hand, the heavily armed force pushed forward, traversing a flat field leading toward the stone fortress with high spiraling tower, its mud-brown turrets and like-colored banners adorned with images of Friga, the earth-god worshipped before the coming of Christianity by locals.

King Fortinbras himself, his woolly hair a brighter shade of crimson than the sky above, spurred his black charger. The beast, as fully armored as his master and better protected than many a humble foot soldier awaiting orders, darted forward with a majestic flourish, seemingly as completely aware of the moment's magnitude as its master.

Fortinbras positioned himself at the furthest extension of his army. Two trusted captains on less spectacular mounts trotted up on either side, flanking their 29-year-old king. The officers awaited his final command, kept secret 'til now, for perchance a traitor lurked in their midst. This was a possibility; someone eager for gold coins to fill a beggar's purse might hurry off and warn Hamblet. "Come, bustle, bustle," the rough king of all far Norsemen roared. "I will myself lead forth soldiers to the plain. Thus, my battle shall be ordered."

Fortinbras handed twin sets of papers, each revealing strategic sketches, to his captains. They considered the plan of action, nodding in solemn agreement that it seemed likely to succeed. One captain turned his mount back toward the first wave of troops, composed of tall men bedecked in chain mail, ready to rush forward. The other eased closer to his leader's side, awaiting specific instructions.

Frightened souls, meanwhile, crouched on the parapet inside Kronborg's walls or huddled in humble cottages just beyond the barricade. Though most Danes still made their homes within the fortress, several dozen squalid structures, crudely fashioned from clay and wood, ranged across the near plain, beyond and adjacent to the castle gate. This constituted the humble origin of an emerging village, Helsingor.

To fearful peasants, shivering in such huts, the initial appearance of advancing troops seemed a nightmarish succession of stark silhouettes, phantom-warriors lumbering against the backdrop of this late medieval morn. Soon enough, huddled Danes noted identifying colors of individual companies: green shields indicating men who prayed to the sea-god Aegir; white-feathers atop helmets for those holding loyalty to the frost-deity Gjalp; *yellow breechcloths on a company owing allegiance to* Dazhbog, *a sun-spirit.*

Inside Kronborg, a smaller but no less dedicated party of five-thousand troops rallied. The Danes' armor was, like their banners snapping in the wind, tinted mud-brown; this, in deference to the rich soil which provided them with an abundant living since, under King Sweyn I a hundred years earlier, they mastered rudiments of farming and accepted The New Religion. Such skills and spirituality were both borrowed from Britons, conquered during four centuries of standhogg—*those lightning raids launched from long wooden ships. Eventually, the Brits ceased all such useless resistance, then set about quietly conquering their conquerors by introducing them to modern forms of industry and prayer.*

In truth, the Danes (even that name derived from the Aenglish) never entirely abandoned their warlike ways. Fortunate, too, as they now prepared to defend their land from a mass of oncoming cousins: fellow members of the Teutonic race, a heritage shared by all people scattered throughout Scandinavia. Such squabbling had been the sad state of affairs since Sweyn's equally revered son, King Canute, died in 1035. With no male heir to assume the throne, only a pair of politically worthless daughters, civil war had engulfed Denmark. Half-a-dozen self-proclaimed 'kings,' lording over their territories, claimed the crown. Shortly, each busied himself with killing former allies in hopes of assuming full power. The effect of such madness was to leave the land vulnerable to invasion by an ambitious man from the north.

So it was that Fortinbras now arrived.

Norway's troops were ranged thusly: three quarters of the advancing horde composed of humble conscripts, wearing woefully thin armor befitting the most expendable foot-soldiers; the remainder, experienced knights on horseback, bedecked in the quarter-inch thick breastplates that, a millennium earlier, Romans had perfected, then begrudgingly shared with the known world. In anticipation of oncoming combat with such fierce souls, the more experienced among Kronborg's foot-soldiers seized broad-swords, for more than two hundred years their weapon of choice; battle-ax remained the preferred fighting-tool for Norwegians. Others among the Danes, new to the experience of war, grasped at long pikes, heavy maces, and shorter blades, all based on weaponry borrowed from Brits, they earlier learning the art of war from occupying Roman armies during the fourth century.

Boasting a head of auburn hair that made him appear more agreeable than his cousin-turned-enemy across the field, King Hamblet, in the center of Kronborg's courtyard, mounted his own royal charger. Like Fortinbras, this was a warrior-king, also approaching 30 years of age, willing to trust no general other than himself at times of crisis. Hamblet's mind, however, threatened to lose focus on the need for effective defense. His wife, Gertrude—coveted queen with green eyes that mesmerized any man who gazed into them—had prematurely slipped into the agony of child-birth. If luck were with them, she might at least deliver the son that, considering what had befallen when Canute left no male issue, this king understandably prayed for.

Beside Hamblet, on his own dependable mount, sat his younger brother by a little less than two years, likewise bedecked in full-armor befitting a member of the royal family. The contrast between them, obvious to all crowded near, suggested that Hamblet ruled not only by birthright but also those qualities which, as a nation, the Danes most admired. The king's dark eyes appeared clear and direct; Fengon inadvertently revealed himself as a man whose gaze never directly met another's. Fengon's soft-hazel eyes—which, to residents of Sjalland, suggested inner weakness despite the fellow's muscular build— invariably shifted to the side while speaking with anyone. Simplest exchanges proved a trial for this peevish fellow.

The king ignored such habits, though, always treating his junior as trusted companion. "A thousand hearts are great within my bosom, brother," Hamblet announced with the high-spirits of one who has never known defeat. Truth be told, Hamblet had avoided failure on the field owing to just such an attitude. "Advance our standard," he called out, "and set upon our most formidable foe!" Hamblet drew his sword, larger and heavier than those of even veteran soldiers, waving it on high.

Simultaneously, Fengon nodded to the nearest of their followers. Stout fellows all, well aware of the danger not only to themselves but their women and children should this day be lost, all lustily roared. While this interchange occurred, rude mechanicals, old or unfit for fighting, feverishly worked rusty metal pulleys, lowering Kronborg's foot thick drawbridge over a surrounding moat.

While Hamblet considered this activity, Fengon glanced to the courtyard's far perimeter some fifty yards away. There, beyond a bubbling fountain, he discerned Polonius, advisor to the king, and his pink-faced wife, Kronborg's only nurse. A thin, angular man accompanied by his comically plump dam, Polonius passed through a doorway erected to keep commoners from slipping inside the royal recesses of Kronborg's castle keep. In their late thirties yet appearing considerably older, the couple flanked Hamblet's queen.

Though most eyes remained trained on the field beyond, it was obvious to anyone who glanced in Gertrude's direction that she was bursting with child. Even her difficult state at this moment could not dim her allure: hair long, golden, naturally curled at the ends; facial features surprisingly fine for a native of this rough land, though with pouty, petulant lips; skin soft as the finest velvet that, in the past year, could finally be imported from Brussels.

Face pinched with pain, Gertrude allowed herself to be bustled past Denmark's massed troops, composed similarly to Norway's of expendable infantry and precious horse soldiers. The trio stumbled toward circular steps at the building's far end. Encrusted with moss and encircled by ivy, the ascending stone slabs led windingly upward to the tower, final hope for safety at times of peril. Despite her anguish, Gertrude stole a peek at the readied army, eyes rushing not to her husband, preoccupied with the oncoming fight and unaware of her presence, but Fengon.

Nervously, he peered back.

Planning to offer strategic advice, Hamblet noticed the silent communication passing between brother and wife. For one moment, the vexed warrior-king considered confronting Fengon, here and now, as he'd long meant to do on this increasingly awkward situation. But for a ruler, country matters come first. However saddened, Hamblet turned away. Still, the king stole several seconds to mutter under his breath a thought which oft haunted him during the past year: "Despiteful love! Inconstant womankind!"

Hamblet's words were phrased so softly even Fengon, a few feet away, did not hear. Sighing deeply, the king again waved sword in air, spurred his mount, then with full ceremony led exuberant troops across the drawbridge and out onto the open field. No one noticed Fengon reining in his horse, waiting 'til the first wave had hurried off.

When they were gone, Fengon slipped down from the worn saddle, cautiously following after Polonius and the nurse. Unaware, Gertrude screamed in anguish as the older couple spirited their charge toward the steps.

2.

Half-a-mile away, on the plain of battle, the first wave of Fortinbras' troops darted forward, pikes and axes ready. Among the cavalry, several—a special few—were bedecked with blood-red helmets, carefully bevered with air shafts for easy breathing. These elite forces, including battle seasoned Fortinbras himself, had traveled together, down to Denmark, accompanied by chosen mounts. First, they had journeyed by land through neutral Sweden, the only Scandinavian province whose rulers steadfastly refused to take sides in internal conflicts. They then boarded wooden rafts to cross the sund separating Sweden from Denmark's militarily significant

Sjalland isle. Such a route allowed those of the highest honour a relatively brief trek.

Others, less fortunate, were in varied Norwegian ports crammed into long ships, still boasting the multi-colored dragonhead bow carvings for which Vikings had become rightfully renown across Europe during the past 500 years. A perilous sailing swept Fortinbras' cannon-fodder from his homeland's southernmost cusp, down across the treacherous North Sea, and finally up onto Denmark's marshy coast. From there, the men trudged 150 miles west, across fertile lowlands, carefully circling occasional bogs. Finally, these exhausted troops reached the Baltic's breeze swept shores, there trans-ported—again by boat—to Sjalland's westernmost finger of land. Now, all ten thousand Norwegians were conjoined into one great force, feverishly intent on victory.

First, infantry pressed forward, dutifully making their way across barren terrain toward the purportedly impregnable fortress Kronborg. Each man knew full well that even if the day were theirs, few would live to savor it.

The castle's six cannons, anchored high on the walls, set to blazing, swiftly transforming dozens of men into bloodied fragments, the second wave carelessly leaping o'er twisted corpses. Accompanied by the trusted captain, Fortinbras scru-tinized every movement, as survivors of this initial assault inched closer toward Hamblet's advancing infantry. Norway's lighter mobile cannons returned fire from the woode, balls smashing into the castle, though doing precious little damage.

Extending a hand before him, Fortinbras shared the final element of his secret plan: "My forward shall be drawn out all in length, consistently of horse and foot. They, thus directed, we will follow in the main battle."

Seconds passed while the officer digested this information. Such an approach was revolutionary at a time when foot-soldiers ordinarily confronted an enemy's infantry, cavalry held in reserve 'til the penultimate pitch of battle. Surprised but fully aware of his commander's brilliance on the field, the captain nodded and spurred his horse, riding off in the direction of eager lieutenants, patiently waiting to learn how the combat would be waged.

The humblest of Hamblet's troops were armed only with the bow and arrow which, since the time of ancient Greeks, had been associated with common men. Nervously, they made ready to fire at the steadily advancing Norwegian line, helmets and high held weapons reflecting five thousand points of light from the rapidly rising sun. On a hillock behind the archers, Hamblet—focused on the enemy's movements to the exclusion of all else—grasped the approach his formidable opponent had taken. At once, he set to mulling over the proper way to repulse such an attack.

"Our ancient world of courage, inspire us with the spleen of dragons," the warrior-king called out, momentarily abandoning his conversion to Christianity at this desperate hour—reverting, if temporarily, to an earlier vision, directly addressing Volundr, smithy-god and designer of celestial swords, and Odin, one-eyed warrior who in tales-out-of-time put his companion's creations to good use. Speaking over his shoulder, Hamblet addressed his seneschal, unaware that Fengon was absent: "Upon them now, brother!"

At last, the king realized what all others already knew: Fengon, second-in-command, was nowhere to be seen.

"Brother?" the dumbfounded king called out.

No answer but the soft whistling of the wind and, from far across the field, fierce cries of battle.

3.

At that moment, Fengon narrowly pursued something far more significant to him even than Kronborg's safety. Remaining a discreetful distance behind, he followed the queen and her companions up lichen encrusted steps circling the tower's exterior. Halfway up, Gertrude slipped into a state of unbearable agony, her head rolling as pain tore through her delicate frame. Desperately, she grasped at the frocks of her helpers, crazed for something to hold on to, as they steadily guided her upward.

Turning a bend by the second floor, Gertrude caught sight of Fengon, shocked but relieved to note her lover of the past year had not deserted her at this moment of crisis, as her husband—Denmark first, wife second—had done. Summoning her remaining strength, the queen managed to call down: "His majesty, tendering my person's safety, hath appointed this conduct to carry me to the tower's top."

Before she could say more, the anguish inside Gertrude seized her wholly. Head hanging loosely, her eyes—green as Njord's underwater kingdom—rolled back in her tortured head. Before she could be whisked away, Fengon managed to furtively nod his understanding. He had wanted for her to see him, if only momentarily, and know that he, the younger brother—the one without *power*—held her safety paramount in mind.

Fengon halted, watching as the trio continued to cautiously ascend, hoping for some gesture of affection before heading back down to remount, fight, possibly die. He had it: *Careful that neither Polonius nor the nurse noticed, Gertrude blew him a subtle kiss, then was gone from sight.* Fortified by the reassurance that this lady remained his, in heart if not title, Fengon paused. There was nothing more to be done here. Ready for whatever might come, he descended the steps. "These times of woe," he sighed to no one in particular, "offer no hours to woo."

Still, Fengon trusted that with a little luck and the support of ancient gods—he was among the few who had never revoked Elder Spirits for that single Father-God of The New Religion—the day might yet be won. Then? Anything *was* possible!

"When peace reclaims the land," he assured himself, "our secret minutes shall be ripe, if few."

4.

Twenty-one years later, on a crisp day in early spring, Fengon's mind drifted back to that dangerous moment in his, and his country's, past. Though born at a time already being described by Denmark's budding historians as the tail end of The Dark Ages, no one would have guessed such a period ever existed on this bright morn. Birds, nesting in the full boughs of trees, chirped gaily, sunlight danced down on all in Fengon's line of sight. The world appeared lush-green thanks to tender vines of sultry late April.

A considerable distance from the clearing in the woode where he and Gertrude nestled close, Fengon could spot, through natural barriers of thick foliage, ever-stately Kronborg, its old gray walls formidable still. During two decades of peace and prosperity that followed Sjalland's greatest challenge and ultimate triumph, Helsingor's village perimeters gradually stretched ever further beyond the castle confines. Warehouses, barns, liveries, makeshift shops selling diverse varieties of merchandise—some homemade, others imported from all across Europe and beyond—mushroomed between the timber halls and earthen cottages that provided housing for a rapidly expanding population. But if the sight of a great past mingling with promises of the exciting future caught Fengon's interest, it did so but briefly. His eyes drifted back to Gertrude, wanton in her nakedness, riding high astride him as they celebrated the end of Denmark's nine month winter by making love in the out-of-doors for the first time since the previous August. This clandestine spot, near to the great meadow, had over the years become their favorite meeting place. How wonderful to return here, after cold winds forced them for so long to quietly couple in the castle's cramped, clammy chambers.

Now nearing fifty, Fengon remained a man of rugged build, even if time's passage added an ever increasing layer of fat to a once trim stomach. Gertrude had changed less during the intervening decades: legs long, torso slender other than bountiful breasts now dangling over Fengon's face. He, spell-bound as always by her sleek beauty and the green eyes that caused some to consider Gertrude a witch from the woode, stared up at the woman he had hungered for from first sight, that day when his brother introduced this daughter of a nearby lord as the king's intended. Gertrude groaned loudly as, a generation earlier, she had in those anguished moments before delivering up to the world her only child. This time, though, her uncontrolled utterings were induced by pleasure, not pain.

For more than an hour, the two had been locked in forbidden embrace, each unwilling to end their stolen joy by reaching climax too quickly. At last, each sensed the other's readiness. They violently came together, cruel and hard, rending their bodies as both froze at precisely the same split-second, a skill perfected by regular practice over many years.

When it was over—mutual hunger seemingly sated—Gertrude allowed her body to slowly roll off Fengon's spent frame. For a man, this was enough. He was dead, done, having experienced what the Normans called *le petite morte*: the little death. Gertrude, conversely, was in a matter of minutes ready to again roll with her husband's brother. Reaching ecstasy only increased her appetite. Raising her head from trampled grass, she turned passionate eyes on Fengon, long ago nicknamed 'Fang' in their private moments, sensuously sweeping a soft hand across his hairy shoulder.

"Once more into the breach," she begged. "Once more?"

Fengon, face down and only half-conscious, twisted about to consider her in disbelief. The sex had been so intense, he half-hoped she might be joking. Couldn't Gertrude grasp there was barely anything left of him? She leaned close, eyes widening seductively, smiling with anticipation of another round.

"Fang?" she pleaded. "Mount thou thy horse, and hide thy spurs in her sides."

Considering her primal need, Fengon determined to at the very least try. Breathing deeply before, like some weary but undaunted general, rallying his forces to yet win the day, Fengon announced with bravado: "Come, wilt thou see me ride?" Pushing her backward, hard on the hillock serving as their rough bed, he tossed Gertrude's equestrian imagery back at her: "That roan shall be my throne. And when I am o' horseback, I will swear I love thee infinitely."

Fengon rolled over on top of Gertrude, forcing himself inside her with more difficulty than he was wont to admit.

5.

Unbeknownst to either of the adulterous (and, in the coda of that time, incestuous) lovers, a vivid image of them together—frightfully close to what was transpiring in the woode—assumed ghostly form in the mind of Denmark's sleeping king. Fifty years of age now, sadly appearing a full decade older, Hamblet rose up from his bed with a start, shouting: "She is the devil's *dam*! The devil's *dam*!"

Osric, a demure courtier who daily attended to Hamblet's needs, lightly pranced across the royal bed-chamber to the king's side. Earlier, he had, on a wooden tray, carried in the king's morning repast of bread, cheese, and a spicey tea from the Orient which Hamblet had come to love since its introduction into northern Europe.

"Sir?" Osric hesitantly addressed the royal presence, noting the king rolled about in furious phantasmagoria, his dark fantasy refusing to subside. "You do but dream."

The sound of a familiar voice snapped Hamblet back to reality. All frantic movements ceased, allowing aging bones—dead-tired, though the day had barely begun—to collapse on his mattress. The fresh straw with which it was stuffed—recently mown by men of the field—squeaked reassuringly.

"Dreams are toys," the king groaned with a sadness that betrayed a soul long-ago adjusted to a life of endless disappointments. "Yet," he added, "for just once, yea, superstitiously, I will be squar'd by this."

Dressing carelessly, quite forgetting to slip on his high leather boots beside the bed, Hamblet darted toward the doorway. Uncertain whether duty prescribed he ought to try and keep his king from rushing off, Osric attempted to speak but could find no appropriate words. By the time he seized on something reassuring to say, Hamblet was out of the room, flying down the long, shadowy corridor connecting his private rooms with the remainder of Kronborg castle.

Muttering under his breath, Hamblet—in a state of physical disarray and mental confusion—rushed he knew-not-where. A few steps down the hall, he found himself face-to-face with Balthazar, a 17-year-old page, taller and more formidable than most boys his age. Whistling absentmindedly as he strolled along, Balthazar carried the king's wine-sack. Earlier, he had sampled the contents, determining no poison had secretly been slipped inside during the night.

"Have you not seen, or heard, Balthazar," Hamblet demanded in quivering voice, "that my wife's slippery?"

The youth was caught off-guard by his master's disheveled appearance and unexpected question. Gazing into Hamblet's eyes, Balthazar feared the madness he saw there. What to say under such circumstances?

"I would not be a stander-by to hear my mistress clouded so, sire," he muttered as Hamblet seized the sack.

Royal eyes askance, the king wondered what the lad meant. Did Balthazar, his words so naive, falsely imply all was right out of sincere concern for his majesty's feelings? Or was the boy being subtly sarcastic?

No matter . . .

And, for now, no time to consider!

Haunted by dark dreams of forbidden passions, recurring throughout the passing decades if never so horridly real as this past night, Hamblet stalked away, hurrying around a corner and out of sight. Stepping out of the bedchamber, Osric exchanged concerned glances with Balthazar, sheepishly explaining: "He hearkens after prophecies and dreams."

"The king dreads his wife?" Balthazar dared ask.

Osric nodded.

Then, thoughts drifting to young Amuleth, far away in

Germany for the better part of a year, Osric added: "And sorely misses his son."

6.

Still designated a medieval city in official records, Wittenberge seemed to Amuleth, particularly in comparison to a fortress-village like Helsingor, the northernmost tip of a cultural-iceberg. A rebirth of love for art and ideas had, during the preceding century, slowly taken root, then flourished in balmier Mediterranean climes. Yet in Denmark, and lands located still further north, such possibilities remained largely unknown. In good time, change would be inevitable, even amid frozen *fjords*. Germany, meanwhile, stretched between the two extremes. Long considered a halfway point between northern and southern Europe, Germany separated the two in orientation as well as geography.

Everywhere, in this sprawling metropolis a week's hard ride due south of Sjalland's salt-stained shores, Amuleth noted vestiges of the past, reminding the prince of Kronborg: stretches of crumbling wall, once lined with citizen-soldiers who bravely repulsed barbarians intent on decimating the city; abandoned armories constructed of now rotting timber, still filled with rusted equipment that had not been called into use during the memory of any living; a lone watch-tower rising high over all other buildings, even those constructed within the past year.

But there was so much more!

Amuleth described, in excited letters home, the city's *modern* aspects: A recently completed cathedral, its complex structure replacing half-a-dozen makeshift churches where German priests had, a century before Denmark's belated conversion, dared practiced the once dreaded New Religion; myriad shops and stalls, from which the slowly increasing number of literate citizens could buy rare books, as well as varied *objects-de-art* from around the world; winding streets where young people, in colored clothing imported from places like Portugal, carried north over newly established trade routes, walked and talked. This new generation ignored the occasional monk in drab attire bustling by, vaguely disapproving of such secular ways, deep in thought about what he believed an important issue: How many angels might at any moment dance on the head of a needle?

In Wittenberge's center stood the university itself. Composed of only three interlocking brick buildings, this academy was not nearly so impressive as the older, larger school in Berlin, one long day's trek to the northeast. Not worthy of mention, certainly, in the same breath with the legendary institution in Bologna, opened in 890, now revered all across the continent. That school had been conceived by Italian intellectuals following visits to Arabic academies. Europe's first university was a precise copy of those found in such lands. The term 'university,' such founders borrowed from the Latin for a broad, deep, general knowledge, a concept unheard of beyond the Near East—a radical idea when contrasted with trade schools and secluded monasteries which had long provided Europe's only education.

A revolutionary vision of learning had begun in Bologna when wealthy youth formed a corporation to pool resources, hiring learned men as teachers. At a snail's pace, such an approach spread ever further north, first to Paris, then up into Germany. Cologne, Heidelberg, Leipzig, and Rostock. Finally, Wittenberge joined the list of older monasteries that, during the past decade, had gradually transformed into something more ambitious. Now each offered classes on the worldly as well as the religious: theology shared time with medicine, law, literature, and the arts.

Initially unsure whether a university education would be of value, Amuleth had fallen in love with this place, and the idea behind it, on that day when Denmark's 21-year-old prince first arrived. Seven months earlier, Amuleth and the commoner Horatio had ridden tired mounts up Wittenberge's narrow, winding streets. Until that moment, Amuleth blithely accepted provincial Denmark as, in miniature, a fair representation of the world at large, assuming what existed beyond Sjalland didn't significantly differ from anything found at home. But first sight of this harbinger of things to come convinced Amuleth otherwise. There was so much to experience and, in time, comprehend.

Amuleth had left the beloved Baltic isle to acquire a contemporary education at Queen Gertrude's insistence. The future—an oncoming century during which, God willing, Amuleth would eventually preside over Sjalland—would scream out for a new kind of leader. One, Amuleth's mother explained, with a greater grasp of things than roughhewn Hamblet had been expected to master. Uncertain if this were so but willing to humor her, Amuleth agreed, providing best friend Horatio were permitted to accompany the prince. In recent years, young men of common birth had, in small numbers, been admitted to university, so Gertrude agreed.

Privately, though, the prince scoffed at this supposed need for education, even to Horatio during their overland trek. Such beliefs were blown away like dead leaves in winter's wind by the sharp breeze of an emerging enlightened age which daily whipped through this city.

On that first day, Horatio and Amuleth were reunited with Amuleth's cousin, young Fortinbras of Norway. The three had been fond friends during their youth, once peace had been established between their countries. Amuleth's companions swiftly headed for a tavern, to consider available wenches. Alone, Amuleth visited the library. Ever since, books had been the prince's primary concern. That remained the case on this sunny spring day. Amuleth paced down busy, bustling Church Street, nose buried in a thick leather-bound manuscript. The work had been copied, word for word in painstaking longhand, from an earlier tome, a task accomplished by some anonymous monk, dedicating his life to transcribing detailed characters so others might read and know. Currently, Amuleth was lost in the dazzling epic of early Britain, as related in that country's *Annals*. The hundred-year-old volume shared the glories of its best loved king, Arthur Pendragon. Ironically, these tales included Arthur's victory over invading Angles—Amuleth's ancient kinsmen—at Badon Hill in 487 A.D. Only after Arthur's death some twenty years later did the Angles of old finally conquer the land, transforming Britain into Aengland. Nonetheless, Amuleth saw in Arthur a kindred soul rather than an enemy of old. Dare Amuleth dream that, in time, Denmark's prince might emerge as just such a beloved leader, forsaking past prejudices, dragging Denmark, as Arthur had his land, into a progressive future?

A consummation, Amuleth thought, *devoutly to be wished!*

Less concerned with daily distractions than other royals, each dividing his time between classroom and tavern, Amuleth now barely noticed several local beauties, drifting by on the street, futilely attempting to catch the prince's eye. The girls whispered among themselves, enamored of Amuleth's visage: better described as "beautiful" than "handsome," these dazzling daughters of merchants agreed. No argument, they buzzed like bees, that this delicate dreamer—who never, like other student-princes, sought out their company—might prove a sweeter companion than rude sometime scholars. This youth was concerned with the finer things in life. Amuleth, they decided, was a mystery; each among them would delight in being the one to penetrate the enigma.

They gazed on, disappointed by Amuleth's apparent lack of interest. The prince strolled by, unconsciously stroking the thin wisps of a moustache that added an element of masculinity to an otherwise epicene appearance. These respectable girls were not the only ones Amuleth ignored. Several chums, familiar with Denmark's prince from classes in ancient Roman literature and recent theories by free thinkers attempting to re-explain the workings of the universe, called out in friendship. Amuleth vaguely waved in polite dismissal, continuing in the direction of The Wild Boar.

This shabby old inn had proven, for two generations of students, the most popular among all crude establishments crowding near the university area. Such places beckoned to the boys, daring them to defer studies 'til another day. More often than not, princes would slip in for wine and wenches. No question, then, that here Amuleth would find Fortinbras and Horatio, who had no classes to attend, this being a Sunday.

Then, Amuleth stopped short. For one person would not make way. A whore—though Amuleth had encountered her before, the woman's name remained unknown—stood squarely in the prince's path. A vulgar girl, pungent with cheap perfume, she grinned from ear-to-ear, twisting her body about 'til her ample bosom threatened to break out of a tight bodice, seeming quite certain that no scholar—not even distracted Amuleth—could resist her shabby charms.

"Soft swain," she cooed, "stay awhile, I beseech you."

Amuleth, nicknamed 'Artist' by friends, indicated the book, a slight smile indicating lack of interest in her offer. "Here is more matter for a hot brain."

This was unheard of!

Anyone, even young men from northern Europe's most respected families, would have reached into his pockets for the necessary coins to insure a day's dalliance. Perhaps a slight insult might help: "Have you a father?"

Confused by the question, Amuleth abandoned all attempts to sidestep the whore, halting and addressing her directly: "I have. What of him?"

The lusty girl's eyes widened as she pointed toward Amuleth's book, hoping to shame the youth into some indiscretion: "Knows he of this?"

Blushing, Amuleth reflected on the once notorious ribaldry of Old Hamblet, in the wild days before his marriage to Amuleth's mother. The prince then countered her question with good humour: "He neither does nor shall!"

With that, Amuleth stepped aside, swiftly turning a sharp corner in the crowded street.

Had Amuleth chosen to glance back, the prince would have briefly caught the rebuffed whore, hands on her hips, stymied by such a reply—attempting to grasp what it was that made this youth so notoriously unseducible.

7.

Unshaven, shoeless, and sloppily attired, Hamblet scrambled through the deserted streets of Kronborg's inner castle city. Most citizens were at home, still asleep following the week's exhausting schedule, or diligently filling the pews of Helsingor's three churches, where priests righteously lectured their congregations.

Rushing he knew not where with manic intensity, the king rounded a sharp corner. On one side, the bend was flanked by a pig sty, home to pink and white porkers rolling about in warm mud and dirty straw. On the other, just across the alley, an open-air butcher shop awaited the oblivious creatures which would, amid snorts of pain and betrayal, shortly be transformed into the fresh hams and slabs of smoked bacon Denmark had become renown for all across Europe. Here, Hamblet brushed past the only other person stirring: Laertes, son of the trusted advisor and his late wife, Sjalland's irre-placeable nurse, gone now for two long years. The lad, at twenty, was likewise in a state of disarray, though his condi-tion hardly compared to that of Hamblet. Laertes stealthily snuck home following an all night tryst at a nearby brothel just beyond the castle.

Before Laertes grasped the identity of this sad shadow of a man before him, uttering the proper words of respect befit-ting a king, Hamblet swept by, apparently unaware of the youth's presence. As he passed, Laertes caught the heady whiff of an unwashed body, and heard Hamblet mumble: "'Tis said, 'many a man has good horns.' Well, that is a dowry of his wife; 'tis none of his own getting."

Renown for sad, shy eyes, betraying a soul that has never known happiness in part because his mind cannot imagine what might actually make him happy, Laertes stared, in shock and disbelief, after the king. Once Hamblet was gone, the youth hurried off toward the handsome stone building he shared with father and younger sister.

"'Tis whispered abroad," Laertes gravely observed, "that 'twixt the sheets, his brother has done his duty."

Perhaps there was truth to the wicked rumor, spoken in secret by Helsingor's lowlifes. If so, the cat had come leaping out of the bag. Surely, this could bode no good. Polonius must be made aware. Saddened by the vision of a great man rendered pitiable, Laertes bolted for his door.

8.

Less than a mile away, in a glen hidden deep within the woode's lush vegetation, Gertrude grinned with amusement as her beloved 'Fang' attempted to bring the queen to full climax for a second time that morning. "You look pained, my love," she naughtily confided, "by the pleasure I bestow."

To Fengon, fully aware that, nearing fifty, he could no longer perform with the energy and audacity of his youth, Gertrude's words added bitter insult to the physical injury he already felt, unable to satisfy her a second time this day. "The sweetest honey," he spat back, "is loathsome in its own deliciousness."

Roaring with the vulgar laughter that this seemingly sophisticated queen held in reserve for such private occasions, Gertrude pressed her ripe chest close to the struggling, threatened male beneath her. With a teasing movement developed over years of experimentation and practice, she brushed her rosy nipples back and forth against his rough, matted bed of chest hair. Thick as a forest hedge, dark brown as Danish mud (if in recent years increasingly marbled with strands of silver gray), Fengon's torso resembled a natural vest of rich fur.

This, as always, proved the gesture that elicited her desired response. Deep inside, Gertrude felt Fengon grow larger even than he had been earlier in the day. Feeling his male flesh expand, the queen's sarcastic giggles suddenly transformed into a wild roar of ecstasy.

9.

The world, in early spring, appeared to Wittenberge's college youth as bright, fresh, and fully renewed. Indeed, this second-coming of a daily life out-of-doors struck the more thoughtful among them as comparable to the intellectual and artistic renaissance currently, if slowly, working its way through society-at-large. The young men forsook The Wild Boar's constraining interiors, where they'd downed horns of sack by the warmth of roaring fires for nine frigid months, along with the similar interiors of this alehouse's numerous competitors. Now, they flocked to raw wooden tables crowding open courtyards, left languishing and unused since early Autumn. In groups of five or six, student-princes basked in the sun, debating issues ranging from Europe's emerging political realignments to the comparable qualities of Wittenberge wenches. What one overheard depended on which table an arriving guest happened to pass.

Huge vats of beer and wine were drained. The young men likewise feasted from heaping platters of sliced apples and roast pork, fresh-cut from a full hog hanging on a spit over the blackened brick fireplace within this building's smoke-filled kitchen. The Wild Boar's serving maids, gussied up in crimson skirts, hoisted high by green suspenders crisscrossing lily-white blouses, boasted the tight-laced bodices The Wild Boar had become infamous for. Imported from Salzburg, these costumes had been designed to emphasize the physical charms of all women who worked here. A dozen overworked wenches hurriedly exited the building with fresh food and drink, delivering orders to twenty tables where youthful appetites ran high, then carried piles of dirty dishes and empty horns back inside.

Prince Fortinbras of Norway—as crimson capped and ruggedly built at 21 as his father had been at that age—preferred the vision of wenches to talk of current affairs. Beside him sat Horatio, a pleasant-visaged lad of near identical age. His yoeman-like demeanor, both the naturally ruddy good looks and humble clothing he found affordable, distinguished Horatio as that rare commoner among princes aplenty. Since arriving, though, he had been fully accepted by his supposed 'betters.' An egregious personality, coupled with a sincere spirit, made him a great favorite. Besides, Horatio's reputation as close friend to both Amuleth and Fortinbras won him immediate acceptance.

Always aware of his inferior social status if never troubled by it, Horatio sipped sack from a horn with the best of them. His own particular mindset? Had Amuleth been with them at this moment, Horatio would have happily discussed politics or philosophy. But he and Fortinbras were alone. So instead, he agreeably joined Young Norway in rating the relative charms of women who earned their living by serving up cool ale, hot pork and, more often than not, bountiful portions of themselves.

One among the girls always caught the eyes of each, indeed of all the assembled youth. For the first time on this Sunday, the brazen one nicknamed *la belle dame sans merci* by student-princes (a result of studies in the Norman language) brushed out the inn's entrance, carrying an oaken tray weighed down by a dozen full horns. At once, the two friends ceased speaking, meticulously observing her every movement. Mistress Quickly, she was called. No one knew for certain if that actually was her name. Several years older than the general company of wenches, she enjoyed considerably higher status. Mistress Quickly shared, with her oft absent brother, ownership of this happy establishment. That in itself was notable. The Wild Boar remained the only business, of any sort in all Wittenberge, boasting a female owner, the term 'proprietress' all but unknown in a city where men ran every institution, women of little distinction laboring for whatever scant wages they could negotiate.

Mistress Quickly was surely as attractive, in a common way, as the giddy girls she employed. But, truth be told, no more so. Not, at least, in terms of physical attributes. Rather, it was her haughty demeanor—she never for a moment forgot her station, never let the young men forget it either, less by word than proud manner—that qualified her as most desirable of the lot. That, and the fact that Mistress Quickly's attentions were far more difficult to acquire than those of the other working girls. As she slipped through the weatherworn wood gateway of her whitewashed-stone building, all eyes darted to her, like a multitude of arrows let fly at a single target. Several students offered shrill whistles that unpleasantly tore through the late morning's drowsy quietude. Others called out epithets best left unrepeated here. However secretly pleased by such attention, Mistress Quickly allowed no sign that she heard any of it. Or, having heard, cared. Without a sideways glance, she proceeded with studied indifference from table to table. Her graceful movements appeared as choreographed as if rehearsed for a midsummer night's masque.

"Why, there's a wench!" Horatio cooed.

"Here's some good pastime toward," Fortinbras added, hoping to wrangle a word or two as she passed.

"I am for her, Fortinbras!" Horatio challenged. Friendly competition for wenches had, from their first week in Wittenberge, constituted something of a merry duel between them.

"And I for her!"

Neither sensed a third presence, though Amuleth had traversed the courtyard, slipping down in an empty chair. "And I?" Amuleth added, voice dripping with the melancholy that oft-characterized young Denmark. "For *no* woman."

Fortinbras and Horatio turned to acknowledge their friend, considering Amuleth's curious choice of words with the fascination Denmark's moody prince always elicited.

10.

Frenzied with fear, several servants standing idly by Kronborg's gate watched in amazement as their distracted king approached. In earlier times, the drawbridge would have been cautiously lowered only upon the declaration of some secret password. Now, there seemed no potent threat to Sjalland. The bridge came clanking down early each morning, allowing denizens of the adjacent village easy access to the castle's inner city before being raised again at twilight, more out of habit than necessity. On this quiet Sunday morn, the area—glutted with people on weekdays—was nearly deserted. Guards sadly watched as Hamblet scampered across, moving as if sleepwalking, his world half dream, half real.

Minutes later, the disheveled monarch—out of breath from earlier, aimless sojourns within the castle proper—crossed the full length of empty field. Forsaking the town of Helsingor stretching far and wide on either side of Kronborg's wall, brick fireplaces of adjacent stone cottages sending black wreathes of smoke circling up into the sky, Hamblet—haunted by the potent image from his dream—headed directly for a line of beech trees signaling the forest's beginning. Over the past two decades, this natural barrier had crept ever closer toward town and castle.

Hamblet halted there, catching his breath. All around, he noted ample evidence of life renewed: the first green buds of spring, hanging overhead, gulls clamoring in the branches after gliding in from the sea. A soothing sound from the river, far off in the forest, fresh water rippling along as it rushed inexorably toward the Baltic.

Then, Hamblet summed up his courage. Tripping over a twisted root, barely regaining balance in order to keep moving, the king lurched past several thick bushes, pushing into the dark woode. Anxiously, this wrinkled man, hair prematurely white from worry, muttered as he moved along: "'Tis a bawdy planet. From east, west, north, south, no barricades for a belly."

11.

In the finest of the older buildings within castle walls, Polonius served himself a simple repaste. Widely revered as a fidgety graybeard possessing vast knowledge and reliable wisdom, he only wished the respect accorded him in public was likewise proffered in this, his private place. Slipping several hard-cooked eggs, a bit of leftover bacon, and some pickled-beets from the well-stocked larder onto a wooden plate, Sjalland's elder statesman glanced into a wall mirror. In this manner, he observed, over his shoulder, his 19-year-old daughter, seated on the room's far side.

Too pretty of face, too trim of figure perhaps for her own good, Ophelia—body carelessly strewn across a plush chair—studied her image in a hand mirror. Absently humming an old ditty, she admired the results of a task that daily consumed several long hours after rising: the methodical application of fashion, adding a sultry aspect to her naturally pouty mouth and a seductive sullenness around the edges of her flirtatious eyes. Such labors enhanced Ophelia's God-given looks, preparing her for yet another full day of breaking local boys' hearts.

Polonius sensed that his precocious daughter revealed unspoken emotions every time Ophelia glanced at a likeness of Amuleth. This remembrance, she had placed in the center of a small, lacquered table's top, the spot where Ophelia displayed her most treasured mementos. All, that is, excepting the gold ring which never left the fourth finger of her right hand. Momentarily, she hesitated in her studied creation of a glamorous image. Such niceties, she had learned from Italian merchants, who recently added Sjalland as the northernmost point on their trade route. These men from the south proffered wondrous cosmetics, carried home by ship following perilous visits to the Orient, then carried upward overland by caravans. Thus, the notion of *haute* fashion had at last extended to new territories. Ophelia brought her right hand to eye level. Studying the delicate band of gold displayed there, the slender girl smiled at the possibilities this ring suggested to a young mind at once romantic and ambitious. It had been her farewell gift from the prince, bestowed on Helsingor's reigning beauty that day when Amuleth and Horatio departed for Wittenberge. Though they promised to return for Yule holidays, a fierce winter altered their best laid plans; since the September morn when last they traded sweet nothings, Ophelia had seen Amuleth only in dreams and, of course, the likeness she always kept close by.

Her father also studied a painting: a somber rendering of his late wife, hanging on the wall near Polonius' place at table. The nurse had been the most respected woman hereabouts, other than ladies of noble birth, owing to her well-reputed medicinal skills. But a cruel winter's storm, sweeping an assortment of deadly illnesses into Denmark, made no fine distinctions between people of diverse worth. One particularly virulent strain extinguished her flame even as she attended to the sicknesses of others. This had left Polonius lonely, if not alone. Ophelia and Laertes shared his house. But the boy was always off romping with women of ill repute. And Ophelia appeared likely to become as enamored of her image as Narcissus in Greek myth, the elegant youth who gazed admiringly at his visage, reflected in a pool, until he lost balance, fell in, and drowned.

Such were the rewards of self-absorption!

Recalling the good old days, Polonius barked between bites: "Fie, daughter; when my old wife lived, this day she was both butler and cook; you are retir'd, as if you were a feasted one, and not the hostess of this house."

A surprised laugh from the far corner was followed by her curt reply: "We modern maids do not live, like our mothers, to be men's slaves."

Before Polonius could offer a huffy protest against such contemporary attitudes, the front door flew open. Tossed in by a combination of his own energies and a sudden gust of wind, Laertes stood before them, eyes wide, brow furrowed. "The king, I fear, is mad!" was all he said.

That proved more than enough: Ophelia immediately ceased her ritual. Their father roughly pushed remnants of his breakfast aside. Both turned to Laertes with rapt attention and deep concern. Moments later, he was seated before them, diligently explaining every detail of the awful sight he'd witnessed.

12.

Finally, Fengon was on the verge of overcoming his earlier exhaustion. He had struggled to satisfy the seemingly insatiable woman astride him, Gertrude now mounted on Fang much as, years earlier, he leaped astride the horse carrying him forward to fierce combat of a different kind. Yet at the onset of their second sensual joust, Gertrude's movements struck him as mechanical. Fengon understood from past experience this derived from his own lack of enthusiasm for an encore into the lists of love. Not wanting to appear a lesser man than he had been in his youth, he increased his effort, gazing up to consider the happy results.

Her green eyes, implacably staring down at him moments earlier, now closed tightly. Gertrude slipped into that sweet surrender that always preceded her final ecstasy.

"Now comes the wanton blood up in your cheeks," Fengon roared lustily.

She tossed her full head of hair back and forth, again and again, until the golden strands flew about like loose shards of wheat in high wind. All the while, the late morning sun, now high in the sky, beamed down its white light on their dark deed. Lost in intense satisfaction of their most basic appetites, the lovers languished in its soothing warmth. Neither noticed as several storm clouds, black as the soot from a village-smithy's shop, appeared on the horizon, drifting ever closer.

13.

The sun blazed every bit as brightly on The Wild Boar's courtyard. Completing her rounds, Mistress Quickly reached the table of *The Inseparables*, as Fortinbras, Horatio, and Amuleth were known. Delivering horns of lukewarm ale, she offered a

generous wink for the triad while avoiding eye-contact with
any one youth in particular.

"Ah, the three princes," she said with a wry smile.

"Nay, lady," Horatio—precise to a fault—corrected. Indicating his companions with a nod, he explained: "*Two* princes,
noble Norway and Denmark; cousins."

"And you, Horatio?" she inquired. Her words happily surprised him. Horatio hadn't been aware that this desirable
wench knew him by name.

"Commoner," Horatio, admired for his inability to mouth
any falsehood, admitted, "not kin."

"Nor common, neither," Fortinbras insisted, rallying to his
friend's defense. "A prince among men!"

Horatio blushed at the compliment.

"Royal ever in thought, if not by blood," Amuleth added,
always ready to say something good about Horatio.

Their words were wasted, for the object of all affections
heard none of it. Furtively, Mistress Quickly snuck a hungry
glance at Amuleth: the spare, slim, elegant frame; sensitive
eyes, burning with intelligence; thin lips, hinting at a subtle
sensuality. Anxiously, Mistress Quickly bit her own lip. Like
many other Wittenberge women of each and every class, Mistress Quickly found herself spellbound by the only student
who didn't appear intoxicated by her own allure. Perhaps
that explained the fascination. There had to be some mystery
here, a logical if unknown reason why this stunning youth,
nicknamed The Delicate Dreamer by some, Artist by others,
never attempted to tread the road to worldly pleasures every
other male longed to explore.

The challenge of benign neglect proved too much for her.
Tray empty of ale horns, Mistress Quickly dropped it down
on the table, sidling over to Amuleth, still lost in that damnable book. As Fortinbras and Horatio gazed on in amazement,
she tousled Amuleth's wispy hair, kept neatly trimmed and
washed in a way other student-princes often didn't bother to
do. Such stimulation would have driven either of Amuleth's
companions to fits of passion; appearing not to notice, Amuleth

made a concerted effort to continue reading, despite a distraction apparently no more important than the mildly annoying presence of a housefly.

The greater the rebuff, the more irresistible the rebuffer! Without warning, Mistress Quickly lunged forward, gaudily painted lips attempting quick contact with Amuleth's intriguingly untouchable mouth. Before she could steal a kiss, the prince strategically turned away, allowing her only a fleeting brush against a soft-as-velvet cheek.

Surely, she thought, this must be heady stuff that Amuleth so seriously considers. "What do you read, my lord?"

"Words, words, words."

Stunned to realize their friend might nonchalantly succeed where their concerted efforts failed, Fortinbras and Horatio observed in amazement as Mistress Quickly followed through with her suit, sliding down onto Amuleth's lap.

14.

"Hurry, hurry!" Polonius commanded son and daughter. "My ancient bones ache with fear of the worst that can be."

All three, having traversed the drawbridge, headed off across the open field. Minutes later, they reached the youngest beeches, a ragged line of freshly sprouted trees. For a moment, they stood still, out of breath, regaining their wind. Then, the father parted company with his grown children, each heading off in some different direction, desperately hopeful one or the other might find their distracted king before, in such a wild state, Hamblet happened across the source of his rage somewhere in a lush forest that, on such days, appeared a second Eden.

15.

No such luck!
Hamblet had, by chance or destiny, arrived at the secluded

glen, at once spotting brother and queen together, naked, lost in each other's arms. While he watched, the illicit pair reached full climax for the second time that morn. Experiencing the unique horror of discovering what, throughout the better part of his life Hamblet vaguely grasped yet hoped never to witness firsthand, the king saw wife and sibling, themselves siblings according to ancient Danish law, twined together as the fabled beast-with-two-backs: eyes locked in rapture, hands hungrily grasping each other's exposed flesh. Lost in carnal pleasure, Gertrude remained blithely unaware of her husband's presence as Hamblet, reduced to sad shadow of a once noble being, hung beside a gnarled tree at clearing's edge. Fengon, out of his eye's corner, spotted the intruder. For reasons he himself could not have explained, the sight thrilled rather than frightened Fengon.

"How like you, the king?" he asked in a stage whisper.

"Very vilely in the morning, when he is sober," she replied, sharply offended by any reminder of the husband that Gertrude long since had lost interest in, "and most vilely in the afternoon, when he is drunk."

Hamblet could take no more. Devastated more by what he'd heard than seen, he stormed away. "What," the broken semblance of a warrior-king mused, "was I married to her in my dream? Or sleep I now, and but think I hear all this?"

Uncorking his wine satchel while plodding down an old path, Hamblet drank deeply. In time, he staggered through a maze of budding beeches, their roots covered with lichen, boughs spiderwebbed together by thick briars. No clear destination existed in the king's mind, only a vague desire to somehow escape harsh reality.

16.

To the amazement of Fortinbras, Horatio, and all other university men relaxing in her crude establishment, Mistress Quickly refused to remove herself from Amuleth's lap until young Denmark agreed to kiss her. With a grand flourish, she forced Amuleth's face away from that apparently all-important tome, the printed page holding as strong a sway over this scholar-prince as her charms did all others. With a good-natured shrug, Amuleth accepted that Mistress Quickly was not to be denied. The prince leaned forward, meeting the lady's richly painted, wide open mouth with parted lips. Once engaged, Amuleth was in no hurry to finish, naughtily nibbling at her fleshy tongue, not with cruelty but enough pressure to inflict a teasing touch of pain.

"I'll call that kiss my payment for thy horn of ale," a startled but pleased Mistress Quickly whispered.

"Cheap payment, Mistress, for so rich a draught."

Giddily, she leaped up from her little victory and darted off, laughingly leaving Horatio and Fortinbras to stare in wonder at their unfathomably demure friend.

"That wench," Horatio allowed, "is stark mad or wonderfully forward."

Lightheaded from more sack than was recommended on such a warm morning, Fortinbras rose and set to strutting about like the poor player who ambles from proud castle to country village in endless search for a new audience. "I burn, I pine, I perish," he wailed in half-hearted imitation of the actor's art, "if I achieve not this 'modest' girl."

Young Norway's sarcasm was not lost on his Danish counterpart. "If she be less than an honest woman," Amuleth admitted, "she is indeed more than I took her for."

"She finds you more attractive than we," Horatio sullenly complained.

"Only as I find her less remarkable; he who would attract fair maid would best repulse her first."

So this was Amuleth's ploy!

Denmark would woo and win, to the chagrin of these sex-starved friends, by feigning no interest. Fortinbras considered the wisdom of such understated seduction. "Still," he argued with a shrug of immense shoulders recalling the similar girth of his father, once Norway's all-powerful king, now reduced to

seneschal, overseer of northern territories belonging to Hamblet,
"she seems much ado to know you better."

Intended as a compliment, his words turned Amuleth
solemn: "I have much ado to know *myself* better."

Aware of Amuleth's altered mood, precipitated by nothing
more than a casual remark, Fortinbras and Horatio silently
considered their friend. This was Amuleth's way, turning
serious—moribund, sometimes!—without warning, or even
a motivation that either could understand.

Neither guessed the prince's mind was drawn back in time,
to the very moment of birth. Though this incident existed
in that early stage of life which no one can recall, Amuleth
had over the years honed a fanciful image, creating a cerebral tapestry from fragments of information culled from
Gertrude, Polonius, and the late nurse during countless con-
versations . . .

. . . *the momentous events of that day were already
recorded, by Scandinavia's recently literate scribes, in immense
volumes collectively called* Historicas Danicas. *Also, interpreted by Europe's early avatars of understanding as the sym-
bolic beginning-of-the-end for The Dark Ages, at least so far
as still-backward northern countries were concerned. The
battle came to be considered an event which, owing to the
end result of a lasting peace, allowed the Renaissance, already ripe in Southern Europe, to belatedly begin its move
beyond Germany's northern border—seeping upward into
ancient Teutonic territory which, in thought and culture, remained frozen as its fjords in winter's darkest hour.*

*Denmark and Norway had, on that famous day, locked
one final time in fierce combat. This had been the morning
when fifteen thousand men of iron, strong and true, met on
the open field before Kronborg castle in a brutal show of
force. The dying screamed in agony as swords and maces,
pikes and arrows, finally bony fingers and sharp teeth ripped
at adversaries, reducing men's bodies to sad fragments of flesh.
A day when, in a cloistered room of the tower spiraling
high above besieged Helsingor, a young queen screamed*

loudly, lost in the paroxysm of pain accompanying her only child's birth, Gertrude's shrieks of pain echoing the frantic howls of doomed men below.

"Day, night, hour, tide, time," the then 22-year-old Gertrude shrieked from her bloodied bed, positioned by the single slit of a window in the cold room, "my care hath been to provide a gentleman of noble parentage."

Polonius and the nurse didn't react, if indeed they heard at all. The two tended a black cauldron of boiling water over a small hearth, taking turns piling sterilized sheets on a nearby table. Such care was necessary—as the nurse had learned from traveling medical men—for the healthy delivery all of Sjalland prayed for.

Gertrude grew vulgar, believing this might win some attention: "Stuffed, as they say, with 'noble parts'? Proportioned as one's thought would with a man!"

Writhing in pain, the queen might have rambled on, only a terrible sensation tore through her body, cruelly rending her flesh as lightning pierces the night sky. Gertrude screamed one final time, her babe inching ever closer toward birth, blindly forcing its way out of her womb and into the world . . .

At least, that was how it all seemed in Amuleth's mind, looking back, composing a mental painting of the event based on details the prince had heard and read . . .

. . . all the while, agonized screams drifted up from the field of battle, where blood streamed like wine across a plain on which even the rankest weeds would not grow for a dozen years. Regaining her senses, and terrified by the battle's possible outcome, Gertrude feebly attempted to rise high enough so she might briefly peer out the window, learning if, despite terrible odds, the day might yet be Denmark's.

"The king!" she gasped, less concerned for him than her own well-being. "If he were dead, what would betide of me?"

If Gertrude were capable of thoughts and feelings beyond her personal safety, they were not for her husband. She cared for herself, her secret paramour, and for the child she would shortly deliver . . . a child born under the threat of premature

death from invading Norway, later on the very day that ear-
lier witnessed its birth.
   Gertrude groaned in horror at the possibility.

17.

What transpired next, Amuleth gradually pieced together from
tales told and retold over the years. Ever the dutiful father,
Hamblet oft sat on the hearth beside his beloved prince, a fire
roaring behind king and child diminishing the chill of
Denmark's nine-month winter, dropping a white blanket of
snow on Sjalland's shores, rendering them all virtual captives
within their solemn grey stone castle. The big, bearded man,
however strong in body, always displayed his gentle side when
with his adored and adoring child. By the hour, Amuleth would
be held spellbound, following a hearty dinner in the great
hall, by well-wrought stories of brutal valor and hard-earned
victory—the defense of Kronborg always a huge favorite of
both the narrator and his audience of one. Further embel-
lished with each subsequent retelling over the years, neither
Hamblet nor Amuleth could separate history from the myth
they had, through the king's words and the prince's imagination, jointly made of it.
   First, advance troops of the two armies—composed mostly
of hapless conscriptees, poor boys unprepared for fighting
yet valiantly willing to do their duty—crashed headlong into
one another. Armed with humble picks or handmade bows
and arrows (and, in some sad cases, only long staves, cut from
nearby beech trees moments before the battle began), they
fought as best they could. And, mostly, died. That occurred
before veteran troops, held in reserve so as not to be wasted
while cannons roared, engaged seasoned opponents wielding
broad-sword and battle-ax.
   Danes and Norsemen carved cousin enemies as sacrificial
dishes fit for the gods with the same wantonness they had, as

allies years earlier, unleashed on defenders of Britain's coasts. Then, as Viking warriors united in pillage, Denmark and Norway had sailed their legendary long ships down from Jutland, journeying southeast to those rich, vulnerable isles across the North Sea. Since the defection of Roman protectors, disorganized Britain invited invasion by conquering Teutons who recognized no mode of life but battle. What an irony, if any chose to note it at a time of civil war, that the Danes, gradually adapting to Brit notions of harvesting crops and raising livestock, now—like their onetime enemies— mounted a hurried defense from far northerners still committed to killing.

Yet Sjalland's men knew something of their heritage. Heavily armored knights hacked away at one another from horseback. Archers unleashed handcrafted arrows in streams that soared through the air like kites, often falling short of their mark, decimating allies instead of enemies. Infantry trudged through a thick mix of mud and blood, the heartier among them slicing into chosen combatants with a sudden, strategic pierce of the metallic-tipped pike, sharp enough to pierce handcrafted chain mail. Death, now as always, proved the great leveler. Shortly, commoner and royalty rolled about on the ground, rendered equal in anguish. The lucky died swiftly, less fortunate souls doomed to languish for grueling hours in painful consideration of a life that must inevitably end that day, though not before a seeming eternity of agony.

Fengon, late arrival to the Danish lines, spurred his horse, then tore up to the top of the highest hillock. From that position, Hamblet, still on horseback, observed the battle below. At the sound of Fengon's mount, panting from a quick gait, Hamblet turned to consider his tardy brother. Guiltily, Fengon smiled, though unconvincingly.

"How is't with you, best brother?" he mumbled. "You look as if you held a brow of great distraction."

No trace of anger could be detected in the king's voice. "If we lose this battle," Hamblet softly replied, "then this is the

very last time we shall speak together."
   "There is the night for talking, day for deeds—"
   "Fengon, I have a wife—"
This was a subject Fengon wished to avoid, feebly attempting to change the subject. "Tut! Come, elder brother. You are too young in this—"
   "Rather, too soon old, if too late wise."
A pregnant pause filled the air around them. Fengon, for once, found himself at a loss for words. The sad eyed king was about to continue when a lieutenant, hardly more than a boy though boasting flashing eyes brimming with the thrill and horror of one's first fight, hurried up.
   "Sire," the young officer announced, "Norwegian forces approach hard upon our flank."
   First things first!
In common cause, at least for the coming hour, Hamblet and Fengon abruptly turned from one another, drew broadswords, spurred their mounts, and pressed forward. Behind them, an odd coterie of volunteers—seasoned men, tender youths—pulled themselves into a makeshift wave and followed, three-quarters of the force on foot, the remainder on horseback. All were ready to fight—and, if necessary, die—for Denmark's greater good.

   That was then; this, now . . .

18.

. . . twenty-one years later, northern Europe's individual states had, one by one, embraced a new order of things. Farming and industry gradually replaced warfare and conquest, civil broil giving way to mutual cooperation. Following that monumental victory over the Norwegians, the isle of Sjalland's ruler had been crowned king of all Denmark. Hamblet, a great warrior when times demanded one, preferred to further the tradition begun by two great kings preceding him: overseeing the conversion of his people to Christian thinking and civilized behavior.

In contrast, Fengon, darkest of the brooding men who took pride in proclaiming themselves staunch holdovers from Medieval times, scoffed at what he considered Hamblet's sentimentality. Denmark's *seneschal*—overseer of all lands, owner of none—could not, or would not, give up the harsher way of life. However necessary it was to publicly swear allegiance to the single God, protector of the meek, Fengon secretly worshipped *Odin* and his more courageous counterparts, inhabiting that celestial storyboard which northmen of his generation once accepted as real.

When their country had been threatened by outside forces, Fengon's inner hostilities were necessarily redirected at Norway. Over the intervening years of peace, Fengon suffered from ever-increasing resentment toward his brother. Hamblet and Fortinbras treated one another as siblings. Hamblet apparently felt more fondness toward his Norwegian cousin—ally turned enemy, now ally once more—than his blood kin. Thus, in that secluded glen where Gertrude now knelt on the grass beside him, humming blissfully while combing her lovely locks, Fengon surprised his paramour by rising abruptly, expressing in every rough movement the anger always boiling just beneath his surface. Thoughts turning from love to war of a personal nature, Fengon sullenly yanked on his flaxen breeches.

"I never loved my brother in my life."

Oh, Gertrude thought, this is one of those days when, ecstasy over, he'll bore me to tears with bitter words. Perhaps sharp humor might puncture that balloon, allowing the queen to continue enjoying spring's paradise: warm sun, gentle breeze, shady boughs, chirping birds . . .

"Therein hangs a tale," she giggled, hoping her double-entendre (Gertrude's irony was derived from French fashions in conversation, even as her clothing was borrowed from the Italian style) would not go unappreciated.

However openly sardonic her tone, Fengon managed to miss the edge in Gertrude's voice, so consumed was he with self-pity. Pulling up his knee-high leather boots, Fengon danced about, venting inner rage in frustrated words.

"I gain nothing under him but growth, for the which his animals on dunghills are as bound to him as I."

"You gain that of me freely," the queen countered, "which he cannot win with words, gifts, or sighs."

"Still, he is lord of this land, compass-wide."

The more serious he waxed, the saucier she grew, twisting her body around to reveal the soft, wavy hair covering her private places, which Fengon admired, coveted: "And you, of uncharted territories . . ."

Gleefully, Gertrude seized her lover's shoulders, pulling his face down to her sweet purse of flesh.

Fengon, less than amused, made great pretense of being offended by the odor encountered there, following this morning's rough usage. Sniffing, he rolled his eyes and railed: "Something's rotten in the state of Denmark!"

With that, he stormed off, leaving the queen alone, naked in the wildwoode, trying to decide if she were more surprised or insulted by her lover's unexpected desertion.

19.

Once Mistress Quickly departed, the other serving wenches paled in comparison. Fortinbras and Horatio continued ogling them, for want of anything better to do other than down more sack. Sensing an opening, Amuleth raised the treasured book on high.

"Here let us breathe and happily institute a course of learning and ingenious studies." That, after all, was why all three had journeyed to Wittenberge. Too often, Fortinbras and Horatio, consumed by sweet seduction of street girls, forgot that higher purpose.

Fortinbras glanced at the leather-bound volume, considered several wenches more readily-available than their employer, and emphatically shook his head 'no.'

"Wine, women, and song," Norway insisted.

A dark look passed over Amuleth's face.

"What ails, my lord?" Horatio inquired.

It had not so much been Fortinbras' superficial edict than a sense of encroaching loss, suddenly passing through Amuleth's mind, that brought on the prince's sudden change.

"Would all were well," Amuleth answered, "but that will never be. I fear our happiness is at its highest."

"Ah," Fortinbras scoffed, not wanting one of his cousin's mood shifts to ruin this glorious day, "you could suck melancholy out of an acorn."

Eyes intense, Amuleth held high an empty ale horn, considering it closely. "Methinks some unborn sorrow, ripe in fortune's womb, moves toward me."

20.

As fate would have it, horns (if invisible) were likewise paramount at that moment in the mind of Amuleth's father. Sodden with drink, Hamblet lay under a towering oak in the darkest recess of Helsingor's woode.

"Take thou no scorn to wear a horn," the king, recalling an ancient ditty, sang out. "It was a crest ere thou was born."

Hamblet's mournful verse drifted to the nearby footpath where his brother sulkily stormed back toward Kronborg. Drawn by an old ballad which, for both men, came fully to life with new meaning, Fengon did not consciously realize he strayed from the path, pushing away thick cords of bramble while nearly slipping on pockets of moss, until he came upon the spot where his brother lay sprawled.

"O monstrous beast!" Fengon cursed. "How like a swine he lays!"

Unaware he was already fingering the sheathed short-sword by his side, Fengon drifted toward Hamblet, suddenly a witless scrap of metal unable to resist the magnet's pull.

"Let me," Fengon muttered, surprising himself by suddenly expressing out loud a long repressed thought following many decades of denial, "if not by birth, have lands by wit."

21.

The travesty that followed in the secluded grove was precisely what Polonius desperately hoped to avoid. He glanced back at majestic Kronborg, where a squad of soldiers, having hopped up from their beds at the sudden alarm, rushed across the bridge, still buckling on sword belts, hurrying to join the family of Polonius in their search. Exhausted, the greybeard feared he might expire at any moment, owing to a growing anxiousness extending far beyond any concern for Hamblet. Inseparable (for him) from the ruler's fate was the ongoing transition of Helsingor from medieval fortress-city to renaissance city-state, something Polonius, more than anyone else, had labored to bring about.

As Polonius made his way around the outer edge of those briars which rendered Sjalland's forest impenetrable to any unaware of its hidden pathways, the old man's offspring pushed deep into the woode. Spreading out on either side, each steadily swept from tree to tree, all youthful self-interest set aside. Neither Laertes nor Ophelia knew anything of their father's long held, deep-seated fears about Fengon, or guessed what such a man was capable of. They only understood their king was sorely distracted, vulnerable to attack by wild animals or passing brigands. As loyal citizens, the youths hoped to locate Hamblet before such things threatened their leader, thereby saving the realm from possible disaster. If only one or the other happened across the principal player in this unfolding drama, tragedy might yet be avoided.

"My grace!" Ophelia called out, peering in vain behind another beech tree.

"My lord?" Laertes screamed, hurrying off to the high grass of a distant hillock.

Unfortunately, tragedy has a way of asserting itself, despite the most sincere of concerted efforts by well-intentioned mortals to prevent it. As if the heavens themselves desired to announce this terrible truth, distant thunder rumbled on high. Within moments, the sky darkened considerably.

22.

In Wittenberge, the weather likewise grew progressively less appealing. Turquoise skies, broken only by white puffs of diverse sizes and shapes, gave way to a harsh gray dome overhead. Clouds remained plentiful, though now all were pitch-black in hue. Nasty, misshapen shards of nothingness, they swept past the sun, blocking out the orb that minutes earlier beamed down brightly on festive youth. Sensing a coming torrent, several students hurried inside to continue their party. Others settled bills, heading off in different directions for sport or study.

This was Horatio's turn to pay (the three alternated rather than bother to split bills), leaving Amuleth free to depart. Fortinbras, after pausing for one final flirtation with a comely new wench, hurried to catch up. "I pray thee, sweet coz," young Norway implored, coming alongside his Danish counterpart, "be merry."

"I show more mirth than I am master of," his moody companion admitted. "Would you yet I were merrier?"

Fortinbras recoiled, his persona of mindless merriment swiftly going the way of the good weather. "Sad, sirrah, when it is *I* who has the cause, but still can smile?"

"You, coz?" Amuleth stopped to consider a sobered Fortinbras. "Fine prince of frolic and fancy-free?"

Such words hardly described the fellow now standing before Amuleth. "Unless you could teach me to forget a conquered father," Fortinbras blurted, eyes sullen, "you must not learn me how to remember extraordinary pleasure."

This statement left Amuleth speechless. Never, during frequent encounters as children or constant companionship since arrival here, had Amuleth heard anything of the sort from this seemingly careless youth. Perhaps there was more to Fortinbras than met the eye!

Always eager to surrender to the past, Amuleth's mind darted back to a mental construction of that decisive day— the all-important battle which paved the way for what Prince Fortinbras now confessed . . .

. . . *after hours of combat, King Fortinbras' forces found themselves completely outmaneuvered, the surviving Norwegian troops brutally beaten back to the woode's edge. Maimed bodies, twisted like grotesque images of lost souls in the aesthetic hell of some seminarian's painting on a chapel wall, were piled high by non-combatants, deliriously trudging about in drifting remnants of cannon-smoke. The wounded, those still able to stumble about, were helped from the field by luckier comrades, the precious few who somehow survived this holocaust unscathed.*

Viewing the continuing carnage from a slight rise on the largely level field, Fortinbras—exhausted from a dozen hand-to-hand combats with fierce Danes, all now dead—breathed heavily. Fortinbras had retired here in hope of regrouping what little was left of his devastated army. Forlorn, Norway's once-glorious king considered what he had yet to admit was proof-positive of his dashed dreams: thousands of brave men, hacked to pieces by an enemy which employed the old Roman notion of the wedge, a triangular shaped fighting force, collectively moving forward as a single unit. Such an approach devastated any disorganized opponents who ruggedly fought as individuals, each for himself. Hamblet had learned the tactic from a Brit general, persuaded years earlier by a purse of gold to instruct Danish troops how to employ the devastating strategy.

A surviving Norwegian, one of the two captains earlier flanking Fortinbras when this oncoming day seemed likely to yield great things, hung by his master's side, imploring: "Fly further off, good king, while time allows—"

Eyes wide, an amazed Fortinbras interrupted the officer. Lifting a weary arm, he pointed toward smoke billowing forth from where his army had camped the previous night. "Are those my tents where I perceive the fire?"

"Aye, my lord. We by King Hamblet are all encircled."

Disbelieving eyes and ears, Norway stared incredulously at the sight. For one brief moment, he remained unable to accept what had happened, much less comprehend the full extent of what this day's bitter loss meant for the future of Northern Europe. Futilely, Fortinbras attempted to imagine some way in which seeming defeat might yet be transformed into a miraculous victory. Then Hamblet and Fengon, on foot, stepped through swirling smoke. A coterie of Danes hurried up behind them, ready to protect the royal brothers with their lives.

"Yield, sir," Hamblet announced. There was no anger or resentment in his voice, only an abiding fatalism, as Denmark continued: "or thou diest."

"Nay," Fortinbras boldly replied. "Still, I will fight on, to the very end."

"Noble heart," Hamblet called out, voice tinged with raw emotion yet surprisingly gentle, considering the toll on his own troops, "think of thy men, my desire for mercy, and so yield?"

A great warrior-king cared little for personal safety. Fortinbras would have preferred to fall fighting, joining the ancient einhorjar high above in Valhal, rather than live the remainder of his life in captivity. Nonetheless, something in Hamblet's words, even more so the striking tone of sincerity with which he spoke, left Norway touched for those others he had persuaded to travel with him. Or, at least, the few remaining alive. Glancing from side to side, hearing carnage to the west where troops clashed in what now qualified as absurdly worthless skirmishes, Fortinbras sucked in what little was left of his fatally wounded pride.

So it was that Fortinbras, now as ever free from any fear, dropped his sword. The gesture relieved his captain, who dared hope he might once again see home and hearth.

"They stand, would parley!" Fengon gasped.

"So call the field to rest," Hamblet commanded.

Fengon nodded, hurrying off to deliver this news in time to perhaps spare a life or two on either side. Danish soldiers rushed to join Hamblet, there awaiting orders.

"Give him all kindness," Denmark calmly proclaimed, indicating Norway with a nod, "for I had rather have such men my friends than enemies."

In the distance, cruel sounds of battle decreased, then hushed altogether. Other members of the Danish force arrived. Showing the respect ordained by Hamblet, they led Fortinbras and his captain away . . .

"I would thou hadst been son to some man else," young Fortinbras admitted to Hamblet's offspring as the two faced one another, oblivious during intense conversation to the dark storm clouds circling overhead. "The world esteems thy father honourable, but as he defeated my father, I did find him always my enemy."

Realizing, for the first time in all these years, how deeply young Fortinbras felt about this, Amuleth stepped close, draping an arm around young Norway's shoulder.

"You know my father hath no child but me, nor none is like to have now?" Amuleth whispered.

Fortinbras, eyes guilty avoiding those of young Denmark, nodded his understanding, saying nothing.

"And truly," Amuleth continued, voice dripping with honest emotion, "when he dies, *thou* shalt be his heir."

Now, it was Fortinbras' turn to disbelieve what he'd heard. "Nay, nay, good coz—"

"Nay? Verily, then we rule together!"

Fortinbras laughed. "Two stars keep not their motion in

one sphere, nor can one country book a double reign."

However inadvertently, Fortinbras raised an issue which Amuleth had seriously considered for some time. Why, when the war between their countries had concluded two decades earlier, should Denmark continue to hold political sway over Norway? Why did Old Fortinbras remain that land's *seneschal,* when full kingship ought to have long since been restored? Perhaps King Hamblet was too set in his ways to change things. Someday, though, Amuleth would reign!

That would likely occur near the century's cusp, as the world discovered its still emerging identity. Didn't sages insist a millennium offers mankind the chance to begin again, opening a new age in the ongoing history of humanity? If so, then in this remote corner of Europe, Amuleth might alter things for the better. Help in some small way to create a better world, sweeping away final vestiges of what here, at university in Wittenberge, were referred to as The Dark Ages.

"Nor shall it. For what he hath taken away from thy father perforce, I will render thee again in affection. Norway shall be free and independent once more; our two lands, as brotherly as we."

Never had Fortinbras been so touched by another person's words. Already aware of how decent his cousin was, Fortinbras grasped the full extent of Amuleth's nobility. Here was a friendship that ran deeper than imagined. Fortinbras knew then that, whatever might come, he would return this wondrous offer with, if need ever arose, his very life. "Generous notion," was all young Norway could utter, so overwhelmed was he.

"So now," Amuleth insisted with a smile, "be merry!"

"From henceforth I will. And devise sports!"

While they spoke so seriously, a gaggle of young women, modestly dressed daughters of the mercantile class and of considerably higher status than Mistress Quickly's brazen wenches, proceeded down the curved cobbled street in their direction. The girls chattered like magpies about perfume, scheduled to arrive soon from the Orient by way of Spanish ports, and the latest in fashions newly delivered to their fathers' shops after long overland treks from Paris and Milan. They were hardly unaware, though, that a pair of attractive nobles stood directly in their way. The secret ambition of every such girl was to marry a man of royal blood. Such a notion— unheard of a generation earlier—was now possible in a rapidly changing world.

"What think thee of falling in love?" Horatio asked, belatedly joining his friends, catching only the final bits of their conversation. Horatio also contemplated the comparative charms of these ladies who pretended not to notice, though in fact were concerned with nothing else.

A shadow of regret passed over Fortinbras' brow. He admitted: "Of all men alive, I alone never yet beheld that special face which I could fancy more than any other."

"'Til then," Horatio suggested, "navigate to the fairest port."

Ordinarily silent while these two made fools of themselves over pretty girls, Amuleth sensed the need to keep everyone's spirits high. At the sight of one young woman's cape fluttering in the rising wind, Amuleth raised hand to forehead, continuing the metaphor: "What ho: A sail! A sail! Covet thee this barge?"

This returned Fortinbras to his former carefree self: "I will board her, coz," he bragged, "though she chide as loud as thunder when clouds in autumn crack."

Sweeping off his hat while he approached the lass, Fortinbras' eyes twinkled.

Amuleth sidled up to Horatio and shrugged. "Off goes his bonnet to another oyster wench."

The two chuckled as Fortinbras, grinning from ear to ear, closed in on the surprised but not unpleased girl.

23.

Fengon leaned over the drunken figure. As his brother's shadow fell across Hamblet's face, Denmark's sodden king stirred, eyes opening slowly, dimly staring up at the menacing figure above him. Dark clouds obscured the sun as Fengon seized Hamblet's collar, pulling him so near, the king's wine-drenched breath caused Fengon to wince.

"Wilt thou lay hands on me, villain?" Hamblet gasped.

"I am no villain," Fengon replied, finally expressing a lifetime of resentment. "I *am* the youngest son."

"The love you owe me is two-fold, then: Brother to brother, subject to sovereign—"

"I do love thee so," he howled, "I will shortly send thy soul to heaven."

Any final whit of self-control falling away, Fengon's free hand unconsciously dropped to the sword hanging by his side. Without hesitation, he drew the blade from its scabbard, shoving it deep into Hamblet's stomach. Fengon remained unaware of the expression on his face 'til the king muttered in amazement: "Thou cutt'st my head off with a golden axe, and smilest upon the stroke that murders us?"

Fengon could find no words adequate to the moment. Instead, he stabbed, again and again, 'til he sensed at last that the king was dead. Royal blood trickled across the ground, mixing with mud from the past week's rainstorms. Finally, shocked at his own brutal deed, Fengon released the corpse and rose, shaking. He stared at his weapon, half disbelieving the unplanned action that had overtaken him.

"The tyrannous and bloody deed is done," he admitted to no one, eyes drawn to the darkening sky following a rumble of distant thunder amid gray angular clouds.

24.

In Wittenberge, Amuleth too noticed menacing skies, though the fate of a faraway father was not at that moment on the prince's mind. Amuleth and Horatio gleefully observed while Fortinbras ventured small talk with the young maids. When the women dared glance in Denmark's direction, Amuleth bowed courteously.

"Fair ladies, you drop scraps in the way of starved men."

They giggled girlishly, flattered, flustered. Any might have been seduced by Amuleth. Why did other men foolishly believe rough behavior would impress modern women? Fortinbras, roughest of the lot, suddenly seized the most attractive maid by her long hair, pulling the stunned girl over and downward. Before she could gather her wits to protest, he kissed her, then in one quick motion returned the maid to a standing position.

Once free, she hurriedly regained composure, slapped Fortinbras across the face hard as she could, then rushed away. Her companions, however intrigued by the prospect of meeting highborn men, had no choice but to huffily follow, with nary a backward glance. Amuleth and Horatio laughed at Fortinbras' failure to win women in the old way; young Norway, embarrassed, rejoined them, eyes downcast.

The three friends continued on their way. "Thou art too wild, too rude, and bold of voice," Horatio suggested.

"Parts that become thee happily enough," Amuleth added, "in such eyes as ours appear not faults. But where thou art not known? Why, there they show something too liberal."

"Pray thee," Horatio concluded, "take pain to ally with some cold drops of modesty thy skipping spirit."

Unwilling to yet admit that the emerging contemporary woman required subtler seduction through cultivated words and fine manners, Fortinbras waved his sword-hand on high.

"Front her, board her—"

Amuleth halted in the road's middle, swirled to face Fortinbras, nodded 'no.' Then, Denmark's delicate dreamer put it so simply, even this rugged throwback could hardly help but comprehend: "*Woo her!*"

Reluctantly, Fortinbras nodded in agreement. Yes, no question about it: Amuleth alone understood what women want.

25.

As the skies over Sjalland further darkened, Fengon employed the kerchief he'd tied round his neck early that morning to wipe coagulating blood from his sword. The task completed, he hurriedly shoved the cloth into the pocket of his breeches, and was ready to return his sword to its scabbard when Gertrude, preceded by the soft patter of her light footsteps, swept past a hedge, entering the clearing. Minutes earlier, the queen had been wending her way back to the castle when queer noises from deep in the woode caused her to abandon the path. What she witnessed in this glen left her momentarily speechless. Trippingly approaching the torn corpse, she at last found her voice.

"Poor key-cold figure of a holy king!" Then, wrathful, she turned on Fengon like a raging banshee. "You—"

Sensing her extreme shock, Fengon raised a battle-scarred finger to Gertrude's mouth, halting her babbling: "Teach not thy lips such scorn, for they were made for kissing, not contempt."

Hissing and spitting, Gertrude threw herself at him, a wildcat now, intent on tearing out Fengon's eyes. "Cursed be the hand that made these fatal holes," she screeched.

Before Gertrude could do serious damage, the still-virile warrior seized her thin right arm, forcing the queen to stop struggling and remain still. A cruel breeze, filled with the pungent odor of sea salt, whipped across their faces. The austere sky, ripe with rain and heavy from oncoming thunder, formed a gray canopy over the couple. Long time lovers stared angrily into one another's eyes, finding themselves in a situation that might yet transform into a sudden death struggle.

Then, to Gertrude's surprise, Fengon relaxed his grip, handing Gertrude his blade. "If thy revengeful heart cannot forgive, lo, here I lend thee this sharp-pointed sword," he explained, "which, if thou please, to hide in this true bosom." Fengon tore open his shirt before continuing: "I lay it naked to the deadly stroke."

For several seconds, Gertrude seemed ready to do just that. Eventually, though, her body untensed. She could not bring herself to end the life of a man who so often provided the satisfaction her husband never brought to their bed.

"Nay, do not pause," he continued, permitting himself a slight smile, "for I did kill Hamblet; thy beauty—which did haunt me in my sleep—did provoke me."

Could this travesty have been *her* fault? Gertrude's guilt was marbled with pride: To think, one man might actually kill another for her love! Surely, there could be no greater compliment to a woman's charms. Ever the romantic, Gertrude—eyes languid, mouth pursed—released her grip. Fengon knew, at her action, he had succeeded. Finally, he was in full power over all that his brother, until minutes earlier, claimed as his own.

Power, though, must be consolidated.

Fengon grasped Gertrude's arm again, pulling her down close to the bloodied corpse, already exuding the stale stench of death. Nauseated, she tried to turn away, yet Fengon forced her to consider Hamblet's torn remains.

"Take up the sword again, or take up me."

Gertrude shivered, almost cried. Instead of calling out for help, or doing as commanded, she crumbled in his arms.

Precisely as he had hoped she would . . .

His task accomplished, Fengon comforted her, gently stroking Gertrude's long hair. In the skies overhead, lightning struck, illuminating the darkening dome, followed by a clap of thunder that might have been a cannon roaring. Gulls clamored in the boughs, concerned at the coming storm. By the sudden blast of light, Gertrude spotted Laertes and Ophelia, hurrying near. Panic-stricken, she whimpered: "We are discovered—"

Fengon, noticing the young people, picked up his sword, sheathing it. "Tut! I can counterfeit the deep tragedian."

Pushing away brush and briar, brother and sister came upon the scene, immediately spying the dead king. The young people stood stock-still, horrified.

"Search, seek," Fengon shouted angrily, "and know how this heinous crime comes about!"

Regaining their wits, the two nodded and rushed off. "Murder!" Ophelia screamed.

"Murder most foul!" Laertes added.

Rain fell, hard and fast. Thunder drowned out their frantic calls. Gertrude and Fengon retreated under a nearby tree, as hailstones swiftly replaced raindrops.

"Who ever knew the heavens menace so?" the queen wept.

26.

The same storm front that, as Gertrude put it, now menaced Denmark stretched far and wide. To the south, precipitation pounded with equal fury on central and northern Germany. Immense hailstones sent those citizens of Wittenberge who had failed to demonstrate good common sense by slipping indoors at the first warning signs frantically scurrying for cover now. Students, some embarrassingly unfamiliar with the library, chose to enter and read books they had too long avoided. Others headed for their homes away from home, the bed-and-breakfasts that provided many a townsman and his *dam* with considerable profits for boarding these rowdy leaders of tomorrow.

The large rooming house where the Three Inseparables lived, located a quarter-mile from university, consisted of a ten-year-old wooden structure (shabby on the outside, snug enough within) and adjoining barn (here, Amuleth and the others kept their mounts). The most expensive closets (single rooms for students who could afford to live alone) were ranged along the third level. Larger suites, shared by two or three boys, dominated the less prestigious second floor. A cavernous lobby, with long tables for breakfast and open spaces for afternoon amusements, stretched the entire house's length adjacent to the main entrance.

It was there, on rainy days, that students lounged. Some sipped hot tea (alcoholic beverages were not permitted by the notoriously strict landlord); others wiled away the hours with games of chess (for those desiring intense competition) or darts (a favorite with young men in search of mindless respite from serious study). As lightning struck again, Fortinbras entered, slipping out of a drenched cloak, shaking himself furiously as if that act would send the chill flying from his bones. Absently tossing his outer garment onto a wall hook, he spotted Amuleth and Horatio, at the room's far end, competing at darts. Several other students, gathered close, offered wagers (also not allowed, though easier to slip by the snoopy owner) on which contestant would likely win.

Fortinbras joined the group: "Who saw the sun today?"

"Not I, my Lord," Horatio replied, taking careful aim.

"A black day," Amuleth insisted, generalizing from the specific, "will it be to somebody."

"Thy countenance appears black enough already," Fortinbras snapped back, in no mood for melancholy.

Another streak of lightning, visible through a large shuttered window, was inevitably followed by deafening thunder. Amuleth's curious eyes, until then considering the perfect construction of a feathered dart, now peered outside at the wild weather. The prince's vision focused on what, a century earlier, would have been explained away as one of Thor's fire bolts ripping through the sky: "When these prodigies do so conjointly meet, let not men say: 'There are reasons, and they are natural.' For I believe they are portentous things upon the climate that they point upon."

Amuleth tossed the dart at a multi-colored target. For the first time that day, the prince hit bull's-eye.

27.

Kronborg's castle guards, frantic after hearing the dreadful news and determined to catch the perpetrators, scrutinized every inch of the woode, then fanned out far beyond its perimeters. Diligently, they searched for wandering brigands, those cut-throats vividly described by Fengon and Gertrude, who explained that they had happened upon the murder scene, tragically arriving too late to save their beloved Hamblet. Despite the best efforts of all, the criminals were not found. Apparently, they had disappeared into thin air after committing the unspeakable deed.

Laertes and Ophelia, meanwhile, scurried about Helsingor, wasting no time making proper arrangements for a royal funeral. The city's strict health laws, central to the modern code of conduct enacted by Polonius to hopefully reduce the risk of plague, dictated that any deceased person, royalty included, be buried as soon as possible.

Deeply disturbed by what he'd been told, hoping against hope that what Gertrude and Fengon related was the truth, Polonius listlessly sat in his small study, penning brief letters which riders would shortly deliver to neighboring nobles, inviting them to attend Hamblet's last rites.

In the most private of all Kronborg's rooms, Gertrude and Fengon quietly stood on either side of an empty throne, the bejeweled crown resting on its cushioned seat.

"In short shrift," he said, "all will be well."

"Save only," Gertrude replied, visibly shivering, "the wrath of my absent son."

At that, Fengon firmly seized Gertrude's hand, insisting: "Amuleth must be made to understand!"

His simplicity of purpose caused her to laugh loudly, if without mirth. "Amuleth," she reminded him, "has a mind all his own, unlike that of any else living!"

Fengon pondered her statement, concerned the prince might prove a fly in his freshly poured buttermilk. Meanwhile, Gertrude closed her eyes, drifting back in time to the odd day of Amuleth's birth . . .

. . . *the battle was done. Hamblet and Fengon, remounting after Norway's surrender, spurred their horses. The royal warriors led the elite detachment known as The King's Guard clomping across Kronborg's lowered drawbridge, back into the castle proper. There, the brothers dismounted and, without exchanging a word, rushed across the courtyard toward the tower steps. Delighted commoners waved and cheered their beloved warrior-saviours.*

High atop the spiraling construction, Gertrude lay abed, straw messily scattered about to cover spilled blood, providing silent testament to an abnormally difficult birth. The queen now gently cradled the crying child she had, half-an-hour earlier, nearly died bringing into the world. Polonius, worn to a frazzle by so much frantic activity, and his wife, seemingly stronger than ever, silently sat on rickety chairs by Gertrude's side. The two loyal souls had, for the past hour, been ready for any emergency that might arise. Since this small pink-faced babe's belated entrance, everything had gone calmly, at least here. Their fear was that those horses rushing into Kronborg might herald Norway's advance force, in which case the day's horrors had hardly begun!

A guard, one of several already informed by Polonius that Denmark boasted a new prince, rushed in. His gleeful demeanor conveyed to all three a sense of relief even before any words were out: "The battle is won! The day is ours."

Surprised, Gertrude exchanged concerned glances with Polonius. He'd feared as deeply as she that Norway's leader might boldly step in, demanding to view the newborn prince. By ancient law and unwritten Scandinavian tradition, obeyed by all members of the Teutonic race, the hours-old heir-apparent could not be put to death; the son of a king must be treated with respect, for that was their heritage. Of late, though, values were so frayed, morality so oft tossed to the wind, the trio worried all the same, praying that, should Fortinbras prove victorious, he would remain true to the ancient Viking code and spare their newborn prince.

In fact, there was no need to worry.

Hamblet bolted in, smiling broadly at the wonderful news gathered from guards: Gertrude had delivered to him the son so necessary if order was to be maintained. Maintaining a polite distance, Fengon and the nobles remained several feet behind, waiting for Gertrude to speak. She did, an obscure smile crossing her face: "Thou meddlest with things dying? I, with those newborn."

The queen extended her swathed babe upward, toward Hamblet. A rousing cheer filled the room.

"Is he of God's making?" the king demanded.

"The heavens have blessed you with a goodly son. I do present you with a man of mine."

Thrilled, Hamblet seized the child, tenderly holding it close, rambling on: "What manner of man? Is his head worth a hat? Or his chin with beard?"

All laughed good-naturedly, this morning's bold warrior-king suddenly sounding like an innocent swain, fit only for tending sheep and writing love ballads. Fengon, feigning joy, quietly observed from the sidelines.

"Nay," Gertrude laughed, "he hath but little beard."

"Why, God will send more."

"It is a gallant child," Polonius ventured, stepping close to his king. "One that indeed pleases the subject, makes old hearts fresh."

Without a word to his trusted advisor, or physical acknowledgment that Polonius had addressed him, Hamblet peered down at the child, gently cradled in his rough arms. Already, Hamblet was lost in love for the infant's closed eyes and furrowed brow, its sulky mouth and austere cheeks. Hamblet carried his babe to the window, holding it close to the great open gash in the grey stones. Peering out, Hamblet carefully extricated one hand, using it to gesture at open fields and thick woode stretching for miles in every direction, a river running through it all and onward to the sea.

"As successively from blood to blood, your right of birth, your empery . . . your own!"

All in the room, save Gertrude and Fengon, cheered. Cautiously, the adulterous couple exchanged the secretive glances that had become their stock in trade when finding themselves in such awkward situations . . .

. . . now, 21 years later, the two were together—and alone!—at last. For reasons neither could comprehend, the

situation did not seem nearly so sweet as they long dreamed it might. Each avoided the other's eyes; both stole furtive glances at the hollow crown.

28.

Later that afternoon, Polonius rushed from his home to the drawbridge, through swirling rain that fell from a sky so black one might have half-believed it to be night. Dependable Balthazar waited, patiently holding a fully tacked horse's reins, the beast's eyes revealing utter confusion at having been forced from the safety of the stable in such dreadful weather. Polonius nodded his appreciation, seizing the leather reins, as Balthazar nodded politely, then hurried off to find cover. Moments later, Laertes approached, full cape held close and tight, taking the reins from his father.

"Let not the creaking of shoes nor the rustling of silks betray thy poor heart to women," Polonius warned as Laertes mounted, ready to depart for Wittenberge. He had been chosen to deliver the dread news to Prince Amuleth. "Keep thy foot out of brothels," Polonius continued, "and defy the foul fiend."

"I am of stronger mettle made," Laertes reassured his father. Polonius' eyes mutely announced that, following years of experience, he didn't believe a word of it.

Also in full cape, Ophelia joined them. "I have seen tempests," she marveled, "when scolding winds rived the knotty oaks. But never 'til now clouds dropping fire!"

"My necessities are embarked," Laertes concluded after a swift check. "Farewell!"

He leaned down, warmly hugging his sister, afterwards shaking his father's hand. No further words were exchanged. Laertes spurred the horse, waving one final time before disappearing from sight into a path that cut through the far end of Helsingor's woode.

"The swifter speed," Ophelia sighed, "the better!"

Arm-in-arm, father and daughter stepped back toward the old buildings, neatly lined against Kronborg's inner walls. Polonius noticed something his daughter, lost in thought, did not see: Fengon, peering down from a high castle window, signaling for Polonius to join him quickly as possible.

BOOK TWO

A MURDER OF CROWS

29.

Amuleth's chamber was located on the third floor, two doors down from Fortinbras' quarters. Horatio, always short on funds, shared a suite on the second floor with three other young men also hailing from humble families. The 'commoner quartet,' as they'd been tagged by their loftier housemates, were among a dozen such students admitted this year. A democratic impulse, steadily working its way upward through Europe, lead to an increasing mix of kings-to-be with commoners at universities. If such a trend were to continue, Fortinbras occasionally complained, what might be next: women students? Most of his fellows scoffed at the thought. The more farsighted among them, Amuleth included, insisted such an idea was not so outrageous as it might at first sound.

Numerous friends had, over the past months, inquired of Fortinbras as to why he and Amuleth did not relinquish their private rooms and share a suite with Horatio. After all, they were absolutely inseparable in all things but living quarters. The reply? Fortinbras adamantly explained he had suggested just such an arrangement on several occasions. Amuleth flatly refused, insisting on absolute privacy. This neither concerned nor insulted Fortinbras or Horatio, both of whom had long since learned to accept Amuleth's plentiful eccentricities.

Now, Amuleth sat alone on the balcony of that third floor sanctuary. A small arena of escape, not only from the world but even close friends, this was the spot to which the moodiest of Wittenberge's student-princes retired when ideas and emotions clashed in a sharp but confused young mind. Lightning tore through the night sky, momentarily illuminating the all-encroaching blackness with a full, terrible white light. Watching these natural forces, Amuleth was seized by the sneaking suspicion that this firestorm served as a visual metaphor for more universal matters. What if, Amuleth mused, life itself were nothing more than vast, eternal darkness, briefly brought to light by sudden thoughts, each vividly exploding for a fleeting moment, only to—with a terrible boom—disappear, never to be recovered?

The past seven months had been cataclysmic for Amuleth, as they would for any impressionable youth existing for more than twenty years in a state of happy oblivion: hunting, riding, sporting in the provincial territories composing Sjalland, isle of thick forests, rocky shores, and rich harvests, and surrounded by salt water on every side, forever thrashing down on rocky coasts. And, truth, be told, little if anything to engage the mind of one born with exceptional potential for creative thought.

Amuleth had grown to maturity in a world which treasured the full experience of everyday life, remaining blithely ignorant of potent alternative realms of the mind including philosophy and the high arts. True, Amuleth had learned ancient Norse myths, then accepted the more recent dismissals of such stuff as nothing more than fairytales when Christian thinking, and its accompanying chivalric code, flourished during Amuleth's youth. Throughout the blissful period of childhood, Amuleth accepted such stuff at face value, never allowing it to cause intellectual concern or moral confusion.

All that changed the moment that Amuleth arrived at university. Before attending even a single class, the prince sensed intellectual stimuli on every side, wholeheartedly surrendering to the world of ideas. Kronborg boasted only a few precious books. Though Gertrude had insisted that Amuleth learn to read, with daily instruction administered by knowledgeable Polonius, Amuleth never considered such stuff anything more than one more skill to be mastered. Reading tales from Norse myth, recently recorded in the annals, or perusing Bible stories already familiar thanks to Sunday sermons, Amuleth felt entertained though hardly enlightened. Reading, it seemed then, was merely a means to reinforce stories that could as easily be verbally conveyed.

At Wittenberge, reading took on another dimension. Amuleth was amazed by the concept, obvious to princes from more civilized areas though new to young Denmark, that books could open one's mind to other universes. Diverse studies, ranging from literature and history recorded by noble Romans to current tomes, daring to call into question the meaning of existence itself, filled the prince with excitement. What, Amuleth hungered to know, was life all about?

If, indeed, anything at all!

The fearsome possibility was that, in the end, *nothing* led, at least in part, to Amuleth's bouts of melancholy—dark moods which friends accepted without comprehending. Fortinbras and Horatio, like most students, managed to study varied subjects, mastering the material well enough to pass examinations without becoming overly concerned with the metaphysical implications of any ideas that they encountered. Amuleth, along with a few like-minded souls, could not so easily put issues aside when class was done, then rush off to The Wild Boar for fun, frivolity, and easily obtainable female companionship. Ideas encountered in books, issues raised in the classroom, and the original thoughts that they inspired within the mind haunted Amuleth during every waking hour. And, more often than not, by night too, when resonating concepts assumed the shadowy form of disturbing dreams.

This evening, though, Amuleth could not fall asleep. With every bolt of lightning, inexorably followed by a resounding clap of thunder, Amuleth's mind was torn by some confounding notion, briefly illuminated in marvelous if harrowing brightness only to slip away before the prince fully grasped its implications. At such moments, Amuleth was drawn to a dark conclusion, leading to encroaching isolation even from friends and fellow scholars exposed to the same theories.

In particular, one notion which no one—teacher or student—dared articulate now recurred in varied forms. The vision derived from comparisons which rose to the surface of Amuleth's mind: similarities between old myths—accepted without question throughout the first millennium by all inhabiting the northlands as the explanation for everything—and the New Religion that had, as the second millennium began, been introduced as their replacement. Why then, Amuleth wondered, did old tales and new parables seem, at least in this singular prince's mind, to be saying the same thing, if in a different manner?

Such concerns originated with explanations of man's creation. Were Adam and Eve, first man and woman according to Christianity, significantly different from *Madder-Atcha* and *Madder-Akka* who, for the ancient Norsemen, were father and mother to all? Gospel insisted that The Holy Trinity resided at the heart of man's moral existence. How were they distinct from the *Norns,* triad of goddesses who, according to Amuleth's ancestors, determined destiny? Satan, beloved angel of the Lord, cast out of heaven after an act of rebellion to visit earth and cause sin, struck Amuleth as no different than *Loki,* mischief maker of the old order, his naughty behaviour in time transforming into something more profoundly negative, the source of all evil. *Einherjar,* the heroic dead inhabiting *Valhal,* were all but indistinguishable, so far as Amuleth was concerned, from those saved souls existing in the Christian's heaven above.

Most profoundly, the theological concept of Apocalypse— that final moment when life on earth would end, all men saved or doomed according to previous actions—appeared identical to *Ragnarok*. This was the Norse vision of the-end-of-all, pre-ordained from the beginning of existence for reasons that mortals could never comprehend, yet always vaguely visible on time's horizon line. Even the New Religion's notion of a single God, replacing the existence of many, struck Amuleth as arbitrary. Vikings hailed *Thor* as supreme spirit, the others nothing more than minor figures in a tapestry-of-tales-out-of-time. Didn't the Bible insist on a hierarchy of angels, surrounding Jehovah even as the minor gods did powerful *Thor?* For that matter, how did the angel with a sword of fire, commanded by God to visit earth whenever mankind found itself most in need of enlightenment, differ from *Hermod*, messenger of the old gods who, carrying an identical weapon, arrived at times of crisis with divine word from on high? Or St. Elmo with his unique fire, prayed to as patron saint of sailors, qualify as unique when compared to *Ran*, sea spirit that caused ocean waves to rise or subside, depending on the sincerity of pleas by endangered Vikings?

Which set Amuleth to abstracting further: How could either of those visions be distinguished from that lord of the seas which earlier Greeks called Poseidon, the Romans transforming into their own Neptune? Having made such specific connections, Amuleth couldn't resist roaming further into the world of free-thought.

The prince's imagination danced on a cerebral stage, improvising outlandish choreographies of the intellect. Following exposure to the history of mankind's struggle since the race's origin to grasp one's place in the universe—which, of course, necessitated a fundamental comprehension of the cosmos itself—Amuleth perceived recurring patterns within supposedly successive world views. This led to a deep conviction that what initially appeared opposing ways of comprehending life were essentially one and the same, altered to make man's self-important notion of himself easily accessible to the next generation.

By this line of reason, the ancients, in the millennium preceding Christ's birth, first created, then inhabited a universe tailored to their specific needs. Another thousand years had passed during which a new religion, with its 'enlightened' view, assumed precedence. A third millennium in man's history on earth had now begun. During its opening century, a viewpoint emerged which, it seemed to Amuleth, would eventually challenge the sense of world-order that Christianity now—however temporarily—imposed. Amuleth's colleagues collectively referred to the still-fresh millennium as a modern age. That word—*modern!*—haunted and thrilled Denmark's prince, since such an age insisted on intense study of all that was past in order to understand the present and properly prepare for any future.

For Amuleth, Christianity—still in the process of spreading to barbaric countries, as it was likely to do for centuries to come—seemed, despite a lingering epithet hailing it as The New Religion, established, perhaps (dare one say it without risking the charge of heresy?) *passe*.

'New' meant something else entirely to Amuleth. For this prince, Christian fact was not so much a rejection of Norse myth as the restatement of identical concepts in alternate terms. If this were true—indeed, a big 'if'—wasn't it possible that, in time, all of what was now accepted as 'fact' might, as this latest millennium crawled to its close, be unmasked as a parallel set of fairytales to what the Norse believed to be 'truth,' or the Greeks and Romans adhered to before them? And, if so, then what was yet to come? Perhaps another series of stories— reworked variations on the same themes—which would eventually cause Christian parable to likewise be discarded as quaint fairytale? Thus, making way for another, supposedly 'true' restatement of the same ideas? Until that temporary version of man's ongoing ordering of his universe gave way once more . . .

Moreover, would there, could there—owing to recent development of a way of seeing which transformed long-feared *alchemy* into something only recently redubbed 'science'— allow a vision to evolve wherein all competing names for metaphysical powers were rejected, man coming to see himself as an insignificant speck on a vast canvas? Horatio, having turned realist since arrival, feared that was the case, accepting it without anguish. Amuleth, on the other hand, felt a profound sense of loss whenever such thoughts occurred.

Born to a man already considered Denmark's final feudal king, Amuleth was destined in time to lead the northlands into an equally perilous, highly different age. Amuleth sensed that when kingship did come, it would be necessary to provide a bridge for the populace. As ruler for a new age, Amuleth must discover a world vision fitting the tenor of the times, leading the people by example into their future.

No mean feat!

Rather, a challenge in excess of any known by previous northern kings, their responsibilities confined to the task of overseeing lands; doling out justice; claiming, taking, then defending ground.

Now, Amuleth studied the merciless sky above, wondering if this image of eternal emptiness might reflect all there was: a sweeping stretch of nothingness, man no more important than any of the myriad stars which, in kinder weather, visibly flickered from far away, yet so easily extinguished, as they were tonight. Yet each time another bolt of lightning cleaved the heavens, Amuleth dared hope all the world's religions—Greek and Roman antiquity, Norse and Celtic during The Dark Ages, Hebrew and Christian in recent years—might be essentially correct in their shared vision: Man's life did indeed have meaning; there was more to heaven and earth than dreamt of in Horatio's philosophy.

Lightning briefly banished the darkness again. Thunder—as always—followed. The Greeks would have claimed Zeus, from on high, hurled down another red-hot spear; Norwegians of the first millennium, that *Perkunu* had done the same thing. Amuleth considered the modern view, insisting this was only natural phenomenon, air temporarily displaced by storm particles.

No!

To exist, on any level above that of animals in the fields, one had to go on believing everything meant something, however challenged such a belief might be.

"Either there is a civil strife in heaven," Amuleth, though alone, insisted out loud, "or else the world, too saucy with the gods, incenses them to send destruction."

30.

"You are come to me in happy time," Fengon whispered to Polonius, ceremoniously ushering the greybeard into Kronborg's most secretive chamber, reserved for royal meetings of a clandestine nature. "For I have some sport in hand wherein your cunning can assist me much."

Visibly shivering at the cryptic undercurrent in Fengon's voice, Polonius nonetheless weakly nodded his acquiescence. A growing fear, deep in his stomach, that Fengon had been involved in Hamblet's death haunted Polonius day and night. Yet there was no proof. If any others shared his suspicions, none dared utter words of accusation, at least none Polonius had heard. A timid man at heart, he would certainly not be the first to do so. For Polonius, the only possible means of dealing with such a horrid situation was to accept that what he'd been told was the truth: Wandering brigands claimed the king's life. From there, Polonius could proceed, owing to his basic nature, in but one way: Like a horse outfitted with blinders, he would do whatever struck him as best for the assurance of continued order in Sjalland.

So the nervous old man allowed himself to be guided by his overbearing companion toward a pair of black stained wooden chairs, their plush cushions covered with bright red velvet, these and other matching objects of furniture imported a year earlier from Paris, now neatly arranged in the center of the small room's shadowy recesses. Once seated, Fengon—grasping the greybeard's simple, unwavering approach to things—shared with Polonius a plan which, Fengon insisted, was designed to insure the necessary order to avoid what could easily degenerate into a state of anarchy.

Though not literate, Fengon was hardly a fool. He knew,

having closely observed Polonius over the years, that nothing frightened the greybeard so much as confusion, and the violence—chaos, even—such a situation engendered. True, the two had often been at odds. Fengon stood foremost among those who refused to renounce the old ways. Polonius was the one who persuaded Hamblet to move the land in modern directions. Now, though, all that seemed beside the point. Old or new, Viking or Christian, Polonius had always, in word and deed, made clear that *order* was the ultimate imperative.

And order could only be achieved through a king. A strong king, at that. The land called out for a ruler, and a formidable one, soon as possible. Still, Polonius countered while half listening to Fengon's discourse as to why he ought to be quickly crowned, wasn't Laertes on his way to Wittenberge, there to locate Amuleth and, swiftly as they could, return, the rightful heir arriving in time to assure Sjalland's populace that the continuity of kingship would be maintained? Polonius actually surprised himself by daring to suggest a patient approach to Fengon.

Fine, then! Let us wait and see, the aging warrior countered, if Amuleth demonstrates the respect of hastily returning, as any proper prince surely would.

31.

At that moment, Laertes spurred his horse as they tore along a rain drenched road leading to the embarkation point for the ferry that would carry them south, toward the Danish mainland, from which they could proceed on down to Germany. On either side, he noted spiraling smoke from a dozen chimneys, thin gray lines wafting upward from behind a belt of trees, and then starkly cutting across the sullen sky. Before long, man and beast would leave Denmark's spinning windmills behind, witnessing the first of Germany's watchtowers.

"Go, horse, go, go!" Laertes encouraged the beast. "For thou and I have thirty miles to ride yet ere dinner time."

Dinner, and perhaps welcome relaxation afterwards. Laertes knew full well that, once he and his mount were ferried across the border, scant miles remained before they reached an old inn called The Halfway Mark. Famous indeed it was to travelers, those weary riders like Laertes, ranging between neighboring northern lands. Such souls arrived there certain of a stable for the horse, then generous servings of food and plentiful drink for themselves, as well as clean beds afterwards. Infamous, too, was The Halfway Mark for the availability of pretty maids to warm their fresh sheets.

Such an appealing stopover was possible for Laertes only because, unbeknownst to Polonius, the ever-plotting Fengon, feigning generosity and friendship, had cannily slipped an abundant supply of gold coins into the youth's purse minutes before Laertes joined his father and sister by Kronborg's drawbridge to say their fond farewells. Thus it was, in spite of repeated assurances to his father, Laertes failed to arrive at Wittenberge in time to spirit Amuleth back to Helsingor on the taxing day-and-night hard ride which would have returned the prince home in time for Hamblet's funeral.

32.

The formal ceremony had been planned to take place six days following discovery of the king's mutilated body. These rites were postponed—despite stern warnings from Polonius, having learned something of preventive medicine from his late wife—yet another day in case Amuleth happened to be temporarily delayed en route. By the time a full week, then eight days, passed, there was clearly no possibility of discussing any further postponement. Nobles from across Denmark, as well as some from neighboring countries to the north, including Old Fortinbras himself, had arrived for the express purpose of bidding fond farewell to their respected comrade. Still, all had country matters to attend at home, demanding swift return. That, coupled with unseasonably warm weather which caused the corpse to rapidly rot, convinced Polonius he must oversee the last rites without further ado.

On the morning of the ninth day, when the rain ceased for several hours, all gathered under a clammy sky to offer up a fitting tribute at Helsingor's old cemetery, located a mile and-a-half south of the city. Fengon, marching stiffly, accompanied the still-shaking queen and helped to hold her in place, Old Fortinbras supporting her other arm. Polonius followed a few paces behind with his daughter, Ophelia appearing as beautiful in basic black (setting off her ghostly white face, austerely powdered for the occasion) as she ordinarily looked in more colorful clothing. Three dozen of Denmark's great men, ranging from young aristocrats to rugged old knights, glumly lined the walkway, flanking the royal party. Behind them, hundreds of commoners—weeping aloud as their well-regarded ruler was slowly lowered into the ground—pressed close for one final glance.

A priest concluded his lengthy valediction, attendants afterwards filling in the cavernous grave with black dirt, carefully smoothing over its gravelly surface. Fengon firmly disengaged Gertrude's claw-like grasp on his arm, stepped up to Hamblet's final resting place, and in quivering voice pronounced: "Death makes no conquest of this conqueror. For now he lives in fame, though not in life."

With that, a dozen rude mechanicals dragged a granite headstone off the wagon that had carried it close, with great effort forcing the fresh cut marker into place. The priest, a tall man with dark, sunken eyes bedecked in flowing black gown, waved his right hand in silent blessing before anxiously hurrying away. In turn, according to rank and station, all others—Old Fortinbras allowed the honour of approaching first—stepped up to the stone, each making his peace with Hamblet in silent acknowledgment of the great things accomplished during this king's reign. Then, one by one, they drifted away in polite quietude. Each noble, man and woman, some solitary and others in small groups, drifted back toward Kronborg, where a simple mid-day meal was being prepared by Osric

and his team of talented cooks, offering these royals suste-
nance before their return to their own corners of the world
and a multitude of responsibilities awaiting them.

The peasants, left as always to fend for themselves, gazed
on until all the great ones were gone. This was the closest
most had come to nobility. They savored every moment, briefly
feeling a part of history in the making.

Fengon rejoined Gertrude, strong arms steadying the silent,
visibly distraught queen. She had mightily impressed everyone present with her stoicism, refusing to cry in public. Then,
following the secret plan Fengon and Polonius had devised as
their course of action in case Amuleth did not return for the
funeral, the greybeard left his daughter in Balthazar's company, scurrying to catch up with the royal couple.

"His silver hairs," Fengon reminded Gertrude, having already
shared the scheme with his intended, "will purchase us a good
opinion and buy men's voices to commend our deeds."

Precisely as the conspirators had devised in secret, the
widely trusted advisor to great ones warily approached.
Polonius' tone, as he addressed Fengon in a stage whisper,
sounded natural enough to those within earshot. Every word
had been scripted, even rehearsed, with nothing left to chance.
Fortunately, Polonius (Denmark's first man of common birth
to attend a German university) had involved himself with amateur theatricals while engaged in serious study of government.
Indeed, Polonius had combined his two great interests—theatre and politics—by playing the glorious Julius Caesar in a
production of a student-authored drama derived from
Plutarch's *Lives*.

"We followed then our lord, our lawful king," he muttered, recalling Sjalland's loyalty to Hamblet, adding: "So
should we you, if you should be our sovereign."

True to plan, Fengon hurled Polonius an annoyed look,
spitting back his reply: "If I should be? I had rather be a
peddler! Far be it from my heart, the very thought of it."

With that, Fengon guided the queen toward town, the small
stone cottages ahead seeming still as death under a placid and

listless sky. Polonius shrugged as if disappointed at this response, disengaging from royal company. Two well regarded knights from seaside castles, Tom of *Kattegat* and Dick of *Skagerrak*, halted in their tracks, trading reactions to what they overheard.

"Mark'd ye his words?" Tom inquired. "He would not take the crown."

"Therefore," Dick agreed, nodding with approval, "it is certain he is not ambitious." Relieved, the two continued on their way.

Fengon, as always, missed nothing: their words, which he strained to hear, precisely what he hoped for. "I will be married," he announced to himself, assured things were going well, "to a wealthy widow!"

33.

The day following Denmark's monumental funeral, Amuleth, Horatio, and Fortinbras—still oblivious to all that had happened—attended morning classes, then hurried off to The Wild Boar for their midday meal. Even as they entered, Laertes—weary from the road and varied diversions encountered along the way—finally dragged into Wittenberge. His head rang madly, as if bells relentlessly clanged in the belfry of his brain—this, the result of too much wine and too many women enjoyed during sojourns at The Halfway Mark and other institutions of dubious repute, all visited by Laertes while slowly wending his way south. Nearly an hour was then lost as Laertes procured a stable for his mount, afterward stopping for a late lunch at one of the open air taverns. The smell of fresh pork roasting on an open-spit proved too strong to resist. Finally, he set out to locate Amuleth's rooming house, upon arrival learning the prince's probable whereabouts from the owner's plump wife, then marching off to locate the heir apparent.

As Amuleth and friends finished off plates of pickled

herring, the front door flew open. "Laertes?" Amuleth gasped. "What happy gale blows you here?"

Slapping grime from the open road off his weather-worn cape, Laertes stepped deeper into the room. "Such wind as scatters young men through the world to seek their fortunes farther than at home, where small experience grows."

Already, Amuleth had risen to greet a youth with whom, if never particularly close, the prince had ever maintained a casually friendly relationship. "What news, what news," Amuleth anxiously asked, "in this our tottering state?"

Suddenly consumed with guilt over his unforgivable delay, and less than anxious to broach the unpleasant subject which had brought him hence, Laertes plopped in an empty chair, carefully avoiding Amuleth's penetrating eyes.

"It is a reeling world, indeed, my lord."

"Why look'st thou sad?" Experiencing an epiphany, Amuleth wondered out loud: "Is my father well?"

Squarely facing his prince, Laertes reached into an inner pocket, drawing forth the note Polonius had penned a full ten days earlier. Silently, he passed it on to Amuleth, who apprehensively tore open the missive and read, initially disbelieving the message discovered there.

Horatio, meanwhile, slipped around to Laertes' far side, softly inquiring: "How fares thy sister?"

"Well, well. She is at the court, no less beloved of Amuleth's uncle than were she his daughter." Such phrasing confused Horatio. Fortinbras, last to sense something was wrong, approached, concerned now.

"O!" Amuleth cried out, as if wounded in battle. "My prophetic soul."

"There are some shrewd contents in that," Fortinbras whispered to Horatio, "that steal color from Amuleth's cheek."

"Some dear friend dead," Horatio grunted, "else nothing in the world could turn so much the contrition."

"Call back yesterday," Amuleth wailed, "bid time return."

"Pardon me," Laertes pleaded. "I am but a guiltless messenger."

Shaking, Amuleth turned to Horatio and Fortinbras. "I must away to-day," the prince announced, "before night comes." Shocked, each was about to protest until Amuleth added: "Make it no wonder. If you knew my business, you would entreat me rather go than stay."

Tossing the note to Horatio, Amuleth hastily exited. Fortinbras peered over Horatio's shoulder, considering the finely penned words. Sensing the jist, Horatio handed Fortinbras the letter, rushing after Amuleth. Young Norway slowly read the missive. A wench, meanwhile, approached Laertes with ale.

Having fully recovered himself, Laertes eyed her closely, concluding: "I like this place, willingly could waste my time in it."

34.

Citizens darted up and down cobblestone streets, spending as little time in the open as possible owing to inclement weather which, for the past ten days, had severely blunted the edge of spring's arrival. Unaware of or unconcerned with light rain and middling wind, Amuleth trudged in the direction of their rooming-house, more deeply lost in thought even than usual. Something was amiss here, and Amuleth's mind immediately turned to Fengon: the crude, boisterous uncle whom Denmark's reserved prince had never been able to like or respect. Always, Amuleth had suspected Fengon of great potential for harm. This was the very man, as vile rumour had it, who secretly saw more of Gertrude than was proper. Amuleth had long harbored negative feelings for this despised uncle. Though the letter did not mention him, Amuleth somehow sensed there must be a connection.

"This day's black fate on more days doth-depend," the prince vowed. "This but begins the woe others must end."

Horatio, catching up, had already decided that lifelong friendship took precedence over scholastic advancement. "Let me go with you," he begged.

Amuleth stopped to consider that rare person on whom the lonely, distracted prince could ever depend. "Thou art not for the fashion of these times," Amuleth replied, "when none will sweat but for promotion."

"I will be your servant," Horatio offered.

"Nay, companion!" Amuleth knew that their own two mounts would not suffice for a forced ride, with little time for rest. "Get thee gone, hire extra horses. I'll be with thee straightaway."

Nodding, Horatio hurried off. Relieved a little to know there remained fine folk in a jaded world, Amuleth continued toward their house.

35.

For Ophelia, spring always meant the happy labor of creating and tending her flower garden. In a narrow stretch of land, the grass-lined alley separating their home from that of their nearest neighbor, she had for the past several years planted seeds on the very day when winter revealed its first signs of receding. Already, initial extensions of gentle green buds peered up through cracks in the rich earth, encouraged by the past week's plentiful rain.

Now, clothed in her oldest dress, Ophelia knelt on the damp earth, deftly employing a dull spade to adjust the dirt around her little ones, daydreaming about the real children she hoped to someday have and, likewise, nurture. Preferably, with Amuleth. Ophelia harbored long-term aspirations to achieve something greater than her current lot in life, however pleasant it might be. An ordinary, average, mundane marriage to some eager local boy—even one as fine and decent as Horatio, often caught gazing at Ophelia like a starving lout standing by a banquet he hadn't been invited to partake of—did not interest her.

Amuleth? Another matter entirely!

She slipped so deep into thought and activity that, without her realizing, Polonius managed to pass by the short iron fence effectively shutting her private place off from the nearby street, standing silent by the gate for several minutes, closely observing his daughter. As perceptive about her as he was sharp witted on courtly matters and political issues, Polonius knew, from Ophelia's dreamy eyes and distant manner, what the girl thought on. Long aware of Ophelia's affections, Polonius regularly lost sleep over the issue. A combination of his presence at Amuleth's birth and more recent occurrences intensified his concern.

"Touching the prince," he awkwardly inquired, "what is between you?"

Without ceasing her digging or looking in Polonius' direction, Ophelia—pretending she'd been aware of his presence all along—replied without hesitation: "He hath, my lord, made many tenders of affection to me."

"Do you believe his 'tenders,' as you call them?"

Ophelia rose, shaking loose bits of dirt from her smock, squarely facing her father. "Upon leaving for university, he left this ring behind him."

She held out her right hand. The gold band sparkled as a rare shaft of sunlight cut through the clouds. Polonius was well aware that the proudly displayed ring had been Amuleth's farewell present. But was it offered as a gesture from one long-time friend to another, or did it symbolize—to Ophelia, to Amuleth—something more serious?

"As sign of undying love, sayeth he?" Polonius asked in a voice laced with trepidation.

With all her heart, Ophelia longed to cry out 'yes!' However desired, that would have been dishonest. For she could vividly recall the uniqueness of their parting moment, how differently Amuleth behaved then in comparison to what she secretly hoped for . . .

. . . they had stood together, high on Kronborg's rear wall, overlooking the narrow river passing some distance from the castle and stretching far into the distant woode. Each enjoyed the soothing sound it made while trickling along to the southwest, eventually emptying into the North Sea. For this was their secluded spot, the private place where two beautiful young people regularly retreated and, by the hour, cuddled close. Amuleth's head cradled in Ophelia's sweet lap, she absently toyed with long strands of the prince's soft hair. In this manner, they spoke of things, momentarily seeming all-important, now long forgotten.

Often, the couple lingered there far later than was proper, silently watching, arm-in-arm as, in the west, a sinking sun tossed oddly appealing hues across the wide curtain of a darkling sky, likewise dappling the surface of Sjalland's swollen river with sudden splashes of bright scarlet. Then, the nightwind whistled through the trees by the woode's nearest extension, chilling the girl to the marrow of her bones. Holding her close, Amuleth gently brushed thin lips against her sultry mouth, though nothing more untoward than that ever occurred. Perfectly polite, Amuleth would abruptly escort Ophelia to her home.

Early on, she feared Amuleth might be playing her so slowly on purpose, in time planning to take advantage of a vulnerable and clearly smitten maid. Ophelia gradually grew frustrated by the incessantly gentleman-like treatment. On this final occasion, Ophelia had grown teary-eyed at the thought of her prince's oncoming departure. Deeply touched by the gift of a golden band, moreso by what she hoped it might mean, the girl closed her eyes, leaned forward, and patiently waited to be kissed long and hard and, following that, willing to surrender herself up to her prince. If Amuleth would not initiate their full-romance, she certainly would!

How stunned Ophelia had been, then, when Amuleth briefly brought those exquisitely thin lips up against her gentle, perfumed cheek before pulling back, refusing to take advantage, less to Ophelia's relief than her chagrin . . .

. . . sadly, she shook her head 'no,' admitting to her father: "As symbol for unyielding friendship, thinks me."

Polonius' relief was all too apparent. "For Amuleth and the trifling of his favour, hold it but a fashion and a toy in his blood."

Ophelia's eyes revealed her disappointment at the wise man's valediction. "No more but so?"

"But *just* so!"

Considering, she shrugged jauntily. A mischievous twinkle in her eyes, Ophelia knelt to tend her first buds.

"Time shall tell," she jauntily replied.

"Time is a thief," Polonius warned, leaning close, "that stealeth away life while seeming only to run free."

If Ophelia heard, she gave no sign in word or gesture.

36.

High above, in the royal chamber, Fengon stood beside the empty throne, staring into a nearby mirror. He had dared pick up the hollow crown, placing it on his head. This was a compulsive gesture which Fengon had, with great difficulty, resisted for the past week and a half. The obsession could no longer be avoided, despite the possible punishment. For this action was considered a capital crime for any man, however noble his birth, until the council met and formally agreed on a new ruler. Fengon didn't care, nor did he fear. Gross ambition, repressed for decades, now ran wild as a sudden spring flood, drowning everything in its path.

"As full of valour as of royal blood," Fengon confessed to himself, increasingly riddled with doubt about his previous gross action that precipitated all the country's current woes, "both I have spill'd. O, would the deed were good! For now, the devil, that told me I did well, says that this deed is chronicled in hell."

His reveries were interrupted by the sound of the door cracking opening. Panic stricken, Fengon yanked off the crown, swirling about. Gertrude stood a few feet away, observing her 'Fang' even as he'd been observing himself. Relieved to encounter none but his co-conspirator, Fengon hurried close, took her hand. From Gertrude's eyes, he grasped that she considered his actions with fascination.

"Men," he awkwardly explained, "are sometimes masters of their fates."

Mulling over his words, Gertrude shook her head 'no.' "Ourselves we do not owe," she insisted. "What is decreed must be, and this is so."

"Tut! I should have been that I am, had the maidenliest star in the firmament twinkled down on my conception."

Gertrude slowly strode to the room's far end. Yanking open the drawer of a large table, she withdrew a Tarot deck. Without a further word, she seated herself on the chair before the table and began dealing cards onto its surface. Fengon warily approached, saying nothing, watching her as critically as she had earlier observed him, realizing finally the vast difference in their approaches to life.

37.

In the narrow room Amuleth had called home for seven months, the prince stood by a wooden bed, methodically stuffing clothes and valuables into a leather traveling bag. The sound of frantic rapping at the doorway failed to snap young Denmark out of this trance-like state. When no reply came, Fortinbras opened the door and peered in, concerned, stepping close in his heavy footed way.

"Good cousin, give me audience a while."

Amuleth did not look up, muttering: "I take my leave before I have begun, for sorrow ends not when it seemeth done."

"I fear you were right," Fortinbras sighed. "Our good times are gone."

That statement allowed Amuleth to momentarily consider something other than consuming grief and intensifying rage. Overcome with rosy reveries of what now seemed a bygone golden age, Amuleth turned to face Fortinbras, offering this good coz a sad smile: "We were two lads that thought there were no more behind but such a day, tomorrow, as today."

Stepping near, Fortinbras added: "And to be boy, eternal. We were as twinned lambs that did frolic in the sun and blast the one at the other."

. . . once, on a bright spring day eleven years earlier, Fortinbras had arrived in Kronborg for his annual month-long visit. During such sojourns, Young Norway resided in the castle, there treated as a happy combination of family member and guest-of-honour, his presence in truth constituting something more on the order of royal hostage. Such yearly visitations had been guaranteed by a formal pact in the peace treaty signed at the end of the Teutonic civil wars. Nonetheless, during the month spent in Kronborg, Fortinbras was accounted a prince of this city, every bit as much as Amuleth.

On this glorious day, the two were playing at being Viking warriors of the sort that ravaged Aengland and other European climes for so many centuries, that harsh age of conquest and killing having finally drawn to an end. Outfitted in makeshift suits of armor, fashioned in secret from bits of metal which the princes discovered in refuse piles or found hidden away in secret cellars, they waved wooden swords in the air, bringing the toy weapons down with surprising violence against each other's shields. In such a manner, the ten-year-olds howled as they tore through Helsingor's streets like twin twisters, carelessly banging into nobles and commoners alike. Such behavior on the part of local street urchins might have resulted in a general clamor. Harsh paddling would have awaited any other perpetrators. These were, after all, sons of great kings, so minor mischief was accepted with good-natured tolerance.

Polonius happened to be crossing a newly cobbled street not far from their wild play. Laertes, also ten, and Ophelia, two months short of nine, flanked the greybeard on either side, as he led his own children along by their hands, lovingly held in his own.

"Two proper young men," Polonius marveled at the sight

of the princes, "of excellent growth and presence." He steered his children toward Amuleth and Fortinbras, trusting they would deign to show proper respect.

The old man was to be sorely disappointed! The princes, leaping about in ever-broadening circles, wild oats screaming to be sown, had decided sometime earlier that they cared little for this pompous fellow, overly eager to please whomever he might meet. Or his shy son, whose passive demeanor and vulnerable eyes suggested Laertes would likely emerge as a precise copy of his pandering father.

On the other hand, there was pretty Ophelia, hair care-fully arranged in a dazzling display of luxurious ringlets, intoxicatingly falling down across her face every time a breeze stirred the air. She shyly held back behind her father. The princes, only recently becoming interested in pretty girls, took mild note of her burgeoning charms.

"Here comes Monsieur Polonius," Amuleth's carrot-topped companion mocked, "with his mouth full of news."

"Which he will put on us," Amuleth replied, voice full of youthful sarcasm, "as pigeons feed their young."

"Then we shall be news-crammed."

"All the better; we shall be more marketable."

Both roared loudly at their own cleverness. As the huddled family drew near, Polonius released his children's hands. Ophelia glanced away, though in truth she, more mature for her years than either Amuleth or Fortinbras, found both princes highly attractive, if in different ways. Laertes stepped forward and smiled, hoping to be invited to join in their rau-cous game. But Polonius had heard the cruel words.

"Young gentlemen," he scolded, "your gests are too bold for your years." He turned on his heels, strutting away in a manner that made him appear more pretentious than before. Amuleth and Fortinbras attempted to control their laughter at the ridiculous sight. Ophelia, however taken with the soft, sensitive Amuleth and rugged, boisterous Fortinbras, none-theless felt deeply wounded for her beloved father's sake, sadly turning away to follow Polonius.

Laertes stood stock still, watching the princes as they darted off for more careless, carefree fun. Bitterness filled his heart. The abandoned boy secretly swore that someday, he'd revenge himself upon both for the mockery they'd made of his father on this unforgettable morn. Oblivious, Amuleth and Fortinbras darted around a corner, past an old stone barn boasting a newly thatched roof, around a wood fence to its adjoining open-air stable.

Roughly the same age, Horatio awaited the princes with rosy cheeks and dancing eyes. The gawky boy tightly grasped reins of three saddled horses. More common by birthright than Laertes, this agreeable lad with cheeks red as apples and uncombed hair resembling fresh gathered straw in spring, as well as a broad, open smile that delighted all, had long since been accepted as equal by the young royals.

"Let's ride!" Fortinbras shouted.

Expert equestrians all, exceptional for their age, the companions slipped polished boots in worn-stirrups, gracefully swirling up and onto their saddles. Three moving as one, they spurred their mounts tearing off down the street, leaving a chubby farm girl and her flock of geese, unfortunate enough to be sauntering down the cobbled avenue at precisely the wrong moment, to rush aside for fear of being trampled, her charges loudly squawking.

Sun shining down brightly, as if in full approval of this giddy activity, the inseparables bolted across the drawbridge. They waved gaily to guards positioned there, then swiftly traversed the field before disappearing into the thick woode beyond. There, hidden trails awaited, leading to enchanted groves where brash boys of today might play for hours at being fearless warriors of yore.

Solitary, Laertes stared down the empty street which, scant moments before, had been bursting with activity. "Punk rampant!" he called out to no one in particular before turning on his heels, following in the direction father and sister had taken . . .

"What we changed was innocence for innocence," Amuleth

recalled from the Wittenberge room that now bore witness to the sudden death of a prince's youth. "We knew not the doctrine of ill-doing, nor dream'd any did."

"And . . . now?"

Amuleth tensed, eyes swelling with sadness, face appearing to Fortinbras as somewhat heavier than usual, already worn with worry, swollen from concern.

Young Denmark, desperate to share a deep inner-fear, blurted out: "O, that I were as great as is my grief, or lesser than my name. Or that I could forget what I have been, or not remember what I must be now." The Danish prince lost control, sobbing like a girl.

Fortinbras, ever his famous father's son, was not pleased to see a fellow future leader drop the stoic demeanor of warrior. He admonished: "Art thou a man? Thy form cries out thou art! Yet thy tears are womanish."

"This is a great action," Amuleth gasped, "laid upon a soul unfit to perform it."

"Still," Fortinbras insisted, tactfully choosing words that might offer comfort, "a great soul."

"Indeed," Amuleth asked between tears, "think'st thou?"

"Aye!" Yet Fortinbras must be honest, awkwardly adding: "The soul of a . . . poet."

"In truth?" Amuleth suddenly admitted. "A woman."

Stunned at this admission, Fortinbras seized Amuleth in his arms. "No, no, coz. I misspoke—"

Amuleth, eyeballing Fortinbras, dared make a stranger, stronger confession still: "*I have a woman's longings!*"

38.

This was too much, even for such a loving relative and blood-brother since boyhood. Fortinbras had heard stories which, out of the extreme discomfort they caused, he chose to disbelieve: rumours concerning men who shared emotions, impulses with the other sex and, as some claimed, even the performance of secretive acts with members of their own. Now, he quickly withdrew from what, until then, had seemed nothing more than a friendly embrace. All at once, the simple hug meant something different, and considerably less acceptable, than simple mutual-admiration of fellow princes.

Inwardly, Fortinbras, in his simple way, struggled to grasp what had brought on this unexpected admission. Already, he wished he had not heard Amuleth's words but, having heard, knew he would never forget them. Apparently, news of Hamblet's death precipitated an uncontrolled flow of feelings within young Denmark. On their own accord, such emotions, long repressed, took the shape of the most dreaded statement a man of action could hear from a brother-in-arms: "I have a woman's longings!"

If nothing else, though, Amuleth had allowed Fortinbras to finally understand why his Danish kin, alone among members of their tight circle of friends, did not visit the plentiful brothels or seduce merchants' daughters. Amuleth, Fortinbras concluded, was one of those 'quare' fellows he knew existed, but had until this moment never encountered. So bizarre, though, that Amuleth would keep this a secret from all, even Fortinbras, for so very long!

Sensing the admission had been too precipitous for Fortinbras to accept, Amuleth broke off eye contact and sullenly returned to packing the necessities. Inadvertently, Fortinbras took several steps backward, silently waiting for Amuleth to finish. When the preparation for a grueling journey was complete, Amuleth brushed by Fortinbras without glance or word, carrying the bag down two flights of stairs. Fortinbras held back a moment before awkwardly following.

Eventually reaching the ground floor, he found Amuleth in the lobby, bidding farewell to friends gathered to offer sympathy. This consumed nearly twenty minutes. Afterwards, Amuleth exited through the main doorway, Fortinbras doggedly following, still silent. Outside, Horatio waited, patient as a saint, holding the reins of four horses. Two would be employed, in the old Viking manner, for the trek's first four hours, the others held in reserve, so the mounts could continue all day with no need for rest stops.

Swinging up into the saddle, Amuleth gazed down at poor, confused Fortinbras. So disoriented he appeared, so incapable of a reply to what had been heard! Amuleth felt sorry now for confessing such bizarre feelings to one clearly incapable of understanding. For a moment, Amuleth doubted the redheaded giant would be able to even muster a fond word of goodbye.

Happily, Amuleth was wrong. "Farewell, coz," Fortinbras at last called out in faltering voice. "If ere in need, think of me!"

Such a relief! To know their bond was strong and permanent enough that Fortinbras could forgive anything, even Amuleth's unwanted revelation of a secret self. "Farewell!" Amuleth replied. "I have a faint cold fear that almost freezes up the heart of life." Then, turning to Horatio, oblivious to all that had passed between the cousins: "Come thy ways; we'll go along together."

Amuleth snapped the reins, trotting off without a backward glance, Horatio following behind.

Fortinbras watched until they were out of sight, then turned back to consider his once-beloved Wittenberge, now uninviting under an oppressive grey sky. With Amuleth and Horatio absent, the pleasure Fortinbras had always taken from being in this place was likewise gone. Though the weather remained warm, Fortinbras was possessed by an inner chill. Never in his life had he felt more alone.

Drifting back toward the university, no particular purpose in mind yet not wanting to return to a solitary room, at least not now, Fortinbras noticed Laertes, conspicuously absent during all the excitement. The young Dane stood before a shabby establishment, conversing with two tawdry street girls, bargaining for their favors.

"Wenches, I'll buy for you both. Follow me, girls!"

"And you shall pay for 'em well," Fortinbras muttered, aware of the decrepit house's ill reputation.

Gleefully, Laertes stepped inside the rough building. For a moment, Fortinbras considered warning him that the place was unsanitary. Then, he thought better of it. Why meddle in another's business? Laertes was no true friend, after all. Let him make, and hopefully learn from, his own mistakes—even if it meant acquiring a touch of the curse between soiled-sheets in that flea-invested place.

Instead, Fortinbras silently continued on his way. Two blocks later, he turned a corner, running smack into Mistress Quickly, untouchable object of so many affections. "Is this not the hostess of my favorite tavern?" he asked, never before happening upon her outside The Boar.

"You do well know it," she coyly replied, happily surprising Fortinbras by stopping for pleasantries. "Thou hast called her to a 'reckoning' many times and oft."

"And a most sweet wench?"

"As the honey of Hybla," she giggled.

"Let me be thy bee-keeper!"

Mistress Quickly rolled her eyes coquettishly before ambling on, Fortinbras hurrying after. Wasn't that the sun peeking through a dark cloud? Wittenberge, even without his great friends, might not be such a bad place after all.

39.

In Kronborg's main courtyard, Fengon stood alone, tossing slabs of raw meat to three growling dogs while secretly dreaming of the crown. Soon, it would be his, at least if all went according to plan. There remained, however, one minor problem. Occasionally, he set pleasing thoughts aside to concentrate on an issue that his bride-to-be had raised two nights earlier: Amuleth. Time enough to worry about that slender youth, if and when the prince returned home. Meanwhile, and in a happier mood, Gertrude had suggested a new name ought to be decided on for Fengon's future use. It would be officially adapted after Polonius—to whom they regularly slipped hints as to what they were up to, he finding himself in a quicksand-like situation of being unable to extricate himself after first stepping in—helped them manipulate Sjalland's nobility into accepting the hasty marriage and Fengon's quick-crowning.

Renaming had become an accepted habit in Denmark following the advent of Christianity one hundred years earlier. As a means of announcing their modernity, onetime warriors renamed—and, in the process, reinvented—themselves, before becoming modern kings. Constantine, Gertrude suggested, would prove a happy choice, considering another of Denmark's recently acquired traditions, the adoption of everything the Brits developed during their own transition from barbarism to civilization half a millennium earlier. Gertrude devoured every volume of lore delivered to Danish shores by traveling merchants, scouring them for any tidbit which might be aped and applied in her own land. Aengland's first great Christian king, she learned, ruled as Ambrosius during their waning pagan era. He demanded all Brits call him Constantine, once the New Religion took hold, in deference to the revered Roman emperor of that name. One hundred years after the death of Christ, and following a century of fervent hostility toward His followers, an inspired Constantine oversaw the conversion of Rome's vast empire to Christianity.

Gertrude's beloved Fang offered his own idea as to what name would best serve him. Among those ancients, whose histories were now told and retold throughout Sjalland, Fengon most admired Claudius, an emperor whose reign preceded that of Constantine by several generations. Here was a man who quietly stood in the shadow of his blood relative, the notorious Caligula, for half his lifetime. Claudius secretively arranged that tyrant's betrayal and death, then assumed full power himself. Better still, Claudius had been wise enough to pretend, during Caligula's infamous rule, that he did not care one whit for power. Such a seeming lack of ambition allowed the public to perceive him as the proper choice to take up the crown following Caligula's demise.

Yes! Claudius I of Denmark would, in due time, be the

name Fengon should assume, and then rule by. As the yap-
ping beasts leaped high, wolfing down ragged chunks of raw
elk caught in midair by sharp fangs, Fengon noted, out of his
eye's corner, Polonius, briskly exiting the castle. Tom and Dick
followed dutifully behind as the greybeard approached
Fengon, affecting a great show of trepidation. Out of respect,
the good knights stood back a bit, allowing Polonius to
approach and state their case.

First, over much growling from the dogs, he engaged Fengon
in polite small talk, inquiring as to his well being, reporting
on the sad failure of Denmark's patrols to catch Hamblet's
killers. Fengon made a great show of personal disappointment upon hearing this. Then, Polonius explained what the
late king's brother already knew full well: Gertrude, who rarely
left her room, was progressing as well as could be hoped for
under difficult circumstances.

Finally, as he and Fengon had planned, Polonius precisely
followed their agreed-upon script: "What were more holy than
to rejoice the queen is well? What holier than, for royalty's
repair and for present comfort as well as future good, to bless
the bed of majesty again with a sweet fellow to it?"

Fengon could not, like Polonius, boast experience as an
amateur actor. Still, he played his part with relish, gusto, and
a starkly authentic aura of conviction. Effectively feigning
horror, he recoiled at the suggestion that he, of all people,
might be the proper one to assume power, thereby guarantee-
ing an avoidance of anarchy. Waving huge hands, still dripping wet and blood-red, in exaggerated gestures of refusal,
Fengon smiled lovingly at his hounds, relentlessly yelping for
more, leaping high as if propelled by coiled springs to clumsily lick his sticky fingers.

"Aye, true. But not I. For Fengon would not, could not,
will not for the world."

Tom and Dick, observing closely, huddled together.

"Yet looks he like a king," Tom softly observed, knowing
the best man for any political position was the one least frantic
with desire to achieve it.

Dick nodded in agreement, impressed. "Behold his eye," he noted, "as bright as is the eagle's, lightens forth controlling majesty."

The two had, for nearly two full weeks, grown ever more concerned for Denmark's continued safety, owing not only to the unexpected death of Hamblet but also Amuleth's failure to return and claim his crown. Could it be, as rumour had it, that this prince had grown so enamored of studies in art and philosophy that country matters—including a murdered father and his homeland's subsequent fate—meant nothing? True, relations between Denmark and Norway had remained stable for better than two decades. And Fortinbras had seemed polite enough—sincerely sorry, even—at the funeral. Some said he appeared more devastated by Hamblet's death than the king's own brother. Yet might not the failure of the crown prince to hurry back suggest to Old Norway, considering Denmark's current situation in leisure, this was the moment to achieve the victory he once dearly sought?

The land must have a king!

According to old Danish tradition, the proper succession of deceased king to incumbent prince remained inviolate always. Nonetheless, a combination of a suddenly perilous state of affairs with the constant modernization of northern Europe convinced Tom, Dick, and other trusted men of good intent that this might be the time to turn away from such an old-fashioned tradition, even as they had recently rejected a scad of others.

Polonius grimly turned from Fengon, back to Tom and Dick, shrugging broadly, as if to say, 'I have done my best to convince him.' He shuffled away, back to personal and political duties, followed by a quiet evening at home.

Fengon, whistling to his dogs, took perverse pleasure watching them wildly hop up in anticipation of more meat, though none was left to proffer. Observing him, and noting Fengon's seeming obliviousness to their presence, Tom and Dick drew close. Perhaps such a respected pair of knights, who ages ago—when the concept of knighthood was still new in this land—

fought alongside Fengon in brutal combat with Denmark's enemies, might succeed in convincing him of the necessity, even where the good old man had failed.

40.

As Tom and Dick eagerly engaged Fengon in conversation, Polonius hurried to the steps lining Kronborg's rear wall. Ascending, Polonius attempted to put his recent bit of play-acting behind him. The greybeard had never cared for Fengon; worse still, he secretly feared this royal brother was at least partly responsible for good Hamblet's death. Yet ever practical to a fault, Polonius now as always pushed such moral issues aside, realistically concentrating instead on the well-being of the state. Now that such matters had been attended to, at least for the moment, he must likewise deal with his own problems, similarly approaching any personal situation. In such a mood did he search for his daughter.

Out of breath from a day filled with emotional and physical exertion, he reached the high turret where Ophelia oft stood, at twilight time, staring off into the distance. Coming up behind her, Polonius watched as she turned to consider the west, a wan look masking her enchanting face. Approaching the lithe girl, Polonius was fascinated to note how closely the image before him now recalled a classic painting: the lovely young woman, dainty and demure in long grey frock, luxurious ringlets of light-brown hair dancing slightly in the soft wind; her entire being framed by the wide sky, now a natural kaleidoscope of light pink, bright red, and dark violet, diverse colors gently bleeding into one another, cut at odd angles by stretches of gray clouds.

Down below, shards of gold from the setting sun reflected on a tight, twisting channel of the river. Its shining waters seemed troubled, their shallows surfeited with dead leaves from the past autumn, long buried under an unrelenting blanket of snow, at last exposed to the air and rapidly decomposing, a process

so strong that Polonius could nose the sickly sweet odor even
from high up and far away. The tranquil vision set to motion
within the greybeard an eerie excitement, not fully understood,
though he sensed that he was gradually becoming enraptured
by it.

And, at the center of all, Ophelia herself. She appeared less
flesh-and-blood woman than a seductive spirit from some old
romance, full cape and shawl suggesting an aura of the
unknown, as her father observed the girl's tightly held hands
and soft sighs. Hearing him approach, she glanced backward,
observing him over her shoulder, revealing dark impassive
eyes hinting at everything, revealing nothing. Her gesture was
accompanied by a strange, sly smile that could have been
borrowed from Egypt's legendary Sphynx. No artist, however talented, could ever capture the atmosphere of heightened melancholy Polonius experienced. It seemed almost sac-
rilegious to disturb the quiet moment.

Still, they must talk!

"Laertes returns soon," Polonius said soothingly, coming
alongside her.

Ophelia laughed, then corrected his false impression as to
the cause of her sweet sadness: "I long with all my heart to
see the prince. I hope he is much grown since last I saw him."

Unhappy to note she harked on Amuleth still, despite his
advice of several days earlier, Polonius grew stiff with seriousness: "Think of him as a star in the sky, out of thy orb."

Insulted, she stepped closer, meeting his weak old eyes with
her own intense orbs. "Look on me as a meteor," Ophelia
announced haughtily, "burning bright by night!"

However concerned for her future, considering all he knew
about this, Polonius couldn't help but be impressed by his
daughter's striking sense of self worth. "What of Horatio?"
he hopefully inquired.

"As a brother, loved even as I do dear Laertes."

"That, I believe," he dared suggest, "is how lord Amuleth
loves you! And how you should him."

Frustrated by the possibility that her father might be correct, yet still spurred on to achieve her ambitions, Ophelia peered into the distance, hopeful she might be the first in Kronborg to catch sight of her prodigal prince.

"I will be joined with nobility," she steadfastly insisted. Polonius could only sigh, shrug, and step away.

41.

Amuleth and Horatio at this very moment remained two full days ride from Helsingor. On exhausted mounts, no longer responding to their masters' spurs even after the scheduled alternation of horses, the companions slowly wound their way across a storm bruised landscape of downed trees, ruined fences, and once tended fields, all swiftly reduced to a scandalous state of slack disorder by wind and rain.

Several days earlier, they had crossed the official barrier separating the two countries, moving steadily upward into beloved Denmark. A ferry from the mainland's northeastern tip and across to Sjalland's shores, which would carry the companions across the notoriously treacherous channel, still remained before they could finally close in on Kronborg. The early evening sky above radiated with a bright crimson sun, now the unseasonable weather of the past ten days had finally subsided. At this hour, the prince and the pauper were intent on discovering some farmhouse where a handful of coins might purchase a pair of rough beds and the stabling of weary horses. An inn would be too much to hope for in this thinly inhabited area.

Certainly, they had no desire to sleep in the woode, as they had, out of necessity, the previous night. Then, they had found themselves far from any outpost of civilization, however humble. Drenched twigs failed to ignite a fire, providing only billowing smoke that choked Amuleth and Horatio without providing hoped-for warmth; cold cheese and stale bread, moldy in their saddlebags, their only provisions for a humble meal. A single blanket apiece provided scant protection from raging winds. Their horses, eager for a warm barn and fresh grain, stared at them incredulously all night long from a tree where they'd been tethered, their wide, unblinking eyes suggesting the animals now believed their masters to be quite mad. Why else spend a miserable night in such wild places?

On this, the following day, men and mounts shared the agony of aching bones and tired flesh. As ribbons of bright color diminished in the sky, swiftly replaced by a stark granite curtain heralding yet another such night nearing, a pair of blackbirds swept down. Like descending phantoms set against a somber curtain, the creatures closed in on the mounted men, cawing as if intent on warning Amuleth and Horatio of trouble ahead. That, at least, was how such phenomenon would have been interpreted in the old days. Amuleth chuckled; a hundred years previous, it was believed by all that *Huginn* and *Muninn*, twin ravens of Odin, regularly carried down messages to mortals. Horatio now openly scoffed at such superstition. Amuleth, if not a true believer, nonetheless acknowledged the possibility that everyday occurrences might in some way represent the hand of providence busily at work in the world.

"Ravens, crows, and kites fly o'er our heads," Amuleth noted, "and downward look on us, as if we were sickly prey."

Then, as the murder of crows departed swifter even than they'd arrived, the riders noticed several farmers a ahead, three stark silhouettes set against a vibrant sky. These men-of-the-earth trudged home following a long day's work in a wide field running parallel to the mud-caked, unpaved highway, its rough edges covered with ivy and bracken. Perhaps such yoemen might provide the grubby sanctuary these tired travelers dreamed of. Amuleth and Horatio clucked to their horses, causing them to lumber forward at least a little more quickly, closing in on the trio. Before either could call out, The two weary riders picked up bits and pieces of an ongoing conversation.

"The old king's dead? Then, masters, look to see a troubled world."

"No, no. By God's grace, his son shall reign."

"What with him? He comes not like to his father's greatness."

"Woe to the land that's governed by a child!"

Those words wounded Amuleth; what followed struck closer still to the heart.

"I saw Polonius offer Fengon a crown. He put it by, but for all that, to my thinking, he would fain have had it."

Amuleth reined in, casting Horatio a look of concern. "Our absence makes us unthrifty to our knowledge," the prince, shocked, confided. "Let's along!"

There would be no rest tonight, for man or beast!

So they continued on for several more miles, until briars hanging from high trees scratched their faces, even Amuleth admitting it was foolish to try riding any further. But the prince would not be halted. Amuleth and Horatio dismounted, the horses momentarily believing they would soon be allowed to sleep. Instead, their masters seized the reins and, with much loud clucking, convinced the animals there were miles yet to go before such a luxury would be proffered. On they went, men leading the beasts, their way now lit only by a dim quarter-moon, a slender sickle of whiteness hanging from the sky and partly concealed by clouds, as well as the stars, twinkling in their courses.

42.

Shortly before noon on the following day, 30 Danish nobles and knights, Polonius positioned several feet ahead of the others and carefully carrying Sjalland's jeweled crown, approached Fengon. They caught him unawares as he stepped down the lengthy corridor leading from Kronborg's state-offices to the private enclave where, as was his habit, Fengon took his midday meal alone. Spotting the body of anxious men and knowing full well the reason for their presence, Fengon feigned disinterest, good-naturedly waving them away as he marched on with nary a sideways glance. Not to be denied, they followed, great men suddenly reduced to a flock of sheep, hurrying after their watchdog.

"How many times must I tell thee?" Fengon called over his shoulder. "I seek not the throne."

"Some are born great," Polonius suggested, "some pursue greatness, while others have greatness thrust upon them."

To the relief of all, Fengon halted, turning to acknowledge the men, noting looks of deep concern on all their faces. Amuleth had not returned, despite ample time to complete the journey three times over. Possibly the prince had, as several feared, been waylaid on the road, perhaps by the same brigands who had murdered Hamblet. More likely, Amuleth's decision was to remain at university, finding the entire business of government tiresome. Even Gertrude, at last relinquishing her period of mourning, admitted publicly it might be best to give up the ever more futile hope of seeing Amuleth soon, instead doing something—*anything*—which would announce to all that Denmark remained well kinged and ready to defend itself.

After all, rumours abounded—perhaps exaggerations, then again possibly true—that Norwegian soldiers had been seen slipping ashore on Sjalland's beaches. There was no proof of such things. What couldn't be denied was the sense of panic spreading throughout the land, growing worse with each day Denmark remained kingless. Polonius gravely explained all this once more. Performing a studied demeanor of exasperation, Fengon shrugged in a way that neatly suggested he might yet relent, solemnly nodding his head in a gesture of capitulation.

A great cheer went up, so loud it threatened to shock the very foundations of Kronborg. Within minutes, preparations were underway for a double ceremony—private marriage followed by public coronation—the following night.

During that afternoon's remaining hours and all through the following day, countless pigs were slaughtered, afterwards slow-smoked over bonfires for a feast unlike any Kronborg had known since the wild days—when Elsinore's old men, mostly farmers and fishermen now, lived the life of warriors.

In honour of that heritage, Fengon decreed the evening's festivities—to be held throughout the castle and adjoining town,
the entire populace invited to partake on some level—would
be staged in the manner of a Viking celebration, including
pagan dancing of the sort popular in pre-Christian times. Grog
would be available late into the night, select knights and nobles
congregating in the great hall with the new royal couple, all
others scattered throughout castle and city. All welcomed such
a revel, save one sober knight, Francis of Aarhus. He alone
expressed concern that the act of descending to such half-
forgotten rituals might, however unintentionally, initiate a
pendulum swing back to the barbarism of old. Sir Francis
could not guess that his deepest fear was precisely what Fengon
hoped for. But the others mostly scoffed at his conservatism,
looking forward to the liberation that such revels would provide. So Francis chose to keep his own peace.

43.

The hours passed quickly, as all in Helsingor labored to make
ready. Early on the next evening, the coronation was held in
the somber recesses of Kronborg's throne room, attended by
a precious few. Those less fortunate, including leading members of the town's middleclass, were allowed to crowd close
to immense iron doors, stretching to see or hear something
through the cracks which, years hence, they might tell their
grandchildren.

Francis, among those invited to attend the formal ceremony,
again kept to himself, gravitating toward the back of the room,
standing there in solitary contemplation. Not far away were
Tom and Dick. Having at last listened to the many qualms
Francis privately expressed, the two knights grew ever more
concerned he was, perhaps, right. They'd been o'er hasty,
deciding to offer Fengon the crown without fully investigat-
ing Amuleth's absence. While others stood spellbound by an
event at once social, political, and religious, Tom and Dick

slowly drifted toward the rear, finally joining Francis by the door. Flanking him on either side, they stood ready to join forces with Francis should he offer a protest. For if this was to happen, Fengon might dare to attempt an act of vengeance on this lone voice, crying out in the wilderness.

A dozen other significant figures of southern Denmark, most accompanied by their ladies in their finery, silently stood between the isolated trio and, on a raised dais, Sjalland's new royal couple, seated on twin thrones. Claudius (as Fengon chose to be called from this moment forth) smiled lovingly at Gertrude, the sight of them together suggesting to all gathered an unlikely union here being achieved. She, ever striving for a greater sense of contemporary worldliness, was bedecked in a luxurious light-blue gown of the finest silk. This had been fashioned in Italy from material imported from the Orient. The gown was patterned by fashion mongers in Venezia, afterwards stitched together by the finest Florentine artisans who ornamented the item with their own fine white lace, before allowing it to be carried along treacherous overland trade routes into the northlands. Though Gertrude ordered the gown a year earlier, she never before wore it in public, insisting the magnificent creation (which, she had known at first sight, would appear stunning on her still slender frame) must be reserved for some special occasion, the likes of which now unfolded.

Claudius, just now her husband but long the queen's unsuspecting foil, earlier entered the room wearing an enormous horned helmet, inherited from a fabled grandfather who had died fighting on the Aenglish coast. Around his shoulders rested a long fur cape, fashioned from skins of silver wolves he himself had hunted down and killed, long tails touching the floor on either side. Had not the guests been intimidated, they might have laughed out loud when the two arrived, considering the contrast. The past appeared to be marrying the future in a strange slice of the present.

In due time, Polonius hesitantly stepped toward the couple, cradling Denmark's golden crown in his thin, feeble, shaking hands. The man now called Claudius rose, removed his helmet, quickly scooped up and carried away by the ever-fawning Osric. Taking the crown from Polonius, he handed it to Gertrude, his wife since a secret ceremony attended only by the couple and a priest half-an-hour earlier.

She slowly rose, every move graceful as would be expected from so elegant a female, and circled behind Claudius. Before setting the crown on his head, Gertrude and Claudius simultaneously turned to the silent assembly. The royal couple said nothing, their fiery eyes announcing this was the final opportunity for any to speak in protest, should someone so choose. The crowd, however dubious they may have grown during the past twenty-four hours as to Claudius' right to rule, sensed itself overwhelmed by the man's strength, cunning, and arrogance. All save Francis, who knew that the final moment of truth was at hand: He must do the right thing.

"To those whose dealings have deserved the place," Claudius began, "and those who have a wit to claim the throne—"

"Prince Amuleth!" Francis called out from the rear.

Claudius' temper rose at the undesired interruption, his face turning a bright shade of scarlet as he shouted back: "This prince has neither claimed, nor deserved it. And therefore, in my opinion, cannot have it."

Tom and Dick moved closer to Francis, who whispered to his trusted friends: "If you crown him, let me prophesy: Future ages will groan for this foul act."

"Well you have argued, sir," Tom sighed, deeply sorry for his hasty decision at the funeral.

"But for your part," Dick added, "keep thee quiet, or for capital treason they will arrest you here."

Francis nodded and said no more, remaining inwardly concerned for their beloved kingdom. One by one, other members of the congregation, observing his silent sadness, likewise experienced second thoughts as to the wisdom of what they were allowing to transpire, the coronation set into motion more by blind fear for Sjalland's well being than any logical progression of thought. The twin ceremonies had seemed acceptable, so long as this man's rule remained only an idea. Actually seeing a rough throwback to an earlier age married to their modern queen, about to receive the crown from her delicate hands filled more than a few souls with a sense of trepidation not easily dismissed.

Yet it was too late now to do, or say, anything. So, as a stony silence descended on all even as the previous week's nasty weather had on Denmark, they watched with growing concern as Claudius turned to Gertrude. She smiled, setting the crown on her husband's thick mane. A husband, who Francis and others believed, remained, according to ancient Nordic lore, her own brother.

44.

Amuleth might have reached Helsingor in time to prevent such maimed rites, had it not been for a series of accidents that overtook them while on the open road. That, at least, is how a realist like Horatio would describe what happened. Viewing the situation from a different perspective, the more spiritually inclined Amuleth firmly believed the hand of fate made itself felt, as it did on all other creatures crawling across the earth, foolishly believing they could determine their own destinies, unknowingly existing as chess pieces in the great game of life.

Before dawn's first light, the travelers had departed from an isolated farmhouse where, after deciding it was impossible to either press on further or sleep upon the hard ground again, they'd taken refuge for the night. Mere minutes later, Horatio's horse, confused in the darkness, slipped on a patch of fresh moss, falling over into a deep rut and nearly crushing Horatio, who luckily managed to leap away at the last possible moment. Sadly, the poor beast's leg was broken. Horatio had no alternative but put the creature out of its misery. After, they stumbled on, on foot, leading their three remaining horses.

At noon, having made little headway owing to paths that promised shortcuts but instead circled backward on themselves, eating away at the precious time, they stopped for a quick, cold meal only to discover their remaining food spoiled. There followed a search, leading to a small cluster of cottages where cheese, sausage, and black bread were purchased, at an exorbitant price, from an unpleasant farmer's wife who flatly refused to believe she was in the presence of her prince. Indeed, Amuleth—caked with mud, clothing torn, hair bedraggled—appeared anything but princely!

Shortly after eating a rancid bit of the meat, Horatio grew sick and could not continue. He lay still and feverish in the balmy shade of a towering tree for several painfully long hours before rising up again on both legs to try and remount. Though he managed, if with great difficulty, to pull himself up into the saddle, they rode slowly as possible for fear Horatio might pass out and fall off.

Finally, they reached the embarkation point where, three times a day, ferries carried travellers back and forth from the Danish mainland to Sjalland's southernmost tip. But the last scheduled run had just concluded; besides, the water appeared churlish, making the always insolent ferrymen more sullen than usual. Experienced sailors all, they nonetheless refused to take the risk, even after the slighter of these two odd fellows insisted he was their prince, a notion the ferrymen scoffed at more nastily than had the farmer's mean-spirited wife earlier that day.

Of the dozen docked boats, only one seemed even a remote possibility. Its elderly captain offered to take them across at an exorbitant rate, but only if they waited until his half-dozen crew members completed patching a gaping hole in the hull. Amuleth and Horatio stood about, hoping the weather might change, allowing them to bargain with this gruff fellow's competitors. By their sides, worn horses pawed at muddy ground adjacent to the water, chewing on whatever meagre bits of grass they could unearth, steam visibly rising from the beasts' tired flesh. A cluster of gulls, cawing incessantly, circled.

Annoyed by these noisy intruders, distracted horses glanced up, snorting at the sky.

Sultry clouds, ripe with rain and heavy with thunder, swept across the heavens without unleashing the expected torrent. Then, they were gone, the sun peeking out again, warming the land. In the west, the sun made ready for its slow descent, its lower rim slipping down past a belt of beech trees lining the horizon, casting odd-shaped traces of a rich orange-glow on the small, spiraling waves. Amuleth was overcome by a profound sense of the scene's sad beauty, moved to sudden and unexpected tears, though they may, in part, have been due to apprehension over what waited at home.

At last, the ferrymen were convinced the channel was safe for crossing. Now, though, the encroaching darkness created new dangers, and so a new demand for higher payment still was made. Besides, the sailors were none too anxious to navigate with these shabby, possibly mad, boys on board! Amuleth negotiated a deal with the old ferryman, his boat finally repaired. At first, their crossing went well enough. The channel remained calm; there was no sound but the gulls above and, below, the slushing sound of heavy wooden oars, repeatedly violating the water's purity as the crew members, three on either side, earned their pay. A westerly breeze, filled with salt smell, announced their nearness to Sjalland. Though the far-shore remained a blur on an uncertain horizon, Amuleth and Horatio were seized with homesickness for the land of their youth.

The ferry pushed closer. Through a rising mist, they could spot the trees thinning out by water's edge, breathed in the tangy odor of fresh moss in the air, and were deeply moved to realize that in moments they would step down on familiar ground. Then, an eerie stillness descended, spooking all aboard. Within seconds, a gale came rushing in out of nowhere, whipping them downstream, even as the sun's last rays faded, leaving all in near-total darkness. At the same time, a fierce current seized the ferry, forcing it miles out of the way, nearly floundering in rough waves. At last, by the rising moon's half-hearted light, the old captain spotted a narrow inlet, and they made for it, aching-arms rowing hard, the tide their mortal enemy.

The captain would not push near to the shore, for fear his barge might become grounded or, worse still, that the already-damaged hull could break apart. Despite Amuleth's offer to pay more money still, the grizzled sailor remained steadfast, so the two companions seized their horse's reins and, amid much horrified whinnying, forced the animals over the side, into the estuary's turbulent waters. There, men and beasts struggled against the current which threatened to drag them off to a sudden drowning. They slipped on jagged rocks, slimy with seaweed, at last crawling up onto a stretch of sandy beach where they lay, exhausted, listening to distant oars carrying the boat back to the far side.

An hour passed before they could rise and proceed. At this point, they could discern no real road, however rough, only a slight pathway, barely detectable in the moonlight now that the abundant grass of early spring had overgrown the slight trace of an escape route. Still, they followed along as best they could, snaking between a belt of beeches, the barely visible pathway twisting and turning in maddening patterns, up and down uneven ground, until finally, and by blind luck, they found themselves at an opening to the main road. So unexpected was this bit of fortune that Amuleth and Horatio leaped, cheered, and embraced before traveling on.

Hours later, the exhausted riders reached Helsingor's furthest outskirts. Despite all these delays, they might yet have arrived at the castle in time to interrupt formal ceremonies. However, Amuleth—blithely unaware of what was occurring little more than a mile away—insisted they stop at the graveyard, so that proper respects might be paid to old Hamblet. The sky had long since passed from fading ribbons of scarlet to a vast black shroud when they drew to a halt atop a hillock overlooking an odd assortment of grey cut stones. A sharp night wind passed through the trees, rustling leaves, leaving both riders feeling haunted.

"O, Jupiter," Amuleth sighed, dismounting, "how weary are my spirits."

Ever precise, Horatio replied: "I care not for my spirits, if my legs were not so worn."

"I am almost afraid to stand alone here in the churchyard," Amuleth admitted as the breeze increased, chilling each to the bone, "yet I will adventure."

From force of habit, Horatio seized the reins, quite unnecessary since the three weary beasts would take no further step unless forced to do so. Horatio then bore silent witness while Amuleth stumbled down a poorly marked path, through natural barriers of high weeds and sharp stones, past an abandoned cathedral and into the graveyard proper.

45.

All members of the royal party had, following the ritual's conclusion, retired to Kronborg's Great Hall. On the wall, torches burned brightly. From an elevated stage, musicians played. All about, horns of beer and wine were passed about by blonde maidens, attired (at Fengon's insistence) in colorful green, white, and red costumes causing the girls to resemble *Valkyries* of ancient lore. To disapproving Francis, it seemed as if time had been turned back, the gathered multitude transported to The Dark Ages, that dread period of abiding ignorance which encompassed Denmark before the new millennium brought with it a more forward looking set of values.

Glancing around, Francis was disappointed to realize any sense of general foreboding noted during the ceremony had faded, washed away by plentiful ale. Apprehension was swiftly set aside by all seated near him, now smiling at the rich smell of peppered mackerel and steamed oysters, first course of the evening's ongoing feast, carried in on huge platters by smiling servants. Swiftly, the lords and their ladies surrendered to an ever-increasing sense of abandonment. They reminded Francis, a devout Christian, of the Bible story in which Israel's children worshipped the golden calf shortly after Moses led them out of Egypt in hope of regaining their true religion.

Surely, he must be alone with such concerns, Francis guessed in his assigned seat at the far end of the hall from Claudius and Gertrude, and insultingly close to the door. Wearing crowns, the royal couple moved to the center of a growing circle of sycophants, each eager to suggest his own essentialness to the coming regime. Stretched out like spokes from a wagon wheel's hub, gathered guests sat at a succession of long oak tables.

As the evening wore on, everyone feasted, drank, sang, laughed, and giddily toasted their generous hosts. Osric could be seen flitting from king to queen, pouring wine for the two-some before hurrying off to oversee delivery of ever larger platters, heaped high with roasted pork, smoked plaice, and pickled beets, to each table. Nearest to the royal couple, Polonius and his daughter sat, enjoying the revelry all around. Gertrude, tipsy, rose with some difficulty, maneuvering around her husband to speak with Ophelia, woman-to-woman. They were, after all, the most beautiful women present, a gorgeous matron and the young heartbreaker. Several members of the knighthood, having stashed any and all fears for the future to the backs of their minds, rose in unison, singing a chorus of the pre-Christian ballad once traditional for such rituals in bygone Denmark of pagan days:

> Wedding is great Juno's crown:
> O blessed bond of board and bed!
> 'Tis Hymen peoples every town,
> High wedlock then be honoured:
> Honour, high honour and renown,
> To Hymen, god of every town!

Claudius drained his cup, only recently refilled, in one great gulp, several drops of the heady liquid afterwards visible on his rough, uncombed beard. Osric poured the king another round from a silver serving goblet. "Fill, 'til the wine o'erwell the cup," Claudius shouted, glancing to his queen. "I cannot drink too much of Gertrude's love."

His words were primitive, shockingly so considering not only the solemnity of their wedding but, more significant, the enormity of the undertaking he, as king, must assume the following morn. This was, after all, the dawn of a new era in which Denmark was expected to continue the social reforms and cultural rebirth which had, like green buds of spring, recently sprouted. For better or worse, Claudius was king now, crowned with unanimous consent of the council. There was nothing to do but tolerate, even embrace his garrulous manner. Most visitors chuckled at his words; Tom and Dick gritted their teeth in grim acknowledgment of the mistake they now knew they had made.

Gertrude's reply made things worse still. In slurred speech, she called back, voice echoing through the cavernous room: "I am the drudge and toil of your delight, but you shall bear the burden soon at night."

This had ever been her way in private, though such antics were new to the public: a careful show of assumed sophistication throughout a day's normal course; shockingly vulgar words and actions followed when alcohol dulled her maintenance of a studied persona as Denmark's most regal woman. Now, she was the actor who, for the moment, forgets his role and the extemporary lines it demands.

Polonius, serving as the chorus of their play, turned to the crowd, smiling broadly while rolling his eyes, each and every gesture intended to indicate to all present that they should take their cue from the king, treating the queen's breach of etiquette with casual good nature. Still, too much was enough. When Gertrude attempted to swig from her silver goblet, only managing to spill most of the wine down the front of her elegant gown, Tom, Dick, and Francis were, though silent still, aghast at the sight.

"Come, madame, wife," Claudius beckoned. "Sit by my side, and let the world slip away. We shall never be younger!"

Gertrude tottered in Claudius' direction. Before she could drop down in her chair, the musicians, who had ceased their playing during the shouting match, caught her eye as, instruments in hand, they awaited a command.

"Yea, musicians, play," Gertrude ordered with a flighty wave. "Give room, and foot it, girls!"

At once, they set about merrily making music. A number of young women scurried to the open floor, dragging male companions in their wake. In a moment, the music was so loud, the dancing so wild, no one observing the scene could have guessed this event was happening in the second millennium. The clock had been turned back. Like some dark beast, crawling out of its cave and yawning while returning to full consciousness, the old ways woke from their long slumber.

46.

After a brief search, the prince located old Hamblet's grave. A long, respectful silence was broken when Amuleth addressed this rough reminder of a bygone father: "In war was never lion raged more fierce, in peace was never gentle lamb more mild, than was that kingly man, god's favorite." Such intense emotions caught in the troubled youth's throat. "Are all thy conquests, glories, triumphs, spoils shrunk to this little measure of land?"

Unable to resist a sudden compulsion for physical contact, Amuleth reached out and touched the fresh cut stone. A sharp wind howled through the surrounding trees, stirring fresh leaves to shudder, as if a ghost slipped by. Horatio, spooked by the sensation, did not want to stand solitary any longer. Leading the fatigued horses, he cautiously descended, joining Amuleth.

"Enough, sire. Come away from this haunted place."

No reaction from Amuleth; perhaps the prince hadn't heard. When Amuleth did deign to speak, the words seemed less directed at Horatio than some lingering memory: "Thou art the ruins of the noblest man that ever lived in the tide of times. Woe to the hand that shed this costly blood."

That final statement caused Horatio to stammer, in reply: "You cannot guess who caused your father's death."

Amuleth whirled, eyeing Horatio as if he had suddenly revealed himself to be an uncomprehending fool. "My *uncle* is to blame for this!"

Where did *this* conclusion hearken from? Horatio could not know that Amuleth, while silently riding side by side with him had, hour after hour, considered, then rejected, the possibility that Hamblet had been done in by wandering outlaws. None of their ilk dared enter Denmark since the initiation, a decade earlier, of citizens' watches all along the border. No, the killer must be someone close at hand. Someone who would profit by his death. Someone who revealed, at least to one as observant as Amuleth, a propensity for violence in the past.

Over the years, Amuleth often noted a touch of jealousy in Fengon's eyes, a sense of constant irritation to his manner. Also, before leaving for Wittenberge, the prince heard rumours concerning Fengon's relationship with Amuleth's mother, rumours too ugly to warrant any hint of credence.

Until now . . .

"We know not—"

"In my heart, I know!" Amuleth waved a fist in the air, angrily cursing the elements all around them. "You live still that shall hereafter for this cry woe."

"Let God revenge it, then," Horatio suggested.

"Indeed! For God helps those who help themselves."

There was no arguing with Amuleth when the prince was so totally consumed by anger. Each summoned up what little energy remained in their depleted frames, hauling themselves up into the saddles, encouraging their horses one final time before journey's end. A slow, plodding gait was the best the beasts could manage. Though less than two miles remained to Kronborg, the better part of an hour passed before they reached the drawbridge, kept lowered this night in case any guests arrived late. While approaching, the riders noted bright lights in adjacent Helsingor, suggesting great excitement in the city.

Balthazar, alone on guard, hurried to see who approached, stopping in his tracks upon recognition. "My liege—"

Amuleth at first seemed not to notice him, preoccupied with flaming candles in every window, intense rhythms of old tunes wafting on the wind from the Great Hall. "Good Balthazar, be this the music of merriment?"

Exasperated, the lad glanced down rather than meet Amuleth's amazed eyes. "In honour, good lords," he admitted, "of the marriage, Claudius to Gertrude." He then explained all that had occurred, including Fengon's changing of his name for this occasion.

Amuleth and Horatio were at first too stunned to speak. Then, Horatio ventured: "So soon after—"

"Thrift, Horatio, thrift!" Amuleth interrupted, bitterly sardonic. "The funeral baked meats did coldly furnish forth the marriage table."

Balthazar led the lathered mounts away for a long rubdown and the comfort of a clean barn. Amuleth and Horatio, bodies stiff, trudged across the courtyard toward the Great Hall, Amuleth's rage rising like a mist at early morn.

47.

Inside, Gertrude ceased her giddy visitation with Ophelia, reeling as she wandered back to her husband's side. While musicians offered up frenzied airs and young people gamboled, Gertrude seized Claudius by the hand. Despite his amused protest, the queen attempted to pull him up and out of his chair.

"Nay, sit," Claudius resisted, bloated from food and drink, "for you and I are past our dancing days."

Never one to be dissuaded from her current purpose, Gertrude gleefully dragged Claudius along behind her. "How long was't now since last yourself and I were in a masque?" she cooed.

"B'yre lady, thirty years."

"What, man! 'Tis not so much. Sure, five and twenty years, and then we were masked."

Everyone made way for king and queen, and then circled the royal couple, watching as they joined in a jig. Gertrude, surprisingly graceful considering the amount of alcohol she'd consumed; Claudius, stumbling over himself and his wife. Guests, aware of proper protocol, laughed good-naturedly at his lame movements. He grinned in return, treating all present to a brief view of his jovial side.

No one present yet noticed Amuleth and Horatio. Following their entrance at the doors, they stood back, staring in disbelief at the grotesque pageant. Then Ophelia, spotting them out of her eye's corner, unceremoniously dropped the hand of a pageboy she'd been dancing with, rushing to join her two favorites.

"Welcome, beloved boys," Ophelia squealed.

Less owing to status than the honest calling of her heart, she approached Amuleth first. The prince barely acknowledged her, angry eyes fuming at the sight of the queen mother, sporting with this despised uncle. Horatio, as always, gazed at Ophelia as a parched man would water: a lovelorn swain from old ballads, lost in secret rapture. Without warning, the outer fringe of partygoers then become aware of intruders, gradually giving way like an old castle wall crumbling to dust, making room for Amuleth to pass. Oblivious still, Gertrude and Claudius danced on.

"From this day forth," she said of his clumsy movement, "I'll use you for my mirth. Yea, for my laughter."

"Is it come to this?" he chuckled.

Surrounding guests, cheering at their antics moments earlier, fell to silence. All noise in the hall gradually ceased, the musicians halting their performance as, one by one, gathered revelers felt a dark presence, then noted the intruders, grim of mien, caked with dirt from the road.

"Shall I hear more," Amuleth asked, "or shall I speak?"

Taken aback, Claudius and Gertrude—somewhat sobered by the unexpected sight—feigned delight.

"The prodigal!" she announced gleefully.

"Welcome, gentlemen," he added with false merriment. Amuleth did not pause to consider Claudius, rather sidling up to Gertrude, staring deep into her eyes, disbelieving she would allow such a thing to happen.

"Ah, me," Amuleth sighed. "How weak a thing the heart of a woman is!"

Personally insulted by these words, Ophelia recoiled. Always ready to support the woman he had yearned for since childhood, Horatio seized her hand comfortingly. Aware of her grown child's disgust at this ribald display, Gertrude stepped forward, hoping to salvage things.

"Our hearts you see not," she chided. "They are pitiful!"

Unable to look on one who would consider such a shabby defense, Amuleth turned away, approaching Claudius. "Thou dost usurp my place," the prince coldly announced, "and doest thou not know the just proportion of my sorrows?"

Claudius thought it best to hide behind a shield of verbal bravado. "Well we know your tenderness of heart and gentle, kind, *effeminate* remorse," he said in a tone that transformed seeming sympathy into suggested reproach, "which we have noted in you to *your* kind."

"If I be so disgracious in your sight," Amuleth spit back, "let me march on, and not offend your grace."

The prince turned, all congregated lords and ladies shifting out of the way for fear Amuleth might run them down. However slight of frame, still there was something threatening about Amuleth when angry. Horatio and Ophelia followed hard upon the prince's heels.

"Thy head is as full of quarrel as an egg is stuffed with meat," Claudius called after.

Amuleth stopped short, standing stock-still a moment before turning to face the bloat king: "I do not like your faults."

"A friendly eye could never see such faults."

Aware of rising tempers, Gertrude—any remnants of her drunken fog banished by sudden fear of total disaster—seized a cup from a server, hurrying over to offer Amuleth wine. "Love, and be friends, as two such men should be."

Smirking, Amuleth accepted the glass, holding it high in

mock toast. "Long may'st thou live to see another, as I see thee now, deck'd in *thy* rights, as thou art stall'd in *mine*." With that, Amuleth drained the glass in one gulp.

Claudius, furious, stalked forward, his hulking frame overshadowing the slender prince. "Away, slight man," he hissed.

"Pray you, no more of this!" Gertrude shrieked, stepping between the two before they came to blows. "'Tis like the howling of Irish wolves at the moon."

Amuleth waved to amazed onlookers in a broad burlesque of graciousness. "Every man hence to his idle bed . . ." Then, Amuleth stormed to the door and left, Horatio in attendance. Ophelia would have followed, but Polonius hurried close, seizing her arm and holding her back.

"Farewell," she whispered, "sweet masters both. I must be gone." Horatio smiled to her over his shoulder, Amuleth barely managing a cursory nod in her direction.

48.

Side-by-side, Amuleth and Horatio mounted the castle stairs on their way to the third floor. There, spare rooms were always available, kept prepared for unexpected guests. For several minutes, neither felt comfortable breaking the oppressive silence.

Finally, Horatio spoke: "Such a mad marriage never was before!"

His words supplied the trigger that released Amuleth's anger: "I'll have this crown of mine cut from my shoulders ere I see the true king's crown so foul misplaced."

Amuleth was so engulfed with fury that, for a moment, continuing on their way proved impossible. They halted, midway between floors, Amuleth staring back down toward the scene they had escaped, Horatio patiently waiting.

In another part of the castle, king and queen hurried down a corridor, silent at first, preferring an alternative stairway to their royal bed-chamber on the second level, so as not to confront Amuleth another time this night. "I had rather been a country servant maid than a great queen, with this coronation," Gertrude whined, all her pretensions to a lofty reign, worthy of Italian nobles whose exploits as set down in weighty tomes she had devoured by the hour, shattered by the intrusion of two unwanted players upon what was to have been her private stage. "To be thus taunted, scorn'd, and baited at!"

Claudius nodded solemnly.

"This was an ill beginning of the night."

"The prince," she admitted guiltily, "hath given me some worthy cause to wish things done, undone."

Turning to consider her closely, Claudius sensed that Gertrude was on the edge of hysteria. Concerned for the woman he truly loved, as well as eager to maintain all he had won, Claudius seized her by the shoulders, swept her close, reminding her: "What's done cannot be undone!"

Ascending once more on the building's far side, Amuleth unleashed a diatribe: "Was ever gentleman thus grieved as I? Office usurped, father slain. And Fengon . . . 'Claudius'! A husband? A king? Nay, *devil!*"

Horatio fully understood how difficult things had become. Also, he was aware that he could provide a service in the coming days, wandering the castle freely as an unvalued commoner, thereby catching bits and pieces of rumour no one would utter in front of Amuleth. "Know this, prince," he interjected. "Nothing can proceed that toucheth us where I shall not have intelligence!"

At that, Amuleth managed a smile, circling Horatio with a loving arm. "My heart doth joy that yet in all my life, I have found one man that was true to me."

Horatio warmed to the compliment. Then Amuleth hugged him tightly. Perhaps, Horatio thought, too tightly . . .

. . . alone in their chamber, Gertrude knelt by a small fireplace, absently stoking glistening embers, gradually bringing them back to full flame. Claudius lay naked under the covers, impatiently waiting for his wife.

"Wilt thou make a fire, or should I complain on thee for being slow in thy hot office?"

She shuddered. "My mind misgives."

"Prince Amuleth?"

Gertrude nodded. "Where two raging fires meet together, they do consume the thing that feeds their fury."

Rising up, Claudius responded: "Save such thoughts for the morrow. Madam, undress you and come to bed now."

Still upset, Gertrude did as told. Once beside him, a pile of heavy covers warming the royal couple, she found it possible to relax. Claudius took her in his rugged arms and, for a moment, the presence of his male strength allowed Gertrude to half-believe everything might turn out alright.

They kissed. His hungry mouth traveled downward, under the covers, across her stomach. He was an army on the move, pushing forward, intent on conquest. "This," Claudius whispered when she finally groaned with pleasure, "is a way to kill a wife with kindness!" His hand joined with his mouth then, revisiting lands well-traveled in the past, much to her delight. "Now," Claudius announced, flipping his wife over and onto her stomach, "I comes behind."

"Ay," Gertrude giggled, all dark thoughts temporarily banished, "and you had an eye behind you, you might see more detraction at your heels than fortunes before you."

As he roughly entered her, purposefully causing a little pain, Gertrude screamed in abandon.

49.

Passing near the royal bedchamber while continuing upward, the friends heard her animal-like yelps from far down the corridor. Horatio wanted to move on quickly as possible. Amuleth insisted on halting for a moment, listening despite— or, perhaps, owing to—the pain such sounds clearly caused one ever-sensitive to any breach of proper conduct. "Frailty," the prince cursed, "thy name is woman." With Horatio's help,

Amuleth, shaken, managed to climb the final set of stairs.

Arriving on the third floor, they halted before an open window, allowing a full view of southern Sjalland. A broad, wide panorama of lush territory stretched for miles in the moon's liquid light, the land appearing as if fresh milk had slowly dripped over plain, forest, farm, and village. Most notably, the river: now-placid waters sparkled, a silver thread winding its inexorable way toward oblivion.

"How bright and goodly shines the moon," Amuleth mused. Nodding in agreement, Horatio could not stifle a long, loud yawn. "What," Amuleth asked, "thou speak'st drowsily?"

"The deep of night is crept upon our talk, and nature must obey necessity."

"Which we will negate with a little rest."

The two ambled on, approaching a pair of open doors, directly across the corridor from one another, each leading to an empty room, made ready for use while visitors were in residence. Before the two could bid one another goodnight, Osric danced up the stairs, bags in hand.

"My lords? Your luggage—"

"Oh," Amuleth complained, "here comes the courageous captain of complements."

If Osric heard, he showed no sign. "A grand night, yes? And fine day for such festivities, though not as nice as some might wish. Still, I—"

"What!" Amuleth asked Horatio in a stage-whisper. "This gentleman will out-talk us all!"

Then, in a mood to bait the pompous courtier, Amuleth bowed low, offering an exaggerated gesture of appreciation for this speedy delivery. Osric dropped the two bags down before either door. Then, as if secretly a student of Terpsichore, Osric bowed lower even than Amuleth, twisting about as he rose, like a human corkscrew.

"I am the very pink of courtesy," Amuleth announced, voice dripping with wicked suggestion.

Osric blushed at the unexpected words while Horatio, hoping to hide his humor, stepped back into shadows. "'Pink,'"

Osric, made bold by Amuleth's implication, dared ask, "for . . . flower?"

"Right," Amuleth replied with a wink.

"Well, then," Osric confided, "is my pump well-flowered!"

"Well said!" Amuleth howled. "Follow me this jest now 'til thou hast worn out thy pump."

Realizing at last that he was the butt of their little joke, Osric quit before suffering further humiliation. "Nay, if thy wits run the wild-goose chase," he huffed, retiring, "I have done." With that, Osric flamboyantly stormed off.

Horatio, watching as Osric whirled round the bend and out of sight, approached Amuleth smiling. "Well said; that was laid on with a trowel."

"Why, is not this better than a groaning for love, that runs up and down to hide his bauble in a hole?"

"Stop there," Horatio begged, sides splitting with laughter, "stop there."

Amuleth's mood abruptly changed from sarcasm to curiosity, the prince turning to consider Horatio. "Thou desirest me to stop in my tale against the hair?"

Not one for punning, Horatio nonetheless decided to give it a try: "Thy wouldn't else have made thy tale large."

Eyes observant, Amuleth stepped closer still. "O, thou art deceived. I would have made it short. For I was come to the whole depth of my tale."

Aware of the rapidly changing tone, Horatio felt confused, threatened even, inquiring: "My lord?"

All mirth gone, Amuleth studied Horatio long and hard before asking, in a detached voice: "What would you?"

"Serve you, sir," he replied without hesitation.

Nodding a full understanding of that loyalty, Amuleth pointed backward, indicating the open door. Partly out of exhaustion, partly due to the emotional pressure since receiving word of Hamblet's death, partly from a difficult reaction to the unexpected events of their strange homecoming, Amuleth uttered an idea long repressed, if secretly present for years. Motioning for Horatio to follow, Amuleth admitted: "I would have you. Come, come with me, and we'll make short work."

At first, the good companion, stunned to total silence, hoped against hope that this was nothing more than a continuation of the joke with which they had belittled Osric. The needy look in Amuleth's eyes made clear that was not the case. "I know not whether to depart in silence," Horatio whispered, "or bitterly to speak in your reproof."

More desperate by the moment, Amuleth came so close they could feel each other's warm breath. "As thou lovest me, Horatio," Amuleth begged, "wipe not out the rest of thy services by leaving now."

Horatio inched backward. "I cannot, nor I will not, yield up to you."

Amuleth gently draped an arm around Horatio's shoulder, as Horatio had earlier done with the prince. "Is it not too far gone?"

"'Tis time to part, then!" Horatio insisted, firmly disengaging. "Goodnight, sweet prince."

Horatio turned, awkwardly grabbed for his bag, then hurried into his own chamber, closing the door firmly, bolting it without looking back.

Heart beating fast, his mind alert with new horror, Horatio muttered in amazement: "Methinks he thinks as though he were in love!" A brief shudder was followed by: "Strange love, of such a sudden grown bold!"

Amuleth hesitated before picking up the other bag, staring long and hard at the closed door. Then, the prince likewise entered a lonely chamber. Once inside, Amuleth strode to a full-length mirror on the far wall, considering the austere image found there: a sad, bitter, confused face. In truth, Amuleth knew, a face better described as beautiful than handsome.

"Who is it," the prince asked in choking voice, "that can tell me who—or what—I am?"

BOOK THREE

BEAUTY IS
A WITCH

50.

Life goes on. This, despite occurrences that momentarily seem likely to plunge the entire world into eternal darkness. No such thing: Next day, the sun rises again, as if nothing out of the ordinary happened in the human sphere. The river still rushes toward the sea; the common folk climb out of bed, trudge off to work, then back home again for a simple meal and sodden sleep, only to repeat the cycle again. A precious few—living within confines of their imaginations, bounded by invisible bars they themselves erect over windows in the prisons of their minds—perceive things differently. To them, life will never again be the same. Yet for the general, the mass, the crowd, and all things in the natural world surrounding them, absolutely nothing has changed.

So it should come as no surprise that by mid-morning the following day, the citizens of Kronborg castle and adjacent Helsingor-town were busily operating as if no untoward event had occurred the preceding night. Before dawn's first harsh shafts descended on Denmark, farmers residing in provincial outskirts woke in darkness, consumed their breakfasts, then stepped out to till the fields, their *dams* having risen earlier still to prepare a humble meal of boiled eggs and cold ham. One by one, shopkeepers opened stalls for business. In the rich and fetid marketplace, everything from fresh vegetables to imported clothing would be bartered throughout the day, even if customers did buzz amongst themselves about the awful scene that apparently had interrupted the aristocrat-party on the previous evening.

Shortly, merchants were hawking wares to a diverse citizenry as, in ever growing numbers, they hurried along cobblestone streets to appointments as important to each as what had occurred among those of royal birth was to those members of the ruling class. In unbearably hot enclaves, blacksmiths banged away at strips of metal, carefully held by tongs over blazing fires, twisting red-hot ore into horseshoes. An occasional apprentice, in training to some master craftsman, rushed off to a nearby store in search of the missing ingredient that must be purchased at once if their product was to be completed on time.

The heady smell of burning meat, carried by a light breeze across countless courtyards, wordlessly announced to all that hogs, butchered early in the day, were already roasting for the afternoon meal. Greasy shanks and juicy slabs would soon be available at indoor taverns and open-air stands. Demure milk-maids, their hair the color of fresh-churned butter, carried huge containers of the precious liquid, to be sold in the central square, high atop surprisingly strong shoulders. Young toughs followed in their wake, hoping for encouragement from young lips which, the boys feared, threatened to remain sweetly sealed forever, at least if one believed the haughty looks in these young ladies' eyes.

Yet one resident did not make an appearance, even if the crowd longed for a look at their prodigal prince. Amuleth was not to be found anywhere. Shortly, hushed-word spread that Sjalland's melancholy prince would not emerge from the third-floor closet where, following the strange homecoming that had awaited Amuleth's return, the prince slept late into the day. Then, food had to be brought up by servants, left by the bolted door, dirty dishes picked up hours later. Since the meals had indeed been eaten, all could assume Amuleth was alive and well inside.

Neither did Gertrude nor Claudius make a public show, preferring to spend their first day as married couple in the privacy of the castle's royal suites. All this gave way to much gossip-mongering. Was something—*everything!*—amiss? So passed three full days following Amuleth's homecoming. Finally, though, Denmark's queen and her husband-king— having officially taken their morning repaste in a private nook reserved for the reigning couple, and attended there by ever-fawning Osric—made ready to offer their little corner of the world an initial daytime appearance as ruling couple. This, on the morning of the fourth day. Exiting the castle's main-building to the riveting accompaniment of a pre-arranged trumpet flourish, Claudius and Gertrude, bedecked in velvet finery, led their entourage through the nearby street, all strutting directly to the royal stable where they were lavishly outfitted for a morning of falconry in the field just beyond Kronborg's heavy drawbridge.

In particular, the women in the party turned the heads of all the common-folk that they passed. Colorfully outfitted in bright sporting costumes, capped by imported felt hats boasting luxurious plumes and silver ornaments, Gertrude (having enthusiastically imported these items at great expense during her first husband's reign, causing Old Hamblet to begrudgingly raise taxes on local farmers) and her ladies-in-waiting had held off wearing the gaudy items, saving them for some special occasion, that date having finally arrived. Highly aware of the thousand eyes upon them, they drew themselves up onto chosen mounts, recently having mastered the art of riding side-saddle, newly popular on the continent's southern tier, where this was now considered the only proper form for women of good breeding. Indeed, every movement and all manners (like the rich garments they displayed) betrayed a highly conscious, if unconsciously exaggerated, imitation of sophisticated styles that had earlier been developed in more culturally advanced lands.

Contrarily, the men took their cue from Claudius, who insisted (over Gertrude's fierce protest) on wearing his favorite cloak, fashioned from the furs of wild silver-wolves. Also, that high-horned helmet (likewise, against his wife's better judgment) that had adorned his head during the wedding and coronation ceremonies. In deference to his recently acquired position of power, knights and nobles likewise dug out Viking vestiges which their fathers—in some cases, fathers' fathers—long ago wore during journeys across the sea, into battle with Brits.

Angular falcons—feathers oily black, harsh faces covered by leather caps—were carefully carried along by terrified pageboys, cautiously handing the potentially deadly creatures up to king and queen. Similar birds were then accordingly distributed to all members of the party. Shortly thereafter, this strange conglomeration of renaissance women and medieval men galloped past the simple folk, halting their work for one brief moment, standing by the roadside where they gazed on in awe as the rainbow of riders tore over the bridge and across the field, then off toward a stretch of beech trees three-quarters of a mile away.

Felt hats from France, never before on view in Denmark, mixing with horned helmets, the like of which had not been seen in the lifetime of Helsingor's younger residents? Mixed messages were being offered to a confused populace, deeply disturbing those merchants and farmers so desperately in search of some clear, simple reassurance as to what was in store for their land, and their own humble futures.

51.

Ophelia stood by her doorway, watching the slowly descending dust—kicked up in the air as the royal party made their way out of Kronborg—settle. Earlier, she had declined an invitation, though no royal blood ran through her veins, to ride out with them. The ambitious side to her personality hungered for possible openings into the land's nobility. Still,

Ophelia preferred to remain behind after learning from several servants that Amuleth had earlier flatly refused Claudius' invitation to join the sporting, and would remain in the castle proper, perhaps to venture out of that third-floor closet at last.

Moreover, Ophelia was shocked to learn the prince was no longer to be addressed as Amuleth! If the king could change his name, thereby reinventing himself for an oncoming future, so too, apparently, could the prince. The very name 'Amuleth' had been Gertrude's creation, her attempt to transform Old Hamblet's good Norse name into something more contemporary. Following the previous night's vulgar display, the person called 'Amuleth' had no patience with anything conceived by the queen mother. Thus, the old king's true-name would be restored, suggesting that, in due time, his lineage might also return to power.

In deference to the fact that this was a modern age, however, Amuleth had decided to drop the ancient 'b.' From this day forward, a pronouncement—carried from Amuleth's closet to the court by Horatio, the only person allowed to briefly visit during the past three days—decreed, the prince must be referred to as 'Hamlet.'

Ophelia darted about, certain this 'Hamlet' would emerge now. She remained eager to track the prince down, whatever name her beloved chose to go by. At first, though, she came into contact only with the normal, everyday activities burgeoning on Helsingor's crowded streets. Then, a burst of feminine instinct guided her eyes upward toward the castle's high tower, that isolated spot where, as she well knew, Hamlet had long ago been born while blood ran in the fields below. On the dark metal walkway surrounding the grey-stone structure's tip, Ophelia spotted Hamlet, garbed entirely in black, solemnly staring at the far field where the royal party gleefully rode back and forth before the woode.

Delighted that an opportunity had so quickly presented itself for her to be alone with the object of her affection—*obsession* perhaps better described the girl's feelings—Ophelia rushed to the steps. She was deliriously out of breath when, several minutes later, Ophelia achieved the spiralling stairwell's highest plane. There, she discovered Hamlet, mournfully leaning against a turret's edge, observing all activity below.

Denmark's newly crowned king pulled the cap from his falcon's head, releasing the bird to tear off after a vulnerable sparrow. In a matter of moments, the small creature was torn to shreds, to the delight of Claudius and his cheering sycophants.

"It is the bright day that brings out the adder," Hamlet mused, "and that craves wary walking."

Hesitating a moment, Ophelia cautiously approached.

Hearing someone intrude on a self-imposed state of solitary sadness, Hamlet turned, relieved to note it was only the sweet girl. Ophelia, smitten as ever, smiled wanly as she drew close. Before Hamlet could offer a belated greeting, Ophelia hushed her prince by gently placing a single finger—the one displaying her beloved gold ring—across Hamlet's soft thin lips.

"I would kiss," she cooed, "before I spoke."

To Ophelia's dismay, Hamlet shuffled back against a shoulder high metal latticework lining the open-air balcony. "Nay," Hamlet insisted, "you were better speak first. And when you grow gravelled for lack of matter? Then, you may take occasion to kiss."

Incredible!

Any other youth in Helsingor, including the prince's closest friend, would swoon at the mere thought of receiving a kiss from Sjalland's reigning beauty. Yet Hamlet—the *rogue!*—brazenly *refused?*

Hiding her deep hurt by affecting a flirtatious mood, she teased: "How if the kiss be denied?"

"Who could deny, being before his beloved mistress?"

"Marry: If I *were* your mistress! Or I should think my honesty ranker than my wit?"

Hamlet's lips parted, ready to proffer further repartee. Before a word was out, Ophelia—without warning—cocked her head sideways. Lunging forward suddenly, she kissed Hamlet, lips slightly parted. Their tender tongues touched, lingered together.

At last, she pulled back, grinning coquettishly, considering the prince she had determined to someday marry.

Hamlet's poise, temporarily thrown off by the sensuous experience, swiftly returned. Assuming a cool, distanced persona, the prince then asked: "Art thou honest?"

"I trust so, my lord," she replied, folding her arms in an unconscious gesture of protection.

"Good. For honesty coupled to beauty is to have honey as sauce to sugar."

"I pray the gods keep me honest, and constant."

The two locked eyes, Ophelia believing Hamlet might be ready to take the initiative, finally kiss her in return. Perhaps she was right; Hamlet *did* lean forward, their gentle encounter rudely interrupted by untimely sounds from below. Jarred back to hateful reality, Hamlet turned away, even as the luxurious ringlets of Ophelia's light-brown hair, gently surrounding her sweet face, were blown by a light breeze across the girl's forehead. Instead of proffering the expected kiss, Hamlet chose to gaze down at a considerably less pleasant sight. At the woode's edge, Gertrude, in a gay sporting mood, rode wildly, Claudius hotly following behind.

"O, what a goodly outside falsehood hath!" Hamlet wailed, the riders too far off to hear. Unable, having witnessed Gertrude's superficiality, to believe any woman could be other than false, Hamlet—in no position to scold the true object of scorn—instead turned a growing fury on the nearest female, however innocent. Whirling about, Hamlet admonished Ophelia: "Constant you are, but . . . a woman."

She blinked, jaw dropping. Ophelia could not form words, confused owing to her lack of awareness as to the cause of Hamlet's bitterness. Flushing scarlet, she knew only that she'd done nothing to deserve such abuse. Hamlet's head sank, the prince's entire frame registering the profound pessimism that had descended, like night's bleak shroud, while observing Gertrude and Claudius together in ribald abandon. Still, Hamlet admitted nothing to Ophelia, leaving her to guess what troubled her prince.

Yes, she mused, Hamlet had a father lost. But that father lost his, and so on, in turn, for time *en memoriam*. True, the queen had remarried. Abruptly, at that. Still, wasn't it for the greater good? Hamlet must be lonely, even lost; couldn't the prince see a loyal friend and willing lover standing here, ready to give herself, fully and without reservation? Life was not all good, nor did any but a blind fool believe it so. Yet were things really *so* bad?

"Art thou wise?" Hamlet inquired in a curious tone.

"I have a pretty wit," she replied, frowning.

"Why, thou say'st well. And yet—"

"Yet?"

Hamlet glanced down, observing the falconry party below, and muttered: "The wiser, the waywarder."

Ophelia placed hands proudly on hips. "A man that had a wife with such a wit, he might say, 'Wit, wither wilt?'"

If Ophelia had hoped, with coy words, to plant the seed of marriage in Hamlet's fertile brain, her plan was dashed by joyful shouts from the field. "'Til you meet your wife's wit going to your neighbor's bed," Hamlet hissed. "What wit could wit have to excuse that?"

"Marry," she countered, "to say she came to seek you there. You should never take her without her answer, unless you take her without her . . . *tongue*."

Ophelia firmly embraced Hamlet again, kissing the prince hard, with wide open-mouth, in the naughty Norman manner.

"Now, 'Madame Tongue'?" Hamlet asked, the kiss finally completed.

"Come, *woo* me. Woo me!" she begged. "For now I am in a holiday humour, and like enough to consent."

She rubbed her soft cheek against Hamlet's equally tender face. For reasons Ophelia couldn't have imagined, the prince refused to yield. "If all the world were playing holidays, to sport would be as tedious as work." More roughly than necessary, Hamlet forced her away. "But when they seldom come? They wish'd for come!" Noting that her eyes registered confusion at this rejection, Hamlet concluded by asking: "Is love a tender thing?"

Knowingly, she shook her head, then—eyes wild, relying on a woman's last resort—Ophelia ground her body hard against Hamlet's. "It is too rough! It pricks like a thorn."

Hamlet attempted to push her away, though Ophelia, seemingly delicate, proved remarkably firm of purpose.

"If love be rough with you," the prince whispered, "be rough with love."

Not wishing to be denied, Ophelia held on tight. "Prick love for pricking," she saucily replied, "and you beat love down."

For a moment, Hamlet seemed ready to relent. Then, the sound of Gertrude's giddy laughter, wafting up from the woode, punctured any yielding mood. Body tensing with blind anger, all reason gone, Hamlet summed up all available strength, crudely repulsing Ophelia. "Is there no manners left among maids?" Hamlet screamed. "Will they wear their plackets where they should bear their faces?"

Free now of the tender-trap her long, lovely arms temporarily threatened to engulf Hamlet in, the prince stormed to the wall, hanging over its edge, glaring furiously at the falconry below. Ophelia, stunned, found herself laying flat on her back, though without the expected companion atop her.

"O, serpent heart," Hamlet churlishly called down to the woman boldly riding below, "hid with a flowery face!"

52.

The queen couldn't hear that admonishment, owing to frenzied squawks of gliding falcons, wild whinnying of horses caught up in the excitement, and loud cheers of all those supporters circling herself and Claudius. She reined in her mount, Claudius trotting up beside her, silently admiring his beautiful queen, momentarily lost in sea-green eyes which never failed to captivate him.

Then, Gertrude pulled the cap from off her falcon's head, watching as the bird blinked twice, adjusting to the sudden intrusion of bright sunlight into its otherwise self-contained existence beneath black leather. Blinking madly, then harshly and swiftly beating its wings, the bird of prey wound its way upward in search of some suitable victim, circling the wide area in gracefully deadly spirals. Watching closely, Claudius' eyes were drawn from the black bird to some equally dark object, high atop the castle's tower. The king's jovial mood dissolved as he realized it was Amuleth—Hamlet—staring down angrily.

Gertrude glanced at her husband, initially unable to understand what had shattered his glorious mood. Claudius thus nodded toward Kronborg. Following suit, Gertrude spotted Hamlet, a black spot on their otherwise bright horizon.

"From forth the kennel of thy womb," Claudius confided, "hath crept a hell-hound, that doth haunt us both to death!"

Her merry mood quickly diminishing, Gertrude shuddered, then confessed: "I fear our purpose is discovered."

"So wise, so young, they say, do never live long."

The queen turned to her husband, shocked. Hamlet was, after all, her only child. Noting a burning intensity in his eyes, and knowing full well his fatal temper, she pleaded: "Let me yet devise some other way, at least try?"

Unable to find anything to kill, her falcon drifted back down, returning to the queen's patiently waiting arm. Quickly capped, he silently surrendered to the oblivion of darkness until the time came for him to be set free to once again search for some gentle life and quickly destroy it.

"Work your wiles swiftly, wife," Claudius sourly explained, "or leave me to mine!"

This was *something*, at least! After all, his rough offer bought her a little time to try and rectify things. Gertrude nodded in agreement.

They rode off, then, into the woode, following a path favored by equestrians, their entire party following.

53.

Hamlet had seen more than enough! Without so much as a word to Ophelia, the prince stormed toward the stairs, huffily descending. The stunned girl hesitated a moment, uncertain whether she should follow. Then, confusion gave way to anger, as Ophelia hurried to catch up.

"And this?" she demanded, holding up her ring finger, coming alongside Hamlet on the circling stairwell.

Turning as they approached ground-level, her prince blushed, insisting: "A trifle. Counterfeit—"

Ridiculous! And *unfair* . . .

"This was *not* counterfeit. There is too great testimony in your complexion that it was a passion of earnest."

"Counterfeit, I assure you."

"Well, then," she continued, voice sarcastic, a flicker of nastiness in her eyes, "take good heart, and counterfeit to be a *man*."

Ophelia meant nothing by these words or, if anything at all, only a fleeting desire to hurt the one who had hurt her. She could not guess how deeply that statement cut through Hamlet. She could not guess what had transpired—or *almost* transpired—between Hamlet and Horatio on the night of their homecoming. Seeing pain in the prince's eyes, she immediately felt sorry for uttering her admonishment, and attempted to come close, withdraw the silly statement, spoken in anger, and so reconcile with warm embrace. By this time, though, they had reached the street level. Embarrassed, as any private person is by an open show of affection in public view, Hamlet stepped away, seizing on her casual words and the damage they had caused.

"So I do! But, i' faith, I should have been a woman by right—by nature."

Hamlet intended only honest admission; Ophelia mistook it for more clever banter. "In nature," she explained, "there's no blemish but the mind; none can be called deform'd but the unkind."

Again, she stepped near. Again, he pushed backward. What was wrong? Didn't the prince realize every man in Helsingor daily dreamed of Ophelia offering him what she openly shared with Hamlet now?

Once more, Hamlet held her at bay. "Will you deny me now?" she asked, on the verge of tears.

A sadness crossed Hamlet's face, like a sudden shadow blocking out the sun. Assuming a confessional tone, the prince sighed: "I would love you, if I could."

This seemed to her so much silliness. "No profit grows," she reminded Hamlet, "where no pleasure is taken."

They gazed deep into one another's eyes, the moment likely to transform, by its own accord, into excited embrace—neither caring a whit now for any who happened to be near and watching. But that was not to be. Horse's hoofs, clomping loud and drawing near, shattered the magic. Hamlet and Ophelia glanced away from one another, as Gertrude and Claudius, flanked by armored nobles and painted ladies, galloped back across the drawbridge and into the castle-proper. As they tore past the young couple, Gertrude glared down at her sullen, dangerous child. Claudius, refusing eye contact, spurred his horse and whirled by.

"Men are April when they woo," Hamlet muttered, "December when they wed. Girls are May when they are maids, but the sky darkens when they turn wives."

With that, the prince wandered away, lost in thought. Ophelia watched Hamlet depart, stunned by all she'd seen and heard. "If I live to be as old as Sibylla," she cursed, "I will die as chaste as Diana."

54.

Before the stable doors, the royal couple dismounted, turning the reins over to attending boys. Watching Hamlet out of the tail of his eye, Claudius stepped near to his queen. "He thinks too much. Such men are dangerous."

Gertrude's eyes filled with dread at the implication. "Wilt thou pluck my fair son from my age, and rob me of a happy mother's name?"

"Thou fond mad woman! Wilt thou not conceal this our dark conspiracy?"

Torn between loyalties to newly acquired husband and long-loved child, Gertrude stumbled away. Claudius, as mad with passion for this woman as ever, reconsidered his plan of action, momentarily setting aside any thought of enlisting Polonius' aide in the swift elimination of Hamlet. Nothing, not even the safety of his own person, was worth the risk of losing green-eyed Gertrude. Still, he feared that failing to seize the moment might spell disaster for them both.

"Under love's heavy burden, do I sink!" he cried.

55.

Overlooking the wide open plain stretching between Kronborg and the distant beech woode, meandering sideways toward the mushrooming metropolis of Helsingor which now flanked the castle on either side, two guards stiffly stood upon a hill-ock. Their backs were turned to Kronborg, allowing them to fully observe all that occurred on the horizon-line. In earlier years, such sentinels had been absolutely necessary for the community's survival, attacks liable to occur at any moment from a variety of potential enemies. Now, in an era of peace and prosperity, their main function was to keep the tradition alive. Villagers had learned to perceive a pair of uniformed soldiers, long pikes in hand, as a potent symbol of their continued safety. While few among the peasants actually thought about such stuff, all were quietly reassured by the presence of two such strong men-at-arms.

Shortly before the noon hour, their interest was piqued when several commoners arrived, heading neither for town nor castle, rather stopping in the center of the plain. Some in the group pushed crude wooden carts, others staggered onto the field hauling sacks along behind them or carrying full packs strapped high on their shoulders. No sooner had the grubby workmen reached the open area than they set to work, pitching open-air tents or setting up temporary stalls.

"Come hence for a faire?" the corporal, recently returned from a visit to his family in the north, asked.

"Grandest ever," the private explained, "to honour coupling king to queen."

More tradesmen arrived, setting up long, unpainted plank-tables, some to display varied wares for sale, others reserved for the consumption of food and drink. Within half-an-hour of the first arrivals, the recently deserted plain, now crowded with vagabonds, burst with frenzied activity.

"Dishonourable marriage," the corporal muttered, "were any to ask me."

Eager to change the subject, his companion replied: "None will."

The corporal winked at his private's wise hint. Only a fool would speak of such things, now the deed was done, a coronation, however dubious, complete. Instead, the corporal focused his attention on the busy-work below, though only after offering one final observation: "True. What great ones do, the less will prattle of."

Tents of every conceivable color had been erected. Village folk, as their workdays ended, poured out of the adjacent village to sample numerous possibilities for pleasure. As always, Denmark's varied denizens seized on any cause for celebration, thrilled to embrace each excuse that allowed them to briefly abandon daily drudgery for a giddy afternoon of enjoyment and, more often than not, excess.

Farm animals were dragged out, displayed in small fenced areas, and then sold to the highest bidder. Obese pink-and-white porkers rolled in warm mud, grinning from ear to ear—oblivious to their oncoming fates—as the sun, achieving its crowning position overhead—increased the thirst of all below, sending them off to purchase wine and beer.

In the royal bedchamber, Claudius stood by the long scrolled window, entranced with the action below. His reverie was distracted by loud weeping. Turning, he observed Gertrude, perched on the wooden edge of their canopied bed, face buried in her hands. Exasperated by the thought that such small pleasures, still open to the ordinary folk, were no longer his for the taking, Claudius joined the maudlin queen, draping a supportive arm around her soft shoulder.

"I am possessed with an adulterous blot," she cried. "My blood is mingled with the crime of lust."

This was too much! There was only one way out, so far as Claudius could see. "It must be by his death!"

His words snapped Gertrude back to reality. "Had'st thou groaned for him as I did at his birth," she scolded, "thou wouldst not so quickly urge his dirth."

Claudius considered her intense loyalty to Hamlet, fearful that their relationship might suffer if he extinguished her only child's life without first trying every other option. "Polonius hath served us well betimes," he suggested. "Perhaps he can observe Amuleth—uh, *Hamlet*—and find some other way besides."

Gertrude, clearly relieved, smiled through her tears, yet able to hope things might somehow right themselves. Then again: Considering the secret she and Polonius alone shared, how could they?

56.

Alone in her home, lost in silent consideration of the morning's bizarre confrontation, Ophelia stood before a mirror, methodically brushing long, luxurious strands of light-brown hair. The face that stared back was beautiful, some said irresistible. The obvious reality of her charms caused Ophelia to consider how incredible it was that her seemingly foolproof stratagem had failed so miserably.

Unbridled sincerity had clearly been a mistake! "I have said too much unto a heart of stone," she concluded, "and laid my honour too unchary out."

In the future, she would, with Hamlet, behave as she did with all other men: feigning a naiveté they found endearing, subtly manipulating events to her own liking. Now, though, noticing the miniature featuring Hamlet's likeness among the collection of treasured objects on her finely polished table, Ophelia's blood began to boil. On impulse, she tossed her brush at the image, knocking the prince's portrait off, down to the floor, as she called out: "Thus hath the candle singed the moth!"

No sooner had it landed with a crash than she was sorry for this uncharacteristic bit of rash behaviour. Hurrying over, Ophelia knelt to retrieve Hamlet's likeness. Scooping it up and brushing dust off the edges, she returned the picture to its place of honour. Then, Ophelia noticed a portrait of Horatio, always kept near, if behind, Hamlet's. The sight provided her with sudden inspiration for winning back her beloved's attention.

"Where flattery failed, jealousy may yet succeed!"

Without acknowledging her full comprehension of the situation to Horatio, Ophelia well understood the nature of his feelings for her. Instinctually, she grasped that they ran far deeper than the sweet-sibling emotions she harbored for him. During every meeting, Ophelia coyly pretended not to notice Horatio's hound-dog eyes whenever he glanced in her direction or, if she did notice, feigned an innocent inability to comprehend the full implications of his demeanor, so utterly guileless was this unique incarnation of herself that Ophelia assumed when alone with Horatio. She sensed, on some semiconscious level, such a persona best suited her purposes. After all, she had long ago decided, it was in her interest not to dismiss Horatio entirely. In case her dreamed-on marriage to Hamlet failed to materialize, Ophelia drew considerable comfort from the knowledge that such an appealing alternative waited patiently in reserve.

Now, though, any loving-yearnings on his part might be put to good use! Didn't they provide Ophelia with a means to spark Hamlet's fading interest, were she to suddenly shift her attentions from prince to companion? True, Horatio remained ever loyal to Hamlet. Then again, a quick glance in the mirror reminded the girl of her rare beauty, not to mention the subtle power it provided: "Who so firm," she reasoned, "that cannot be seduced?"

Admiring her own appearance, Ophelia smiled as a plan of action took shape in her sharp young mind. During the next half-hour, she developed a plot while dutifully brushing her hair into the particular pattern Horatio had wordlessly revealed, from the starved look in his eyes, that he most admired. Certain, Ophelia had no wish to hurt Horatio. Still, her ambition would not go unfulfilled.

"My thoughts are ripe in mischief. I'll sacrifice the lamb I do love, to spite a raven's heart within a dove."

57.

In the queen's study, where the recently literate lady retired each afternoon to scribble letters, Gertrude—having left Polonius in their chamber some thirty-minutes earlier—sat at a mahogany stained desk. The considerable cost of its construction in Brussels and careful overland importation to Sjalland had caused Old Hamblet, against his better judgment, to raise taxes of village merchants some two years earlier. Unwise, yet he had always been unable to deny his wife anything. Diligently, she worked with her goose quill, putting something down on paper that surely must be of great significance. Or so Claudius believed when, searching for her out of concern, he discovered Gertrude here.

He was in for a surprise. Instead of writing some nice note to a neighboring lady, he noticed, glancing over her shoulder, that the queen doodled aimlessly, intensely sketching an ever-expanding set of concentric circles on the parchment before her. This shocked Claudius. He hadn't until this moment grasped how seriously Hamlet's return had impacted her. Deeply worried about her well-being, and aware of how quickly such a high-strung person can snap, Claudius gently took the ink-tipped feather from Gertrude's hand, holding it firmly until Polonius—ever the obedient dog, hurrying to hear-out and then help execute his latest-master's request—arrived, out of breath from running.

Claudius explained his strategy in full, making clear that Hamlet's life was—at least, for now—in no way endangered. All the king wanted was information as to what the prince might be up to, and how Hamlet might yet be appeased.

Polonius nodded at what he heard. "In all ways," the greybeard insisted, cautiously sneaking a peek at the dim, distracted Gertrude while considering the secret they two shared, "I will ever serve thee as you wilt."

"Spy on Hamlet; learn what is that spirits him ill. Then make known to us, if we may suffer him still."

"Your bidding, I do. And now, my lords, adieu!"

Courteously exiting the room, Polonius left Claudius alone with his downtrodden queen. Gertrude refused to meet her husband's eyes, staring at the empty tabletop, lost in the dark thoughts she had throughout the day found herself surrendering to, embracing the horror they suggested.

Her precious Fang, as adulterous lover, knew no peer. Now, as husband, he seemed somehow inferior to her late Hamblet. Ironic, she thought, that after decades of dreaming about how wonderful it would be to share every waking moment with this man, and now the two of them finally having no need to hide their love, she found this long-sought situation only caused her to wish for a return to the way things were.

58.

In another part of the castle, another woman went about the task of attempting to manipulate events to her liking. Ophelia, of course, was an entirely different person than the queen. Essentially a tragic figure, Gertrude had found herself trapped between two conflicting ways of thinking; born into medieval times, doomed to forever carry their dark heritage in every ounce of her flesh, blood and brain, she nonetheless aspired to something greater; the still embryonic Renaissance mindset had seized hold of her imagination, causing Gertrude to ape its outward semblances with the skill of an accomplished actress. For her, though, this could never be anything more than an elaborate show—studying, and then performing the superficial styles of a modern sophistication without truly understanding their essence.

Ophelia, on the other hand, was in all respects a woman of her time, fully belonging to the exciting future that someone like Gertrude could only dream on, desire to achieve, pretend to be part of. Ophelia was the new woman incarnate, an unconscious pioneer of an emerging breed—able to think for herself, decide what she wanted, then go out and seize it, with little concern for old-fashioned notions of image or protocol. Should this cause some pain, so be it. If men must be toyed with in the service of her unwavering commitment to burning personal ambition, then they would suffer the consequences. Ophelia meant no harm to any one. Still, she clung to an agenda that would not be denied.

So it was that, having brushed her full head of hair until it gleamed as close to perfection as possible, Ophelia left her home and dared to stroll unannounced onto the practice field, a half-acre plot tucked away in a quiet corner around the bend from the tower steps. Until this moment, the area had always been strictly reserved for men. Such an appearance was unheard of, particularly for a young woman of her crystal reputation and social standing.

A dozen young knights, nobles, and courtiers, all wearing tight-breeches and shirtless from the waist up, sweated profusely while honing their skills with sword, javelin, and battle mace. Such training was more out of respect for honoured heritage than any fear their country might be menaced in the foreseeable future. Still, one never knew for certain when hard times might return. It was best to be ever-prepared for the worst. The sight of so lovely a girl in a beige silk sheath, the garment clinging tight to her slender frame thanks to a bright-yellow sash casually wrapped around her hourglass waist (Ophelia was, by anyone's definition, overdressed for the occasion) caused all to cease activity and marvel at the poetry-in-motion provided by her unexpected arrival.

Among them stood Horatio, sword in hand, halting in mid-swing at an over-stuffed leather target. Eyes radiant, ringlets carefully arranged to fall across the delicate features of her smiling face with every calculated step, Ophelia ventured close. She considered Horatio's rugged torso, as wet with sweat as if he'd been caught in a rainstorm. The embarrassed youth was thrilled to realize that Ophelia, object of his heart's desire, had sought him out.

"I feared thou had'st avoided me since thy hasty return," she whispered sweetly, setting her tender trap, waiting for the young elk to step directly in, naively as an inexperienced fawn.

"Fair lady, not so," Horatio stammered, reaching to a nearby pole, where his shirt hung, grasping for it and swiftly covering his torso. "Where you chance to walk, Horatio's eyes do follow."

"Good," she replied, affecting a little-girl-lost voice that never failed to serve her in such situations, "for once you swore to protect me always."

"Your worth is very dear in my regard, believe me!" Horatio's statement, like everything else he said or did, resonated with sincerity.

"Then this could be written in stone, for all believe all honest Horatio says."

Exchanging smiles—his real, hers carefully executed—the attractive youths stepped closer. "Inform me, then," he asked, "of thy own affairs. While we were hence in Wittenberge, how have you occupied your idle hours?"

Her playing of Horatio, now reduced to a viol, was less schematized than organic—more on the order of inspired riff than carefully orchestrated composition. Ophelia had arrived with a general plan for swiftly transforming Hamlet's best friend into her unwitting pawn. Horatio's innocent words allowed her a fuller sense as to how she might achieve that aim, which she then improvised upon.

"Have you seen my garden?"

"Indeed, I have not."

She swept a delicate hand in the direction of the practice field's exit, cooing: "Away before me to sweet beds of flowers. Love thoughts lie rich when canopied with bowers." Ophelia gracefully swirled about, drifting past other strapping young men, all remaining stock still, worthless weapons held in ridiculous poses of readiness. They stood, watching and wishing, each in his own way, that he were the one she had come to seek.

"Love sought is good," Horatio muttered under his breath, "but given unsought—*better!*"

Tossing his sword down on a pile of practice weapons, he hurried after, knowing all eyes were upon him, enjoying every second of the impossibly happy experience, hoping against hope he wouldn't wake at any moment.

59.

Hamlet, source of all intrigue currently practiced in Kronborg—political on Claudius' part, romantic for Ophelia—hid just beyond the drawbridge, camouflaged from sight within a clump of closely-rooted beeches. Shortly, Balthazar led a fresh horse out of the castle, appearing to guards on duty merely another of the king's many messengers. In fact, Balthazar was heading to a secret appointment with Hamlet at this pre-arranged place.

"Now, Balthazar, as I have ever found thee true, so let me find thee still," Hamlet implored as the boy stepped close.

"I will not sleep, my lord," Balthazar brightly replied, "'til I have delivered your letter."

He joined Hamlet in the privacy afforded by thick foliage within the brace of trees. Here, they could speak without being seen or heard by any within the castle. Hamlet handed the youth a sealed note, intended for Fortinbras. The missive explained in detail all that had happened since the prince's return, beckoning the Norwegian prince to hurry along— if indeed he held true to his profound promise—and help to extricate Hamlet from this impossible situation. Knowing full well the purpose, and as fiercely loyal to the prince as he had ever been to Old Hamblet, Balthazar was willing to risk a charge of treason, if only he could do service to the rightful ruler.

"Vie thee all the endeavor of a man in speed to Wittenberge," Hamlet begged.

"I do not stop to sleep 'til I render this into thy cousin's hand," Balthazar assured him. Unlike Laertes, Balthazar now and ever meant what he said.

Hamlet seized Balthazar's hand, shaking it in the manner of friend-to-friend rather than ruler-to-subject. Deeply touched, both by the gesture's sincerity and its hint of a democratic spirit, Balthazar packed the missive into his saddlebag, lifted himself up and into the saddle, then dug in spurs and, with a quick gesture of farewell, hurried away.

Hamlet watched until Balthazar turned a corner in the woode, disappearing from sight. Only then did the prince head back across the drawbridge and into Kronborg.

60.

Horatio, whom Hamlet hoped to locate, stood face-to-face with Ophelia in the narrow stretch of sweet-smelling, richly colored paradise which she proudly called her private place. He marveled at the sight. The grass ranged along the area's edges was kept meticulously trimmed. A surrounding wall of hedge, neatly clipped, created a natural protection that cast cooling shadows in early afternoon. Tight rows of flowers were arranged in painstakingly planned lines. Formal in design, the garden had been brilliantly conceived, then filled with diverse choices, all—as spring asserted its full presence— now radiantly in bloom: primroses, bluebells, daisies, honey-suckles and countless others, including some Horatio couldn't identify—their pink, blue, yellow, tan and white petals con-joined in a charming phantasmagoria of conflicting hues, resulting in a pretty pastel rainbow, pollens co-mingling into a collective scent, seductively sweet as any drug imported from the Orient. Horatio had no notion what he ought to do or say under such circumstances.

Ophelia, as always, knew full well where the conversation would go, and how she would, as if composing an extemporary script, arrange for their dialogue to convey the two of them there. "What sport shall we devise here in this garden to drive away the heavy thought of care?" she asked.

Despite her almond-shaped eyes, devilish with provoca-tion, Horatio didn't dare hope, much less believe, that this living-goddess might have finally given up trying to snare the ever-elusive Hamlet, thus turning her attention to him. Surely, she wanted nothing more than for a trusted friend to momen-tarily amuse her. Ever the good soldier, Horatio was willing to serve. "Madam," he suggested, "we'll tell tales."

"Of sorrow, or joy?"

"Either, Madam."

"Neither." She breathed deeply, affecting an air of roman-tic loneliness. "For if joy, being altogether wanting, it doth remember me the more of sorrows. Or if grief, being alto-gether had, it adds more sorry to my want of joy."

"I could weep, madam, would it do you good."

"And I could sing, would weeping do me good, and never borrow any tear of thee."

Histrionically, she sadly shook her head, back and forth, ringlets teasingly dancing about her eyes. Ophelia mincingly walked about in concentric circles, acting thoroughly distracted, all the while blinking a great deal. That combina-tion of gestures, she long-ago learned, could seep away the resolution of even the most formidable men, Hamlet the only apparent exception. Which, of course, only made her want Hamlet all the more, and all the more madly.

"Were I, in truth, fairer of form," Horatio mourned, "I could cheer thee with my very visage."

Perfect! His honest humility allowed Ophelia the opening she'd been searching for, prying to discover his weakness through seemingly spontaneous small-talk. So she swirled about, baby-stepped precariously close, performing perfectly in a seemingly unguarded, open-manner. "In terms of choice," she lectured, "I am not solely led by nice direction of a maiden's eye."

Nonetheless, Horatio remained the ever loyal Horatio. And so he interjected what few others would have brought up at such a moment: "Are you not betrothed to my friend, the prince?"

Ophelia rolled her eyes with consternation, pursing her mouth artfully to convey an aura of innocent concern. "That is a question! Would I knew the answer. Is he inconstant in his favours?"

"Hamlet? No, believe me."

She shrugged, coming to rest on a small wrought-iron bench, snaked with ivy, set firmly against her house's side wall. Ophelia indicated for Horatio to join her. "Then, I have bought the mansion of a love," she complained, "but not possessed it."

Her words gave Horatio courage. Eyes flashing ardently, he sat, trembling at the experience of lightly brushing against her, albeit briefly. "You are free?"

"As a crone who hears the chimes at midnight."

"Dare I hope—"

"Hope, Horatio, springs eternal."

Warily, Horatio slid closer still.

61.

Hamlet, searching for Horatio, entered the practice field, where such a youth would likely be found at this time of day.

The dozen men exercising there, resuming careful imitations of combat following Horatio's hasty exit, ceased all action the moment their prince arrived. Hamlet glanced around, surprised to find the favorite companion—neither in his room nor partaking of a meal, both possibilities checked by Hamlet before coming here—not present.

"Horatio?" Francis, guessing Hamlet's purpose, inquired. The prince nodded. Outspoken and honest as Horatio himself, Francis revealed what little he knew: "Gone these past ten minutes."

Hamlet sensed, from the trepidation in the knight's voice, something amiss. "Where, and with who?"

Not wanting to publicly embarrass Hamlet, Francis shuffled close, whispering in Hamlet's ear. Stunned, and far less naive than Horatio as to such matters, Hamlet hurried off toward Ophelia's home.

62.

There, in the garden, Ophelia decided that the right moment had arrived to firmly take Horatio's hand in her own. She could feel him shaking at the subtle sensuousness of this experience, masculine power diminishing in the presence of what, ironically, was oft-tagged 'the weaker sex.' Then, she treated him to her most special smile, the one Ophelia held in reserve for important occasions only.

"I have neither wit, nor words, nor worth, nor the power of speech to stir men's blood," he confessed. "I only speak right-on. I tell you that which you yourself do know."

"I would hear," she said, carefully projecting an aura of innocence combined with encouragement, "all the same."

"I know no ways to mince in love, but directly to say: *I love you.*"

The situation was ripe now for Ophelia, up until this moment presenting herself as a fiercely independent woman, to reveal a more conservative side. Neatly switching personas, like a wandering player discarding one mask for another, she instantly shifted to an old-fashioned aura. "And yet a maiden hath no tongue, but thought."

"Still, speak; Give me your answer: 'I' faith, I do!'"

"Then, if you urge me farther than to say, 'do you in faith?' I wear out my suit."

This confused Horatio, a simple man hungry to have everything clean and clear: "How say you, lady?"

She, subtle and complex, must be careful to remain ambiguous, never making an absolute commitment yet providing Horatio with precisely enough information that would allow him to believe she'd done just so. By such a tactic, Ophelia could sidestep his request for openness and honesty while appearing open and honest in all things. During the split-second it takes a sharp-witted woman to size up any social situation, rapidly changing strategies as necessity demands, she seized on the idea of appearing humorously charmed by his bold forthrightness.

"And so clap hands and a bargain?" she laughed.

Horatio grew more serious still: "I pray thee, Ophelia, understand a plain man in his plain meaning."

Hamlet turned the corner then, saw them together, and stood observing—silent, still, remote. Horatio's back, turned toward Hamlet, left the youth utterly unaware of his prince's presence. Ophelia noticed Hamlet at once, spotting the prince over Horatio's shoulder. Now, Horatio—formerly fellow-player *and* audience-of-one for her improvisation—unwittingly found himself reduced to actor-only—Hamlet now the all-important viewer. She purposefully fumbled with the tie on Horatio's shirt, pulling it loose to reveal a little more of his rugged chest, eyes rolling so as to encourage Hamlet to believe their conversation was far more intimate than the case truly happened to be. Responding as she hoped, Hamlet was seized by a fit. The irony, lost on her: Hamlet's jealous feelings were not for Ophelia's favors, but Horatio's!

Was this girl no better than Gertrude, queen mother who, in short shrift, wantonly married the man Hamlet held responsible for Old Hamblet's death? "Beauty is a witch," the prince snarled to no one in particular, "against whom there is no protection."

Excited by Hamlet's growing anger, Ophelia slipped out of character, allowing her true thoughts sudden expression: "O, what a deal of scorn looks beautiful in the contempt and anger of his lip!"

"What, fair maid?" Horatio asked, confused.

She turned her attention back to Horatio, never allowing Hamlet to perceive how fully aware she was of the prince's nearby presence. Hamlet, meanwhile, continued spying, which was fine with Ophelia! In a slightly-larger-than-life gesture, she slipped the gold ring off her finger. To the amazement of the commoner beside her and the prince observing from across the way, Ophelia theatrically pushed it onto Horatio's fourth finger, right hand. "Wear this for me, one out of suits with fortune."

For a moment that remained pregnant with possibilities, absolute silence shrouded the scene. Finally able to form words, Horatio gasped: "You pay too dear for what's given freely."

"This ring, good sir—alas, it is a trifle." Then, without warning, she deftly slipped it back off Horatio's hand. "I will not shame myself to give you this."

Desperately, Horatio pulled the ring away from her, forcing it back to its recent if temporary home. "I will have nothing else *but* this!"

"The venom clamours of a jealous woman poisons more deadly than a mad dog's tooth," Hamlet, half hidden, concluded. Having seen and heard more than enough, the prince stepped out from behind the foliage and marched in their direction. Before Hamlet had a chance to cross the cobbled street and join them, Ophelia seized the moment, moving in new directions.

"Kiss me!" she demanded.

"What," Horatio—unable to grasp that his fondest dream had come true—questioned, "in the midst of the street?"

In fact, they were off the main street, though in full public view through a gap in the garden's surrounding hedge. "What," she peevishly replied, "art thou ashamed of me?"

"No, God forbid."

"What, then?"

"Ashamed to kiss."

"Why?"

"Here, all eyes gaze on us."

Petulantly, Ophelia again reached for her gold band, the girl's voice of a sudden grown icy. "The ring, if you please."

Panic seized Horatio: "But, lady, why?"

"I fear, on second thought, it is not mine to give."

Panic gave way to concern: "How came you by it?"

"A present from Hamlet."

That was all Horatio needed to hear. "Then to him it must be returned," he flatly stated.

"I thank thee." As Hamlet stepped closer still, Ophelia pretended to finally notice the royal presence. "Oh! Here comes the prince!"

Horatio rose, eager to make things right. "I'll do it anon," he volunteered.

Ophelia also stood, seizing the collar of Horatio's shirt. "I will have my kiss first!" Catching him off-guard, Ophelia pulled Horatio close, pecking him quickly on the cheek. Then—casting eyes at once flirtatious, innocent, and coy, this constituting one of her specialities—she turned, hurrying off into her house, and slammed the door behind.

This left Horatio standing awkwardly, alone in the garden, staring down at the ring on his hand, while recalling the soft kiss that, in his mind, had been lovingly branded into his very soul. "This is the air," he marveled, "that is the glorious sun. This the ring she gave me, I do feel and see it."

Still, serious issues remained. Horatio turned to confront Hamlet. But the prince was nowhere to be found. The kiss, too much to bear, had sent an outraged Hamlet stalking away rather than stand by and helplessly watch.

"But no, not for the likes of me," Horatio concluded. "The

ring must be returned, if I am to ever hold the girl." He hurried down the rough street, intent on finding and openly confronting his sweet prince.

63.

Like a lap pet, lost without a current master and embarrassingly eager to be adopted by a likely prospect, Fortinbras followed Mistress Quickly into The Wild Boar. Once within the dimly lit building, smelling of spilt wine and baking meats, she sauntered to the oak bar, there running through her litany of orders to men and women in her employ.

Though of exceedingly common birth, Mistress Quickly had come to enjoy her status (at least, within the small circle of life she reigned over here) and power (likewise extending no further than the sportive *demi-monde* she had fashioned with considerable care). Such an enviable situation, for a working girl, derived from an impressive combination of lusty good-looks, a sharp-witted mind and, most significant, a highly individualistic spirit. Combined with a steadfast refusal to give of herself too easily or too often, such qualities made her more desirable than most other women of her class.

So Norway, born a prince among men, stood silently beside her, hoping this commoner might deign to allow him a moment of her time once the staff was versed as to the evening's meal and the choice of grog that would flow all night long. Her workers nodded their understanding, then scattered in a dozen different directions. Mistress Quickly at last turned, seeming surprised to see the rugged redhead. "You hound my every step like a little dog," she laughed good-naturedly.

"Still," he whined, "you pet me not."

Her eyes rolling naughtily, she replied: "I may yet put a collar round your neck."

"Your property, lush lady, I long to be."

Though his words were an exaggeration, Fortinbras had learned, following a great deal of coaching from Amuleth and

Horatio, that for a man to sound desperately in love with whatever woman he happened to encounter worked wonders while trying to win the wench's favor—particularly a woman as selective as Mistress Quickly was known to be when it came to bedmates.

Considering Fortinbras closely, impressed by the ardor of his pursuit, Mistress Quickly nodded in the direction of a corner booth. There, Laertes sat, sodden with drink, between a pair of tawdry working girls. "Why not join your friend?" she sniffed. "His hands are more than full, I think."

Fortinbras glanced briefly at the sight, afterwards casting intense eyes on her and making his best case, precisely as Amuleth had instructed. "For a prince such as I," he insisted, "only a true queen of the night maketh me blink!"

The words won him a coy smile. No question, Fortinbras decided, this desirable wench—if not entirely won over—was weakening by the moment. The prize might yet be his! He did hope this would soon prove true, for Fortinbras sensed a need to enter into something as exciting as a love affair with the supposedly 'untouchable' object of so many affections now that his best friends were absent.

64.

Those best friends were, in fact, less congenially met than ere before! Horatio finally discovered Hamlet a short distance beyond Kronborg's drawbridge, around a corner of the castle, at the point where a line of circular targets stood, ranged along Kronborg's side wall. These were set in place here each morning by squires so that Danish men-at-arms could practice archery whenever they chose. Now, though, Hamlet stood alone, taking careful aim with a longbow. Sensing at once that the prince was not in an agreeable mood, Horatio eased up alongside.

"Will you hunt, my lord?" he asked, desperate to initiate small-talk.

"What, pray tell?" Hamlet loosed an arrow, then considered the result: shaft deep in the yellow circle, half-an-inch from dead-center. Without hesitating so much as to acknowledge Horatio with a quick look, Hamlet drew another arrow from a leather quiver, taking aim once more.

"The hart."

"Her love is not the hare that I do hunt; for Lady Ophelia you speak on, if indirectly?"

Hamlet loosed another shaft, the arrow grazing only the outer ring this time. Swiftly, the bow was readied for a third attempt.

"My lady will hang thee for thy absence."

"Let her hang me. He that is well-hanged in this world needs fear no betrayal."

Subtle wit was not Horatio's forte: "Make that good."

"Many a good hanging prevents a bad marriage."

Clearly, Hamlet understood what had brought Horatio here. The companion decided it would be best to hand over the gold band without further discussion, flatly stating: "She returns this ring to you, sir."

Hamlet glanced at the object, then returned to archery. "She took the ring of me," the prince said, dismissing it with casual words. "I'll none of it. I know not what use to put her to but to make a lamp of her and run from her own light."

At this reference to Ophelia, Horatio's eyes lit up: "Indeed, her smile burns bright, by day and night."

"'Tis written," Hamlet replied, every word tinged with envy, "girls appear to men like angels of light."

"So?"

"So: Light is an effect of fire; fire will burn."

"Ergo?"

"Light wenches will burn." Hamlet twisted around to consider Horatio, eye-to-eye. "Come not near her, for fear of flames."

"Your words flicker with cruel fire, kindled fast."

"Ay, but I do know—"

"What dost thou know?"

"Too well what love women to men may owe."

"In faith, they are as true of heart as we!"

A nasty snort. Then: "Think thee so?"

"With all my heart."

"Be happy as a fool in May, then, 'til though know more of the wide-world's way."

With trepidation, Horatio inched closer. "Might I, then, entreat the lady you so scorn?"

Hamlet spoke, not directly to Horatio but to some secret self: "Self-harming jealousy! Fie, beat it hence."

"Pardon, prince?"

Without warning, Hamlet bellowed: "Carouse you full measure to her maidenhead. Be mad and merry, or go hang yourself."

This devastated Horatio. Never before had Hamlet spoken so! The prince didn't appear interested in Ophelia. Why, then, such hostility if a friend hoped to pursue her? "How now, sir? Is your merry humour alter'd?"

Hamlet threw down bow and arrow, hissing: "I am not in a sportive humour now! Farewell, and take her. But direct thy feet where thou and I henceforth may n'er again meet."

Stunned, Horatio replied: "My lord, I do protest—"

Hamlet turned away, refusing Horatio any further acknowledgment. For a long, awkward moment, Horatio stood in place, hoping time might heal whatever wound he had inadvertently inflicted, and Hamlet would return. The prince did not. Accepting that the conversation—perhaps their friendship—was over, Horatio staggered away.

Only then did Hamlet glance back at a friend loved more dearly than Horatio could guess, moaning: "How bitter a thing it is to look into happiness through another's eyes."

Likewise, Horatio was consumed with heavy thoughts and tattered emotions: "How will this fudge? My master, she loves dearly. And I, poor monster, fond as much of him, yet dote on her, as he seems to do on me." Horatio shook his head sadly, concluding. "O, time, thou must entangle this, not I; it is too hard a knot for me to untie."

65.

Fearing that she might be in danger of losing all semblance of control, her tortured mind every bit as uncertain as Sjalland's seashore at ebb tide, Gertrude desperately seized on the idea of occupying each waking hour with small tasks she could concentrate on to the exclusion of all else. One possibility was to fiercely focus attention on something as harmless as helping Ophelia prepare for her role as the May Queen in Helsingor's upcoming outdoor celebrations. The festivities had originally been planned for two weeks hence, the date abruptly moved-up in honour of the recent royal marriage. Polonius' lithe, charming daughter had easily won the previous week's province-wide informal election, even as she had the year before; Ophelia seemed to all as natural a choice for the coveted role of nature-goddess as Gertrude in her own youth. Now, though, everyone understood the queen to be a mature beauty, unfit for such silly stuff. They would have been amazed to learn that, deep in her covetous heart, Gertrude secretly hungered for the excitement of old, when all eyes were cast on her.

The crowd, however, must have its exalted young woman of the moment. For the time being, that meant Ophelia. Such an honour necessitated she outfit herself in the manner of a woode-sprite from ancient myth. So she now modeled for Gertrude a gown which the girl had cleverly designed, improving on the previous year's costume: soft-green in hue, long strands of brown fringe extending downward from both sleeves, a matching earth-brown sash swept around her perfect waist. Her hair, Ophelia had combed into a luxurious spiral of curls—the color halfway between winter rye and spring wheat—now piled high atop her head.

Girlishly giddy hours were spent in a secretive closet, reserved for private use by Kronborg's distinguished women, during this final fashioning of Ophelia's image. Relaxing for the first time that day, the distraught queen opened wide her soul to this sweet child whom, as Gertrude well knew, coveted Hamlet. Gertrude confided all her concern for the prince's sanity. Several times during their intense conversation, she reiterated to Ophelia that, so far as the queen was concerned, a royal marriage to some local lord's daughter was not necessary. Rarely speaking openly on the subject, Gertrude always hoped, even trusted, sometimes secretly schemed for an eventual wedding between Amuleth—Hamlet, now—and excellent Ophelia, whose good looks, some said, drove all young men to utter distraction.

Hearing these words, Ophelia danced about, gown billowing outward, strands of fringe flying wildly in mid-air. For the moment, any observer would have truly believed her to be the magical spirit of spring. Ophelia had hoped against hope Gertrude hadn't forgotten what, years earlier, the queen once confided to this impressionable girl: Owing to what Gertrude considered certain 'peculiarities' (the term had never been fully explained to Ophelia) on the part of Denmark's prince, it might be for the best if Amuleth married someone close to the royal family, preferably the daughter of ever-loyal Polonius, to 'cover' (again, Gertrude's term) any possible public revelations which might otherwise cause awkwardness. Ophelia had no idea what Gertrude might mean by any of this jabbering. All that mattered, in her mind, was that the queen apparently could be trusted as her ally in Ophelia's ongoing quest to marry Hamlet and, as she herself put it, be joined with nobility. That was good enough!

"I but hope, dear Ophelia, your good beauties be sole cause of our Hamlet's sore distraction."

Her assertion inadvertently deflated Ophelia's giddy mood. "I think not, Madam, for since his coming hither, I have known only rejection by our sweet prince."

Claudius stormed in, uninvited, his huge, crude male bulk diminishing the sisterly spirit so ripe in the room until his unwished appearance destroyed the delicate mood. "'Sweet' to some, perforce," he grumpily asserted.

"Go, now, child," Gertrude—sensing her husband had weighty matters to privately discuss—commanded. "You are young; seize the day!"

Nodding, Ophelia rushed to the door, darted out into the adjoining corridor and then down the stairwell to join the revellers below, already partaking of a carnival atmosphere.

"Be careful what you speak," Claudius reminded his wife. "She has the prince's ear."

"Tut, never fear. I am as vigilant as a cat that steals the cream."

"I think, to steal cream indeed," he snarled, turning lascivious, "for my theft hath already made thee butter." Always eager for a taste of Gertrude's flesh, Claudius hurried close, set about to fondling her breasts. How often, during the past twenty years, Gertrude thrilled to such secret passions in places like this! Now, though, the rough hands which once struck her as marvelously strong seemed only brutal, his grasp more on the order of an unwanted assault than sweet-seduction. How different the same pair of hands felt after formal marriage to the man, allowing him the right that Old Hamblet had once called, to her eternal resentment, his own: total freedom to touch her any time he liked . . . the woman as man's possession.

Gertrude didn't appreciate that. She missed the forbidden thrills of adultery, which in the past served their passion as grains of salt do meat. Today, what they shared was a marriage, no better or worse than any other, including her own to the late, and lately lamented, king. Pretending to respond in hopes of avoiding once more having to listen to his whining, Gertrude glanced down, out of the corner of her eye and through an opening in the shuttered window. On the field moved hordes of people, congregating between brightly colored tents and open-air stalls, the common-folk watching wide-eyed as jugglers demonstrated skills with flamed-sticks, jesters meanwhile rushing up to compete for their laughter and possible coins.

A bear, captured two days earlier in the woode's north-sector, growled while led off to be baited, then put to death. Men and women in their early twenties held hands, exchanging flirtatious glances of youth. Such happy sights depressed her. Gertrude cared naught about being queen at this moment. All the supposed power and glory attending her crown meant nothing. She wanted only to once more join in the merriment which all others, even the poorest of the poor, enjoyed, while she, the bird in a gilded cage, must remain aloof, not allowed to participate.

It wasn't fair!

Then, Gertrude spotted Ophelia, hurrying across the drawbridge to sweetly mingle with the masses. All eyes immediately turned to her. All men wanted her, all women wanted to be like her. A quarter-century earlier, Gertrude invariably won such attention. Gertrude, the girl all boys desired, some secretly, others openly.

Oh, to be young again!

She would, without hesitation, trade all her fine jewelry, elegant gowns, her rights and privileges to be at one with them all. Provided, of course, that she be allowed to occupy a position at the very center of attention.

66.

Hamlet stood by an open-air beer tent, purchasing a horn of ale, distractedly observing all the comings and goings. On a nearby spit, the meat of an entire pig, still bloody from slaughter, sizzled. As flames crackled below, small bubbles rose to the burnt surface of its skin, lathered with a tangy-scented vinegar-and-pepper sauce. Wailing gulls, thick in the sky, flapped their wings in hysteria while glaring down at the feast below, crazed with concern that they might not find a way to partake of the sweet-smelling bounty. Visitors from outlying sections of Sjalland, late to arrive owing to a long work-day and the considerable trip, poured into the area. The crowd thickened, making even the simplest movements something of a challenge. Yet all were in good spirits, most of the men inebriated, leading to a general tipsy atmosphere. A happy hum rose from the field; people who had not met and greeted one another since the previous year's celebration were giddy at being reunited.

Hesitantly, Horatio forced his way through the shifting mass. Finally, he spotted Hamlet, noting that the prince vividly stood out from all the others, bedecked in their most gaily colored costumes, owing to the nondescript black-garb Hamlet had favored since their dark homecoming. Horatio nervously stepped up to the tent, glancing over awkwardly, apologetic eyes begging permission to approach and, perhaps, speak. Hamlet, sipping sack, spotted him, the prince's own eyes immediately bursting with delight.

For already, Hamlet regretted the earlier reaction to this honest friend's understandable inclinations. "Good Horatio, forgive my rash words," the prince shouted over the buzzing mob. "Like the weather, my hot temper dost subside. Join me for ale, as in fond Wittenberge."

Horatio's face lit up at the offer. "What I hoped to hear!" came his relieved reply. He pushed and shoved his way up alongside Hamlet, there purchasing a horn. The two toasted their friendship. Then, sipping sack, they navigated, like twin trading ships on the storm-tossed Baltic, through a shifting sea of merrymakers, friends once more. Not that, hot tempers and bad moments aside, they could ever be anything else.

"Speak," Hamlet commanded. "What did you learn in the castle?"

"We are at the stake," Horatio, already witness to numerous rumours of a possible plot against the prince, confided, "buoyed about with many enemies."

People brushed past, raising horns in happy toasts. "And some that smile," Hamlet noted, "have in their hearts, I fear, millions of mischiefs."

Horatio nodded glumly. As was their habit in more innocent years, before their minds had been opened to the intellectual world and their lives thusly changed forever, the two strolled to a nearby hillock, where the ground rose slightly above the general plain. This was the very place where, decades ago, King Fortinbras had retired to try and regroup his

devastated army shortly before final defeat. They sat on the
damp grass, observing others making merry from a discrete
distance, Horatio slowly sharing with Hamlet all that he had
heard and seen.

67.

From her position by the window, Gertrude noticed the two
huddled conspiratorially on their hillock. Frightened by the
implications of intense conversation passing between Horatio
and Hamlet, she turned to Claudius, eyes wild with concern.
He, sensing her sudden removal from all but gross physical
contact, ceased his heated groping and peered into her terrified eyes. Like Gertrude, Claudius had found marriage to the
object of his dreams something other than the glorious experience he'd so often fantasized about. Still, there was something of the practical man to him, in contrast to her wild
romantic leanings which, more often than not, led Gertrude
down dangerous paths she could not navigate, much less control. Claudius knew the queen, in all her complexity, full-
well, having experienced—and survived—her sudden whims
and changing moods, unexpected bursts of savage humor and
inexplicable bouts with deep-depression.

Now, her lower-lip trembled, eyes flickering with reproach.
Taking her cue, Claudius glanced out onto the field, noting
Hamlet and Horatio together, at once understanding—and
sharing—her concern. "So shaken as we are," he noted, "so
wan with care."

Gertrude's eyes revealed a mind on the edge of hysteria.
She desperately desired to confess all: "An admission, husband? At my nativity, the font of heaven was full of fiery
shapes, burning cressets—"

"So?" he snapped. As much the cynic as Horatio was a
realist, Claudius had no truck, particularly at such difficult
times, with Gertrude's paralyzing fatalism.

"And the frame and huge foundation of the earth shaked,

like a coward," she continued as if he had said nothing.

Claudius openly scoffed at her superstitions: "So it would have done at the same season if your mother's cat had but kittened, though you yourself had ne'er been born."

Sarcasm only made her all the more adamant. "I say the earth *did* shake when I was born," she wailed.

"And I say," he replied, flushing crimson, "the earth was not of my mind if you suppose as *fearing you,* it shook."

She turned from him, disgusted with his narrow, limited way of perceiving the universe. Once more, Gertrude glanced out the long window. Hamlet and Horatio, a pair of animated puppets on their little rise, talked, talked, talked. Of what? That, Gertrude burned to know.

"Yet I would we were well rid of this knavery," she gasped, overcome by a growing sense of trepidation, a vast shadow overpowering her vulnerable mind, and implying to one such as she—forever searching for signs and symbols—that the darkness before dawn had now arrived in their lives.

Looking to the spot that so transfixed his wife, Claudius fixated all anger on Hamlet, and the king's temper threatened to roar out of control: "If he be conveniently delivered, I would he were."

One side of Gertrude's mind sensed Claudius was right. Eliminating the prince was the only way to insure a peaceful reign, allowing them to enjoy the future they had wistfully spoken of, so many times, over so many years. Truth was, though, she remained as much a mother as wife. "Still, he be my own," she reminded Claudius. "I must speak to him alone, before—"

"At first occasion, then!"

Gertrude nodded in solemn agreement.

A sudden rapping was followed by Polonius' gaunt frame in the doorway: "How now, noble lords. A moment?"

They waved him in, Gertrude seating herself daintily, at once affecting a half-convincing performance as the kingdom's calm, controlled, charming queen.

68.

Having revealed all that he knew, in fact little more than the whisperings of servants and squires overheard as they gossiped in Kronborg's shadowy corridors or the ale-houses of nearby Helsingor, Horatio tried his best to lift the prince's dashed spirits. "'Twill be the grandest ere held hereabouts," he noted of the burgeoning faire, as ever more people poured in from outlying farming communities and seaside cottages. Many who had been unable to abandon their duties in order to attend, if only at a discrete distance, the marriage and coronation ceremonies had planned all year long to visit the province's largest city for May Day celebrations. Now, that annual faire was taking on a special aura, transforming into a major event—allowing all to celebrate, if belatedly, the great changes occurring in their land.

Some carried along their wares in brown sacks, and set about selling baked-barley or smoked-oysters to the village folk. Others were present only to enjoy the giddy atmosphere, hoisting their children high atop rugged shoulders. Happy couples, or so they seemed on this warm afternoon, stood patiently in line for games of chance, the rougher men hoping to knock over wooden clogs by tossing stuffed bean-bags, netting prizes for their ladies. The more intelligent among them were eager to challenge chess champions in hopes of winning a full, rich purse.

"There is sure another flood moving toward," Hamlet scoffed, "and these couples are coming to the ark."

Horatio laughed, eager to believe Hamlet might be recovering from the shock of their strange homecoming. Soon, though, the prince again waxed serious, this time haunted by personal rather than political problems. "I thought you were my man, Horatio."

"I am, sirrah. As constant as the north star."

"I believed you so."

"My life I never held but as a pawn to wage against thy

enemies; nor fear to lose it, thy safety being the motive."

Hamlet considered Horatio, who could feel the prince's warm, sweet breath on his cheek. "Yet the other night, you denied me."

"I denied you not."

"You did."

"I did not."

With a sudden lunge, Hamlet attempted to grab hold of Horatio's right hand. Chilled more by the possible implication than the deed itself, Horatio pulled away, then addressed his prince more seriously than he ever before dared: "You bear too stubborn and too strange a hand over your friend that loves you."

To Horatio's surprise, hints of tears appeared at the edges of Hamlet's eyes: "Better not to have had thee as friend than thus to want thee in vain."

The moment proved catastrophic for Horatio, who could not have been more deeply devoted to Hamlet if the prince had been his own brother. "Good gentle youth," he implored, "tempt not a desperate man. For sure, thou hast my love."

Unable to meet the tragic mask of Hamlet's face, Horatio turned, glancing off to the field. Not far away, loving parents placed small children on frisky ponies for circular rides, then chewed on roasted meats carried about at the ends of sharp sticks while their little ones howled with glee. This was the kind of day Horatio hoped to someday share with Ophelia, if only she would deign to marry him.

"Horatio," Hamlet pleaded, "the need I have of thee, thine own goodness hath made. What, am I so ugly?"

That was clearly ridiculous. Hamlet, as wenches of Wittenberge oft declared, had been rated as the most attractive of all student-princes. "Were you a woman as the rest goes even," Horatio replied, "I should my tears let fall upon your cheek, and cry: 'My own true love!'"

Smiling strangely, Hamlet reached up, unhooking the frock's top-button, apparently willing to strip in full public view if only that would please. "If nothing lets to make us happy both but this my masculine usurp'd attire," Hamlet chuckled, "do not embrace me 'til each circumstance of time, place and fortune do cohere and jump as I these rags drop."

"'Tis no time for jest."

"Wit to cover wisdom. Horatio, I cannot be mine own, nor anything to any, if I be not thine."

For the first time, in all their years as friends, Horatio admonished Hamlet: "I am due to a woman; one that claims me, one that haunts me, one that I do believe will have me."

Ophelia! This was all her doing, Hamlet knew.

As fate would have it, the beautiful girl passed through the crowd, spotted them and mounted the hillock, all smiles. "Here comes the lady," Horatio exclaimed, thrilled at the sudden sight of her. "Now, heaven walks on earth."

Joining them, she dropped to the ground between Hamlet and Horatio, delighted by the ecstatic reception she had received while strolling about, flirtatiously playing her fairy-sprite to the hilt: "Sirs, welcome! It is my father's will I should on me the hostess-ship of the May-day assume."

Horatio considered her closely: all foolish and vain, drunk with the sweet-spirit of spring. When her delicious lips parted slightly to speak, a quick view of her perfect little white teeth and sharp pink tongue made him woozy.

Ophelia pointed to a distant spot, off near the woode's edge. There, a dozen women danced around a maypole, hanging on tight to its long ribbons. Though leaders of the church now considered this an obscene ceremony, some unsavory throwback to open pagan-worship of the male sexual organ, the commoners were too enamored of their timeworn ritual to give it up, despite their own conversions to Christianity. "After so long grief," Ophelia marveled, "such festivity!"

69.

Gertrude, unable to sit still in her plush chair owing to thoughts and emotions that wickedly danced about in her grim imagination, gradually became aware, once again, of gay merrymaking below. She rose, drifting to the long window, staring down at the fun and frolic, feeling very much a prisoner here. Momentarily halting their discussion of various ways in which the current crisis might yet be resolved, Claudius and Polonius joined her. They came alongside Gertrude, one on either side, all three gazing at the faire below, in particular focusing on the trio, seemingly so happy on their little hillock, yet consumed with problems of their own: the difficulties of being young and in love.

"I am afraid my daughter will run mad," Polonius complained, "so much she doteth on her Hamlet."

"But thou aidest us in our strategies against the prince," Claudius hopefully opined, "and thy salvage thy daughter's mind and reputation at once."

The greybeard shrugged, concluding: "And so we kill two birds with but a single stone?"

Gertrude, turning to observe him, noted the sadness in the old man's eyes: "Yet still you sigh?"

Without hesitation, Polonius blurted out the true reason for his misery. Laertes, not Ophelia, was foremost in his mind. "Can no man tell me of my untardy son?" he wept. "In Wittenberge, 'mongst the taverns there, they say, he daily doth frequent, with unrestrained loose companies."

70.

In a dank closet of a shabby Wittenberge brothel, Laertes slipped out of his clothes, crawling under the torn blankets of an unmade bed. The stale scent of soiled sheets and an unwashed coverlet, reminders of the many men who had passed this way in recent hours, gave him pause. So did the rough surface of an exposed mattress, still wet with the coagulating remains of those other fellows who briefly occupied this room earlier that very day. Already arrayed on the bed and covered up to her waist by a rough blanket, a young, foul-smelling whore awaited Laertes with something less than unbridled enthusiasm for the coming bout.

She had serviced a university youth minutes earlier, and felt that she could use—indeed, had *earned*—a rest, a drink, a little conversation even. In fact, on his way in, Laertes passed the exiting-fellow, the two lads exchanging furtive, guilty glances during their brief moment of awkward recognition. Now, though, he was already forgotten. Laertes was set for his turn, and excited at the prospect. Curling a finger provocatively and rolling her eyes in mute invitation, the wench signaled for him to come closer. Laertes had already financially settled for her services, in advance, in the lobby below. Naively, the provincial youth attempted to kiss her on the mouth, unaware that this wasn't allowed—not since the last bout of plague caused officials throughout Europe to outlaw mouth-to-mouth contact between prostitutes and their clients. Though whores in the hinterlands of Sjalland paid scant attention to such restrictions, particularly for the son of Polonius, Germany was another matter. Here, no one knew his name, or cared for his father's lofty reputation.

Thwarted in his attempt to steal a kiss by the sudden presence of her strong arm, so impressively firm in barring his way that the flesh and bone could readily have belonged to a Viking warrior, Laertes nodded his understanding. She relaxed, as he brought his eager mouth down over her body and across the rippling, unclean flesh, holding his breath to avert recognition of the pungent odor encountered while lips and tongue feasted, in turn, on neck, breasts, stomach . . .

. . . then, Laertes reached the whore's waist, and halted. Awaiting him there, under the covers, he discovered a belt-like stretch of black-satin, interwoven with like-colored lace. He had heard of such stuff: Those irrepressible Normans had (if claims of experienced travelers could be believed) invented a series of garments for women to wear during erotic encounters, such ribbon-like underthings purportedly adding to the man's sensuous-experience. "Better than naked," a visitor from Gaul once confided while they whispered of such stuff during a late night encounter in a Sjalland inn. This marvel before him now must be what experienced lovers referred to as a garterbelt; additional stretches of satin were attached, by metallic hooks adorned with small scarlet bows, to flesh-tight black stockings, designed in the style of those fishnets the Danes employed for more practical purposes along the Baltic coast.

Flipping the remaining portion of sheet away to view these previously concealed treasures, Laertes was fascinated to note a single, continuous line of black thread, running up along the backside of each leg, from toe to the very tip of her fleshy buttocks. This was not unlike those similar contraptions which visibly held a peasant's clothes together. Why, then, did it now stir within him a rumbling inner passion, quite unlike anything Laertes had ever known? Tracing a finger along the entire length of leg, Laertes marveled that a simple tailor's device could be put to such wickedly enchanting purpose.

Noticing that the whore stared at him, confused by his obvious amazement at the sight, he asked: "Seams?"

She nodded in agreement.

This was a first for him, so Laertes dutifully if excitedly admitted: "I know not seams!"

71.

Hamlet, Horatio, and Ophelia silently observed all activity on the grounds below. Slowly emerging from out of the crowd, a gypsy-wagon kicked up dust as it drew near. A cloaked driver, perched atop the brightly colored contraption, reined in his weary team several feet below the trio, hot steam visibly rising from the horses' tired flesh. At once, various performers, bedecked with bits and pieces of costumes hanging over everyday clothes, hopped out and stretched. Their ragtag outfits would shortly be employed for an early evening show which rich and poor alike would be invited to attend. The players set to work without hesitation, constructing a simple stage of long timbers which they carried along with them, attached by thick ropes to the wagon's sides. Overseeing the activity, an elderly Player King, adorned with *faux* crown, barked orders. By his side, a dwarf, wearing torn rags of English motley and the ornate bell-strung headpiece of an Italian Fool, danced.

"The best is yet to do," Hamlet remarked, "and here, where you are, they are coming to perform it."

"How now, rustics," Horatio called out. "Whither are you bound?"

The Player King and his Fool approached the extraordinarily attractive young people. "To the palace," the old one modestly said, "an' it like your worship."

The three youths rose to meet these antic newcomers. "Your affairs there?" Hamlet inquired. "Your names, ages, breeding? Discover."

"We are but plain fellows, sir."

This admission allowed Hamlet an opportunity for the verbal repartee the prince had come in contact with, and proven a master of, during the term at Wittenberge. "A lie!" Hamlet asserted, chuckling. "You are rough and hairy; do not give us the lie."

Grinning madly with the realization that here stood a worthy opponent at jest, the Fool darted close, speaking directly to Hamlet: "Your worship had like to have given us one, if you had not taken yourself with the manner."

All the while, the Player King studied Hamlet and Ophelia, standing near to one another, Horatio remaining a discrete distance away. "You two are married?" he asked.

"We are not," Hamlet sharply replied.

Blinking nervously, Ophelia crossed her arms over her chest. When she spoke, her voice inadvertently revealed a touch of bitterness: "Nor are we likely to be!"

For reasons known only to the prince, Hamlet chose to add levity to her heartfelt admission: "The stars, I say, will kiss the valleys first."

If the intent had been to remove any awkwardness from the situation, Hamlet's words had the opposite effect. Hurt to the quick, her elegant cheekbones glowing with embarrassment, Ophelia sidled closer to Horatio. The Fool, hopping like a toad toward Hamlet, scrutinized the youth.

"If an eye may profit by a tongue, then should I know you by description."

"In truth?"

"The prince!"

Hamlet wore no identifying signs of royalty, bedecked only in dark clothing; the Fool's observation thus amazed Horatio: "He hits the mark with first arrow!"

"How know me, fool?" a curious Hamlet asked.

Parading up and down, the Fool naughtily mimicked a woman's manner and movements. "Such garments and such years; 'the prince is fair, of female favour, and bestows himself like a ripe sister,' all say."

Hamlet blushed at this harsh honesty: "A witty fool!"

"Better witty fool than foolish wit."

Fools were notorious for their ability to utter cleverly phrased admissions of truth that would have demanded an immediate beheading for anyone else. Still, Horatio felt it might be wise to change the subject, addressing the Player King: "What art thou?"

"A very honest-hearted fellow, as poor as the king."

"If thou be as poor for a subject as he is for a king," Hamlet scoffed, "thou art poor enough."

Now, it was Ophelia's turn: "What would'st thou?"

"Service."

"What service cans't thou do?" Horatio wondered.

The Fool answered, in an ironic manner, for his simple-spoken master: "I can mar a curious tale in telling it, and deliver a plain message bluntly."

Unbeknownst to the others, Hamlet—luminous with inspiration—muttered: "This weaves itself perforce into my business!"

"Some sorrowful tragedy?" Ophelia suggested.

"Nay," Hamlet scoffed, gazing around at the lovely day. "A sad tale's best for winter."

"Comedy, then?" Horatio hopefully asked.

"With masque to follow!" Ophelia squealed.

Unconsciously, she danced in anticipation of the fun, in which her glorious ability to create poetry in motion always drew all eyes to Ophelia. Even as she did, Hamlet took the Fool aside, whispering: "I have a jest to execute that I cannot manage alone."

"Pastoral, historical—," the Player King rambled on, Horatio and Ophelia so entranced with his resume of possible shows that they did not hear what passed between Hamlet and the Fool: "Might thou, perchance, before tonight's performance, coin in your memory a few lines I might yet compose?"

"Of course, sirrah. I wear not motley in my brain."

"You are a merry man, sir. Fare thee well." Hamlet motioned toward Horatio, adding: "This good youth will see you to quarters."

Waving for the players to follow, Horatio departed toward Kronborg. All members of the company scurried off for a hot meal, followed by a much needed nap and then, of course, the show! Hamlet and Ophelia found themselves alone, though for all intents, she might not have been there at all. Already, Hamlet was mentally tearing through multiple versions of an emerging strategy that had seized the prince's active imagination, a way in which these poor players might reveal to all what Hamlet deeply believed: Claudius, whom Hamlet suspected all along of coveting both crown and queen, was responsible for Old Hamblet's death.

"Time shall unfold what plaited cunning hides," Hamlet muttered, thinking out loud.

Ever hopeful, Ophelia stepped close: "You spoke, my lord?"

Startled by her presence, Hamlet whirled about. "All shall be clear, in God's good time." Suddenly self-conscious, the prince added: "I must away."

"Why, my lord?"

"Why, to write a play!"

Hamlet marched toward the castle. Still unwilling to admit defeat, Ophelia dutifully trudged along behind. "I would have stayed 'til I made you merry. Well, I commend thee to thine own content."

Hamlet glanced back, offering her a set of sad eyes: "He that commends me to mine own content commends me to the thing I cannot get."

This stopped the girl in her tracks. Ophelia stood, silently watching as Hamlet continued on, alone.

72.

On a quiet mid-afternoon following a full day of classes, Fortinbras sat on a raw-wood stool by The Wild Boar's indoor bar. Sipping a horn of lukewarm sack, he attempted, without notable success, to initiate some conversation with the distracted Mistress Quickly. However friendly she might have seemed several days earlier, the object of his affections had noticeably cooled to him once more, leaving Fortinbras wondering if he would ever comprehend the shifting moods of the fairer sex. A few feet away, meanwhile, at a private booth, Laertes—unshaven, stale-smelling even from a distance—sat, hunched over a full horn.

Draining the contents in one long swallow, Laertes glanced over to the bar, eyes red and bulbous, clumsily attempting to signal a serving wench by snapping his fingers. None came near. Though Laertes had been in town little more than a week, most of that time had been spent roistering at pubs and brothels. Already he was infamously regarded as a stingy tipper. Indeed, Laertes was likely to forget such amenities altogether, more often than not. The bedraggled youth pulled himself up and out of the shadowy corner. He reeled over to the bar, and loudly hailed Mistress Quickly's brother stationed there.

"Give me a cup of sack, boy!"

"Thy lips are scarce wiped since thou drunk'st last," Fortinbras snarled under his breath. Laertes tossed the Norwegian prince a hostile look, seizing a newly filled horn, begrudgingly handed to him by the stout, pug-nosed bartender. Mistress Quickly, not pleased to have Laertes in her establishment, cast him an askance glance to fully convey her ill-feelings.

Catching the haughty woman's drift, Laertes turned his temper on her: "How now, Mistress Quickly. Have you inquired yet who picked my pocket?"

He here referred to a complaint registered, amid much huffing and cajoling, the previous day. After being asked to settle his afternoon bill in full and make at least partial payment on the considerable balance he had amassed, the slovenly youth made a great show of trying to find his money, only to insist, upon discovering no coins in his purse, that they must have been stolen.

"Why," she yelped, "Do you think I keep thieves in my house? The tithe of a hair was never lost in here before."

"Go to, go to," Laertes muttered, sipping his grog. "I know you well enough."

Drifting back toward the booth, Laertes discovered that Mistress Quickly, swift to defend her reputation as owner of an honest house, had circled around the bar, now standing directly before him, boldly blocking his way.

"No, sir. You owe me money, and pick a quarrel to beguile me of it!"

Unable, owing to his inebriated state, to form a worthy answer, Laertes slowly brought the horn up to his lips. He hoped to buy a bit of thinking time while drinking and, with a little luck, devise some clever quip. Before he could, Fortinbras, having slipped off his stool and sidled around to stand by Mistress Quickly, added his considerable presence to the human wall barring Laertes' way. Firmly, Fortinbras removed the beverage from the stunned Dane's grasp, and coldly announced: "A little more than a little is by much too much."

Terrified since childhood of this burly carrot-top, Laertes desperately seized on another ploy. Scratching himself all over, he insisted: "I think this be the most villainous house in all Wittenberge for fleas. I am stung like a tench."

Mistress Quickly eased closer to Fortinbras, the two moving as one, precisely what young Norway had hoped to achieve. "Like a tench! By the mass," she wailed, "there's not a cleaner club here 'bouts."

"I vouch for that!" Fortinbras chimed in.

Shamed and scared, Laertes bolted for the door, vaguely aware that The Wild Boar must be added to the growing list of Wittenberge houses from which his presence was barred. Once the sour fellow was gone, Mistress Quickly turned to consider Fortinbras. Her eyes danced with delight. The high-spirited wench was impressed to realize that he would stand with her, even against a fellow Teuton from the far north. She smiled at him, more warmly than before.

Returning the gesture, Fortinbras leaned close, whispering: "Now, what say. Shall we be . . . *merry?*"

Raising a pencil-darkened eyebrow provocatively, she winked: "Merry as crickets, my lord!"

Seizing one another's hands, without uttering so much as a single word more, they swiftly proceeded to the stairs.

73.

Hamlet sat before a mahogany desk in one of Kronborg's hidden enclaves. All the rooms lining this lengthy corridor had recently been transformed from storehouses, piled high with extra weapons, into chambers designed to serve more contemporary purposes. This particular room now presented a most princely study. Sunlight streamed in through cracks in the whitewashed shutters, fashioned in the Portuguese style and installed over an immense slash of a window. The queen herself had overseen the remodeling during one of Gertrude's frequent attempts to bring some sense of modern architectural-fashion to the medieval fortress she remained obliged to call her home.

Situated with back to window, in order to take maximum advantage of the natural warmth and abundant brightness,

Hamlet had, during the past hour, filled a large parchment with neatly penned characters, thanks to the handy quill and plentiful supply of ink which Gertrude, who often retreated to this spot, kept ready on the desk. Finally finished, Hamlet glanced over all those words and phrases, rapidly yet thoughtfully jotted down during the late-afternoon's concentrated work. In consideration, the prince decided, this little addition to the play that the troupe would perform was, from a literary standpoint, nothing to be ashamed of.

"I'll lay a plot shall show us all a merry day!"

A shuffling near the door caused Hamlet to glance up. There, Ophelia stood: Silent, patient, eager for a word of encouragement from her prince, some small ray of hope that she did not pursue entirely in vain.

"If you will see a pageant truly play'd," Hamlet, gently dismissive, muttered, "go hence a little and I shall conduct you."

Uninvited, she entered, approaching Hamlet with eyes that guilelessly projected her deep concern. Ophelia's disastrous attempt to create, at Horatio's expense, an aura of jealousy had achieved nothing, muddling matters worse even than they'd been before. So she had, returning home to collect her wits, determined that a show of sensitivity to Hamlet's problems—obviously great, though still unknown to her—might better serve her purpose: "I do observe you now of late," Ophelia ventured.

"Aye, madam?"

She reached out, absently toying with the lace band of one of Hamlet's shirt-cuffs, her small gesture conveying a full measure of feminine concern. "I have not from your eyes that gentleness and show of love I was wont to have."

Hamlet shrugged: "I have not the alacrity of spirits, nor cheer of mind, that I was wont to have."

Asserting herself so as not to appear hopelessly weak, Ophelia, uninvited, seated herself in a nearby chair, seizing one of her prince's hands: "Dear my lord, make me acquainted with your cause of grief."

For the first time since witnessing her arch flirtation with poor gullible Horatio, Hamlet softened toward the girl. She had, after all, ever proven a tender comrade and fond friend. However dark Hamlet's present mood might be, the prince had no desire to hurt one who harbored sincere love in her heart, even if Ophelia's honest affections were obviously mixed with intense ambition. "Be not deceived," Hamlet whispered sweetly. "If I have veiled my look, I turn the trouble of my countenance merely upon myself."

Discerning a tone of reconciliation in Hamlet's voice, Ophelia leaned close, eyes batting hopefully. "Since you know you cannot see yourself so well as by reflection," she suggested, "I, your glass, will modestly discover to yourself that of yourself which you yet know not of."

Visibly upset by her offer, though the girl's words were in truth gentle and fair, the prince rose, turned, stepped lightly to the window. There, Hamlet toyed with the shutters, opening them wider, and gazed out at the country faire, with its grand display of the human comedy spread far and wide below. "Vexed I am of late," Hamlet admitted, "with passions of some difference, conceptions only proper to myself, which give soil perhaps to my foul behaviors."

Without hesitation, Ophelia joined Hamlet there, still trusting in the idea that by throwing her earlier attempt at manipulation to the wind, she might yet rekindle the old intimacy between them: "This morning, I wished to smother your sadness with happy love."

Hamlet, feeling her warm breath draw near, deftly avoided any physical contact. Turning to face Ophelia, the young prince gazed deep into her eyes: "Your honour not o'erthrown by your desires, I am friend to them and you."

"Friend?" she wept. "When love is what I wish?"

Hamlet then once again felt engulfed by sadness, truly touched by the impossibility of her desire. "Poor lady, you were better to love a dream."

Why, she marveled, did Hamlet speak so? Only a year earlier, the two danced together in fresh green fields, laughing with innocent delight at the budding foliage all around. The whole wide world had appeared their oyster! "Once," she reminded Hamlet, "we did frolic in a kind of dream. Now: The daylight hours bring a nightmare's visage, with your fickle playing on my harp."

"Fickle?"

This last proved difficult for Ophelia to express in words. Still, what must be done, must be done; what must be said, said. "Rumour ran before you," she continued, pained eyes dropping to the floor, "of your hours with a Mistress Quickly in Wittenberge."

To Ophelia's surprise, Hamlet roared with laughter at the mere thought. Once some semblance of control returned, young Denmark, still smiling at what she had said, insisted: "By innocence I swear, and by my youth: I have one heart, one bosom, and one truth."

"And that," she ventured, "no woman has?"

Drawing near, Hamlet tried to explain the situation without revealing more than was safe to say at this moment in time: "No—nor never shall."

Sensitivity, Ophelia realized, was not achieving her purpose any more than open flirtation with Horatio had earlier in the day. Options rapidly diminishing, she returned, out of sheer desperation, to a play on jealousy: "Honest Horatio would care to have me."

Hamlet flushed bright crimson—jealous enough, certainly, though not in any way Ophelia might understand. "T'would be a sad waste."

"In truth?"

Hamlet pulled away, disgusted by her proximity, and stalked about the sparely furnished room in a state of utter remorse. For a moment, the prince actually frightened Ophelia, so near to madness did Hamlet suddenly seem. "Truly!" the prince hissed. "For to cast away honesty upon a foul slut were to put good meat into an unclean dish."

Ophelia hadn't expected foul language or cruel sentiments. Holding back tears, the girl asserted: "I am not a slut, though thank the gods if I am found foul."

"Well, praised be the gods for thy foulness, then." Hamlet hissed. "Sluttishness may come hereafter."

Tears flowing, Ophelia waved an elegant little fist in Hamlet's direction: "Oh! vile, vile—"

"What? Not a slut, then?"

"No!"

Without warning, Hamlet bore down on the amazed girl so menacingly that, for an instant, Ophelia feared she might faint dead away if Hamlet did not kill her first. "Give me the ring of mine you had this morning," the prince coldly demanded.

This caught her off-guard, and her face blanched: "What ring gave you me, my lord?"

Seizing her right hand, Hamlet yanked it upward to reveal a naked finger where the object had for so long been proudly displayed: "I gave my love a ring, and made her swear ne'er to part with it, and here she stands."

"But you see my finger hath not the ring on it."

"Is't gone?"

Attempting to assert herself, Ophelia yanked her arm away, wiping tears from her cheek while insisting: "If you did know to whom I *gave* the ring, and how *unwillingly* I left the ring, when naught else would be accepted *but* the ring, you would abate the strength of your displeasure."

Hamlet was not about to be outmaneuvered: "If you knew the *worth* of the ring, or your honour to *contain* the ring, you would not then have *parted* with the ring."

Polonius appeared in the doorway, staring at the young people, askance. "A quarrel? What's the matter?"

"About a hoop of gold," Ophelia wept, "a paltry ring he did give me."

"Whose poesy was," Hamlet added, quoting the inscription from memory, "for all the world, like cutler's words upon a knife: 'Love me, and leave me not.'"

"What," Polonius interceded, coming between them, "talk you of the poesy, or the value?"

The prince turned a cold shoulder to the greybeard, peering

at Ophelia out of Hamlet's eye's corner: "You swore to me, when I did give it you, that you would wear it 'til your hour of death."

Since she did not have it now, did the prince plan to murder her on the spot? Hamlet was, so far as Ophelia could determine, making a mountain out of a molehill. She grew more exasperated by the moment: "Why, I were best to cut my left hand off and say I lost the ring, defending it."

"Though not for me, yet for your vehement oaths, you should have been respective, and kept it."

While Polonius glanced back and forth, from one to the other, Ophelia recoiled at Hamlet's icy manner and cruel tone. "Cold indeed?" she wept. "My labor lost. Then, farewell heat, and welcome frost. Hamlet, adieu! I have too grieved a heart to take a tedious leave." She swept out of the room without uttering another word, Hamlet and Polonius watching her go.

"Thus," the prince sighed, "losers part."

"My daughter weeps," the old man sadly observed. "She would not part from you."

This, Hamlet thought, from Polonius? One of only two living people, other than myself, who knows full well Denmark's most carefully guarded secret? Still, the greybeard stared at Hamlet as if he, Polonius, who above all should have known better, believed the prince had all a sudden gone quite mad.

Then again, Hamlet pondered, that might not be such a bad idea! Indeed, this might provide inspiration, and also fit in nicely with Hamlet's gradually emerging plan to engage and then destroy despised Claudius, along with his entire court of fawning fools. "Thou cans't tell me why one's nose stands i' the middle of one's face?" Hamlet intoned, his tone of voice suddenly strange.

"No."

"Why," Hamlet explained, grinning from ear to ear, "to keep one's eyes on either side o' one's nose; that way, what a man cannot smell, he may spy into."

"In truth," Polonius added, "had he eyeglasses."

"Get thee eyeglasses, then," Hamlet ordered, waving a hand in the air like some frantic madman, "and, like a scurvy politician, seem to see the things thou dost not."

"With what a sharp-provided wit he reasons!" Polonius noted. Certainly, he must report this latest aberration to king and queen, as quickly as possible.

"Peace, doting wizard, peace. I am not mad."

As all knew, the maddest among us always insist they are perfectly sane. That, in fact, verifies their madness!

"O, that thou were not," Polonius mourned, "poor distressed soul."

Abruptly, Hamlet waved the old man away. "I hold your dainties cheap, sir," the prince howled, "and your welcome dear."

"Dainties?"

"Dainties, daughter—"

"Huh!" Polonius took serious note of that last word. "Harping on her?" Since the good nurse had taken leave of this fertile promontory, only Polonius and Gertrude, of all living beings, grasped the full truth as to why Ophelia's insistent flirtations might well drive Hamlet, more even than any other, to such extremities of distemper.

"For you know, uncle," Hamlet continued, appearing and sounding madder by the moment, "the hedge-sparrow fed the cuckoo so long, that it had its head bit off by the young. So—out went the candle, and we were left darkling."

"Though this be madness," Polonius pondered, "yet there's method in 't."

Hamlet began wildly dancing about the room. "If thou wert my subject," the prince howled, "I'd have thee beaten for being old before thy time."

Polonius stepped backward, curious as to Hamlet's reason for asserting this: "How's that?"

"Thou should'st not have been old," Hamlet screamed, "'til thou hast been wise. Begone!"

With that, Polonius scurried off in the direction his daughter had lately taken.

"Mad, is it?" Hamlet carefully considered how this turn of events might benefit a still in-embryo plan. "Fine, then. I shall, henceforth, affect an antic disposition."

74.

Slipping between the sheets with Mistress Quickly, Fortinbras had months ago decided, was a consummation devoutly to be wished. Now, to his delight and near-disbelief, the moment was at hand. Norway's rugged, rough-complexioned prince embraced and then rolled together in a great ball of flesh with the lush object of his desire, alone at last in an ornate bed which all but filled her small private closet on The Wild Boar's third floor—reserved for herself and several trusted employees, all guests required to remain on the sporting levels below. What made the moment more wonderful still: An urban legend, spoken of throughout Wittenberge, held that no man had been fortunate enough to find himself entertained here before. Perhaps the dreamy woman's lovemaking would prove no more accomplished than that of any other wench whom Fortinbras might, without so much difficulty, have bedded.

No matter. While hunting wild wolves, the one that came closest to slipping away always provided a discriminating marksman with the greatest satisfaction. Likewise, the awesome sense of accomplishment rushing through Fortinbras' frame elevated this coupling to a whole other plane. Though he had never locked in mortal combat, young Norway knew the joy he experienced at this thrilling moment must be precisely how his father had felt when, on the battlefield, diligent planning proved successful; this truly constituted a great conquest.

Damn!

A sudden rapping at the locked door disturbed their retreat, at least for Mistress Quickly. For while he would have ignored the noise, his companion responded: "Who comes so fast?"

He, meanwhile, strained to avoid an early climax. Fortinbras struggled desperately to remain firm within the soft recesses of her sweet flesh, thereby insuring he would be invited back, yet he was on the verge of losing control owing to pleasurable intensity. At first oblivious to the loud rapping beyond the door and utterly immersed in ecstasy, he momentarily had feared that her words were directed at him.

"A friend," a nervous voice responded from the hall.

"No 'friend' would come afore I have," Fortinbras, now aware of the rude interruption, shouted. "Your name, I pray you, 'friend.'"

"One Balthazar, loyal servant to young Denmark."

That was all Fortinbras needed to hear. With a sudden start, he pulled out of Mistress Quickly and leaped up off the bed without consideration for the woman he had so long doted on. Such frantic movements stunned the wench. After sitting upright in an attempt to recover her bearings, Mistress Quickly hastily seized the sheets, pulling them up and over her breasts. Having covered her nakedness, at least in part, she watched, wide-eyed, anxious to see what might transpire next. The sight was certainly something to behold! Dancing about on his way across the room, while struggling into crumpled breaches he'd carelessly discarded halfway to the bed, Fortinbras reached his destination and fully flung himself at the door. Hurriedly loosening the bolt, he then threw the door open, standing face to face with a weary youth, covered from head to foot in dust from the open road.

Unlike Laertes, this messenger had wasted no time along the way, nor any after arrival. Immediately, Balthazar had sought out the prince's rooming house, there learning that young Norway would likely be found at The Boar. After much persuasion and the exchange of several coins, Mistress Quickly's brother, still serving drinks from behind the bar, shared with him the precise whereabouts of Fortinbras. Now, nodding in recognition, Fortinbras seized the envelope Balthazar held forward and frantically tore it open, reading Hamlet's missive.

Halfway through, his face went ashen. "That's the worst tidings that I heard of yet."

"Aye, Aye, by my faith. It calls for a frosty sword."

Leaving the door ajar, Fortinbras rushed back inside and searched for his shirt, finding it a wrinkled mess under an overturned chair. No sooner had he slipped it on than he clumsily strapped on belt and sword. All the while, Mistress Quickly, her initial surprise giving way to a sense of having been entirely overwhelmed by events, observed from her spot on the big luxurious bed, astonished by jerky movements that would have seemed more appropriate for wooden puppets than a prince.

"Why, what is it, my lord?" she asked at last, rising from the bed while wrapping the sheet around herself in a half-hearted gesture of modesty.

"Saddle my horse!" Fortinbras, still ignoring her, screamed to Balthazar, who remained hanging in the doorway. The lad, all the while sneaking furtive peeks at Mistress Quickly, was shocked back to reality by the order and darted down the corridor.

"What is the matter?"

"Peace, foolish woman!"

Foolish? Why, mere minutes ago, she had been worshipped as a goddess come to life! Now . . . *foolish?*

Initially, Mistress Quickly couldn't imagine what might be significant enough to lure Fortinbras away, after all the effort he'd expended. Could there be someone he loved, indeed worshipped, more than her? By forming that question in her mind, she realized that she herself had provided the likely answer. "Is your sweet, soft friend in trouble?"

Having thrown himself together, however haphazardly, Fortinbras spun on his heels to face Mistress Quickly one final time and shouted like a bad stage actor: "The dearest friend to me, the kindest man, the best condition'd and unweary spirit in doing courtesies—" (here he paused to catch his breath) "—and one in whom the ancient Roman honour more appears than any draws breath in Italy today!"

With that, Fortinbras blew the lady a fond kiss and rushed off, if not without slamming the door behind him. At first, she simply stood there, frozen in shocked fascination at what had so quickly transpired. How rare it was that she, since becoming proprietress, gave herself to any customer, and at no charge? And how ironic that, having finally done so, she could be deserted before achieving mutually desired satisfaction! Tears then flowed. "As always," she complained aloud, if to none but the walls, "men's love of women lead to harms; for in their hearts, they love best other men-of-arms!"

75.

In Kronborg's main dining hall, members of the nobility and invited knights assumed their assigned places at table for evening meal. This event had been rescheduled for several hours earlier than the norm so that all might have time to prepare for the upcoming performance. Moments before their arrival, Osric and his courtiers had pranced about, lighting wall candles and setting plush cushions down on hardwood seats. According to the wishes of Claudius, his beloved dogs—three Danes he claimed were as great in courage and noble in character as any man present—lay restlessly on the cold stone floor, ready to leap at any dropped bit of bone or grissle. The beasts warily eyed each other, growling under their breaths for fear that one of their companions might be first to move and gulp down any greasy morsel.

Some in the current assembly secretly regretted such an obvious throwback to earlier, primitive ways, all but abandoned during the past decade. The custom reeked of those gross manners which Sjalland's forward thinking believed were best left consigned to their dubious place in the country's heritage. Yet Claudius reigned as king now, so none dared question his edicts. Thus, the dogs were begrudgingly tolerated.

Last to arrive, slowly strolling toward the oak table where all rose in deference, Claudius chatted with Horatio. What, the king hoped to learn, was the reason for Hamlet's absence during this afternoon's waning hours, not to mention three full days' seclusion following the homecoming of Kronborg's two university students? The question saddened the least royal of this evening's guests: "Sir, it is three hours since I saw the prince. What his happier affairs may be are to me unknown."

Thinking out loud, revealing more in front of Hamlet's friend than he would have allowed to slip had he been more cautious, the king countered: "I have missingly noted he is of late much retired from the court."

"From my company, as well," Horatio wanely admitted.

They arrived at table then, all gathered guests still standing in deference as Claudius took his place and snuggled close beside Gertrude in all her early evening finery. The queen had served as hostess while the others had earlier entered, holding her guests spellbound with lavish descriptions of dancing styles, recently originated in Spain. Such devices might soon be practiced here as well, if only an instructor could be persuaded, at considerable cost that would be covered by further raising of taxes on farmers and shopkeepers, to make the perilous journey to the northlands. Horatio, meanwhile noting with delight that his place was to the direct left of Ophelia (her father ensconced on her right-hand side), seated himself. She smiled sweetly, but said nothing. Horatio couldn't be sure whether this implied further invitation to courtship, or a return to the demure distance she had, in the past, always gently wedged between them.

At a snap of Osric's fingers, servants rushed about, delivering platters of fresh-caught cod, slow-baked in seaweed and vinegar. There were steaming bowls of boiled potatoes and hard-cooked eggs, as well as immense earthen pots filled with a thick brown gravy, fashioned from homegrown onions and imported herbs. Everyone waited for Claudius to help himself first and then wildly spear at his food. No sooner had he taken his initial bite than all others fell to loud gourmandizing.

Hamlet remained conspicuously absent. Though all observed a single vacant seat, none dared acknowledge it.

Then, a sudden stirring from atop the stairwell at the room's far end drew all eyes in that direction. The guests glanced up in unison to see if this late-arrival might be Denmark's ever-more-obscure prince, joining them with faint apologies which, in respect for Hamlet's status, would be readily accepted. As light footsteps descended, the sound preceding first sight of the prince, a casual interest in each guest's eyes transformed, as Hamlet emerged into their lines of vision, to utter astonishment, then abject shock. For what they witnessed could not be; somehow, all must have simultaneously slipped into the same horrid dream.

And yet . . . *yet* . . .

"Who have we here?" Gertrude gasped, first to break the stony silence.

"Tongue-tied, my queen?" Hamlet replied, halfway down and coming into full view. "Speak you!"

Instead of answering, Gertrude exchanged confused glances with Ophelia, who mumbled: "Some odd humour pricks him in this fashion."

"Melancholy is the nurse of such frenzy," Claudius griped, spitting several fish-bones onto the tabletop.

"He hath some meaning in his mad attire," Horatio suggested, hoping to explain the strange sight or, at least, offer some acceptable motivation.

Old Polonius, jaw dropping a full inch, nodded in his daughter's direction: "By this reckoning, he's more shrew than she."

At that, Hamlet—having purposefully descended slowly as possible—reached the bottom step. Smiling cat-like, Denmark's prince stood before them, fully revealed in a flowing cream-colored gown of fine imported silk, with a bright pink sash wrapped tightly around the waist, held in place by a frilly bow. In one hand, Hamlet carried a fan, the type recently introduced from the Orient, now all the rage with local girls of a coquettish nature who employed the objects to partly hide behind, as this allowed them to assume a pose that was at once modest and mysterious. Hamlet likewise held such a delicate object close to and over the royal mouth. Nonchalantly ignoring the flurry of activity this unexpected costume elicited, Hamlet strolled to the only empty chair and sat to Gertrude's right, gracefully setting the fan down on the tabletop.

Only then did the guests note Hamlet's whisp of a moustache, grotesquely conflicting with the feminine attire. Until that single reminder of masculinity became visible, all would have agreed the figure before them gave Ophelia competition as fairest female in the land.

Hamlet, feigning obliviousness to exasperated reactions, reached for the nearest platter and employed a huge serving spoon to gather potatoes onto a plate. All others, Horatio included, sat motionless, staring incredulously.

"How oddly he is suited," Polonius whispered.

"I think he bought his doublet in Italy, his round hose in France, his bonnet in Germany, and his behaviour everywhere!" Ophelia, long since infected by Gertrude's mania for fashion, replied.

Ignoring all, Hamlet considered the clean spoon placed by the prince's spot, carefully set on a napkin and awaiting use. Hamlet raised it high for close inspection, then theatrically cast the spoon aside, drawing another, with notably longer stem, from a hiding-place within the gown's billowing sleeve. Noting Horatio's wide-eyed confusion at this elaborate gesture, Hamlet smiled knowingly before offering an explanation: "Merry, he would have a long spoon that would sup with the devil." While speaking these words, Hamlet nodded gravely in Claudius' direction.

"I knew he was not in his perfect wits," Polonius reminded everyone.

"You're much deceived," Hamlet called across the table. "In nothing am I changed but in my garments."

Gertrude, ever desirous of orchestrating an evening's event into an approximation of what she believed to be the current manner in more advanced lands, attempted to soothe rising tempers: "'Tis nothing but some bond that he is enter'd into, for gay apparel'd 'gainst the triumph day."

Harshly, Hamlet stared at the queen mother before shifting about to face Claudius: "Look to her, man. She has deceived my father, and may thee."

Gertrude continued in her valiant effort to make light of all that was happening. The king, outraged and with blood visibly rising in his eyes, stormed up out and of his place. Claudius' bulky body thrust forward at a harsh angle as he made ready to seize Hamlet by the neck and wring the very life out of the prince. Gertrude, grasping what was about to happen, hurriedly grabbed hold his arm and restrained Claudius, who, after a moment's reflection, thought better of such open conflict.

"Go hang thyself, in thine own heir apparent garters!" the king then bellowed, hurling the insult over his shoulder as he hurried out of the room.

Slipping close to her only child, still beloved despite the ever-more-serious danger Hamlet spelled to her reign, Gertrude stooped low and spoke, reprimanding him: "I warrant you, the man is not alive might so have tempted him as you have done, without taste of danger and reproof."

"Well, I am school'd," came Hamlet's sarcastic reply. "Good manners be your speed."

Hamlet indicated, with a nasty nod, for Gertrude to follow along behind her husband, as his dogs—snapping and growling at the assemblage to express their dumb, dull anger at the feast concluding far too soon—had already done. Exasperated, the queen did precisely that, leaving the court to watch silently as Hamlet neatly sliced a potato, then heartily consumed it, careful not to let any of the gravy drop down and stain the remarkably beautiful dress.

BOOK FOUR

ᴛʜᴇ ᴄᴜᴄᴋᴏᴏ
ɪɴ ᴊᴜɴᴇ

76.

Methodically, Claudius marched back and forth across the royal bedchamber's polished hardwood floor, all the while cursing and spitting over the incredible audacity of this effeminate youth. Hamlet had dared insult a true warrior-king in front of his honoured guests. Worse still, owing to the exasperatingly antic ploy of a woman's garb, Hamlet had gotten away with it. Had the queen not quickly moved to restrain him, Claudius would have surrendered to his sudden burst of temper, thrown caution to the wind, and killed Hamlet on the spot with his bare hands.

Hesitantly, Gertrude entered, standing by the doorway as the dimming late afternoon sun cut through scrolled windows, bathing them both in the eerie pink light that briefly appears in Denmark as evening's shade emerges.

"A woeful pageant have we here beheld!" he shrieked upon catching sight of her.

Sullen and shrill, Gertrude nodded in agreement, still in a state of shock following Hamlet's grand promenade. For the first time in all the many years that they had secretly shared before marriage, she half-considered telling Claudius all there was to know. But that, Gertrude swiftly decided, might be more than even he could bear. Instead, she muttered: "He was perfumed like a French milliner. Were't not for laughing, I should pity him."

Momentarily forgetting they were shortly due at an open-air performance, the players already assembled and now awaiting the royal personages on the far end of Helsingor's fairground, Gertrude drifted over to the small table. Methodically, she opened a drawer, drew out her beloved Ouija board—a farewell present from Rumanian gypsies whom she had treated exceptionally well when they visited a decade earlier—and set it up for play.

"Zounds," Claudius continued, oblivious to nimble hands manipulating the pieces, "an' were I now by this rascal, I could brain him with his lady's fan."

"In time, perchance, his mad mood may pass, like the changeling moon on high. The late eclipses of the sun and moon portend no good to us."

He halted in his tracks, made aware, by the clicking of pieces, what she was up to. Claudius, who despised all superstition, raged in offense at her words. "This," he bellowed, drawing close, "is the excellent foppery of the world! That—when we are sick in fortune by the surfeit of our own behavior—we swiftly make of our disasters spawn of sun, moon, stars."

Gertrude paid him no never-mind. Deftly working old pieces of stone and bone with slender fingers, the queen fully believed that such objects could foretell, and occasionally even alter, the future. Frustrated by her refusal to acknowledge his objection, and suffering under incredible pressure, Claudius swung a meaty hand across her line of vision. This sudden action sent the board and its playing-pieces flying against the wall, most of the elements shattering before they fell to the floor.

"I can call to the spirits of the vastly deep with that!" she wailed.

"Why," he replied, sarcasm dripping from every word, "so can I; so can any man." Claudius leaned close before adding:

"But will they come when you call for them?"

Gertrude fell to weeping, and then collapsed in his arms—a ploy she had discovered early on in life would end any argument with a man, so long as she appeared to completely surrender to his strong masculine presence. As always, it worked. Even as Old Hamblet had done countless times during such confrontations during his lifetime, Claudius quickly calmed down, and then soothingly stroked her still beautiful hair. "Come, now," he reminded her, "and dress yourself, the players await us in open air."

After several more sobs, some sincere and others strictly for dramatic effect, Gertrude mechanically rose to make ready. Let's see, she thought . . . which of the newly-imported gowns—all recent arrivals from Firenze, none ever worn in public before—would most effectively whisk the breath away from all, women and men alike, lucky enough to lay eyes on her tonight?

77.

While Mistress Quickly wept alone in her bed on The Wild Boar's third floor, Fortinbras danced atop a table in the bar below. Exuding unbounded enthusiasm, the carrot-topped prince roused all in attendance, young lords and old louts alike. Already, he had fully explained Sjalland's tenuous situation: Upon arriving home, their friend Amuleth—the prince formerly known as Artist, now called 'Hamlet' according to Balthazar—had discovered a serpent of an uncle wore the crown. The monstrous man had seized it less than two weeks after old Hamblet's death. Doubtless, the scoundrel was deeply involved in the king's untimely demise. Worse, this self-proclaimed 'Claudius' now lived openly with the queen, flaunting an ancient Norse taboo, as marriage to the brother of a deceased husband could only be considered incest.

"Wasn't that Denmark's problem?" one man replied.

"Shouldn't we remain here, continue our studies?"

"What was Hamlet to them, or they to Hamlet?"

Such hesitant souls, as it turned out, were clearly in the minority. Many princes, who did not happen to be wearing weapons at the moment, stormed off to buckle on swords which ornamentally adorned hearths in their private suites. Plentiful commoners and townies, having slipped into The Wild Boar after dark, likewise hurried away to gather up axes and staffs. Substantial helpings of sack made them brave men of strong carriage, at least for the time being.

"I press me none but good householders, yeoman's sons," Fortinbras insisted, sword in hand. At this memorable moment, he appeared all but identical to his famous father when, as a warrior-king, Old Norway proved similarly gifted at rousing the rabble to arms. "A commodity of fond slaves and brave knaves," Fortinbras continued, carried away with the thrill of coming battle and, in all honesty, the sound of his own voice, "as had as lieu wrestle the devil as march to a drum."

"I'm for you, sir," a noble from Sweden shouted.

"And I!" a local storeowner joined in.

A general cheer of approval filled the room. This military campaign would, at the least, break their monotony. "I will lift the downtrodden Hamlet," Fortinbras vowed, "as high in the air as the unthinkable king, this canker'd Claudius."

In a shadowy corner sat Laertes. Restricted from drinking here, he had cautiously slipped back inside while Mistress Quickly was not in attendance, now turning a jaundiced eye to the self-proclaimed avenger. "Rare words," he hissed, head reeling from too much wine, "and brave world!"

Leaping from his perch, Fortinbras approached the Danish youth who, since arrival, had degenerated into this sad state. Young Norway enthusiastically proffered a fair offer: "Wilt join us, Laertes? Time serves wherein you may redeem your trampled honours and restore yourself into the good graces of this world once more."

Rather than rise to meet the challenge, as most others in the room had done, Laertes turned away. He waved to a serving wench, beating the tabletop with his fist. "Hostess, my breakfast, come." Nastily, Laertes then addressed Norway: "I could wish this tavern were my drum." With that, he continued hammering away at the table.

"Breakfast at this hour?" a student, unfamiliar with Laertes until now, asked.

"For him, now, night is day, day seems night," a fellow scholar explained.

Disgusted, Fortinbras wrote Laertes off as a hopeless cause and returned his attention to the others. "The land is burning," he called out boldly. "Claudius stands high, and either we or they must fall low and die."

Sophistication, civilization, all other rewards of careful study were forgotten in a flash. With a hearty cry that distinguished Norsemen of an earlier era, the crowd wildly raised Fortinbras onto their shoulders and, cheering, carried him out to make ready for their oncoming adventure.

78.

Throughout the day, the fairground that stretched between stately Kronborg castle and the thatched stone cottages of nearby Helsingor had played host to myriad activities as the common folk, gleeful at an opportunity to celebrate, set aside farming tools and city crafts. Deserting tightly fenced fields where unmilked cows were left to agonizingly moo for the expected attention, yoeman with necks burned red from daily exposure to the relentless sun joined with creamier colored shopkeepers, who locked up their establishments for a rare day of sport and frivolity. As they arrived in large number, the visitors found beer and wine available in half a dozen tents. There was much to eat, too, among the most popular items rich sausages of every variety—some stuffed with seafood, others with pork, all seasoned with imported spice—all roasting on spits over roaring cookfires, the diverse scents mixing seductively.

As a mild breeze carried the smells and smoke from barbeque pits over the entire area, other revelers danced in the field to tunes performed by local musicians. Gambling with dice and cards had halted at noon, when a dozen fully armored knights, bright shields sparkling in the high sun, engaged in non-deadly jousts. The sharp tips of their lances had been carefully capped so that the worst any warrior might experience was a rough fall off his huffing horse. Cheering wildly, while openly making wagers on their favorites, commoners crowded close against the rough wooden fence set up to restrict any unwanted entry into the lists.

Ophelia, her green scarves and long fringe dancing in the wind, was treated by all she passed as if Kronborg's reigning young beauty truly had transformed into the mythic May Queen. As the day wore on, though, all such activities were, in turn, abandoned. Those in attendance drifted, as if summoned by some shared ancient instinct, toward the makeshift stage assembled atop the same hillock where Hamlet, Horatio, and Ophelia first encountered the company of players. When all was said and done, nothing caught the imagination of noble and commoner alike so fully as a theatrical performance which might make them laugh, cry, or perhaps—and best of all!—a bit of both.

Much to Horatio's relief, Hamlet no longer wore the woman's attire that had caused such consternation during the disastrous late lunch. Instead, the prince was bedecked in tight breeches and vest, an intriguing costume that might have been worn by either man or woman. Only Hamlet's moustache announced to all which of the two this happened to be. Spotting Ophelia, Hamlet and Horatio sifted their way through the thickening crowd, at last joining her on a tuft of grass and sat close together, awaiting the show.

As Ophelia moved in between the two, Hamlet saucily whispered: "Come, thou art perfect in lying down. Come quickly, quick-quick, that I may lay my head in thy lap."

She was in no mood for such insolence, not even from a prince, particularly considering the rejection she had earlier suffered at Hamlet's hands. "Would'st thou have thy head broken?" Ophelia answered, flashing a deadly smile.

"No."

"Good. Then be still."

Hamlet glanced to her finger; no ring resided there to reflect the fast fading sunlight. The prince then looked to Horatio, absently fingering the ring, visible on the fourth finger of his right hand. Before Hamlet could comment, king and queen arrived, accompanied by a full royal party of knights in armor and older nobles in their finery. All in attendance rose at their entrance. Claudius and Gertrude, after a round of polite smiles and formal waves, took their cushioned seats on an elevated platform erected to allow the land's rulers a perfect view. At no point did either acknowledge the presence of Hamlet, though they could not have missed the highly visible prince in such vividly ambiguous attire.

Having followed the royal couple into the audience, Polonius drifted over to the trio of young people and stood directly behind his daughter. She smiled up at him, dancing eyes wordlessly reminding the old man of her claim: 'I will be married to royalty!' As if to compensate for the king and queen's slight, Polonius attempted small talk. "Will art, as Aristotle of old claimed, truly imitate life, Hamlet?"

A noncommittal tone underlined Hamlet's words: "And rather than it shall, I will be free ever to the uttermost, as I please in words. If you cannot, best stop your ears."

Polonius attempted to formulate some reply. Before he could, the Player King stormed onto the stage from behind a shabby, faded curtain. In a matter of moments, all who stood about talking and sipping ale from horns, hushed and found places on the ground, where they awaited the show with eager silence. Behind the makeshift theatre, the sun—threatening to momentarily sink below a stretch of tall trees lining the horizon—painted a darkening sky with wild splashes of color. Gashes of red, orange, and yellow added a majestic backdrop to the human proceedings which they now dwarfed.

Behind the Player King, his Fool, to whom Hamlet had

earlier entrusted additional lines for the script, followed along, bent over like a hunchback. The Player King wore a crown; the Fool clutched a shawl close, indicating that he represented a woman. As they staggered about on the rough stage, everyone laughed loudly. "O mistress mine," the Player King muttered some several seconds after a hush descended on the gathered multitude. "Where are you roaming? O, stay and hear, your true love's coming!"

"Trip no further, pretty sweeting; Journey's end in lovers meeting."

At that, the Fool, following Hamlet's precise instructions, produced a knife from beneath the shawl.

"Fair lady, do you think you have fob in hand?"

"Sir, I have not *you* by hand." The Fool rolled his eyes wildly, much to the crowd's delight.

"Marry, but you shall have. And here's my hand."

"Now, sir, thought is free. I pray you, bring your hand to the buttery bar, and let it dawdle."

With that, the Fool slapped away the Player King's extended hand of love and friendship, grasping at a bulge threatening to burst from out of the heavy crotch in his drooping pantaloons. The commoners laughed loudly at this vulgarity. Polonius, already fearful that something might be amiss, glanced to king and queen. Gertrude, as was her fashion, had affected a pose of outrage and offense at any public show of vulgarity. In truth, this minor frivolity seemed mild in comparison to the stunning variety of unspeakable things she secretly did and said during the early years of her marriage to Old Hamblet. Or, following that, further improved on while Claudius remained her beloved 'Fang,' the adventurous Gertrude's adulterous lover. Always, though, she remained conscious and cautious of her public image. When in the general eye, Gertrude assumed a studied demeanor of innocence, gentility, and conservatism.

"Wherefore, sweetheart?" the Player King continued. "Where's your metaphor?"

"It's dry, sir."

"Why, I think so. I am not such an ass but I can keep my head dry. Where's your jest?"

An exaggerated shrug, accompanied by the unsubtle widening of the Fool's bulbuous eyes, was followed by: "A dry jest, sir."

"Are you full of them?"

"I have them at my fingers' ends."

Claudius stirred uneasily in his seat. Members of the royal party noted his discomfort. Some among the commoners sensed this performance was drifting in dangerous directions. Yet all remained riveted in their places, so forceful was the unfolding performance which, for all in attendance, had truly taken on a life of its own—one that seemed strangely informed by, and relevant to, their own current situation.

"Come away, come away, death," The Player King mourned, "and in sad cypress, let me be laid."

"As you wish."

The Fool then pretended to stab the Player King, repeatedly and violently whacking away with his *faux* weapon. A pig's bladder, filled to overflowing with the butchered animal's blood, had been until this point kept carefully hidden beneath the Player King's waistcoat. Now, he skillfully allowed the contents to pour out onto the makeshift stage. Men in the audience gasped, while several women fainted.

Hamlet leaned close to Ophelia, speaking in a stage whisper loud enough to be heard by any and all around: "Jesters do oft prove prophets, I have heard."

The Player King fell to his knees, flailing about in fiery imitation of agony. "Fly away, fly away, breath," he muttered. "I am slain by a fair cruel maid."

That was more than enough!

Claudius, seized all a sudden by some inner frenzy, leaped up from his seat, screaming: "Horrid words! Horrid—"

Immediately realizing they had, without intending to, sorely offended, and fearing for their heads, the players at once abandoned the stage. First, the troupe darted behind the curtain to collect their wits, and then rushed off in the direction of the woode. What had gone so terribly wrong, they did not know. Obviously, though, their only hope was to hide away somewhere until their gypsy wagon could be readied to whisk them away, off (hopefully!) to other lands and further shows.

Hamlet gleefully took the onus off them. Rising, the prince addressed Claudius, speaking calmly: "Pardon me your evening's bad entertainment, 'gracious' uncle."

Hands tearing impotently at the air, eyes rolling back in his head like a man consumed by the falling sickness that long ago overcame the great Julius Caesar of Rome, Claudius surrendered to his rising fury. All at once, he lost all semblance of control. "Grace me no grace, nor uncle no uncle," he screamed at a fever-pitch. "I am no traitor's uncle, and that word 'grace' in an ungracious mouth is profane."

Tom, Dick, and Francis, seated among the nobles, exchanged concerned glances. For several days, they had secretly debated the worthiness of Claudius to reign as Denmark's king. This display proved the final straw. Now, they were certain that, by remaining silent at the coronation and attempting to remain loyal supporters for whoever wore the crown, they had committed a grievous error. As knights of the realm, such men of valor were now responsible for its correction, one way or another. So without anyone noticing, they drifted toward Hamlet's side.

"*Thou* art the traitor," Hamlet called back, clearly in control of all faculties, "and too bad to live."

Gertrude's difficult attempt to rise up and out of her place of honour was interrupted by the sudden darting of a delicate hand to her woozy head. The queen fainted dead away, or at least mimicked such a sudden fall realistically enough that all in attendance, save perhaps Hamlet, believed what they saw. Whatever the case might be, real or feigned, this unexpected occurrence drew the eyes of all from her husband's tantrum, thereby salvaging a bad situation. Polonius and Osric hurried up to seize her limp body before it could make contact with the hard ground. Swooping Gertrude up in their arms, they rushed through the swiftly parting crowd and carried their queen back to Kronborg.

If Claudius noticed any of this, he gave no hint, standing stock-still in place, eyes trained on Hamlet. If looks could truly kill, the young prince would have died then and there. "Boys," Claudius hissed, pushing forward toward Hamlet, "with women's voices, strive to speak big and clap their female joints in stiff, unwieldy arms against the crown."

Despite the considerable threat of Claudius' massive frame, already casting a great shadow over the slender youth, Hamlet refused to yield even an inch of ground. Hamlet softly insisted: "I am the one and only rightful heir to the self-said crown!"

"A king's son?" Claudius screeched, further closing the distance between them. "If I do not beat thee out of thy kingdom with a dagger of lath, I'll never wear hair more on my face!" The king indicated his own rough beard, notably masculine in comparison to Hamlet's cheek: soft, gentle, elegant as velvet.

Fearful that Claudius might lose all control and wildly strike out, Horatio had hurriedly risen and, ever loyal, assumed a place directly in front of Hamlet. He stood ready to interrupt any possible attack—deflecting it if possible, absorbing the blow himself if need be. As king and prince stood in defiant confrontation, their mutual hatred at last obvious to one and all, Tom, Dick and Francis made their way around the king, reinforcing Horatio by flanking him on either side. Their simple movement made clear to the other nobles and awe-struck commoners that three of Sjalland's most formidable knights had no intention of allowing anyone to lay so much as a finger on Old Hamblet's offspring.

No one—not even the current king!

The sight of four rugged men standing close to Hamlet, hands resting lightly on temporarily sheathed swords yet ready for anything, was enough to shock Claudius to his senses. Moreover, the vivid image of Hamlet's mushrooming coterie of followers forced the king to acknowledge that the tide was likely to turn against him. Burning with anger and betrayal, he stormed off in sullen fury, everyone unlucky enough to be standing in his path rushing now to get out of the way before being trampled.

"What trick, what device, what startling-hole," Hamlet dared call after him, "canst thou now find to hide thee from this open and apparent shame?"

Once more pricked near to hysteria, Claudius turned on his heels, hurling back a rough insult. "I can teach thee, nephew, to command the devil."

"And I content thee, uncle," Hamlet answered with a wry laugh, "to shame the devil by telling truth: tell truth and shame the devil!"

Several nobles, dedicated to the Old Ways and loyal to Claudius long before he had claimed the crown, spirited the king away before their leader could utter anything of an incriminating nature. Nervously, the crowd dispersed, even as the sun finally slipped out of sight, like a coastal swimmer disappearing into the Baltic at its calmest ebb. Seconds later, richly painted heavens were obliterated by darkness, shrouding the countryside until one by one stars twinkled above, their merry light providing sharp contrast to the heady human-drama unfolding below. Lighting tapers and firing up torches, the confused multitude wandered away. Most remained silent following the strange spectacle they had witnessed, and surely having been treated to a grander show than any had bargained for. Tom, Dick and Francis held back, huddling close in tense conversation. Each fully knew he had reached a point that called for weighty decisions.

"This man cried out abuses," Tom recalled, "seemed to weep over his country's wrongs."

"And by this face, this seeming brow of justice," Dick added, "did he win the hearts of all he did angle for."

"Indeed, not I," Francis reminded them. "Do recall, though I stayed silent, I did scream in my very soul."

Delighted with the end result of the quickly penned show, Hamlet studied the abandoned stage. Leaning close to Ophelia, the prince naughtily confided: "The mousetrap!"

79.

Working as an impromptu team, Polonius and Osric maneuvered Gertrude, still reeling in confusion, through Kronborg's shadowy corridors and up a winding staircase. There, staggered wall candles offered a feeble glow by which the little party picked its way, at last reaching the second floor. They gently manipulated their queen into the royal chamber, then cautiously lifted the near-lifeless lady onto her bed. Finally, these attendants blanketed Gertrude with a thick coverlet. Polonius placed an aged palm across her forehead, fearful that a fever-fit may have left his queen in such a sorry state forever. While the greybeard tended to Gertrude, Osric hurried to a hearth on the far side, fervently stoking dormant ashes. Gradually, he breathed life into a small fire that would, he hoped, banish an evening chill already seeping into the room, and perhaps help restore their lady to some semblance of her former self.

"Go," Polonius, more worried than usual, commanded the shuddering courtier, "see to the king!"

No sooner had Osric darted off than Gertrude moaned. Waking in agony, she then restlessly pawed at the sheets. Slowly regaining consciousness, Gertrude noticed the loyal old man by her side, as he had been since that day—it felt like centuries ago—of her marriage to Hamblet. Such loyalty had a calming effect, and Gertrude managed a slight smile.

"This was, truly," she whispered, "what poets of yore tagged 'the final straw.'"

"Indeed," Polonius agreed.

He was, after all, the only person alive, save she and Hamlet, who knew the entire story. Gertrude always retained a few secrets. Hamblet, then Claudius would each have been amazed to realize how completely they'd been kept in the dark all these years.

"I fear, Madam," the greybeard nervously added, "*all* will soon be known."

Even in her current state, Gertrude had over the years become so ingrained in the craft of withholding truth as her best means to survive that she now tried to deny the obvious wisdom of his words: "The brutal murder that haunts us so—"

"That," Polonius nodded, still resentful over the reigning couple's decision to gradually take him into their full confidence concerning the true fate of Old Hamblet, "and more— *what e'en your current husband does not know!*"

Fear danced in her eyes, the horror of full, final discovery a potent reality at long last. Before she could reply, there came the sound of soft footsteps ascending nearby stairs, heralding the presence of someone moving upward, inexorably headed toward them.

"My mother calls me?" Hamlet, rounding the circular stairwell, announced. "I must not say 'no.'"

This was enough to force Gertrude back down on the bed, cringing against fur pillows, wishing she could dissolve into them and disappear. "A fear o'ertakes me—"

"Fear not," Polonius assured her. "I'll behind the curtain hide—if trouble brews, to be by your side!"

With surprising dexterity, the old man scampered over to an immense tapestry hanging on the far wall. On its surface, colorful images of bold crusaders crossing Europe, en route to the Holy Land, had lavishly been embroidered by Brussels-based artisans across a rich burgundy backdrop. Polonius slid into the open space between curtain and wall, and there assumed a hiding spot from which he could listen—remaining near enough to rush in and rescue Gertrude should the need arise. Then, Hamlet stormed into the room: eyes furious, demeanor arrogant, slamming the door behind.

Frightened by this spectacle, Gertrude assumed her bold front. She scolded Hamlet as if her child were an errant puppy: "Hamlet, you your father have much offended."

For a long moment, pregnant with menace, Hamlet incredulously stared at her. Then, the prince turned to a table where paintings of Hamblet and the man formerly known as Fengon sat, arranged amid bowls of fresh-cut flowers. Hamlet indicated the former king. "Mother," the prince hissed, "*you*, my father have much offended."

"What? Was never widow had so dear a loss!"

Ignoring her false words of defense and denial, Hamlet lovingly seized Hamblet's likeness and held it close. The prince examined the late-king's rugged mien, old Hamblet's rough yet kindly face marked by honest, sensitive eyes.

"What?" Hamlet sighed, on the verge of tears. "Was never orphan had so dear a loss."

Gertrude would not, could not suffer further insults from her own offspring. "So young, and so untender?"

"So young, and so *true*."

Having momentarily faltered, Gertrude resumed her wavering display of self-confidence. Summing up her courage, she approached Hamlet. "As to the late king—"

Carefully returning Hamblet's image to its appointed place, Hamlet, waving both hands in the air, set to storming about, refusing to meet Gertrude's pleading eyes: "Prithee, no more. Cease! He dies to me again when talk'd of."

She withdrew, letting Hamlet alone for a while, afraid of possible violence, secretly calmed a little by her knowledge of the greybeard's hidden presence. "How sharper than a serpent's tooth it is to have a thankless child," she finally huffed, adding: "All I did was done for *thee*!"

Hamlet halted in mid-step, laughing at Gertrude's words. Self-serving, she had always been. Now, to gussy up unforgivable acts in a cloak of selflessness? "For *me*? Kill a king, and marry with his brother?"

"O, the woman that cannot make her fault her husband's occasion," Gertrude wailed, "let her never nurse her child herself, for she will breed it like a fool!"

Hamlet rushed back to the table. This time grabbing hold of Claudius' likeness, Hamlet raised it high and darted across the room to Gertrude's side. Then Hamlet shoved the painting before her line of vision, forcing her to consider it closely. And all the while, Hamlet screamed, "Fool for love!"

Perhaps if she tried another tact! "Thou didst not know how many fathoms deep I am in love!"

Her approach only made Hamlet all the angrier. "O, rather bottomless," the prince shrieked, "that as fast as you pour affection in, it runs out."

"If thou remember'st not the slightest folly ever love did make thee run unto, thou has not loved."

Dare she utter the words Hamlet had just heard? Knowing full well the truth of the prince's predicament, and her own involvement in the creation of this ever gnawing problem?

This issue could be left dangling no longer!

Now, at last, it was time for these two, mother and child, to confront not only each other, but her momentous decision—the desperate ploy assumed so long ago, a single false statement on her part which had forced Hamlet to live a lie during every waking hour of every single day for each of the past 21 years. "Love is blind," the prince lectured, "and lovers cannot see the pretty follies they themselves commit. For if they could, cupid himself would blush, to see me thus transformed into a *boy*."

Gertrude wept, as each considered the results of the choice she had made. The queen recalled, as she oft did in nightmares, what had happened through the mists of time—quite unable now to picture the truth as it had transpired, able only to sum up an image in her mind that had been polished, altered, reinvented with each and every endless replaying. Hamlet, of course, could but construct a mental myth, imagining the incident as one might picture some tale out of time, derived from ancient Norse legend . . .

80.

. . . *fiercely, the armies of Denmark and Norway had plunged into that historic day's final combat. Warriors screamed in pain—brave men who in the past had stoically suffered their wounds in silence, yet could not now deny the primordial terror of a virtual holocaust occurring on the bloodied field before Kronborg castle. High in the tower, Gertrude echoed their screams. Her baby, the longed-for child, fought its way out of her womb and into the awesome, immense, intimidating world at large. Only the nurse attended Gertrude at this juncture; Polonius had briefly slipped into the adjoining corridor, hoping to learn what the day's outcome might be, while secretly doubting that the results could be happy for Denmark. At last, he returned, moving sluggishly, face ashen.*

"How goes the battle?" the nurse inquired. From the look of devastation in his eyes, she grasped the answer without Polonius needing to reply. No one yet knew the outcome, leastways not for certain. Still, survivors of the early fighting, crawling in morbid disarray back to the castle where women nursed their gaping wounds in the open courtyard, did not offer much in the way of optimism. Too depressed to share the specifics of what he'd learned, Polonius shrugged sadly. His solemn gesture proved more than enough to communicate an assessment of their chances.

The nurse rolled her eyes in horror: What might momentarily betide them? The answer was too terrible to consider. She must force herself to focus on the task at hand, caring for their queen and her newborn child.

"How fares our gracious lady?" Polonius asked, coming close.

"She is, something before her time, delivered."

"A boy?"

No, the nurse gestured, holding up for his observation a perfect little girl: "A daughter, and goodly babe: Lusty, and likely to live."

The nurse carefully swaddled the infant, cradling her close. Gertrude, meanwhile, slowly returned to consciousness. For several seconds, she lay still, uncertain as to her precise whereabouts. Then, her eyes lit up like twin lightning bugs on midsummer's eve. Reality closed in; Gertrude recalled everything all a sudden and, like any new mother, hungered to inspect her child.

No yabbering or crying was to be heard! Gertrude's eyes flickered fearfully. "Lives my sweet son?"

Nervously, the nurse held the girl-child before the queen's blurry line-of-vision. "Sweet daughter.*"*

To the nurse's surprise, Gertrude recoiled in horror, abruptly turning away, which set her babe to bawling. "If the king had no son," Gertrude reasoned, "the populace would desire to live on crutches 'til he had one."

"Care not for the issue," Polonius, hoping to right things, insisted. "The crown will find an heir."

"And then," Gertrude mumbled, "to have a wretched puling fool, a whining mammet in her fortune's tender? God's bread, it makes me mad. Leave her to heaven!"

Gertrude hid her face amid the pillows, unable to consider her child. Fool! Didn't the nurse realize this situation's seriousness? Even in the best of times, Gertrude would have been expected to deliver a prince—not only for her husband's sake but, more significant still, the greater good of Denmark. And these, obviously, were the worst *of times!*

She quivered at the sound of mighty men, screaming in agony below. No doubt they were Danes, dying in a final vain attempt to protect Helsingor . . . terribly outnumbered by Norway's warriors, who were considerably more proficient at the brutal Viking skills of war, pillage, rape, and . . . as invariably followed in such situations . . . the murder of innocents!

A woman herself, despite advancing years still hopeful for children of her own, the nurse felt sorely offended by Gertrude's negativism. Without being aware of moving, she had stepped back in dismay at what, to her, had on the queen's part been an unconscionable reaction.

Perhaps, Polonius thought, a man's assurance might succeed where a woman's words, even from one so revered as the nurse, had not. "Heaven and yourself had part in this fair maid," he suggested. "Do you love your child so ill that you run mad, seeing that she is well?" Polonius turned, cross-

ing to his wife's side, and carefully took the girl in his own arms, carrying the babe back.

"Only look on this sweet child and sense your duty," the nurse sobbed from her spot in the shadows, even as Polonius firmly handed the baby girl to Gertrude. This time, she relented, took the child, and gazed into its half-open eyes; soft hazel, yet as intense and mesmerizing as her own green orbs.

"Is there no pity," Gertrude imagined her babe asking, "sitting in the clouds? O, sweet mother, cast me not away."

Gertrude sobbed, loud and uncontrollable. When, at last, her tears were done, she lovingly brought the baby girl down to her ample chest. The queen allowed the child to suckle there, all the while stroking her soft little head. Polonius smiled with relief at Gertrude's unexpected show of tenderness.

Pleased by this gesture, the nurse sighed: "Aye, that is more natural!"

Cruel sounds of battle gradually diminished on the field. That could mean but one thing: The fighting was done. Little doubt that soon hulking crimson-capped Fortinbras would, his victorious army following hard upon, come crashing into the castle. Then, the far Norsemen would do as they wished with the lost souls found there. Women would be raped, the prettiest among them carried off as spoils of war, others put to quick death after use and abuse. Men and boys, certain, would be massacred where they stood. Little girls, dangled over bonfires until their tender bodies burst into flames, exploding before their mothers' eyes.

It had all happened before, at other castles unable to mount sufficient defense. Doubtless, from the dark early reports carried back, such would be their fate now. Too late to hope, Gertrude knew, that she might save herself: Both husband and paramour were doubtless dead, equally unable to help at the moment when she most needed one or the other. Likely, her fabled beauty would permit Gertrude to live, if as slave for Fortinbras to use as he pleased.

Fatalistic about her chances for anything better, her thoughts turned to this lovely girl-child, cradled in her arm, suckling at her breast. If only Gertrude could somehow save her infant daughter, the baby she had, after coaxing from Polonius and the nurse, come to accept, even love. *A sudden rage tore through Gertrude's body at the possibility that her tiny girl's fresh life might be extinguished little more than an hour following her birth. She could not, would not let the child die.*

There had to be a way to save her babe, and no tactic, however strange, would be discounted . . .

If only the child had been born a boy, everything would be different! Ancient Nordic law dictated that, without exception, the only son of a defeated king could not be summarily executed, though any—indeed, every!—worthless daughter might—would! Such a one—a male, a prince—must be treated with respect and dignity, allowed to live, if in captivity. This tradition, always kept by all, owed to a long-held belief that the male offspring of any Teuton king was descended from Odin, and thus could only be killed in combat after reaching manhood—though never summarily executed the way lesser persons, particularly girls, indiscriminately were.

If only her babe had been a boy!

Gertrude's eyes burned with strange fire as a bizarre, risky, difficult yet altogether possible plan took form. Glancing down at her child, the queen's eyes closed as she surrendered to the sweet sound of the girl's suckling. Then, the queen insisted, *"Why, how now. This is a man, and not a maiden, as thou say'st he is."*

Husband and wife exchanged confused glances. *"Oh, great queen, no—,"* Polonius, gathering her drift, argued in vain.

One final scream rose from the field below. Death had already taken so many; it would not claim her baby! *"To save your life in this extremity,"* she whispered to the oblivious girl, *"this favor will I do you. Hamlet's name and credit shall you undertake."*

The nurse argued: *"There's no way under heaven—"*

Now, Gertrude was sitting up in bed, her strength suddenly restored owing to a sense of mission: *"I am to get a man, what ere he be. It skills not much! We'll fit 'him' to our turn."*

Clucking her teeth, the nurse nervously paced about. Ever the diplomat, Polonius reconsidered his initial objection: *"Perhaps 'tis possible—"*

"Ay," his wife shouted in a rare display of hot temper, *"if a woman live to be a man."*

Gertrude scornfully cowed them both: *"If you would not do so, you pity not the state, nor the remembrance of his most sovereign name. Consider little what dangers, by his highness' fail of male issue, may drop upon his kingdom and devour us all."*

Polonius was won over. Taking up the child again, he bounced her in mid-air, pronouncing: *"He'll make a proper man!"*

Commandingly, Gertrude pointed to the only book in the room, an immense Bible resting on an old oak-table, and demanded: *"Swear!"*

Polonius, the realm's most devout Christian, rested a weary hand on the leather-bound volume. *"I swear."*

"Now," Gertrude continued, to the nurse, *"you!"*

Reluctantly, she obeyed. *"I, too, swear."*

Gertrude then sent both into the corridor and on down to the great hall, with orders to announce to all there—old men and young boys, the wounded and the women caring for them, and anyone else encountered along the way—that the land did indeed have a prince, the future king all so yearned for. If the day was Denmark's, he would someday reign. If not, there would at least be the solace of knowing Fortinbras could not kill this child. This insured hope for the future, the very thing Sjalland's population always needed most.

While they were gone, Gertrude formulated plans on how best to keep the child's form from ever being seen, her blatantly brilliant lie thus unmasked. She would tell the conquering Fortinbras—or Hamblet, in the unlikely case that he had won—that her newborn son suffered from a rare condition, a tenderness of flesh requiring careful attention from its mother. Viking males—of Norway and

Denmark alike, however courageous in mortal combat with powerful enemies—retreated in abject fear from situations such as that. Royal male-children were considered holy; the mothers who nursed and cared for them, enchanted beings.

This would not be such a difficult ruse to maintain, after all!

Gertrude named her babe Amuleth, adjusting the king's own title for a more sophisticated century. Then, they heard the sound of distant drums, coming close and in a hurry. Polonius rushed back in, the nurse following. Amazingly, Gertrude learned, the day was Denmark's.

"*Your husband is at hand,*" *Polonius announced in happy disbelief.* "*We hear his trumpet.*"

Desperately, the nurse attempted, in the few seconds that she had left, to convince her queen it was not too late to call off a charade that, if allowed to continue, must be carried on throughout this child's entire life. And how difficult that would be upon reaching maturity! Yet Gertrude would not be moved. The castle was already informed; ignorant masses grow confused by sudden reversals. The king, who would surely have heard the happy news on his way to the tower, might grow furious upon having his happiest dream shattered upon arrival.

No! What was done, was done. Only, could she trust them?

"*We are no tell-tales, madam,*" *the nurse sighed.*

"*Fear not,*" *Polonius added.*

Relieved, Gertrude kissed her child on its gentle head. "*See?*" *she cooed.* "*What a man you are now!*"

81.

"Harp not on that string, Madam," Hamlet coldly informed Gertrude. "That is the past."

"'Past' is but present," she countered, "that's danced its hour and fast-faded."

"My present thought?" Hamlet mused. "The spirit of my father, which I think is within me, begins to mutiny against this servitude."

Without hesitation, Hamlet drew her sword, turning the blade against her own stomach, ready to take her life rather than continue the masquerade any longer.

"Wilt thou slay thyself?" Gertrude hurried close, once again as concerned for her daughter as that day when the girl-child had been born. "And slay the lady too that lives in thee, by doing damned hate upon thyself?"

Her words had their intended effect. Considering what Gertrude said, Hamlet slowly turned the sword away from her torso. Then, consumed by a growing fury over the dishonest life this loved-and-hated mother had forced her child to suffer during every waking hour, Hamlet turned the blade toward Gertrude. This sudden act caused the queen to recoil in amazement.

"The shame itself doth speak for instant remedy," Hamlet shouted, on the verge of hysteria.

"What? My own flesh and blood rebel?"

"You have misused your sex in your love-prate," Hamlet continued, perhaps willing to forgive Gertrude her decision of 21 years earlier, yet quite unable to overcome absolute rage over the queen's relationship with Hamlet's damned satyr of an uncle.

"Do not presume too much upon my love," Gertrude, pulling herself together only with considerable effort, reprimanded. The child she once felt a need to protect was grown, and thus able to fend for herself. Gertrude must look out for Gertrude, and the future she had chosen, first.

"Presume? *Presume?*" Hamlet closed the distance between them, eyes ablaze, waving her sword wildly.

"Better thou had not been born," the queen wept, "than not to have pleased me better."

Her words pushed Hamlet over the brink: "O, that e're I was born!" With her free hand, Hamlet seized Gertrude by the neck, threatening to throttle her. Before Hamlet's fingers could close tightly enough to end Gertrude's life, she wailed, long and loud.

"What?" Polonius—until then frozen in fear at the overheard conversation, followed by such intense commotion—called from his hiding place. "What, ho?"

The old man's voice was muffled by the very curtain hiding him from sight. Hamlet, in her heightened state, imagined that she'd heard Claudius there, perhaps plotting Hamlet's murder.

"My enemy? To you, woe!"

Without hesitation, Hamlet let go Gertrude and lunged forward, sword tearing through the thick curtain at the precise spot from which the voice had emerged. There followed the sound of cold steel ripping through soft flesh, then a muffled yelp of pain and surprise. After, Hamlet and Gertrude witnessed frantic movements of a still unseen body, thrashing against the worthless shield of the wall-hanging.

Hamlet stabbed again, then a third time. Death to the damned uncle, the bloat king!

Gertrude screamed as Polonius, breathing his last, slipped out from his hiding place. Old hands covered wounds as if, in final agony, the greybeard half-believed he might yet prevent his life's blood from spilling out onto the stone floor. For one terrible split second, Polonius locked eyes with Hamlet. Brittle thoughts and bitter emotions consumed the greybeard's last moments: This was his reward for having, all these years, kept the terrible secret to himself? Doing all that could be done to maintain the charade, convince everyone in Denmark Hamlet truly was a man? Allow his own beloved daughter to pine away for love of this supposed 'prince' rather than tell her the truth—thereby bringing a swift end to Ophelia's obsession? Agreeing with Gertrude that Ophelia might best be married to Hamlet, to serve as a cover so the great lie could be maintained?

To die all a sudden, without having made proper confession to a priest . . . die alone, neither son nor daughter near to hold his hand while he expired . . . die at the hands of she, the self-important, self-serving little she-brat whose well-being had always taken precedence, for Polonius, over all else in his life . . .

It wasn't fair!

With such thoughts, but no time for a single spoken word, Polonius fell forward, dead. Hot blood trickled out from his corpse in extending circles.

"You have killed the good old man," Gertrude muttered when, minutes later, she could finally form words.

Stunned at the consequence of her rash action, Hamlet unconsciously dropped the sword and addressed the corpse: "Forgive me, doddering fool. I mistook thee for thy better."

"Here," Gertrude proclaimed, distancing herself from a daughter who had carelessly shattered, in a rash moment, all that the queen had labored, long and hard and over so many years, to build and protect, "I disclaim all parental care, and as a stranger from my heart to me, hold thee, from now 'til forever, my despised daughter."

Tears rolled down Hamlet's cheeks as she locked eyes with her mother: "Call you me *daughter?*"

"Onetime daughter, sometime son."

"God be wi' you, then," Hamlet replied, offering a mock curtsy before sauntering toward the door. "Let's meet as little as we can."

"I do desire we be better strangers," Gertrude replied.

"Perfect strangers, from this day forth."

With that, Hamlet was gone, out into the corridor, down the circling steps. Gertrude fell to her knees, sobbing—sincerely, for once—beside the body of her trusted friend.

82.

Storming out of Gertrude's room, Hamlet turned a bend in the corridor, proceeding down the circular stairwell in a state of utter confusion. How might this awful mistake be reported to poor Ophelia? Hamlet had taken only a few steps when Claudius appeared directly in her path, the king slowly mounting the steps on his way up to visit Gertrude. At the sight of Denmark's despised 'prince' blocking his way, the look of concern vanished from Claudius' face, replaced by a shock that swiftly gave way to rage, potent as Hamlet's own. One quick look, and she sensed mortal danger; large, crude Claudius might grab hold of what he still believed to be a man, furiously tearing him—her!—to pieces.

Bravado was Hamlet's only hope, as feigning casualness might diffuse danger. "Why, the king of smiles!"

"Young, wanton, and effeminate boy!" Claudius growled. Muted light from a long line of candles, staggered in an upward arc along the stonewall, sent strange shadows flickering across his face, causing Claudius to appear, at least in Hamlet's perception, utterly demonic. "So, thou art midwife to my woe."

"I swear—"

"Swearest thou, ungracious boy? I say unto you again, you are a shallow, cowardly hind."

"I am none of these."

"What, then?"

"Hamlet; y'know," she laughed. "Old Hamblet's boy."

Claudius also emitted a laugh, if one with no hint of humor: "Can sick men play so nicely with their names?"

"No, misery makes sport to mock itself. Since thou dost seek to kill my name in me, I mock my name, 'great' king, to flatter thee."

Unschooled in the art of clever repartee, Claudius could abide no more of this prattle. Yet few could match him as warrior. Drawing his long-sword, the king pushed forward. "Should dying men flatter with those that live?"

Hamlet was consumed by a sudden instinct to turn and run. Yet she would not, could not let this moral monster see how terrified she was, instead affecting a bold demeanor: "O, no! Thou diest, though I the sicker be." Hamlet reached for her own sword, surprised to feel only an empty scabbard.

Damn! The blade remained in Gertrude's room, on the floor, dropped during the struggle, never retrieved.

"Think so, effeminate boy?" Claudius growled, lumbering closer. "Come on, then; I can no longer brook thy vanities." Another step and Claudius stood face-to-face with unarmed Hamlet, the king's huge frame dwarfing her.

"Thy deathbed is no lesser than the land wherein thou liest in reputation sick," Hamlet asserted. Claudius would have run Hamlet through with a single fierce stroke had not Osric appeared without warning at the top of the stairs. After delivering Gertrude's message to Claudius, Osric had set about busily preparing medicines for her in the apothecary room, down the corridor from Gertrude's chamber. Hearing her screams, the confused courtier came hurrying along, finding his queen sprawled on the floor, weeping uncontrollably beside dead Polonius. Osric then rushed about, desperate to find help. Descending from behind Hamlet and spotting Claudius, he waved his thin hands, fluttering like the wings of a wounded bird.

"Claudius! Come quick. The queen, the queen!"

The king hesitated, considering whether it might be wise to kill Hamlet first, and then attend to Gertrude.

"Help!" Osric screamed again. "The queen—"

Out of love for his green-eyed enchantress, Claudius sheathed his sword, rudely as possible brushing past Hamlet. A broad shoulder hit hard against her delicate frame with bullying forcefulness, knocking Hamlet aside. Passing, Claudius hissed in her ear: "This but doth buy thee momentary respite; in due time, I will set things right." Then, he was gone, hurrying along after Osric, who had already turned to rush ahead and rejoin Gertrude.

Bitterly, Hamlet stared up after them for several long seconds, before continuing down the stairwell.

83.

Osric hurried into the queen's room. Gertrude, he noted at once, remained where he had left her, kneeling beside the old man's body, weeping loudly still. "When troubles come," she called out, chest heaving, for once, in an honest display of agony, "they come not singly, but in waves."

Claudius stormed in then, stunned to see his poised wife engulfed by such a distraught state, absolutely unconcerned as to her appearance in front of others. Deeply moved by the intensity of her hysteria, Claudius vowed revenge on the source of their trouble. "I told you he was a frantic fool," the king confided, "hiding bitter jests in blunt behavior."

"I, me," she sighed. "I see the downfall of our house. I see, as in a map, the worst that can befall."

There was no calming her now, try as he might. Claudius quickly sensed that. Instead, he turned to Osric, admitting: "Uneasy is the head that wears the crown."

The courtier nodded in dutiful agreement as three knights, known for loyalty to Claudius, entered the room. They had been sipping ale in a public room far down the corridor when they had heard strange sounds. So the men hurried along to the source, and now stood, troubled and amazed, in the doorway.

"Have I no friend," Claudius called out to the armed men, "will rid me of this living fear?"

Three moving as one, they nodded their understanding before retreating to the shadowy corridor. There, they regrouped under a flickering torch where, by its uncertain light, the men considered how best to serve their master.

"Dids'st thou not hear the king, what words he spoke?"

"'Have I no friend, will rid me of this living fear'? Was it not so?"

Osric, exiting on orders from Claudius, cautiously slipped past, unnoticed by the three conspirators who sought means to win the king's approval.

"Those were the very words. Speaking, he looked at me!"

"Come, let's go. I am the king's friend, and will rid him of this foe."

The man's fellows nodded in grim agreement. With that, they marched down the stairwell, planning to accomplish what would most please Claudius: The murder of Prince Hamlet.

84.

Lost in a waking-dream from which no escape apparently existed, Hamlet drifted across the courtyard in the general direction of Kronborg's drawbridge. In all the evening's confusion and excitement, it had not been raised as darkness set in, as ordinarily would have been the case. Momentarily, Hamlet considered crossing over, to wander she knew not where. About to step onto the ancient wooden planks with trepidation, she halted upon hearing the clanking of a courtier's metal-healed boots on the same sharp cobblestone path that Hamlet had crossed moments earlier. Turning, she noted Osric straining to catch up.

"Sirrah, if you please," Osric huffed, out of breath. "Your father—"

"God forbid! Uncle."

"The *king* requests you rejoin your queen mother—"

"Return with her? No, rather I abjure all roofs, and choose to be comrade with the wolf, fawn, owl."

This confused Osric. "To live in wild-woode?"

"Aye," Hamlet said, recalling philosophic works encountered in Wittenberge's classrooms, as well as subsequent debates between eager young minds as to whether a life lived close to the earth might be morally superior to one spent in cloistered civilization: "As a *natural* man!"

There was nothing more to say. Hamlet spun about, crossed over the bridge, and headed off into the woode.

85.

Gertrude cringed in a corner at the room's far wall. After rising, she had retreated there in hopes of dissolving into its dark shadows, furtively watching as Claudius oversaw the removal of the old man's corpse. In time, the distraught queen regained something of her composure. Her mind functioning again, she sensed it must be she who informed Ophelia of the horrible news. Sending a member of her court to do such dirty work would seem grossly insensitive, not only to the devastated girl but to others—people of influence and importance—as well. If there was one thing neither she nor Claudius needed at this point, it was to make enemies of possible allies.

So Gertrude excused herself and wandered away, seeking out Ophelia. Shortly, she confronted her, all in a flurry, en route to the queen's chamber. Polonius' daughter had heard, from men at-arms whispering as they rushed about the open courtyard or pausing to gossip in lengthy corridors, that someone had apparently been murdered. In her heart, Ophelia immediately feared for her father, though she knew not why. Darting about the castle, attempting to disbelieve in her head what her heart already confirmed as known-fact, Ophelia arrived in the hallway leading to Gertrude's room just in time to see the greybeard, partly shrouded by a bloody sheet, carried off by four grim-faced servants.

Ophelia's entire frame shook uncontrollably. She might start screaming at any second. Concerned for the sweet child and, as always, for appearances, Gertrude seized Ophelia's arm and drew her inside the room, firmly shutting the door behind them. For a while, no words were spoken by either girl or woman; the two held one another tightly, mourning together without need of speech, tears intermingling as their cheeks touched. In due time, there was much to say. Gertrude slowly explained what had happened, though doing so from a point-of-view calculated to make the queen and her Claudius appear victims, not unlike Ophelia. Hamlet—still a man, so far as

Ophelia knew—was cast as the crazed, unsympathetic villain. "What!" Ophelia cried out upon learning who had done the deed. "My greatest hate, sprung from my only love?" "Cry, cry on my shoulder, all you care, gentle child."

Instead, Ophelia held her head high, tears all done. Once again, she emerged as a modern woman with her own approach to life, including the act of mourning. "I am not prone to weeping, as our sex commonly is," she announced in a voice so calm that it frightened Gertrude. "But I have that honourable grief lodg'd here, which burns worse than tears that drown a poor player."

Gertrude attempted to come close again, perhaps drape an arm around the girl. Ophelia, sensing what Gertrude intended and not eager to be patronized, stepped away. Mad thoughts danced on the stage of her nimble mind: How could Hamlet have done such a thing? If it proved to be true, then she might well murder the prince whom she had ever loved.

Then again, could Gertrude be believed? Think clearly, now, girl! Had not Amuleth—Hamlet—insisted only days earlier that Gertrude and Claudius were not to be trusted? Perhaps it was they who had killed her father, casting blame on Hamlet!

Ophelia couldn't conceive of how such an undeserved murder might have occurred, or guess who had actually perpetrated this rueful act. She only knew, deep in her heart, that she loved Hamlet still. A woman's emotions will not allow her to believe a man she has fallen in love with is capable of such dreadful acts, no matter how seemingly obvious the evidence. Not without proof positive.

Before acting rashly, she would learn for certain if the prince were guilty.

With that, Ophelia determined to inquire where Hamlet had gone. Then? Follow, confront, and resolve the issue, one way or another. Without a further word, Ophelia deserted Gertrude, hurrying down the stairwell, out of the castle's main building and back toward her home. Once inside, the house suddenly empty and cold owing to her knowledge that

Polonius would never grace its rooms again, Ophelia seized a shawl to protect her from the evening's chill before setting off in search of Hamlet.

86.

Exhausted from the hard ride, Balthazar urged his spent horse along a well-worn trail circling around the woode. He cut across the deserted field, so full of activity only a few hours earlier. Shortly, his mount clobbered over the rough wood drawbridge. Entering Kronborg, Balthazar wearily slid from the saddle, handing reins to a pageboy, as Horatio strolled up alongside his friend.

"The prince . . .?" Balthazar inquired.

"I go to seek him anon," Horatio explained, his tone tinged with sadness; eyes distant, removed, and fearful.

Balthazar reached into his vest, pulling out a sealed letter which he turned over to one he knew to be as loyal to Hamlet as himself: "Tell him there's a post from Fortinbras with his horn full of good news: Young Norway will be here two days hence, with a small army besides!"

"This fair tiding may indeed help restore his wits."

"What! The prince is distracted?"

"Sadly so." Horatio hadn't confided even a word about Hamlet's unspeakable overtures to anyone, trusting none except Ophelia, who couldn't be told for obvious reasons. If there was one person both he and Hamlet could depend upon, other than Fortinbras, it was Balthazar. Considering the profound decision he had made in his chamber's privacy, Horatio hungered to share his awesome burden with someone.

"His humour is that he . . . *loves* me."

"As brother in arms—"

Horatio sadly shook his head: "More and less."

Even naive Balthazar could hardly fail to grasp Horatio's drift, wondering out loud: "And, to his remedy?"

Here, Horatio breathed-in deeply before admitting what,

after hours of difficult consideration, he'd decided: "Be he as he will, yet ere this night be done, I will embrace him with a soldier's arm." Horatio hesitated briefly before concluding: "And, if need be, a lover's hand."

"No, *no!*"

Balthazar's protest had no effect, for Horatio had made up his mind. "I will not let him stir 'til I have used the approved means I have to make him a formal man again."

"Truly, sirrah?"

"It is branch and parcel of mine oath, a charitable duty of my order. Therefore, depart, and leave me to find him."

With a fatalistic air, Horatio marched across the draw-bridge, heading toward the woode. From Osric, whom Horatio had needed to calm down before the courtier could speak, Horatio had learned that Hamlet had last been seen heading in that direction. Balthazar stood watching until Horatio disappeared into a shroud of tall trees, bathed with a soft silver sheen thanks to the full moon's light.

"Truly," Balthazar announced out loud, to no one in particular, "greater love than this knows no man!"

87.

Slightly dazed and utterly confused, Ophelia drifted through the castle courtyard and down its cobbled streets. Her movements were shrouded by the night, its blackness melding with the spectral cloak that the delirious girl held tight under her chin. All the while, she muttered words that, if any had heard, would not be easily understood: "Being fed by us, you used us as that ungentle gull, the cuckoo bird, views the sparrow; did oppress our nest, grew by our feeding to so great a bulk that even our love durst not come near your sight for fear of swallowing."

She couldn't have explained, on penalty of death, what any of it meant. Her spontaneous outburst combined bits of old ballads, heard in her youth and dimly recalled now, with shards of emotions new to her experience. Along with them were sharp-edged ideas, cutting through her gentle mind like a hunting knife. Occasionally forgetting her self-divined mission and halting to inspect a chipped statue of some Norse god or visit a fat pig squealing from behind its prison fence of rough sticks, Ophelia drifted toward the drawbridge, drawn by some vague inner instinct to visit the woode.

88.

Hamlet was already deep in the forest, relishing the manner in which the moon bathed tall trees in a shimmering gel of white-light, thus causing the entire area to momentarily seem a magical place. Following a barely visible footpath to beloved childhood haunts, shared long ago with Horatio and Fortinbras during their carefree years, Hamlet halted at the sudden sound of fumbling noises in a clump of beeches fifty feet ahead. The three knights who had vowed eternal loyalty to Claudius had, upon learning that the prince was walking in the woode, hurried ahead while planning an ambush. Now, realizing that Hamlet had arrived and was aware of their presence, all three arrogantly marched from out of their hiding place to block Hamlet's way.

"Ill met my moonlight!" she sighed, as men of iron drew swords, approaching. Their movements were cautious, for these would-be assassins were fearful of the thin figure positioned, swordless and seemingly without means of defense, before them. Hamlet, they knew, was unpredictable, and might yet prove dangerous if they weren't careful.

"Hamlet," the chosen leader announced, "thy time is near." While the others drifted sideways to flank her, this knight boldly stepped forward.

"Villain, thy own hand yields thy death's instrument," Hamlet replied without a trace of fear.

Swiftly, she swung about like some deadly ballerina. For Hamlet employed a technique learned at Wittenberge, thanks to an instructor who had journeyed north from the Orient. Proficient in Asian arts of self-defense, the sage had been delighted to share such rare hand-to-hand combat skills with Europe's student-princes. Hamlet's foot, flying through the air faster than an arrow toward its target, knocked the shining sword from her lumbering opponent's mailed hand before the stunned adversary could grasp that anything untoward had happened. Catching its hilt in midair as if the weapon were no heavier or more dangerous than a feather quill, Hamlet then turned the sword on its previous owner and, in a single continuous movement, ran the knight through. Too stunned to scream out, he had only several seconds to grasp what had happened. Then his life's blood gushed forth like water from a fountain and the man fell dead.

Shocked by this unexpected occurrence, which caused them to remain frozen in their places for several long seconds, the two surviving knights, considerably more cautious now, resumed their purpose. Warily, the two heavyset figures circled Hamlet. She held the sword ready, grinning like a madman, waiting for either or both to dare make a move. Before they could, the sound of heavy footsteps treading over fresh grass and dead twigs announced yet another interloper arriving from the trail on which Hamlet had appeared.

The knights were distracted; Hamlet glanced over her shoulder. Horatio rushed up, out of breath from his trek through the forest. One quick look at the bloody scene and he grasped what was happening. Without hesitation, Horatio drew his own sword. "How now? What means death in this rude assault?"

The larger of the two remaining knights shifted his line of attack, waving his heavy blade in the air while lunging toward Horatio. The other closed in on Hamlet. All at once, a flurry of silver blades flickered in the eerie moonlight. Then, anguished screams from wounded men tore through the air like an owl's call. Finally, the scene evidenced a fitful gushing of more blood onto muddied ground. All this sudden and rough action was followed by a silence so profound those

few remaining birds which hadn't already flown away in fear
now did so.

"Go," Horatio addressed the blood-splattered body spread
out before him, "and fill another room in hell."

The knight who dared encounter Hamlet, sorely wounded
yet still alive, hurried away as best he could. The maimed
man whined in misery like a wounded jackal while leaving a
trail of fresh blood as his wake. Hamlet and Horatio stood at
a distance from one another, breathing heavily, smiling at their
joint victory.

Noticing a dark shadow pass over her friend's beloved face,
Hamlet remarked: "What! Good Horatio? Approach."

"Aye, my lord."

"Not to be abed after midnight is to be up betimes."

Awkwardly, Horatio likewise diminished the distance
between them. Standing close, two lifelong friends considered one another curiously. "A kind of witchcraft drew me
hither," Horatio admitted, voice uncharacteristically soft
and sad.

Fully understanding the implication, Hamlet's eyes lit up
at his friend's obvious intent. "Come," she cooed, "we'll away
from this place of dirth and death, to find one more suited for
birth of love."

Gently grasping Horatio's hand, Hamlet abandoned the
bloodied clearing and continued further down the path, into
the forest's thickest stretch. There, she followed the footprints
of countless others who had ventured this way in centuries
past, searching out a clandestine spot for reasons known only
to themselves. Their diverse motivations had passed, over the
years, into oblivion as they—so vividly alive for so short a
time—returned to dust and were forgotten.

At last, the companions came upon a small glen, the fresh
blades of grass lush with early spring's bloom. Unseen, a single
bird gaily sang from its chosen spot high atop a tree. Close
by, a branch of the river reflected twinkling stars while rushing headlong to the sea, offering gurgling noises as the pure

water, from secret springs in bracken-encrusted hills, passed through Denmark on its way to the source of all life. Hamlet sensed this to be the perfect place for the two to consummate, as she long dreamed of doing, their great love. Stepping to the enclave's center, she there discovered a bed of moss and turned to her friend, who was trying to conceal his horror at what was about to happen.

Hamlet could have said something, of course, thereby relieving Horatio's anxiety. But a twinge of naughtiness in her feminine spirit wouldn't allow it. Save the surprise as long as possible, hold off full recognition to the last moment! *Make Horatio sweat.* Then, he'll enjoy the coming rewards all the more.

Hamlet's voice danced giddily: "Spread thy close-curtain, love performing night, that runaway eyes may wink."

Consumed with dread, Horatio appeared to his scholar-friend as a Danish incarnation of doomed Hector, ready to march without hope past walled Troy's gates, ready to die at the hands of unconquerable Achilles. "Or," Horatio sighed, "if love be blind, it best agrees with night."

Smiling wickedly, Hamlet drew close for their first kiss, so long anticipated. And, after, the moment of full recognition which would follow as night does day.

89.

Claudius and Gertrude stood in the open doorway to the royal bedchamber, holding hands like frightened children who have just heard a ghost story. Crouched before them, the sole surviving knight, blood trickling from his open wound, fitfully recounted the terrible fight in the woode.

"For ever will I walk upon my knees," Claudius mumbled to absent Hamlet, "and never see day that the happy sees, 'til thou give me joy by thy death, transgressing boy."

Fully won over now to his way of thinking, Gertrude nodded in solemn agreement: "If so, then be not tongue-tied."

Eyes filled with resentment, she bolted toward the corridor, ready to hurry off and do the deed herself. "Go with me, and let's murder my dear son!"

As the wounded knight gazed on in amazement, Claudius took her arm, restraining his queen: "Fools rush in. If it is to be done, this deed must follow thought."

His words sobered Gertrude. She made a conscious effort to force her heart to cease fluttering. Then, turning on her heels, the queen deserted the doorway and re-entered the room, patiently waiting for Claudius to dispatch the knight—who might, with swift medical attention, yet live—and rejoin her. Together, they would chart Hamlet's demise.

Too much, after all, was enough! The time had come to concern herself with her own survival.

The wounded man shuffled down the corridor, aided by several pageboys. Gertrude considered, upon her husband's return, seizing the opportunity to finally reveal the truth about Hamlet's identity. The idea proved short-lived; she had kept her secret so long, it would be difficult to frame it in words now, particularly at such a taxing time. Claudius was, she sensed, beginning to suspect her sanity had been strained to the breaking point; likely, he would disbelieve what she said, and call out for his minions to come running, then order them to cart the queen off to the keep, where crazy people were stowed.

No, Gertrude decided as his footsteps resounded behind her. She would keep her secret a little longer!

90.

Hamlet, however, was at that moment ready to reveal the truth. She and Horatio stood a distance apart, their vision of one another obscured as night clouds swept over the moon, momentarily extinguishing its silver-light. Then, all such obstructions were gone, swiftly as they had come; the moon once more beamed down brightly, reinforced on all sides by a multitude of sparkling stars. Utter stillness might have made the moment too eerie, but the single bird continued its merry concert, while the slow-running river's sounds proved soothing to frayed nerves. Even Horatio, who believed himself to be shortly going to his doom, appreciated the idyllic atmosphere, their secret spot a piece of pastoral poetry come to life for one haunting if lurid moment.

Awkwardly, Horatio felt compelled to state the obvious: "How bright shines down the inconstant moon."

Hamlet smiled: "Were it dark this night, no matter. Lovers can see to do their amorous rites by their own beauties that shine as bright."

Sad resignation overtook a youthful spirit, and Horatio hung his head in grim anticipation: "I am here, sir, to do your service, as you require." Then, his body betrayed him. Exhausted from the evening's excitement, Horatio's shoulders slumped as he yawned.

Hamlet stepped close, taking one of Horatio's trembling hands in her own and gently drew it toward her waist. "Canst thou hold up thy heavy eyes awhile, and touch my instrument a strain or two?"

"Ay, ay, my lord, an't please you."

"It does, my boy! I trouble thee too much, but thou art willing?"

Horatio shrugged: "It is my duty, sir."

"I should not urge thy duty past thy might; I know young bloods look for a time of rest."

"I have slept, my lord, already."

"It was well done. And thou shalt sleep again. I will not hold thee long."

Eager to have the ordeal over and done, Horatio nodded in agreement, imploring: "Unbuckle, unbuckle."

Hamlet's left hand swept upward, seizing her *faux* moustache. She yanked it off with a single movement, tossing the carefully knitted hairs to the ground. Horatio's jaw dropped.

He still didn't grasp what was happening, as Hamlet withdrew several feet and began stripping, slowly as possible, out of her clothing.

Why, Hamlet wondered, did she so enjoy keeping poor, dear Horatio in his state of utter horror? Perhaps to increase, through greater relief, his ultimate joy once reality was finally, fully grasped. Confused, and averting his eyes at the first glimmer of white flesh, Horatio drew in his breath, awaiting the worst. As Hamlet's frock fell away, slowly sweeping to the ground like an autumn leaf gliding down from a tree, Horatio caught, out of his eye's corner, a glimmer of full, ripe breasts, free now after being kept for so long pressed flat by a tight corset designed specifically for that purpose.

A moment later, the curvaceous waist could be glimpsed. And below that, a gleaming navel; then the private parts, surrounded by the sleek, soft hidden-hair of a slender, elegant woman. For Horatio, the moment seemed fiction, not fact—some fantastical tale-out-of-time actually occurring. This must be a fairy-fable, stuffed full of impossible transformations, usurping the reality that he had inhabited moments ago . . . a midsummer night's dream, arriving early, in spring.

Horatio almost spoke, and then thought better of it. A sudden gust tore through the boughs, rustling fresh leaves, visibly chilling the nude maid before him.

"Too long a pause," Hamlet chided, "for that which you find there."

"I am . . . dumb."

Inadvertently, Horatio stepped closer, considering a body more perfectly proportioned than any wench he had bedded in Wittenberge, their number considerable.

"Stand not amazed."

For 21 years, Amuleth—Hamlet—had been Horatio's constant friend; a companion, brave and true. They had never bathed together as other men did, Hamlet too demure, too shy. At least, that had been the story, never questioned. Now, a greater understanding of Hamlet's propensity for privacy dawned on Horatio. Disbelieving, he stared at the spot where

Hamlet's masculinity, if he were what he had so long seemed, ought to announce itself.

"Where is thy instrument?"

"'Tis a long story."

"Rather," Horatio replied, seized by an inspiration to mimic his friend's wit, "shorter than short."

Hamlet laughed, then rushed forward without warning—thin, feminine arms seductively enclosing Horatio.

"Is it fantasy that plays upon our eyesight?" Horatio continued. "I prithee, speak. We will not trust our eyes without our ears. Thou art not what thou always seem'st."

"No, that's certain. Yet I am not a double man."

"What, then?"

"A single woman." Suddenly nervous, Hamlet whispered in her companion's ear: "No man must know, Horatio!"

"Nor none shall, from my lips."

Satisfied that her secret remained safe for as long as she chose to keep it so, Hamlet set to stripping away Horatio's garments. "Ever loyal, Horatio?" she cooed.

Before an answer could be formulated, much less out, Hamlet slowly, gently, firmly kissed the man whom she had loved, and desperately craved, all these many years.

91.

Her wits sorely challenged, Ophelia rushed across the courtyard toward the still lowered drawbridge. Balthazar, attending to his half-dead horse in a quiet corner by an abandoned guard's booth, spotted the girl, incongruously clad in her gaily colored May Queen costume but with black shawl now draped over her milky shoulders. The lad noted a strained quality to Ophelia's every movement and, concerned, hurried forward, blocking her way.

"Hamlet?" she asked at the sight of a shrouded figure, drawing near.

"Gone, m' lady."

"Horatio—"

"He, too; to him, that is gone before."

Eyes blazing, Ophelia peered about, not readily believing what Balthazar said. After all, it was unwise to trust anyone, she had learned from cruel experience. Surely, Hamlet and Horatio were lurking just out of sight. "Gone, all—," she stammered.

"Mistress," Balthazar blurted, on the verge of tears, "both man and master are possess'd. I know it by the pale and deadly look in Horatio's eyes."

"Mad, mad, mad—"

"Aye. They must be bound and laid in some dark room."

She turned on the boy then, cat-like, seemingly ready to scratch out Balthazar's eyes: "And you?"

"I, lady?" he asked, stepping back and out of reach.

"If you be not mad, be gone," she said, flightily dismissive, "if you have reason, be brief. 'Tis not that time o' the moon with me to make one in so skipping a dialogue."

Spinning about like a toy top, Ophelia danced across the bridge, her gestures suggested the delirium of one who inhabits a forbidden dream of darkness. She lived so fully in fearful fantasy that its bat-wing sounds and shadowy sights are mistaken for the greater reality all others share. Something must be done, before she harmed herself, so Balthazar scurried off toward the main building. He hoped that some guards might still remain awake, perhaps help him return this sorely distracted girl to the castle's safety.

Ophelia, meanwhile, darted across the field, littered with remnants of the afternoon's activities. Reaching its far end, she plunged into an opening in the wall of beech trees. Leaving the little outpost of civilization which she had always called home behind, she penetrated the natural world beyond. Still humming and singing to herself, Ophelia moved not by any inclination of her will—rather drawn, like metal fragments to a magnet, in the direction Hamlet and Horatio had taken. The girl barely paused as she stumbled over the dead bodies of two fallen knights.

Pushing briars and brambles out of her way, Ophelia darted over a virtual sea of high grass. Eventually, she gravitated toward that hidden glen where Hamlet and Horatio already stood in fond embrace. Plentiful foliage yet obscured them from her sight. Nonetheless, muffled voices could be detected, as well as the subtle sound of flesh undulating against flesh.

Ophelia was seized by an epiphany; something—some voice deep inside her—insisted this was not the way to go. She ought to hurry off in the opposite direction, at once. Only her womanly will would not permit it. Fumbling momentarily, and shaking more from some vague, unformed fear than the cold, Ophelia stepped forward.

92.

A sudden shaft of moonlight, penetrating foliage overhead, spotlighted a pair of firm bodies, glistening in their nakedness, as a cool breeze swept by. Hamlet and Horatio, standing face to face, lost in one another's eyes, warmed each other with close contact.

"Do I dream?" Horatio mused. "Or have I dreamed 'til now?"

Pulling back, Hamlet considered Horatio's rugged frame, eyes relishing the strong shoulders as fully as her hands had earlier done. One small bit of clothing yet remained, the scarf he wore wrapped about his neck. Hamlet grasped its knot with her teeth, tore it away, spit it aside.

"Sans everything," she giggled.

"Of all matches," Horatio marveled, "never was the like!"

Hamlet's arms wrapped about Horatio once more. As she hung on tightly, meeting his masculine lips with her hungry open mouth, Hamlet pulled herself upward. She circled Horatio's hard male buttocks with her long thin legs, feeling the rigid power of his manhood force itself against her yielding pink slit, sweetly hidden beneath a gentle jungle of hair.

"Sheathe your dagger," she demanded.

With a sudden plunge, Horatio entered Hamlet. Together, they fell to the ground, writhing in sublime ecstasy, true friends who have discovered their spiritual love can be made physical as well, without detracting from what they so long shared. Rather, the sudden sensuality enhanced their wonderful, if previously incomplete, relationship. The polar emotions of friendship and lust were not new to either. For the first time, though, the far ranging instincts came crashing together, changing a pair of young lives forever.

Horatio experienced a glow of satisfaction ranging beyond anything he'd imagined possible. "Why," he marveled, "'tis an office of discovery, love!"

"And I should be obscured!"

"So you were, sweet, even in the lovely garnish of a boy."

Together, they rolled over, again and again. Each took turns on top, bodies becoming indistinguishable as another stretch of clouds rolled across the moon, obscuring its milky light, several flickering stars providing but mild illumination. Oblivious and uncaring, Hamlet and Horatio each locked arms so tightly around the beloved companion that it grew ever more difficult to breath. This experience only served to increase the intensity of their abandonment.

93.

Ophelia, too, had trouble breathing, if for other reasons. Drawn by unfamiliar sounds emanating from the glen, she had wandered off the footpath. Tripping over the exposed root of a gnarled tree, the girl fell forward and slipped in mud, a thick, black lingering reminder of recent rains. Bruised and disoriented, she lay still a while. Then, pulling what little was left of her wits together, she managed, if with difficulty, to rise up. Shortly, though, she fell again while attempting to mount a mossy hillock.

For a while, she sat where she had fallen, on the cold ground, unable to even consider continuing on her way to she knew not where.

Then, a murder of crows passed overhead, cawing and dropping wet pellets of dung on the tormented girl. As their excrement fell like some vile rain on her once-elegant, now-tattered costume, torn shawl and mussed hair, ringlets wildly scattered in every direction over the scratched white skin of her delicate face, Ophelia was seized by a sudden burst of energy.

For there were those strange sounds again!

Forcing herself to rise a final time, she regained her bearings and staggered on, overcoming the slope that had earlier defeated her. She pushed away the tangled branches barring her path only to have them slap back roughly on her already tingling cheeks. Ophelia felt her soft skin glow with pain, yet also with life. A burning sensation spurred her on, despite an encroaching sense of exhaustion that overtook her body once the initial explosion of vitality was depleted.

Still, she stepped forward, if shakily; a woman possessed, boasting a modern female will that would not, could not be denied. She would, come what may, find her man, Hamlet, accused of killing her father.

What she would do then, Ophelia didn't know.

Kill him? Perhaps.

Kiss him? As likely!

Perhaps kiss, then kill.

Or the other way around . . .

She didn't know, couldn't think, and was no longer capable of clearing her head of the wild notions rushing through it. Conflicting ideas and changeling emotions thrashed madly about, not unlike those small animals she could hear scurrying in the nearby brush, fearful of this sudden intruder.

"Since the more fair and crystal is the sky," she suddenly sang out, without intending to, "the ugliness uglier in it seems—dark clouds that in the heavens fly."

94.

Horatio rolled over on top of Hamlet, plunging deeper into her yielding flesh. As he did, the first premature rays of oncoming dawn presented themselves; a vague, clammy haze, shyly peeking up from the east, hinting at the full light to follow within the hour. Then, at least if quaint legends were to be believed, night spirits would be dispelled to their dark daylight lairs somewhere far beneath the earth.

How wonderful this is, Horatio thought, penetrating Hamlet's body as he had so often done her mind.

"What," Hamlet chided mischievously, "is my beaver easier than it was?"

"This is the very ecstasy of love," Horatio groaned.

"O, happy dagger!" Hamlet replied. "This is thy sheath!"

They came together then, surrendering to a sudden rush of excitement. In the following torrent, the companions screamed their pleasure out loud, two voices fused into one as their souls had done long ago; their bodies, only minutes before. When his desperate thrusting was done, and her sweet submission complete, Horatio dropped down beside his lover.

"Spit in the hole, man," Hamlet chided, "and tune again!"

My God! Was she insatiable?

Horatio proved as loyal to lover as he'd always been to friend, prince, and companion. Hamlet now, after all, incarnated four in one. So they embraced again, made love another time, oblivious to a lightly hesitant set of footsteps, approaching from the nearby trees.

95.

Castle guards, caught napping by Balthazar, were quickly roused from their pre-dawn slumber. Once wakened, they remained unsure about leaving their posts to follow this hysterical youth. But this was Ophelia, Balthazar insisted; even to search for someone worshipped as all did treasure their May Queen, the men were loathe to exit the castle without first receiving official permission. Distraught, Balthazar finally accepted their decision, hurrying on to a stairwell leading to the royal chamber. Arriving out of breath, he banged rudely on the door, thus waking king and queen, who had finally fallen into a fitful sleep.

As calmly as possible, Balthazar reported what he'd witnessed below as Ophelia forsook the castle's safety for the wilds: "Faith, once or twice, she heaved the name of 'father,' pantingly forth, as if it were pressed by her heart. Then, she shook holy water from her heavenly eyes, and away she started, to deal with grief alone."

Aghast at the thought of further complications, Claudius signaled for several men-at-arms, never far from his presence, ordering them: "Search every acre in high grown field, and return her to our eye."

At once, all hurried into the corridor, then down the steps and, collecting any and all persons they passed on their way, across the drawbridge to the woode. Pausing only long enough to slip into breeches and buckle on a sword, Claudius followed hard upon.

Left alone, Balthazar pondered what he ought to do. Part of him yearned to join the search, but he sensed a greater responsibility. "And I will to horse, once again," he decided, "rejoin young Norway and hasten him here."

Then, he too was off on an equally important mission.

96.

Backs and bones aching from coupling on hard ground, Hamlet and Horatio crawled back to the rich bed of moss where their lovemaking had begun. There, the two lay wrapped in one another's arms, half-asleep, gently touching and kissing. Too spent to enter Hamlet again, Horatio and his lover shifted positions, enjoying each other's bodies in varying ways. Both dropped their heads down on the partner's private parts, tongues extended, slowly bringing their lovers to one final climax, mouths serving now as exquisite mechanisms of arousal.

"Such pleasure is far and away beyond belief," Horatio purred. He pulled his head away to briefly glance at Hamlet, still busily employing her talented tongue to harden Horatio. Releasing his pulsating organ, Hamlet likewise pulled back, however temporarily, nodding in solemn agreement.

Then, they returned to their positions, continuing on as before.

97.

A few feet away, Ophelia pushed through the last layer of brush. Still, the girl searched for something she sensed was significant, though she was no longer able to recall the precise nature of what she had come here for. Her mind waxed every bit as brittle as the pre-dawn sky, stars one-by-one extinguished by the first weak rays of an encroaching sun, the fading moon once again obliterated by oblong clouds. What ranged before her troubled line of vision seemed dank and swollen, an early morning mist distorting all present into a gray phantasmagoria.

"My tongue will tell the anger of my heart," she announced to hare and owl, "or else my heart concealing it will break."

Stealthily, she passed through the brush. Then, hearing the sound again, Ophelia found herself inexorably drawn to its source. At last, she stepped full into the glen, halting in her tracks at an unexpected sight: a pair of human figures, hazy and indistinct, dimly perceived in the uncertain light as luxuriously intertwined. Her vulnerable mind misgave, rejecting information offered by weary eyes. Fragments of flesh, she could sharply discern: one person's hand, gently stroking another's back. Each lover's knees locked around the other's head in forbidden pleasure; bits and pieces of faces, kissing the other's secret spots with hungry lips, could be discerned. Faces, Ophelia feared, she knew. Now, though, in this altered context, faces which seemed unfamiliar, removed from the known world she had inhabited for twenty years. Vaguely recognizable faces, contained here in some awful, awesome nightmare-land; engaged in an impossible act, one a maid such as she could never have imagined.

All a sudden, the palms of her hands went clammy. Her throat felt rough and parched, and a strange spasm—part fear, part fascination—rippled along Ophelia's spine. The girl's mind, desperate to maintain some semblance of sanity, initially rejected all she saw. In a matter of moments, there was no doubting that these were the faces of the two men Ophelia loved, had assumed someday she would be forced to choose between for husband: Hamlet, princely object of romantic obsession; Horatio, solid yeoman, trusted friend, good soldier.

Hamlet and Horatio, together.

In the flesh.

Instinctively, Ophelia withdrew from the glen's edge to partial cover provided by nearby beeches, their branches softly stirring as a light whisper of wind passed through leaves. There she crouched; remote, silent, trembling from her vision of an unfathomable act taking place only a stone's throw away. Ophelia clutched at her shawl, fingers stiff and unresponsive to what little was left of her frayed will, then dug sharp nails into soft palms. Her mind was overcome by a shroud of hopelessness. Something inside her snapped, like one of the weak twigs she trod upon.

"He was but as the cuckoo in June," she sang, turning away from a sight so shocking that she no longer considered it horrible, rather unthinkable, something to be denied. "Heard, not regarded; seen, but with such eyes as is bent on sun-like majesty when it shines seldom in admiring eyes."

Ophelia wandered away, aimlessly, careless for her own safety, off onto the mudflats leading to the nearby river.

98.

"Did'st hear a voice?" Hamlet whispered.

With a start, Horatio sat up, gathering his wits, grasping what must have happened: "Alack, 'tis *her*."

"Why," Hamlet moaned, reaching for her clothes, "she was met even now as mad as the vex'd sea, ringing aloud."

Horatio nodded in solemn agreement. Pulling on his breeches, he leaped up to search for the girl in hopes he might catch Ophelia before calamity could befall her.

99.

Already, she had drifted a considerable distance away, escaping from the glen, desperate to put as much distance as possible between herself and what existed there. If only that might extinguish the horrible mental image of her best suitors in secret, damnable embrace!

"By my troth," she laughed out loud, reaching the very river she and Hamlet so oft observed from Kronborg's high walls. Glimmering dots of milky light now appeared and disappeared across its rippling surface. "My little lady is a-weary of this great world."

Ophelia—feet chilled, head aching—reached the curving bankside. Without hesitation, she plunged into the shallows, thick and muddy from ebb tide. The cruel shafts of a rapidly breaking-dawn dissolved what little was left of the moon's white circle into its daily oblivion. Rippling waters, passing about her uncertain legs, grew troubled all of a sudden as a wicked wind shimmered across their surface. A half dozen gulls, drifted in from the sea to visit the flats for their morning's fishing, protectively drew wings up around their heads.

The river, seemingly bright blue from distant castle, appeared brown, tepid, utterly unpleasant up close. Brackish smelling owing to dead leaves, oddly shaped twigs, and small drowned creatures collected in the weeds by its edges. From a distance, this had seemed a pastoral paradise; up close, the river—like everything else in life, Ophelia feared—proved less bright dream than grim nightmare.

Perhaps she belonged with those sad, furry corpses half-buried there. How bright and good life must have seemed to these small things on the day they were born, nursing warm milk from dear mothers. How horrible it must have been when, starved and freezing in the unyielding blanket of a northern winter, they comprehended, in their simple yet crudely intelligent way, that death would shortly claim them before life had had a chance to even properly begin.

Scant realizing what she did, Ophelia plunged up to her naked knees, exposed by tattered remnants of a once gay costume. The water felt warm around her legs, soft like velvet to the touch. Still, the night wind, whistling as it passed through low hanging branches, chilled the girl to the marrow of her bones. Clinging weeds slowed Ophelia's movements as she pushed forward, best as she could, overcome all of a sudden by an encroaching sensation of fatigue. A ghostly voice from somewhere deep under the water seeming to seductively whisper: "Surrender! Surrender!"

She paused, wits all but gone. Then, caught up by the current, Ophelia felt herself carried along, unaware of what was happening or why. She was blithely unconcerned with any of it any more, the living and the dead, and her own life as well.

100.

"I pray we are not too late," Horatio declared as he and Hamlet attempted to follow broken grass and fading footprints, scant evidence that indicated the direction Ophelia had taken.

"Yet my mind misgives," Hamlet—the fatalist always, even more so as woman than man, inherited no doubt from her mother—"I fear we are!"

Exchanging brief glances of concern, they doggedly continued on. Not far away, soldiers and guards, pouring out of the castle, likewise traipsed about, eager for any hopeful sign. Claudius himself, more deeply disturbed than he might have believed possible over Polonius' death, wished to wreak no more havoc on this loyal family. The king drew forth his sword, furiously slashing away at the thick vegetation slowing his gait.

Eventually, though, it was Hamlet and Horatio who came across that point on the riverbed where Ophelia's shawl, torn in several places, was discovered. They found it twisted around the claw-shaped branch of a dead tree like the deserted shard of a once perfect cobweb.

"Alas," Horatio wept, guessing what Ophelia must have seen upon entering the glen, as well as how wrongly she interpreted the image, "thou has misconstrued everything!"

Hamlet slung a comforting arm around her friend, as Horatio oft did to bolster Hamlet's spirit. "I drove my suitor from her mad humour of love," she admitted tearfully, "to a living humour of madness."

In the distance, they heard a multitude of searchers, vainly calling out Ophelia's name. Sensing the futility of any further effort, Hamlet and Horatio, entirely spent, gave up. Each sensed and accepted, in his or her heart of hearts, a responsibility for what had happened to this poor girl whom both had loved well, if not wisely.

BOOK FIVE

The Whirligig of Time

101.

Another day, another funeral.

With considerably less pomp and ceremony than had been lavished on Hamblet less than two weeks earlier, Polonius' body was lowered into yet another yawning grave. The old man's final resting place had been dug as near to that of the late king as permissible for one of common birth. This honour was bestowed owing to the great distinction he had achieved in life, as well as years of service to the general good of Helsingor. Nobles from the court were again present. In addition, many of the townsfolk turned out, though in truth they were waxing weary as such unpleasant events, which ought to have been rare, grew depressingly commonplace.

Hamlet stood in solemn attendance, wearing a simple, single-piece suit of black material which could have comfortably accommodated either man or woman. Her *faux* moustache, recovered following a fitful search in the woode from a pile of rotting leaves, once more sat firmly in place, so none would guess what only Horatio and Gertrude now knew. Filled with sincere sorrow, Hamlet quietly stood among the mourners, brooding on the hazy horizon line created by an unseasonably bright midday sun.

At least this burial had been scheduled for a day marked by a harsh clarity from its opening hour. The crisp atmosphere helped keep spirits as high as possible under such dour circumstances. With Ophelia absent, there were no tears, only a solemn sense of respect for one who had done much to modernize Denmark. Indeed, Polonius had so unassumingly gone about the business of enriching everyone's lives over the years that few noticed, much less properly acknowledged, his considerable contribution. Until now; once gone, all in Sjalland belatedly grasped the greatness of a nearly invisible man who had exerted his effect by seeming to remain on the sidelines of life.

Stony silence was broken by the heavy clip-clop of an approaching horse. Collectively, the crowd turned in the direction from where that sound emanated to observe the late arrival. Laertes, digging spurs into a weary horse's sides, appeared from around a bend, then cantered up the rocky pathway. Purse empty, unable to borrow money from any in Wittenberge owing to swift spreading word of his dishonourable habits, the youth had decided it was due time to head home. The embarrassing drunkard who had scoffed when Fortinbras suggested that Laertes ought to join his volunteers—sobered now, less by desire than necessity—reconsidered Norway's declarations. He was stirred to immediate action, if not the sort Fortinbras had intended or of which he would approve. Perhaps, Laertes thought, he might win a rich reward from Claudius by hurrying back and being first to impart information about a coming invasion.

Following five days on the open road, with less than one full afternoon's travel remaining, Laertes had heard wild rumors while lunching in an out-of-the-way farming village. The commoners whispered about the strange death of old Polonius! Forsaking his humble repaste of cheese, bread, and wine, Laertes leapt upon his horse. Rendered serious in a way he'd never before been by this bit of gossip, he furiously pushed on, hoping against hope that, upon arrival, such overheard whisperings would prove nothing more than some grotesque mistake.

Nearing the graveyard, his horse galloping wildly now and kicking up stones which giddily danced in the air behind man and mount, Laertes sensed at once that this was not the case. "Father?" he called out in desperation, leaping down from his saddle as he approached the funeral party. "Where—"

No one spoke. Laertes knew then, and for certain, that the rumour was true. The youth staggered, red-eyed, to the open grave, peering down at his beloved father. Polonius was there, shrouded in a white sheet. Laertes barely stifled a sob: "Why should a dog, a horse, a rat have life," he called out in honest anguish, "and thou no breath at all?"

Gradually, Laertes realized someone was missing. The rumor of Polonius' death, obviously, was true. The good greybeard's daughter ought to be here, no matter how terribly this crime may have impacted on her. But . . . where was she?

"Ophelia? Sister—"

Someone had to take responsibility and, at the least, try and calm the youth while admitting that the worst was, in fact, yet to come. Gertrude seized the initiative, stepping close, pressing a gentle hand on Laertes' rattling arm. "Gone," she said stiffly, confirming his worst suspicion. "Feared drowned."

This was too much! "What? Father and sister? Double-dealt, twice-trounced? Fickle fate!" Moaning, Laertes threw himself on the ground, sobbing like a babe, scratching at the dirt and stones.

Deeply moved, Hamlet approached, kneeling by Laertes' side: "No body was found. Perchance she lives yet."

"Howl, howl, howl, howl," Laertes continued, the prince's words apparently not registering. "O, you men of stones. Had I your tongues and eyes, I'd use them so that heaven's fault should crack. She's gone—gone forever!"

Rolling about, any semblance of control gone now, Laertes beat his head against the hard ground until blood flowed freely from mouth and nose. Stunned and truly saddened, Hamlet edged nearer. She placed an arm around the distraught lad, hoping to console him with supportive words: "She bore a mind that envy could not but call fair."

Recognition of the voice, brutally cutting through his agony and anger, recalled Laertes to consciousness. Gasping, he realized who offered these feeble stabs at comfort: the very person who, according to advance word, had slain Polonius. If one half of the rumor was true, did it not follow that the other must be, too?

Tears abruptly ceasing, Laertes drew himself up from the ground like a stiff corpse and grotesquely returned to some semblance of life: "She is drowned already, sir, with water, though I drown her remembrance again with my tears."

So often perceptive about others, Hamlet mistook Laertes' anger for the bittersweet sentiment of shared sadness. "I loved thy sister, too," she said with a sad smile. "A thousand brothers could not have loved her more."

Without warning, Laertes bolted forward, seizing Hamlet by the neck, intent on strangling the prince before any in attendance could grasp what was happening. As she gagged, Laertes hissed: "Fie on thee, wretch! 'Tis pity thou livest to walk where any honest men may resort."

Caught completely off guard, Hamlet fitfully fought back. Guards, initially frozen with shock, quickly recovered and rushed forward, pulling the youths apart, afterwards forcibly restraining them. "I prithee thee," Hamlet coughed, bending over in pain, "vent thy folly elsewhere."

Caught up in a mad fury, Laertes shook off both of the guards holding him and unsheathed his sword. "If thou darest tempt me further," he screamed, "draw!"

Regaining composure, Hamlet likewise pushed away a soldier's grasp, and then drew the sword hanging by her side. Before the two could lunge forward and lock in mortal combat, Horatio slipped between them, calmly addressing Laertes: "Put up your sword. If this young gentleman have done offence, I take the fault on me."

Laertes turned his wrath on Horatio. Like Hamlet, this

unaccountably well-regarded lout had displayed little interest in, and less time for, Polonius' son during childhood. As the offspring of a humble farmer, Horatio deserved considerably less status than Laertes. Yet this commoner had inexplicably enjoyed the close friendship with Amuleth that Laertes secretly coveted throughout his youth.

"He, gentleman?" Laertes railed. "And me, what: Common? Gentleman, non: *churlish* boy!"

For Hamlet, this proved one insult too many. Still prince of this land and, however unlikely it might seem during these current circumstances, heir to the crown so long as Claudius and Gertrude remained childless, Hamlet exploded at such an open display of disrespect. "I could fight, and win, if I chose," she howled. Calming, Hamlet added: "Yet I have done enough damage to your house anon."

Laertes calmed, too, at least a little. The guards, concerned and frightened, inched away, while nonetheless keeping a watchful eye on all. "Prince or no, come not near me for fear of death!" Laertes hissed, turning to wave his free fist at the others congregated in this place of woe: "I'll be revenged on the whole pack of you."

Eyes brimming with tears, Laertes huffily stormed away. All in attendance observed him in stunned silence. Moved by his plight, Claudius whispered in Gertrude's ear: "He hath been most notoriously abused."

"Pursue him," she coldly suggested, "and entreat him to a peace."

"Ay, but he will not be pacified."

"He will," she added with a subtle wink, "should you use your wiles well." Gathering his queen's drift, Claudius nodded in agreement, following Laertes back toward the castle.

"I know we shall have him wed to friend in good time," Horatio hopefully confided to Hamlet as the crowd broke up, dispersing in a dozen directions.

The 'prince' shook her head *no*: "I wish we may. Yet I have a mind that fears him much."

Tom, Dick, and Francis, last of those in attendance to remain by the grave, awkwardly approached. "I would a word with you, sirrah!" Tom ventured.

"And I!" Dick joined in.

"Serve you, we will," Francis added in turn.

"To sleep under stars?" Hamlet asked, indicating the vast woode. In the wake of this latest outrage, she had no intention of returning to Kronborg and, Hamlet wisely feared, certain death during the dark of night.

"Far from these star-crossed rulers," Francis said.

"And their incestuous bed," Tom grunted.

Their loyalty and decency moved Hamlet: "Come, comrades. We'll none of this court of cowards." She turned; Horatio following, they headed for the woode in bounding strides.

"I'll follow this man," Dick said of Hamlet to Horatio, "and go with you."

"And having sworn thus," Francis added, hurrying to join the others, "ever will be true."

102.

Initially, Fortinbras had worried about the likelihood of rounding up a full-scale volunteer army, composed entirely of students and farmers, and then successfully invading Denmark with such a highly irregular force. After all, his far more experienced father had tried to conquer Kronborg's sea-swept fortress a generation earlier, and failed miserably despite the presence of well outfitted regular soldiers as well as a solid support convoy hurrying along behind with plentiful food supplies and additional weaponry. For one awkward moment, young Norway actually considered hesitating, long enough to send missives home, requesting that his aged parent hurry along and help, accompanied by as many good men as he could muster. Then he experienced second thoughts: His father had, the youth recalled, sworn a sacred oath, in return for the sparing of his own life and those of his surviving troops, never again to approach Sjalland's shores with intent to conquer. Old Fortinbras could not now be asked to violate that promise, even in support of Hamlet, son of his enemy-turned-ally.

On the other hand, young Fortinbras had taken no such vow. So he threw himself fully into a mission which, in truth, he thoroughly enjoyed: There was enough of the warrior heritage running through his blood to leave Fortinbras bored by endless days spent in intellectual pursuit. Indeed, the university experience left him eager for an excuse to pursue some heady adventure.

In Wittenberge, he had no difficulty discovering men aplenty who likewise were eager for action: student-princes and bored sons of yeoman farmers; street urchins hungry for glory, working-class louts desperate to escape dull lives and heckling wives. The more well stationed among them owned swords, even armor. Others seized rusty axes intended only for farm work, carrying them along atop their shoulders. Those with horses set about filling leather traveling bags with basic necessities, afterwards hurriedly mounting for the long, hard ride. Others trailed behind, marching on foot past whirling windmill, up toward thawing fjord, gathering strength as they steadily welcomed newcomers to their cause. All the while, this humble band of brothers pushed ever further through Germany, up into the Danish mainland, then veered northeastward to ferry across to their final destination.

Volunteers proved surprisingly easy to come by, once they traversed the craggy peninsula and crossed over the channel. This was achieved at a considerable expense, owing to insolent ferrymen who were amazed to learn, from the obviously princely leader of this makeshift military force, that the eccentric youth encountered a week earlier had indeed been Denmark's royal prince! Once transported to the rough island, Fortinbras pursued an indirect path toward Kronborg, allowing for brief stopovers in every seaport, farming village, and a host of isolated inns encountered along the way. The men he met in such places expressed discomfort with the hasty coronation and incestuous union, and made clear that they were unable to grasp why such a thing had been allowed by their supposedly wise council of elders. Apparently, young Norway concluded, many in the land had become convinced that only the rightful heir could insure lasting peace and prosperity.

Now, their makeshift banners flailing in the wind, Fortinbras' rag-tag army inched closer to its destination. Fearing Claudius might have received advance word of their presence, the brash leader ordered his men off main roads, instead cutting their way through high field and lush forest. Nearing noon on their second day in Sjalland, Fortinbras ordered all to camp by a narrow creek, a feeble offshoot of the nearby river which, if they were to follow along its circuitous route, would windingly lead them up toward Helsingor. By avoiding clearly marked paths, they could avoid the risk of losing what Fortinbras knew, for such an insurgent fighting force, to be their greatest strength: surprise.

Like all armies throughout history, this one traveled on its stomach. The time had come for noon meal. Men and animals rested in the shade of trees boasting full foliage, lounging beneath shady boughs on beds of moss. There, they recouped the necessary strength to make a show of it were they destined to meet Claudius' troops on the field before Kronborg. Fortinbras grasped full well that his volunteers, however enthusiastic, could not possibly defeat Denmark's well equipped army in such full open combat, even under the best of circumstances. Their only hope for success, he had decided, would be a sudden show of support for Amuleth, as broad as it was deep, causing like-minded men among Denmark's regular soldiers to abandon Claudius and come over to the rebellion's side. If that transpired, victory would be theirs!

And . . . if not?

Fortinbras had promised, if necessary, to lay his own life on the line for that delicate dreamer, Amuleth—now, as Balthazar had informed Fortinbras, called Hamlet. It might yet come to that, though only time would tell.

Having rejoined the main party earlier that day, Balthazar had been discovered patiently waiting by Sjalland's southern-most ferry stop when Fortinbras crossed over with the first boatload. While waiting for the others—or, at least, those composing their advance guard—to join them, Balthazar reported all he had seen and heard during his brief sojourn in Helsingor. Now, the youth conferred once more with Fortinbras over a hasty meal of hard-cooked eggs and cold ham. Having heard Balthazar's report and given the situation much thought, young Norway shared his best possible strat-egy: "Let's march without the noise of threatening drum, that from castle Kronborg's brutal battlements, our fair appoint-ments will not be perused."

"I pray we are in time."

A forced march, to begin that very afternoon, initially seemed the right course of action. Unwise, though, Fortinbras realized upon closer consideration: These exhausted souls needed to recoup their strength before proceeding and, per-haps, encountering a mighty enemy. How awful it would be to arrive in time, only to prove too weak to properly fight. However foolish it seemed, lolling about on the grass and basking in the sun's warmth, such a respite was necessary if they were to eventually achieve their end.

"Yet the men must have their rest, or be too tired on ar-rival to serve our purpose," he insisted when Balthazar begged the prince to rouse his men and move on. Sensing the wisdom of this approach, Balthazar leaned against a tree's lichen-encrusted bark. Closing his eyes, the loyal servant felt hun-grier for sleep than he had been for food. Fortinbras, unable to sit still, seized a metal cup, strolling toward the creek for a drink. Halfway down the hillock, he halted, spotting some-thing strange. Among dead branches and lush vegetation lining the muddied bed, the Norwegian prince thought for a fleet-ing moment that he spied a human form, drenched from brackish water, tangled in weeds, shrouded in rags.

His mind must be playing tricks on one who had not prop-erly slept or eaten in days . . .

Still, Fortinbras dared ventured closer. Lo and behold, it was indeed a person! Or, more likely, the corpse of some poor fool, drowned during the night, then borne downriver to this spot by a current at once steady and fierce. He called back, over his shoulder, to Balthazar, who woke from a dream of happier days.

Sodden from lack of sleep, Balthazar hurried down the incline. "Sirrah?" he asked.

Fortinbras pointed to what he now perceived as a distinctly female form, be it quick or dead, stretched out in the bright sunlight that sharply cut through a sparse line of trees. Then, to the amazement of both observers, the girl stirred ever so slightly, shakily attempting to rise up on her knees and focus her blurred vision on the two men hurrying near. She was drained—if not of life, then certainly of the necessary energy to manage any recovery on her own. Her head fell again, into the mud, where she lay still.

Fortinbras, first to arrive, stood over her, marveling at the young woman's appearance, for a remarkable natural beauty radiated through her current bedraggled state. For one brief moment, his mind played tricks on him. Fortinbras thought he had seen her somewhere, once before, and her lovely visage had been stored away in the recesses of his memory ever since. That was unlikely, though. Perhaps he had glimpsed her in a half forgotten dream, in which his youthful imagination summed up the perfect woman—perfect, at least, for him.

"Be I Britain's Arthur of old all a sudden," he mused, "she our own fair Lady of the Lake?"

"I know her!" Balthazar gasped. "One called Ophelia."

Fortinbras scooped the maid up in his arms, proceeding to carry her up the incline to their camp, where food and drink might yet revive the delirious beauty. "I do not like her name," he absently concluded.

"There was no thought of pleasing you when she was christened," servant reminded master.

"True 'nough there," Fortinbras chuckled.

They reached the tallest tree, around which the makeshift

camp was structured. Soldiers gathered close at the sight of what appeared a half-drowned wood nymph from some ancient fable. Moving as carefully as possible, Fortinbras set her down on his blanket, while barking orders for preparation of hot broth in hopes of nourishing her back to health. So lovely, Fortinbras mused as he whisked wet weeds away from the perfect features of Ophelia's face, while gently fingering locks of light-brown hair hanging in vaguely formed ringlets. The very face, a smitten Fortinbras knew, he had been searching for all these many years!

103.

In a small shrine tucked away between a pair of the myriad meeting rooms that lined Kronborg's first floor, Laertes knelt before an image of the Holy Virgin. He prayed with an intensity he hadn't expressed since boyhood. Claudius, frantically searching for the anguished youth ever since the fiasco at the graveyard, at last found him here, candles burning brightly on either side of the small enclave. Crosses on the walls reassured those in an extreme state of need that life did indeed have meaning, even if—at difficult times like the ones that brought each newly desperate soul here—such a belief seemed ever less likely.

Pausing out of respect owing to the moment's demand for privacy, the king listened as Laertes wailed: "Villainous company hath been the spoil of me!"

"Good Laertes—," Claudius cautiously ventured.

Laertes only continued his rambling confession, unaware of or unconcerned with any other person present: "I had a sister, whom the blind waves and surges have devour'd."

In the extremity of his despair, Laertes clearly required a father figure. Claudius knew he could play that role! "Rise," he commanded, "and be a man."

Laertes spit back over his shoulder: "Come not between the dragon and his wrath."

"Impartial are our eyes and ears," Claudius, his voice calm, assured the youth. "Were Hamlet my own son, as he is but my brother's, I vow, it should not privilege him."

Rising, Laertes turned to face Claudius. "Truly?"

"Anon." As the youth quieted, the king stepped forward, if with some trepidation. "Besides," he confided, "here is one who hates Hamlet more than you." Laertes gazed into his eyes and knew Claudius spoke the truth; no one could feign such rank emotion. "Methinks I see a way by which thou can redeem thy soiled honour," the king continued.

"Yet, Hamlet is a prince. What shall be done?"

This would be easier even than Claudius dared hope! "Challenge the brash youth to fight with him."

Considering this, Laertes announced: "I will meditate the while upon some horrid message for a challenge."

Reassuringly, Claudius patted the vulnerable young man's shoulder.

104.

In the center of Helsingor's far-reaching woode, other souls devised alternative plans for Sjalland's future. All morning, Horatio had busied himself with overseeing the creation of a makeshift camp, which was constructed by recent converts to their cause. Their number ever increasing, noble and commoner alike joined him in collaborating on two dozen temporary shelters. This, they crafted from an ample supply of wood, generously provided by fallen trees, and the abundant earth which, for generations, Danes had employed to fashion crude living quarters. These were now inhabited by the first to join their mushrooming rebellion: Tom, Dick, and Francis, as well as a score of other knights who had suffered enough of the now despised Claudius, not to mention his incestuous union with beloved old Hamblet's wife.

Others, of all social classes and like mind, had heard rumors of the insurgency taking shape in the woode and wandered in, one by one. In short shrift, each new recruit was set to some work, fashioning similar hovels to those already constructed or erecting a series of tents similar to the one Hamlet and Horatio had chosen for their own living quarters while encamped here. Several volunteers brought their women along; members of the fairer sex labored at preparing a noon meal over roaring cook fires. Others devised a simple laundry by the nearby riverbank while men practiced archery or sparred with spear and sword.

The current picnic atmosphere, all knew, would not last long. In the meantime, though, there was entertainment, for the players were there as well. Initially, they had desired only to leave Denmark as quickly as possible. But the Player King had determined that their creaking wagon was in no condition for travel, for a rusted axel and rear wheel sorely needed repair. Had they tried to escape on the open road, there likely would have been an immediate breakdown, leading to their quick arrest, and then they would surely face the wrath of Claudius. So instead, they drifted to the camp, for word of Hamlet's burgeoning group had reached them. Once there, the Player King begged admission until the necessary repairs were complete. Already guilty over the difficulty she had caused these innocent dupes, Hamlet happily admitted their party.

She had not been disturbed during the remainder of this day, for the loyal followers hoped that their prince would, through sleep's soothing balm, recover from a case of extreme exhaustion. Dozing in the tent, Hamlet was finally roused to full consciousness by the ever louder work sounds from just outside. Dressing quickly, she briefly considered revealing her secret to the gathered men, then decided that it might be too much for them at this point. Instead, wearing male garb and with *faux* moustache once more properly in place, she stepped forth, surveying the growing endeavor. Strolling through camp, Hamlet joined Horatio by a large oak and nodded approval at the work in progress.

"They are up already, and call for eggs and butter," Horatio informed her.

"Sirrah," Hamlet said, observing her ever more formidable band, "I am sworn brother to a brace of nobles, and I can call them by their Christian names: Tom, Dick, and Francis."

"More arrive by the moment," Horatio noted. Several stragglers, including an elderly knight atop an ancient horse, followed by a dozen rough yoemen, trotted through the thick woode and into camp. Once there, they reported to Francis, then set to picking out spots for themselves amid myriad tents and huts.

For several hours, Hamlet and Horatio joined in the activities. They made certain that their followers were well fed from bounteous contributions offered by local farmers and nearby fishermen, unable to join the company owing to family commitments yet wishing to lend some support. There would be no shortage of fresh cheese, smoked plaice, baked ham, or hard-cooked eggs. After, they instructed novices on the art of self-defense, pleased to observe how quickly these inexperienced village boys were able to master their new weapons. Then, all took part in a crude feast served round a crackling campfire. It was mid-afternoon when they finished, and naptime. One by one, they retreated to the shade of their quarters to escape the intensity of the harsh sun.

Seized by intense desire, Horatio indicated their tent, whispering suggestively: "Prince Hamlet, come."

She smiled coyly in return. "'Prince'?" Hamlet countered. "You are betrothed both to man and maid."

Lifting the flap, Horatio motioned for royalty to enter first. As Hamlet did, Horatio cooed: "Give me thy hand, and let me see thee again in thy woman's tweeds."

Hamlet rolled her pretty eyes while slipping inside. Horatio glowed, charmed by an elegant edge to Hamlet's subtlest movements which, for 20 years, he oft observed but thought best ignored. Now, he delighted in every little gesture.

"Maid!" Horatio insisted. "For so you shall be, while you are a man. But when in other habits you are seen, Horatio's mistress—and his fancy's queen!"

Laughing conspiratorially, they grasped one another's hands

and slipped inside. Horatio hurriedly fastened the tent-flap behind them for a sense of privacy. Tom and Dick, who had chosen to forego the rest period so as to stand guard while also initiating the construction of a sharp tipped wooden fence around their compound, raised eyebrows and flashed one another amazed glances.

"Brave new world," Francis muttered from where he stood sentinel, "that hath such people in 't!"

105.

"He is in the forest," Osric reported to king and queen, "and a many merry men with him. There, they live like Robin Hood of England, and fleet the time carelessly, as outlaws did in the golden world."

Bowing low, the courtier slipped from the royal study, leaving Claudius and Gertrude to their own designs. Once he was gone, she marched directly to the polished mahogany desk without noticeable hesitation or even so much as a single word to her husband. Seated there, vexed and frowning with intense concentration, Gertrude seized a quill and set to work, hastily scribbling a note.

"'Tis thought among the prudent," her husband snorted, "he would quickly have the gift of a grave."

Gertrude did not reply until having finished. Once done, she turned to Claudius, reading out loud: "'O, noble lord, call home thy ancient thoughts from banishment and banish hence these abject lowly dreams.'"

"You would forgive?" he marveled, coming close.

"Nay, *entrap!*" She signed the parchment, sullenly announcing: "Look! How I damn him with a spot."

Though Hamlet may have been her son—*daughter*—that hardly allowed him—*her*—the right to behave abominably. None could argue the simple truth: She had extended to Hamlet ample opportunity for redemption in her eyes, extended each and every option open to her. Indeed, Gertrude concluded, she had done her best to reconcile all these situations, however difficult; had held out far too long against her husband's violent inclinations. Now, she understood and accepted that Claudius' brutal bent was the only way. Pushed beyond her capacity for tolerance, Gertrude finally embraced, even exceeded, her current husband in bitterness. For when it came down to it, her own survival took precedence; she must harden herself, even toward her only child.

Disheveled in appearance, and moving with the clumsiness of one who has lost all sense of bearings, Laertes shuffled into the doorway. Drawing near to Gertrude, Claudius whispered: "I have persuaded him the youth's a devil."

"This well fits our scheme."

Storming in without waiting for proper invite, Laertes shoved a note of his own making under the king's nose. "Here's the challenge; read it."

"I warrant there's vinegar and pepper in 't?"

"An' bitter herbs, too!"

Without glancing at the missive, Claudius tore the thin parchment to shreds, afterwards tossing its remnants into a nearby receptacle. Luxuriously, Gertrude had stretched her arms above her head while watching this, looking for all the world like a large, lazy, self-satisfied cat. Then, in a silent expression of respect for this ill-used youth, Gertrude gracefully rose, indicating for him to take her usual place at the writing table, to compose anew.

"Challenge Hamlet to a 'friendly' duel," she said, handing him her quill.

Disappointed but obedient, Laertes dropped down into the cushioned chair: "With blunted swords?"

"His, yea," she explained. "Yours? *Sharp!*"

Cheered by the deadly plot, Laertes dabbed the quill into ink, then leaned over a parchment, ready to write. Gertrude dictated: "'I hold the olive in my hand; my words are as full of peace as matter.'"

Absently tilting forward in his chair, Laertes scratched away, as quickly as possible, attempting to keep up with her hurried dictation. Claudius, leaning close, archly reminded Laertes: "He is indeed the most skillful, bloody, and fatal opposite you could have found."

The letter complete, Gertrude drew from the billowing folds of her gown a single pellet, sickly yellow in hue, and displayed it for the astounded men. Gravely, she explained: "And, should his skill with sword be too sure, this gelatin, interred in his drink, will do the rest."

Nodding, Laertes reached for the poisoned capsule and stuffed it into a pocket. "The villainy you teach me," he urgently replied, "I will execute. And it should go hard, but I will better the instructor!"

Claudius and Gertrude stepped near to him on either side, embracing Laertes as if he were their very own son. Then, Claudius poured wine. The three toasted the imminent death of Hamlet, sipping the red liquid from long-stemmed glasses, each considering the others over the rim's circular edge.

106.

Late afternoon, an hour's hard ride south of Helsingor, found the army of Fortinbras in good humor. Having eaten and drunk their full, then afterwards enjoying a much needed rest, the men roused themselves at last and groggily made ready to proceed toward Kronborg. Observing the buzz of activity, young Norway sat beside Ophelia, still stretched out beneath the tree. She had never stirred from the mossy spot where the rough prince had gently deposited her several hours earlier, afterwards tightly wrapping a blanket around the beautiful creature's shivering frame. Ophelia had slept soundly since, and Fortinbras never ventured from her side.

This is the face, he knew for certain, the one face in all the world to which I could be loyal always! If only Hamlet and Horatio were here to share this wonderful moment. Once more, though, his memory played strange tricks on the prince; in some other place, at another time, he sensed that he had observed this perfect beauty with both those best friends present.

Ophelia shivered, frowning fretfully. Had she but dreamed those unlikely visions which had haunted her since the previous night? Unaware of how anguished her movements appeared, the girl grappled for her forehead, unconsciously brushing soft ringlets from a bruised but no less beautiful face. Slowly, she opened her eyes, noting that the red-headed lad sitting close by, his solid frame shading her from sunlight cutting through thick leaves overhead.

"Love's night is noon," Fortinbras proclaimed, fondly recalling the hour in which he had found and rescued her. His voice sounded surprisingly gentle for so rugged a fellow, his eyes wide and adoring, leaving her intrigued and amused.

Ophelia blinked, then extended a shaky arm, and weakly requested: "Give me your hand, sir."

"My duty, madam, and most humbly happy service."

Carefully, Fortinbras helped her sit up, then handed Ophelia a mug of the warm broth bubbling, in anticipation of her need, atop a nearby fire. Visibly shaking, she took the mug and slowly drained its contents, not speaking again until all the life sustaining liquid was gone.

"What is your name?" she softly inquired.

"Fortinbras is your servant's title, sprite."

With that, Ophelia regained a modicum of composure: "Prince of Norway, cousin to Lord Hamlet?"

"The same."

Yes, of course; the freckled skin, carrot color hair, and immense shoulders! "I saw you, in my youth."

That was it, then; he *had* glimpsed her before, and not in a dream. "Methinks I never saw the world at all, 'til now," he sighed.

His unguarded ardor embarrassed her. Secretly, though, Ophelia was relieved to learn that, even with all cosmetic art removed, she could still charm a man.

"'Twas never a merry world, since such lowly feigning passed for fair compliment," she answered coyly, for Ophelia was fully aware from his sweet, sad eyes that his words had been sincere. Recovering from her recent trauma, she automatically assumed the innocent pose that always proved successful in fashioning a tender trap. Thus, Ophelia swiftly assumed control of the situation by allowing her latest smitten male the sense of power and importance that these silly creatures—these *men*—obviously required.

"Feigning? Nay. All else said to women, preceding this, was but play-acting."

"If so," she continued, voice purposefully small, as she hoped to elicit further compliment, "why should I believe this true, and not show?"

"Never beheld I true beauty, 'til now."

At this, Ophelia laughed out loud. "Is the plague caught so quickly, then?"

Hardly suffering from that dread disease, Fortinbras did in fact momentarily feel weak, in a way that no physical contest with any man, however powerful, could impact upon him. "Whoever loved," he replied, "who loved not at first sight?"

She cast him her most adoring smile, taking great pleasure in witnessing his tender heart break then, there, and forever.

107.

Miles to the north, Hamlet and Horatio sat together, under a similar oak, immense as the one sheltering Ophelia and Fortinbras at that very moment. In the glen before them, Francis oversaw the completion of a wooden wall, nearly six feet high, which now protectively circled the compound. This formidable barrier was composed of logs, buried in the ground, the tips sharpened to better repel any possible attack. Such a forest fortress represented yet another style adapted from Brits; so necessary, Hamlet mused, if a last stand must be made here against Claudius' army.

Their attention was caught by a sudden flurry of color, quickly identified as the latest costume to adorn Denmark's most self-conscious courtier. Osric, carrying a missive from the royal couple, won admission to the compound following a brief interview with the guard. He sent this unexpected visitor strolling to where Hamlet and Horatio sat, closely considering Osric's every move. As always, they felt themselves filling with mean-spirited humor at the very sight of him displaying those pretensions so despised by university wits: of particular note on this day, Osric's hair had been altered, now worn long and straight in the manner of his Gallic counterparts. His gait more affected than ever, Osric waved affably, much to their amusement.

"Here comes the trout must be caught with tickling," Hamlet scoffed.

"That ever this fellow should have fewer words than a parrot!" Horatio agreed.

Sensing, as he approached, that their mutual compact of sarcasm hadn't diminished, Osric huffily assumed an aloof manner, whining: "Sirs, the king hath bade me all day look for you."

"I have been busy all this day to avoid him, courtier," Hamlet stiffly answered.

Osric shrugged, hoping yet to convince these men of station he was not particularly fond of the lot life had cast him in: "Such political persuasions are not for me, I fear."

"Would thou had bestowed thy time in study of fencing, dance, and poesy?" Horatio asked.

Horatio and Hamlet rose from their resting spots to circle Osric, scrutinizing the affected one from all sides while, over his shoulders, casting askance glances at each other.

"O," Osric reflected, "had I but followed the arts!"

"Then hadst thou had an excellent head o' hair," Horatio caustically observed.

Horrified, Osric replied: "Why, would that have mended my hair?"

"Past question!" Hamlet insisted. "For thou seest it will not curl by nature."

Osric was aghast!

He had been well aware, moments after washing his

now fashionably long locks that they flatly refused to respond to comb or brush, no matter how methodically he attempted to bring the long strands to some sense of order. In truth, though, did he look *that* poorly? "But it becomes me well enough, does't not?" he asked, exasperated.

"Excellent," Horatio exclaimed. "It hangs like flax on a distaff."

"I hope to see a housewife take thee between her legs and spin it off," Hamlet added.

Any intellectual limitations aside, Osric didn't qualify as such a total buffoon that he could fail to realize he was, once more, being put on by these cruel characters. "You have too courtly a wit for me," he sighed. "I'll rest."

Now, Hamlet's words rang with undisguised anger for any who blindly continued to obey the king: "Wilt thou rest damned? God help thee, shallow man!"

Deeply wounded by this unexpected affront, Osric shakily handed the missive to Hamlet, then prepared to take leave as swiftly as convention might allow.

"Here are a few of the pleasantest words e're blotted paper!" were his final words, before Osric hurried off and out of the makeshift fence.

Once the intruder was gone, Hamlet tore open the envelope, pouring over its contents. Horatio leaned close: "What employment have we here?"

Worried that the friendly words found there might likely disguise some deadly trick, Hamlet handed the paper to Horatio. He read closely and grew concerned.

A 'friendly' duel, the following day at noon!

108.

Early the next morning, in a stark, airy room adjacent to Kronborg's armory, Laertes diligently practiced with a well-balanced sword, chosen from all on display, for the afternoon's duel. As he lunged at stuffed semblances of adversaries hanging from a high cathedral ceiling, Gertrude and Claudius observed every move from the small balcony above, taking close note of the young man's particular style. In conclusion, they agreed that Laertes, at best a provincial youth, could never stand up to a truly accomplished and university trained duellist like Hamlet in a fair fight. Then again, though, there would be nothing fair about the fight.

"O," Gertrude sighed, pessimism overcoming her desire to believe, as Claudius insisted, that their troubles might soon be over, "that one might know the end of the day's business ere it comes."

Considering, Claudius shrugged: "But it sufficeth that the day *will* end, and then the end *is* known."

Below, Laertes danced about on the stone floor, then violently thrust his perfectly modulated blade deep into a mannequin made up to resemble, as much as possible, Prince Hamlet. King and queen nodded their shared approval.

"No contraries hold more antipathy than I and such a knave," Laertes, halting his efforts, called up. Already, he anticipated that glorious moment later in the day when he would similarly stab Hamlet and, at last, end the life of his despised adversary.

109.

Hamlet stepped from the tent that she and Horatio had happily shared for the past several days into the calm midmorning air. All the volunteers, commoner and noble alike, had been fully informed by Horatio as to the rules for this oncoming contest. Now, they stood at attention, ready to accompany their prince to the reckoning place. All fully understood this was to be a 'friendly' duel, yet each man feared the worst, and to the last man they had prepared for any possible trick. Long-swords dangled in the sunlight at every knight's side; yoemen carried heavy farm tools, converted to weapons, high atop their heavyset shoulders. Following a morning meal, consumed in silence, all had gathered, ready to expend their lives, if necessary, should the 'harmless' exchange transform into something else.

So far as any knew, Hamlet was a man, if a delicate one, slender of frame, elegant in carriage. When the prince exited her tent, she gave them no reason to suspect anything other than that. The womanly body, which Horatio had explored and enjoyed only hours earlier, was now completely covered by a thick, long cape—black as the night—stretching from neck to toe. And her moustache, having been removed for her dalliance with Horatio, now once more had been firmly fastened in place. Finally, her hair had been pulled back into a simple bun, hidden under the cape's circular shawl.

"I never in my life did read a challenge urged more modestly," Hamlet confided to Horatio, as he followed her out into daylight, "unless brother should brother dare to gentle exercise and proof of arms."

Horatio, holding the flap high for Hamlet to exit, allowed his hand to drop and reassuringly touch his sword's hilt. "Do you not fear a trap?"

"It seems to me," Hamlet mused, "most strange that men should fear; seeing that death, a necessary end, will come when it will come."

How cool Hamlet remained!

Could nothing emotionally unhorse this prince of philosophic jousters? Horatio glanced at an hourglass, set down by one of the villagers upon a nearby tree stump, so all would know when the time had finally arrived to march out of the woode and approach the field before Kronborg.

"The bawdy hand of the dial," Horatio reminded his beloved, "is now upon the very prick of noon."

"Come," Hamlet announced. "We trifle time with words. This day, 'tis deeds must win the prize."

Cape billowing about her, allowing no hint as to the carefully chosen costume hidden beneath, Hamlet stepped toward the rough gate, composed of fresh-cut branches held firmly together by leather chords. The position was currently manned by several youths, newly arrived from a Baltic seaport. The rugged boys respectfully opened the way, allowing Hamlet access to the forest path, before joining in at the procession's rear. All followed in Hamlet's wake like a pride of lions, resolutely marching behind their king, unaware that their leader would, in fact, more correctly be referred to as a queen.

When they were gone, only the players inhabited the quiet fortress. The little band sat silently at the camp's far end, knowing too well that their fates hung on what happened next to Hamlet.

110.

Less than five miles to the south, Fortinbras' army crept steadily closer. They had marched throughout the late-afternoon and evening of the previous day, as well as most of the preceding night. The men were then allowed a brief rest during the dark hours before dawn; Fortinbras knew it would be difficult to make their way through thick forest without benefit of a proper road, also that his men must sleep, at least for a while, if they were to be ready for anything that might occur the following day.

Once more on the move, young Norway led the way, mounted on a large grey horse, some distance ahead of the cavalry. His forces struggled to keep up, their leader's mount encouraged, by jabs of sharp spurs into soft undersides, to trot along the muddy riverbank. Some distance to the rear, the infantry huffed along as best it could, though falling ever further behind fast moving horse soldiers. Beside the prince, Ophelia rode a brown roan assigned by Balthazar, the hearty animal picked from the company's meagre supply of extra mounts. Fortinbras smiled with fascination, noting that this charming girl, seemingly so delicate while near-death throughout the previous day, now proved herself a marvelous horsewoman. Apparently, Ophelia's spirits had been revived somewhat by joining this grand adventure.

"You will conquer Denmark, then?" she nervously inquired. Whatever horrible things had happened in Helsingor, Sjalland did remain her beloved homeland.

Firmly, Fortinbras shook his head, insisting: "No blown ambition doth our arms incite, but love, dear love, for our thwarted cousin's right."

Relieved by his admission, Ophelia nodded her full agreement as to the rightness of the mission. Clicking to their horses, they pushed on.

111.

Likewise mounted, the knights and nobles of Kronborg, their number sorely depleted during the past several days (these were the remaining court members who hadn't chosen to desert Claudius and join Hamlet in the woode), galloped in full armor across the drawbridge and out onto the far stretching field. Polished breastplates and embossed shields reflected the late-morning sun, threatening to blind the multitude of peasants which crowded as close to the pathway as was permitted. Restrained there by guards carrying long pikes, the humble folk were yet ever hopeful of catching quick glimpses of the rich and powerful—images that would be transformed, in time, into vivid memories of this monumental day, told and retold to their children as the years slowly passed.

Multi-colored banners, all containing some touch of the rich earthen tone that signified Sjalland, fluttered in a gentle wind. Fine ladies in silken sheaths drenched in pastel hues followed along behind, mounted sidesaddle to display their recently affected sophistication. Delighted to be the center of attention, they waved gaily to farmers, smithies, and merchants lining the way on either side of a rocky path, all awe-struck at the sight of so much splendor.

At last, Gertrude and Claudius appeared on a pair of matched white mounts. Those in attendance pressed close to catch a quick peek as king and queen, majestically cantering at an awesome gait, proceeded without so much as a sideways glance to the central spot upon the field. This spot, throughout the morning hours, had been prepared by pageboys and squires for a monumental meeting of two remarkable adversaries. As had been the case with the disastrous play several evenings earlier, the stretch of ground closest to the tight circle now designated as dueling area was left open for peasants, who crowded close, horns of ale in hand, strips of roasted meat held high on skewers. Further back, rough benches had been set in place for the city's recently emerged middleclass. A dozen plush seats, carefully carted out from the castle, were set in appointed spots on higher ground for the royalty, thus allowing them a more vivid and distinct view than the others.

Further back still, constructed on a slight incline for the best possible viewing, twin thrones awaited king and queen. Dismounting, Claudius and Gertrude, escorted by armed guards who immediately formed a protective circle around the royals, forced their way through the braying multitude to their designated places. They sat, attended by Osric and a flock of overdressed servants who regularly rushed up with goblets of wine, as well as fans to keep king and queen cool whenever the soft breeze relinquished and an unseasonably hot sun became unbearable.

Gertrude, as was her habit, had chosen the loveliest gown in her collection for the public spectacle: a breathtaking beige sheath adorned with lavender-tinted lace at the cuffs and neck. Atop her head sat a felt hat, its beige color matching the gown, with an immense ostrich feather, tinted the same light shade of lavender as her dress, sweeping down on the right side to conceal half her face, thereby creating an aura of mystery around the lovely lady. Claudius, true to a deep-rooted vision of himself as final champion of a dying tradition—the man who might yet return Denmark to its era of past glories on the field of battle—had outfitted himself in the brown leather breeches and matching jacket of a Viking warrior. On his head rested the horned helmet, his most prized possession.

Though they didn't possess the vocabulary to express deep thoughts and emotions, even the simplest of peasants gathered here to watch the oncoming duel were aware, on some basic level, of the grotesque sight that these two provided for all who considered them closely: a woman striving for the heightened elegance she could not truly master, wed to a man desperate to retrieve the primitive state most others had abandoned.

"How bloodily the sun begins to peer above yon bushy hill," Claudius observed.

"The day looks pale," Gertrude added, "at his distemperature."

Shortly, the cloaked Hamlet and her party of rebels—considerably larger than Claudius had suspected—could be glimpsed. The rebels emerged from the protective line of beech trees at woode's edge, then boldly made their way onto the open field. Traipsing slowly but without a hint of hesitation, the patchwork military force—dedicated soldiers or menacing outlaws, depending on how one perceived their cause— steadily continued across the flats. All eyes in the assembled multitude one by one deserted the affected grandeur of the court, drawn now to the spontaneous majesty of Hamlet's improvised army. Despite the gathered crowd's enormity, not one whisper broke the profound silence.

"Come," Claudius finally hissed under his breath, "tread the path that thou shal't ne'er return from."

Standing in the center of the designated circle, Laertes drew his sword and leaned upon it as if the blade were naught but some casual cane. Commoners, crowding forward to get a look at the challenger, would have poured into the marked-off area but for staggered guards, who carefully restrained them with sharp pikes.

At last, flanked by followers, Hamlet reached the appointed spot. Peasants, guards, even several nobles who had taken standing positions nearby hastily made way for the prince to pass. Smiling cryptically, Hamlet stepped toward the circle's center and confidently faced Laertes. Horatio, keeping as close to Hamlet as possible, accompanied his lover to a line in the sand that marked off the dueling circle, only to be roughly restrained there by unrelenting guards, who followed Claudius' strict orders to the letter.

"As gentle and jocund as to jest go I to fight," Hamlet called back to Horatio as they separated. "Truth hath a quiet breast."

Spooked by the eerie undercurrent in Hamlet's tone, Horatio whispered while being forced back to the sidelines: "There is some strange thing toward. Pray you, be careful."

Hamlet and Laertes stood close in the circle's center. Hamlet attempted to make eye contact with her adversary, but Laertes guiltily refused. Turning away, the prince stared at Claudius, who downed a pint of ale from a curved horn.

"High noon, mighty king," Hamlet shouted. "And high time!"

Gertrude answered in her husband's place: "For reckoning?"

Slowly, Hamlet moved away from the reigning king to consider her, more in pity than hostility now. For all the hatred yet residing in Hamlet's breast had since the difficult meeting between parent and child become focused on ever-more despised Claudius. "Aye, mother," Hamlet muttered, without a hint of the old anger that had reached its crescendo in those hours between the play's conclusion and the death of old Polonius.

Considerably skilled as performers, Claudius and Gertrude then affected a giddy, frivolous mood, according to their plan of action. "Know, Hamlet," Claudius cooed after finishing his draught, "that we are in a forgiving mood. Pity me my earlier anger."

At a snap of the king's fingers, the guards restraining Horatio stepped aside, thus allowing him temporary entrance into the circle. As Hamlet's 'second,' Horatio was responsible to remove, then carry away the prince's cape. Hearing not only the king's words but also a subtle undercurrent of irony, Horatio, stepping close, whispered in Hamlet's ear: "Fear, and not love, begets his penitence."

"Let's forget to pity him," Hamlet agreed with a wink, "lest our pity prove a serpent that will sting us from heel to heart."

Claudius rose from his place, holding his horn, already refilled by Osric, high and forward in toast. "But, Hamlet," he called out, "knoweth this be but sport, mere play—"

"Good," Hamlet retorted. "For I hold the world but as a stage, where every man must play a part."

"And, yours?" Gertrude asked from where she sat, hunched over, seized all a sudden by a cold sweat.

"Mine, mother? A sad one. Whilst there is time, give me your blessing."

Hamlet veered forward, as if to approach Gertrude. The queen recoiled, clearly made uncomfortable by the thought of any close encounter with this grown child whose fate— she, far more than Claudius—had sealed.

What, she feared, was Hamlet up to now? "Of course, my son—" she replied, stumbling on her words.

Hamlet stepped in Gertrude's direction. Horatio, having reached up to Hamlet's shoulders, with both hands grabbed hold of the cape and held on tightly, then whisked it away— and, with it, the camouflage it had provided, even as 'the prince' took several steps toward the queen.

In unison, all present gasped at what they saw: Hamlet's outfit of choice for the duel, now at last revealed . . . a skin-tight, scandalously short skirt of black leather, adorned with shiny silver studs. The immodest length allowed everyone to observe Hamlet's long, shapely legs. Imported black stockings covered the flesh between this dazzling garment and a matching pair of boots, also studded with silver decorations. As the public's eyes moved up and down the stunning torso, amply on display, they couldn't help but notice Hamlet's considerable chest—large twin breasts pressing hard against the matching black leather jacket.

Swiftly, Hamlet tore away the *faux* moustache with one hand. The other simultaneously released her bunned hair, dropping down suddenly in a luxurious mane. "Should I meet my father now," Hamlet stated, "he would not call me son."

Standing proudly before the crowd now stood a modern

incarnation of the Amazon women of ancient myth, feminine yet formidable, beautiful and deadly. At first, no one dared speak. All knew, in a single instant, the carefully kept secret only Gertrude and Horatio, among the living—along with Polonius and the nurse, now both with the dead—shared a moment before. Far from the womanly man some suspected—and others feared—their prince might be, Hamlet appeared every inch a woman; lithe, graceful, and charming. Yet, strangely enough, strong as a man all the same.

Minutes passed in awkward silence before Claudius croaked: "If this were played upon a stage now, I could condemn it as an improbable fiction."

The king, amazed, turned toward Gertrude. She avoided his eyes: "Truth will out, as sages say."

Gertrude's words caused her daughter's eyes to bulge with anticipated vengeance. As end-game approached, Hamlet desired nothing less than their own little *ragnarok*—an irrefutable final reckoning. "Aye, mother," Hamlet said with quiet composure. "E'en murder cannot be hid long."

Claudius, the life force seemingly sucked out of him, guiltily dropped back down into his plush cushioned seat. Laertes approached Hamlet, barely containing his venom while staring at the 'prince' with new hatred.

"Why look you strange on me?" Hamlet asked. "You know me well."

"In truth? I never saw you in my life 'til now." Laertes sheathed his sword, preparing to leave. "Fight I not thee, gentlewoman."

Claudius, concerned, interrupted. "He—"

"*She!*" Laertes shouted, correcting the king.

"——will fight with you for oath's sake." Then, turning to Hamlet: "Marry, Laertes better bethought him of his quarrel, and he finds that now scarce to be worth talking of. Therefore, draw, for the sincerity of his vow. He protests, he will not hurt you."

Eyes aglow, Hamlet swirled about, facing Laertes with

mocking smile, honestly stating: "I'm for you, sir."

Sudden fury rippled through her opponent's frame, the face of Laertes turning crimson with embarrassment. "You denied to fight with me this other day, because I was no gentleman born. See you these clothes? Say you see them and think me still no gentleman?"

Humbly, Hamlet replied: "I know you are now, sir, a gentleman."

"Ay, ay, and have been so in time these many hours of my life."

"And I," Hamlet chuckled. "'Til now."

Others laughed as well, though no merriment could be detected in the sound. Hamlet stepped nearer to Laertes, speaking with the utmost sincerity: "And, gentlewoman to gentleman, I do humbly beseech you, sir, pardon me all the faults I have committed to your person."

For a moment, Laertes appeared as if he might be won over by the sincere hunger for reconciliation in Hamlet's voice. Then, his mind drifted to his father, the old greybeard Laertes had loved so dearly, yet to whom the callow son had never shown, or expressed in words, proper appreciation. Then, to the tender sister whose sweetness brightened all their days, robbed of any future by Hamlet's neglect. Laertes also recalled the unforgivable arrogance with which Hamlet, throughout their boyhood, always treated him—this youth never invited to run off and play with the prince. Yet Horatio—son of a peasant, more common than common—somehow merited just such inclusion.

No, it was too late for any reconciliation now, despite the impact of this amazing revelation. For Laertes, the despised past remained all too vivid a reality in the lonely present. All that had happened caused him to bristle with an insatiable, and as yet unsatisfied, lust for Hamlet's blood.

"Prithee, I do," Laertes lied. "For we must be gentle, now we are gentleman and woman."

The sarcasm oozing from Laertes' statement could neither

be missed nor ignored. Hamlet stiffened with the realization that their quarrel must be resolved, once and for all, with swords.

"Sound, trumpets," Claudius called out, anxious to see this over and done. "Set forward, combatants."

All those standing then crowded as close as they could to the circle. Those seated rose up in their spots to observe the coming conflict, sensing some heightened excitement in the air. As Hamlet drew her sword, Laertes raised his on high. Then, the two warily circled one another within the confines of the tight ring.

112.

Laertes, first to make a move, rushed forward, swinging wildly at Hamlet in the Old Norse style. That was his first mistake. Wittenberge's most skillful fencing instructors had taught her how to deftly raise a sword, meeting such an awkward blow while forcing an adversary back and off balance by a subtle angling of the blade.

"Now, sir," Hamlet confidently announced, "have I met you again? There's for you."

Furious at being casually dismissed by his mortal enemy— a *woman*, as it turned out—Laertes rushed in once more. He swung harder still, as if a greater expenditure of energy might yet do the trick, while countering: "You are well met, sir."

Their swords clanked loudly. Hamlet again forced Laertes back, as everyone—king, commoner, and all those ranked at various stations in-between—remained spellbound by the action. "Of more fierce endeavor," Claudius called out, true to his Viking heritage and so ever-anxious for rough entertainment. "I have seen drunkards do more than this in sport."

Hamlet noted that Laertes, forced further and further back by her own more accomplished swordplay, maintained balance only with great difficulty. Mercifully, Hamlet wheeled about to step away, giving her clumsy opponent time to regain footing and carry on. Instead, Laertes seized the opportunity to slash away while her back remained briefly turned.

"Beware, Hamlet!" Horatio, observing, screamed.

Hamlet had no time to so much as glance behind her. Nimbly she sidestepped, allowing Laertes to rush by, slashing furiously at the air and in the process losing his balance, then falling to the ground. Thanks to Horatio, the lowly trick failed. Nonetheless, Laertes did manage slight if cruel contact. The black-leather sleeve covering Hamlet's right arm had been sliced through, a light scratch on her arm evidenced now by dripping blood.

Clearly, only one sword had been blunted according to those rules of chivalry recently introduced into northern Europe! Laertes, huffing, guiltily glanced at Hamlet while recovering his stance. No doubt that Hamlet now knew full the true danger of the situation she found herself in.

"What a slave art thou," Hamlet hissed, "to hack thy sword as thou hast done, then say it was a fair fight!"

The crowd, realizing a foul trick had been played, reeled in amazement. Fully aware that the unfolding events were not going according to plan, Claudius hastily rose, announcing: "Stop a moment; take a spot of wine."

At the king's command, the combatants backed away from one another, both breathing hard from exertion. Gertrude poured wine from a vase, handing a pair of full horns to Claudius. Carefully taking them, he at last rose from his elevated throne approaching Hamlet and Horatio. Each duelist thrust his sword deep into the ground, as Claudius came close, proffering the first drink to Laertes. While accepting his beverage, Laertes secretively palmed the poison pellet, hidden deep in his breeches pocket 'til that very moment, into Hamlet's horn without any but Claudius noticing.

Exuding false jollity, Claudius then approached Hamlet: "A cool draught?"

Thirsty from the activity, Hamlet seized the horn and was about to drain its contents. And would have, except that he happened to notice Horatio standing in the first line of spectators, shaking his head firmly in protest. Though the loyal friend hadn't spotted Laertes' sly maneuver, Horatio sensed something amiss. The concern in this loyal friend's eyes was all it took to alert Hamlet, who swiftly declined.

"Skill," he said, "knows not thirst."

Claudius had no choice but to retreat to his throne, carrying the horn with him. Once there, he deposited the now-potent brew on a nearby stand. As soon as the fight resumed, all eyes trained once more upon the duelists, he would secretively dump its deadly contents onto the ground.

Having drained his horn and feeling fully refreshed, Laertes moved toward his sunken sword, its hilt waving ever-so-slightly in the gentle afternoon breeze. Before he could yank the weapon from its earthen sheath, though, Hamlet stepped up and did so. She motioned with a cruel smile for Laertes to take Hamlet's sword in its stead. Uncertain as to what he ought to do, Laertes, eyes begging for help, turned to Claudius.

The king could only motion for them continue. Otherwise, of course, he would have supplied proof positive to all that the duel was dishonest.

113.

Eyes dancing nervously, Gertrude glanced back and forth from Hamlet, the daughter she had sacrificed so much for, to Claudius, the husband she had risked everything to be with. Beads of sweat formed on her brow as the queen fully grasped this current confrontation would prove to be her moment of truth—the brief piece of time in which she must finally choose between the only two people alive who meant anything to her. She understood, too, that in making such a choice, Gertrude would finally define her values in life, as well as her future reputation in the annals of Danish history.

This was her moment of truth.

Within the tight circle, fenced in by a seething wall of dazzled spectators, Hamlet and Laertes faced one another, each prepared for the final struggle. Wielding the sharp sword, Hamlet glided close to her opponent, swinging upward and forward with a detached, objective skill, effortlessly displaying the approach favored at Wittenberge's revered gymnasium. Laertes' only training had been on Kronborg's practice fields where one such as he was allowed to watch and imitate sons of knights as they received instruction. Now, he could do little but lift his worthless sword in sad defense as Hamlet's blows sliced downward.

A whistling of the wind, eerily blowing past the gathered Danes, preceded the clash of weapons. Hamlet slammed past the worthless blunt blade, squarely skewering Laertes. A sudden yelp of pain, like that of a disobedient puppy being slapped. Then, Laertes ceased all attempts at self-defense, dropping his useless weapon while reaching under his tunic. The youth groped at the gash where Hamlet's blade had penetrated his flesh. Staggering back, away from Hamlet, Laertes drew forth his wet, red hand, holding it up for the king to see.

"Look, sir," he muttered to Claudius, as if only half believing what had happened, "I bleed."

On the lookout for foul-play, Tom, Dick, and Francis leaped up from their seats, pushing forward through the mass of people that crowded in for a peek of liquid crimson. "What," Tom called out. "Treachery?" He forced his way through the crowd, approaching Laertes. The vast crowd swayed backward, like a Baltic wave retreating from the sandy white shore at ebb tide.

Dick, however, reached Laertes first, and held the swooning youth upright as best he could. "Is the wound serious?" he asked.

"A scratch," Laertes—fearful he might entrap himself by revealing the conspiracy he'd taken part in—lied.

Meanwhile, wearied from combat and consumed by a thirst that rendered her barely capable of speech, Hamlet stepped away from the commotion. She approached the table where that horn of poisoned wine yet sat, forgotten in the excitement by Claudius and everyone save the parched prince. "Now," she croaked, "refreshment!"

Stunned by her daughter's words, and fully aware of what would happen if she chose not to intervene, Gertrude stood. She almost spoke, thought better of it, then instead hurried forward and grasped the horn before Hamlet could—seizing the mortal liquid, holding it close . . .

. . . *all at once, she was 20 again, at least in her mind. Mother to a newborn babe, squeezing her daughter close as any such a one might . . . peering down at trusting eyes while the dear little girl suckled. That small, trusting face caused Gertrude to reconsider her initial impulse. Had she really planned to abandon this child simply because her babe hadn't shown the common sense to be born a boy?*

"Is there no pity, sitting in the clouds?" the child, staring up her mother and somehow seeming to comprehend the terrible act being contemplated, communicated without words. *"O, sweet mother, cast me not away."*

She had relented then . . .

. . . sensing what his queen was about to do, Claudius—absolutely panic-stricken—turned to her in horror. "Gertrude! Do not drink—"

Slowly, she turned to face him, one final time. Her green eyes, gorgeous as ever, now seemed full of a strange mockery. Not at him, the man for whom she had thrown all caution to the wind, but their situation, the madness of it and, for that matter, generalizing from the specific, the absurdity of life itself. "I will, my lord!" she calmly replied.

Turning to Hamlet, gazing on at all this in total confusion, Gertrude lifted the horn to her lips, winked, then drained its contents. Horrified at the inevitable result, Claudius dropped back down into his seat, visibly shaking. For the moment, Gertrude still stood before him, irresistible as ever. She was his queen; he, king. Kronborg castle, the province of Sjalland, all of Denmark stretched in every direction, at their command. In time, the entire Northlands might yet fall under their power. At this juncture in time, this split second out of all eternity, everything either had ever hoped for, dreamed and schemed to achieve, was theirs.

Yet the victory was hollow; in a matter of moments, she would die—nothing could prevent that now—dooming him to a life worse than death. A life without *her*.

What a difference a day makes, he recalled someone had once written. For Claudius, the loss of everything he held most dear would require not a full day, merely one minute more. The old ones spoke of *ragnarok*, the end of all, a final reckoning. This sad spectacle, unfolding before his eyes as he stood by, powerless to prevent it, seemed to Claudius his own private incarnation of that vision. The world might well go on, but he would not share in its pleasures ever again.

Unable to feign any longer, Laertes collapsed in Dick's arms. "I have wasted time," he wept. "Now, time doth waste me!" As blood gushed from the youth's mouth, women screamed in horror, shading children's eyes.

"Hamlet hath murdered Laertes," Claudius bellowed, consumed still by an instinct for self-preservation. "Seize him!"

Obeying, several armed guards lurched toward Hamlet, their lances ready. Before they could move far, though, Horatio and other members of their entourage drew forth swords, leaping forward to surround Hamlet, ready to shield her with their lives. At this, the guards halted. Though they vastly outnumbered the outlaws, there remained the question of loyalty. Who was the rightful ruler of Denmark, after all, Claudius or Hamlet? Whose orders should they follow?

As they hesitated, the sound of a hundred horses' hoofs, pounding hard on soft ground, rattled through the woode sending gathered birds cawing off in terror. Glancing toward the path leading past a thick stretch of beeches, all suddenly saw bright banners waving high. Then, Fortinbras himself, bedecked in princely armor and mounted on a great charger, came tearing out of the forest, his sword held high.

"He is come to open the purple testament of bleeding war," Claudius shouted to his remaining knights.

Balthazar and Ophelia, one on each side, flanked Norway.

Dozens of mounted volunteers followed close behind. As they hurried up, the crowd gave way. Fortinbras and his followers leaped down from their saddles. In a matter of moments, the invading force reinforced Hamlet, Horatio, and their volunteers. Refraining from taking first blood, the now considerable force stood ready to counter anyone who dared oppose them.

"Herein fortune shows herself more kind than is her custom," Hamlet sighed in relief.

Fortinbras stood by Hamlet's side. Horatio, Tom, Dick, and Francis were directly behind them, on the ready. Every man present was dedicated to protecting their lord and lady— both being, however incongruously, one and the same.

Fortinbras glanced at the lithe maid he had so long called 'brother,' unable to believe his eyes.

"O, this?" Hamlet laughed, peering down to consider her shapely figure. "Grief hath changed me since you saw me last."

Fortinbras called over his shoulder to Horatio. "Beseech you, were you present at this revelation?"

Recalling their night of passion, Horatio shrugged, nodded, whispered: "I was by at the opening of the fardel."

At Claudius' incessant urging, a dozen more Danish guards closed in, swords held high, ready for a fight.

"Do not fear," Fortinbras informed Hamlet. "Upon mine honour, I will stand 'twixt you and danger."

The nerve of that carrot-top! So Hamlet had turned out to be a woman. Did that mean she should now shiver and hide behind Norway's coattails? "Rather," Hamlet corrected him, "stand beside me as *equal*."

"Cry havoc!" Fortinbras shouted to his followers, "and let slip the dogs of war."

The few Danish troops still loyal to Claudius advanced, swords flashing in the afternoon sun. Their number had been further diminished, for half the men threw down their weapons and, owing to the situation's complexity, refusing to take sides. The remaining party proved no match for the combination of Fortinbras' collected volunteers and Hamlet's dedicated supporters. Knowing right was on their side, and would surely supply them with might, they lunged forward in a mass and swiftly lay their remaining adversaries to waste.

A few reinforcements did arrive from Kronborg, fresh troops hurrying to replace those falling before Hamlet and Fortinbras. Even as they arrived, though, Norway's infantry emerged from the woode in time to meet, pike-to-pike, these Danes. In the ensuing scuffle, Hamlet received another minor wound.

"Hamlet," Fortinbras cautioned, "withdraw thyself. Thou bleed'st too much."

"God forbid," Hamlet scoffed, "a shallow scratch should drive me from a field such as this, where strain'd nobility triumphs over injustice."

The fight, or what there was of one, lasted only a matter of minutes. Denmark's soldiers, unconvinced that they ought to bear arms against the offspring—son or daughter—of old Hamblet, had no heart for the fight, and quickly surrendered.

Then, a sudden scream pierced the silence, as all turned to the source of that tragic sound. Ophelia, forgotten in the action, fell on her knees, bending over dying Laertes. "O," she wept, "my poor brother!"

Guilt ridden for being the source of yet more pain to Ophelia, while greatly relieved to find her alive, Hamlet staggered over, leaning close, both to comfort her and hear the dying youth.

"I pant for life," Laertes muttered. "Some good I mean to do, despite my own nature."

Hamlet softly demanded: "Sharp sword supplied by?"

Burning eyes turned now toward the bloat king, Laertes hissed: "Claudius!" A gasp of horror passed, like foul wind, from the crowd. "Hamlet," Laertes continued, "thou hast robbed me of my youth. O, I could prophesy, but that the cold hard hand of death hath made me meat for—"

Before he could finish, Laertes died. Ophelia dropped her head down on her brother's chest and wept.

"For worms, brave Laertes," Hamlet pronounced, finishing the sentence for one who had, she now knew, ever deserved better treatment at Hamlet's hands. "Adieu, and take my praise to heaven with you."

No such kindness, though, for the despised and utterly unforgiven Claudius! Grip tightening on her sword's hilt, Hamlet rose, moving toward the king, who stood in fearful anticipation.

"The wheel is come full circle," Gertrude, a few feet from Claudius, calmly announced before falling to the ground. Unaware that this might be anything other than a fainting spell, Hamlet stepped to her side, as did Osric.

"Mother—," Hamlet queried, staring deep into her green eyes, suddenly sensing that something was seriously amiss.

"Son," she smiled strangely. "Daughter . . ."

"*Either*," Hamlet replied in a voice tinged with forgiveness. "Your *child!*"

"The draught of poison," she explained, "intended for you, I took unto myself."

A deadly silence, followed by: "Why?"

"Blood runs thicker than water. Your forgiveness—"

"You did have that before you asked."

She smiled strangely, turning to Claudius. He stood motionless, a hulking giant rendered powerless, and therefore pitiable, by events beyond his control. For once, despite his body's considerable mass, Claudius appeared weak, pale, and entirely vulnerable.

"You were right, my lord," Gertrude called to him, considering her own act. "Men—and women—*are* sometimes masters of their fates!" Before Claudius could manage an answer, she died.

"Woe!" Osric wailed. "The queen, the queen, the sweetest, dearest creature's dead."

Hamlet's frame was overcome with anger so intense that it far surpassed any rage she had known before. Members of the crowd, feeling the fury rise from her nearby body like heavy air preceding a thunderstorm on a still summer's day, drew back in fear and awe.

"I know my hour is come," Claudius announced, watching

as even the most loyal followers cast down arms and backed away. "What you have charged me with, that have I done."

"Aye?" Hamlet asked.

"And much, much more."

"Time will bring it out."

"Time is past; so am I."

Claudius drew his sword. If Hamlet expected the king to rush forward for one last fight, she was quite mistaken. Instead, Claudius staggered to the body of his queen. "If I did take the kingdom from your son," he whispered to the corpse, "to make amends, I'll give it to your daughter." Without hesitation, Claudius fell on his own sword, in the style of stoic Romans. "O King Hamblet," he shrieked in self-wrought pain, "thou art mighty yet! Thy spirit walks abroad, and turns our swords in our own proper entrails."

Claudius pushed down hard toward the ground, thus forcing the sword deeper into his body. People screamed in horror, blood flowing from the king as if his frame was a sieve. Then, Claudius collapsed beside Gertrude. "My brother, now be still," he muttered while peering up toward the sky. "I killed not thee with half so good a will."

Hamlet likewise glanced heavenward. "Father, thou art revenged. Even with the sword that kill'd thee."

Yet Claudius, not yet dead, was far from done. "Thou art thy father's daughter," he cackled.

"Aye, uncle. I am that!"

"Father, Hamlet. *Thy* father."

Hamlet's face went ashen. "Whoah! How now—"

"If there be truth in sight, you are *my* daughter!"

In the dying man's eyes, Hamlet saw a terrible map of the past, coming to light after so long a time . . .

114.

. . . *five years following the great battle on the field before Kronborg, an immense celebration, attended by king and commoner alike, commemorated the end of the final civil war between people of Teutonic heritage. Simple folk spent the morning at games of chance and sports, later circling around the great bonfire where a fresh killed pig had been slow-roasting over a spit, while sucking down sack in great quantities throughout the day; visiting royalty, following journeys from as far away as Norway, embraced the ruler of Denmark in full public view, thereby insuring that the peace was a good, strong, and lasting one.*

Side by side, Old Hamblet and King Fortinbras stood atop a high hillock, arm-in-arm, their brotherly love a potent symbol for all who gazed in their direction. The image of them together mutely announced that old enmities had matured into true friendship. Down below, on the field where others sported, the man yet known as Fengon approached the festivities in progress. This day, he served as escort to the queen, whose giddy girlish charms had, during the intervening years, given way to a woman's ripe sensuality.

Together, they proceeded to a spot where peasants danced about a tall maypole, its tip rounded and indented with a single deep slice so that it might resemble a giant male organ. Fiddlers played, horns trumpeted; each participant in the dance held tightly to a long, brightly colored ribbon, these strands connecting all revelers to the great wooden phallus dominating the field. A concerned Polonius suggested that this pagan rite, celebrating the natural side of man's existence, ought to be eliminated now that Christianity held sway in Sjalland. After much pondering, Hamblet had decided to allow his people their fun. True, the barbarian ways were receding; yet this dance might yet be enjoyed as a merry rite, any darker implications gradually forgotten as time obscured the original intent.

Amuleth, a delicate youth of five years, hurried up the hillock, directly to Hamblet's side, thin arms lovingly embracing the rugged man who stood strong as a statue. Though Amuleth was, as always, disguised in the garb of a boy, any who looked closely could not help but notice certain feminine qualities.

Still, this was the 'son' of a great king. Even the least observant of those gathered here knew better than call attention to
anything out of the ordinary.

Fortinbras, who had never before cast eyes on Denmark's
prince, was stunned to note the child's gentle demeanor. Without hesitating, he muttered in honest amazement to Hamblet:
"Art thou his father?"

Polonius, approaching and accompanied by his own children, overheard this potent comment, as well as what Denmark said in reply.

"Aye," Hamblet sighed. "Or so his mother says."

The king lifted his child high in the air, studying the face of
his sweet prince—the delicate babe so dearly loved by a king
whose political woes waxed insignificant when compared to
his deep personal fears. Observing Amuleth's features,
Hamblet hopefully—desperately—searched for some trace of
himself in the child's features. Finally, the king exhaled, glanced
down at the field where Fengon and Gertrude enjoyed each
other's company more than was deemed proper, muttering:
"If I can believe her."

Grasping his cousin's drift, Fortinbras was touched to the
quick by this unguarded hint. "'Tis a wise father that knows
his own child," he whispered, deeply concerned.

Ever fearful of any developing situation that might lead to
unrest and, ultimately, dreaded anarchy, Polonius pointed to
the happy couple, sporting with commoners in utter abandonment. "This, sir, is nothing."

Unable to repress a growing inner rage, Hamblet wheeled
about, his fiery orbs staring into Polonius' soft eyes. "Is whispering nothing?" the king hissed. "Is leaning cheek-to-cheek?
Meeting noses? Stopping laughter with a sigh? Why, then, the
world and all that's in 't is nothing."

Unsure as to how he might appease everyone, Polonius
could only try to assuage the king's temper with a poor jest:
"Nothing shall come of nothing."

Regaining some semblance of self-control, Hamblet yet
bridled at all he'd silently suffered for more than five years.

Despite deep trepidations, the king sweetly kissed Amuleth's
gentle forehead. Yet his words, though addressed to the child,
were of a more general nature: "That thou art my own son, I
have partly thy mother's word, plus my own prayer. If then
thou be son to me, here lies a question: Why do people point,
and stare?"

Confused by the uproar, Amuleth motioned to the ground,
ready to run off. Hamblet carefully deposited his prince—
watching the youth hurry away, affection fused with concern,
as Amuleth darted off to children's games, young Fortinbras
and Horatio awaiting their friend.

"Go!" Hamblet called after him. "Play, boy, play; thy
mother plays. And I play, too, but so disgraced a part."

All the while, Gertrude frivolously danced with her par-
amour, barely bothering to hide her feelings for 'Fang' from
the nearby peasants, simple folk filled with deep regret and
an awful sense of embarrassment . . .

. . . a generation later, the young people who had then
danced with Gertrude and Fengon were, like the main players in this strange drama, middle-aged. Once more, they leaned
close, eager to watch as the final curtain closed on what, long
ago, had on this very field served as their introduction to a
great, abiding, yet largely unspoken scandal. No mirth now,
only death. Gertrude, already gone; Claudius, her lover of
more than twenty years, husband for less than twenty days,
agonized through his final moments by her side.

Gazing up at the encroaching crowd, Claudius smiled. Blood
dripping down, over his lips and across his cheek, he nodded
toward Hamlet. "Though this knave came something saucily
into the world before he was sent for, yet was his mother fair.
There was good sport at his—*her*—making."

"Oh, heavens," Hamlet wailed, finally facing a truth that
had struggled toward consciousness for years, only to be
rejected by her mind and denied by her heart, too terrible to
contemplate. "*This* is my true begotten father?"

"I'll be sworn," Claudius replied, coughing up blood. "Thou

art my own flesh and blood. And thus, the whirligig of time brings his revenges."

Stepping close to Hamlet, offering his strong arm for support, Francis reminded the prince: "They breathe truth, that breathe their words in pain."

Summing up a final burst of strength, Claudius crawled closer to Gertrude and draped an arm over her lifeless body. "You were right, my love," he whispered into her ear, forever deaf now. "A greater power than we can contradict hath thwarted our intents."

He died then, too. And they lay together in death. Drawing close, Amuleth knelt beside the bodies and wept, as much for herself as for either of her parents.

115.

For seven difficult days, the population of Sjalland anxiously awaited some word as to the future of their apparent leader, and—as things went in those days—the fate awaiting them all. Shortly after that remarkable afternoon's carnage, riders had been dispatched, the incredible news spreading far and wide. Eventually, the bizarre truth had reached every inland village, each shipbuilding seaport, even the isolated provincial farms. Hamlet, accepted by all in Denmark for more than two decades as a feminine young man, was in fact a lovely woman. The revelation was greeted, in each and every place, first with skepticism, then denial, followed by shock, acceptance, and trepidation.

Would Hamlet ascend to the throne? If so, as king or queen? Some could not conceive of such a thing—particularly those who had admired Claudius and, like him, secretly wished for the old days, when rough Viking warriors ruled, to return. A few even spoke of taking up arms and assailing Kronborg. Such whispers of revolution were swiftly quelled by the presence of Fortinbras. The fiery Norwegian swept all Denmark's soldiers under his wing. These, along with members of his own volunteer army, were dispersed far and wide, from salt-stained shanties to isolated mountain outposts. No turmoil, the military men made clear, would be tolerated.

All the while, Hamlet kept to herself, locked away in one of the castle's small studies. Dressed in simple gowns and stark sheaths befitting a young woman of royal stature during a period of mourning, she incessantly poured over tomes of ancient lore, then turned to recent books carried with her, by saddlebag, back from Wittenberge. In volumes of wisdom, old and new, Hamlet searched for inspiration, hoping against hope that she might discover the right thing to do.

Outside, Hamlet noticed through the slit of a window, the season of rain and dark clouds had, at least for the time being, completely passed. Bright blue skies, interrupted only by an occasional puff of a cloud, formed the bright backdrop to Helsingor's long stretch of wooden shops and earthen cottages. Yet it seemed a single black cloud lingered still over Hamlet's head, hailing down torrents of private sadness. Hamlet had revealed her secret self to the world, though any sense of liberation from a stifling role proved sadly short-lived. Destiny once more played a mean trick on the prince. Claudius' dying words had forced Hamlet to face the truth of her lineage—a revelation more difficult to bear than anything the Danes learned and begrudgingly accepted about her true identity.

"O Gods!" she finally muttered, throwing down a heavy volume in desolation. "Who is 't can say, 'I am the worst?' I am e'en now worse e'er I was. My shame knows no bounds."

Horatio, the only person allowed to enter during this difficult week, sat across from her, waiting for his lover to speak, now nodding in solemn agreement. "The worst is not so long as we can say, 'This is the worst.'"

"Alack!" Hamlet wept, tears streaming down elegant high cheekbones. "What heinous sin is it to me to be asham'd to be my father's child!"

Horatio's practical view of all things might yet serve to

help the one who, as friend or lover, remained to Hamlet the most important person in the world. "Why rail'st thou on thy birth," he argued, rising, "like heaven upon earth? Since birth, and heavens, and earth all three do meet in thee at once— which thou at once would'st lose."

That made sense, more profound in the purity of its simplicity than any intellectual arguments Hamlet had encountered in books. Summing up her courage, Hamlet rose, nodding in agreement. "True. Though I am daughter to his blood, I am not to his manners."

Heartened, Horatio stepped close, embracing Hamlet and kissing her gently on the forehead. They might have made love then, something they hadn't done since their final time in the encampment before being summoned to duel, only a sudden rapping at the door caused the two to furtively pull apart. Fortinbras stormed in, hoping for some final decision on Hamlet's part that might help young Norway quell any hints of unrest, yet equally troubled by his own private affairs.

Hamlet, noting concern in Norway's eyes, hoped to set any sadness aside. "Coz," Hamlet said, "I am too young to be your father, though you are old enough to be my heir. What you will have, I'll give away; willing, too."

"Would I could have that which eludes me else."

"The lady Ophelia?" Horatio asked. Then, it seemed as if all three were miraculously transported from this dark place of bitterness and blood, back to the sacrosanct world of Wittenberge, where a student need worry only worry about balancing serious studies with wine and wenching.

"Like a cloistress," Fortinbras explained, "she will veiled walk to season a dead brother's love, which she would keep fresh and lasting in sad remembrance."

Hamlet was glad to have something to occupy her mind other than the terrible truth of her origins and a mountingly complex political situation. "Her brother Laertes," Hamlet said, "for his dear memory, they say, she hath abjured the company and sight of men."

Nodding, Fortinbras dropped down in a nearby chair,

moaning: "O, that I served that lady, and might not be destined to the world, 'til I had made my own occasions mellow."

Horatio approached Hamlet, lovingly taking her hand while
chiding their friend: "What happened to our Fortinbras of
old? 'Front her, board her—'"

"*Woo* her!" Hamlet, interrupting, reminded Fortinbras.

116.

In her secluded garden, at full bloom appearing as a rich rainbow descended to earth, Ophelia sat, alone on her wrought-
iron bench, holding the first bright flowers of spring to reach
maturity. She had, an hour earlier, cut them close at the stalk,
and now methodically crumbled the delicate petals, one after
another, afterwards letting them drop. She glumly observed
as the powdery remnants drifted to the ground, dead before
they had a chance to enjoy the rich warmth of this bright day.
Her action was cruel, she knew, yet somehow appropriate.
Glancing down at the sweet shards, Ophelia believed that
they provided a mute metaphor for herself and her own tragic
state of affairs.

Warily, Fortinbras approached, noting an extreme contrast
between the burst of rich colors on all sides of the slender
girl, set against the cryptic figure she cut: long black shroud
circling head and shoulders, emphasizing the ghostly whiteness of her face. Hearing an intruder, Ophelia glanced up
without apparent interest. Noting that young Norway had
come again to call, she offered curtly polite words of rejection: "My stars shine darkly on me; I shall crave your leave
that I may bear my loss alone."

For several days, Fortinbras had done as commanded when
visiting the object of his affections only to be summarily
sent away each and every time. Heartened by poetic Hamlet
and realistic Horatio, he dared try a new tactic: "Sorrow
would be a rarity most beloved, if all could so beautifully
become it." As she managed a small smile, Fortinbras

summed up his courage, cautiously venturing: "Why mournest thou?"

Such a question, the answer obvious to all, shocked Ophelia enough that she deigned to look him in the eyes. "For my brother's death," she harshly reminded Fortinbras.

Daring sit beside her, he calmly inquired: "Do you fear his soul is in hell?"

"I know," she hissed, "it inhabits heaven."

Cautiously, he continued: "Then, rejoice his good fortune. He is better removed from this foul world."

Spoken by Fortinbras, though in truth devised by Hamlet and Horatio, the words gave her reason to pause in her abundant self-pity. "True, there," she admitted.

"Comfort's in heaven," he continued, hopeful for a breakthrough, "and we on this earth, where nothing lives but crosses, cares, and grief."

"Which," she added, picking up on his drift, "only love can ease."

Gently, Fortinbras took her hand, bidding Ophelia rise. "Live, then, and love me."

"Would I could, fair sir—"

"Lady, you are the cruel'st she alive, if you will leave these graces to the grave and bless the world with no copy."

Ophelia gazed into the eyes of the young man she had found most agreeable during their initial meeting, when the rough Norwegian interrupted his great crusade to gently nurse a Danish beauty back to health. "Perhaps in time—" she suggested.

"What is yours to bestow is not yours to reserve!"

Then, they both knew a period of healing was at hand. The past must be set behind them, Fortinbras and Ophelia afterwards moving on to a life of rich experience and enduring love.

117.

The four young people agreed, owing to the effort of messengers sent darting back and forth between them, that they would meet one another in the castle's main courtyard at high noon. The appointed place was Kronborg's oldest fountain, blackened by years of neglect. Long ago, a local artisan, his identity long since forgotten, had fashioned his master-work in the likeness of *Luonnotar*, earliest of those goddesses in their mythology. The female spirit was here depicted bathing in a placid sea, blissfully oblivious to a female eagle constructing a nest in her lap. The eggs, all Danes knew, would someday break open, spill out into surging waters, and result in the creation of the earth on which all men now walked.

Hamlet arrived first, bedecked in an elegant satin gown befitting her royal beauty, showing it off for all to see. Nonetheless, she wore the crown not of her mother but her father, asserting full rights of kingship. Fortinbras approached, amazed by the vision awaiting him, chuckling gently at the sight.

"What means our cousin," Hamlet asked with wry smile, "that he stares so wildly?"

"I fear thou art another counterfeit. And yet, in faith, thou bear'st thee like a true leader. But mine, I am sure thou art, who'ere or what ever you be. And thus I pledge love and loyalty to thee."

Precisely what Hamlet hoped to hear! "Love," she said, "like a Greek tragedian, wears many masks, reveals many faces."

"Before," Fortinbras admitted, "I loved thee as a brother. Now, I accept thee as my sister."

Ophelia, having cast off her shroud of mourning and slipped into a simple white sheath, appeared next. "As do I!" she informed Hamlet, embracing her.

"What?" Hamlet asked, merrily winking. "She who would have bade me to her boudoir days ago?"

Ophelia blushed. "My lord, so please you, these things further considered: Think of me as sister, not as wife."

"Madam, I am most apt to embrace your offer."

Ophelia hugged Hamlet tightly before gliding back to Fortinbras' side. He took her hand; they gazed into one another's eyes. "I am joined with nobility!" she giddily exclaimed to each and all.

Horatio arrived, taking Hamlet's hand. Walking together as a foursome, the quartet approaching the drawbridge, cranked down for their benefit by several rude mechanicals. On the far side, nearly a thousand citizens—women and men, young and old—were held at bay by guards wielding long pikes. Tom, Dick, and Francis stepped forward from the crowd, chosen to address those even now exiting the castle. "Who will rule now?" Tom called out over all the shouting, as the crowd calmed, their roar subsiding.

"I, once our prince," Hamlet explained, "am now your sovereign." With a few catcalls from those unable to imagine a female ruler, most people cheered.

"What," Dick asked, "no king?"

"I grant I am a woman. But withal, a woman well-reputed."

"Strong enough to reign?" Francis wanted to know.

"Think you I am no stronger than my sex, being so father'd and husbanded?" With that, Hamlet nodded to Horatio, standing by her side.

In case some serious objection might be raised, Fortinbras bounded forward, glaring at all before him with fierce eyes that broached no argument. "As king of Norway, I say our lands will henceforth exist as sister states." That was all the Danes needed to hear; another cheer, louder and more enthusiastic than the first, went up.

"What of the recent rebellion?" Balthazar inquired.

"Some shall be pardoned," Hamlet insisted, "and some punished."

At that, Osric darted out from the crowd and hurried up to the drawbridge. "I never longed to hear a word 'til now," he wept to Hamlet. "Say 'pardon,' lord—"

"Lady," Hamlet corrected.

"King/queen, lady-lord; still, that word is short, but not so short as sweet."

"No word like 'pardon,' for rulers' mouths so meet. With Cain, go wander through the shades of night, and never show thy head again here, for wrong or right."

"Happily, I take my leave."

"You have good leave to leave us to our happiness."

As Osric rushed off, Tom raised a cup of ale in merry salute. "Many years of happy days befall my gracious sovereign, my most loving liege and lady, two in one."

Dick and Francis followed suit. "Each day still better other's happiness,' Dick called out.

"Until the heavens," Francis added, "envying earth's good hap, add an immortal talent to your eternal crown."

Now, it was Hamlet's turn: "We shall forthwith shake off our slavish yoke, imp out our drooping country's broken wing, redeem from pandering pawn the blemished crown."

More cheers, louder still than before. Then, Balthazar wanted to know: "Your first command?"

"Every one of this happy number that hath endured shrewd day and strange nights shall share the good of our returned fortune, according to the measure of their states. Meantime, forget all care, fall into rustic revelry."

That was the kind of regime all Danes could happily embrace. Momentarily, everyone could be seen making merry . . . singing, dancing, enjoying a makeshift celebration.

"Well begins these rites," Horatio observed.

"As we do trust they'll end," Hamlet said, "in true delights."

118.

While the people reveled, Hamlet shared with her companions the ways in which Denmark would forthwith be managed by its new and young regime. Having studied diverse strategies through which civilization had successfully asserted itself in southern Europe, Hamlet would apply everything she had so diligently learned at Wittenberge to the guidance of this, their own state . . .

Laws would be enacted, making it impossible for members of the royalty to ever again build up large estates which stretched across entire provinces. Instead, humble farmers would be forever guaranteed the right to own as well as manage small farms, providing such people with a sense of dignity that could only increase the intensity of their work and, in turn, the national productivity level.

Rotation of crops would keep such lands from being worn thin; beets, barley, wheat, rye, oats and potatoes would be raised on alternate stretches of farmland each year.

Fertilizers would help keep these fields rich and abundant.

Wet, wasted stretches of marshland would be drained; their waters carefully run off into reservoirs, there stored for use during the annual dry seasons.

Before any could drink this water, it would be boiled to insure health and safety.

Trees would, for the first time in Denmark's history, be planted along the edge of every beach, thus preventing sand from being blown inland and ruining farming lands.

Each time a grown tree was leveled for any purpose, a sapling must be planted to take its place for the benefit of future generations.

Those would be but the first edicts; others would follow, gradually transforming Sjalland into a modern state.

"Why, this is it," Fortinbras marveled, "when men are ruled by women?"

"Women will love her," Ophelia happily insisted, "that she is a woman of more worth than any man; men, that she is the rarest of all women."

"Give me your hands, all over, one by one," Hamlet gently commanded.

Each did as told. Hamlet carefully slipped the ring off Horatio's finger, handing it to Fortinbras, who in turn placed it on Ophelia's fourth-finger, right hand.

"When golden time converts," Hamlet concluded, "a solemn combination shall be made of our dear souls."

"And, now?" Horatio inquired.

"Come," Hamlet whispered, "we'll to bed. We four are married, but you two are sped."

How much they all loved one another! The foursome might yet prove 'modern,' Hamlet considered, in private as well as public. A quartet of highly attractive friends: her eager, nimble mind quickly counted the possibilities . . .

Each linking hands with the others, they turned their backs on the general merry-making, crossing over the bridge and back into Kronborg, there to while away the lazy afternoon in pleasurable mischief of their own inventive making.

119.

Watching from high atop their gypsy wagon, the Player King and his faithful Fool observed all that had happened on the field, even as their lackeys oiled the wheels and made ready to push on to the next castle, there to perform another show. Certain, its plot must be drawn from what had happened here; nothing had ever caught the players' imagination like Hamlet, the woman-prince, and her charmed circle of friends.

"In truth," the Player King admitted, "this was the strangest tale e're I heard."

Other members of their company, tucked away inside the wagon, shoved heads out windows as their six horses, snapped by the driver's reins, pushed forward and headed toward the woode. Each of the actors craved one last look at this land called Sjalland, a place none would soon forget.

"And, in good time," the Fool noted, "'twill be played by us, cousins to the mocking cuckoo bird."

"At least," the Player King sighed, "villainy in this land hath lost its sway, meeting check of such a grand-odd day."

"And since our hand in the business is done," the Fool noted as they circled round Helsinborg over an old trail, "let us move on, to perform this story for profit and fun."

"Oft said before," the Player King concluded with nary a backward glance, "yet still rings true as a bell; all's well that ends well."

Then, they were gone from sight of those ranging across the field before Kronborg on that glorious day in 1071. For on that afternoon, as carefully recorded in ancient volumes of lore, the Old Ways were banished forever and a modern era, augmented in southern lands nearly a century earlier at the millennium's onset, finally stretched as far north as Denmark. In due time, this new order of things—scientific, social, religious, and personal—would extend further still, up into the frozen reaches of Sweden and Norway, until in time the modern way of living would be accepted in all those lands that make up Europe, and by all the many and diverse groups of people inhabiting them.

The End

ABOUT THE AUTHOR:

DOUGLAS BRODE is the author of twenty-five books on mass media, the performing arts, cinema aesthetics and popular culture. Most famous among them is SHAKESPEARE IN THE MOVIES (Oxford University Press). Other volumes include in-depth studies of actors Denzel Washington, Robert De Niro, and Jack Nicholson; directors Steven Spielberg and Woody Allen; such genres as gangster films, psychological thrillers, and erotic movies; and studies of several key decades (the 1950s and 1980s) in film history. The translation of such works into numerous languages for international publication ranks Brode alongside Leonard Maltin and Roger Ebert as one of the most widely read experts on the Hollywood film. Brode's controversial interpretations of famous films have earned him an international cult following and comparison to such legendary iconoclastic critics as Raymond Durgnat, Manny Farber, and Parker Tyler.

Brode grew up on Long Island in the shadow of New York City. Following graduation from the State University of New York, Geneseo, in 1965, he went 'on the road,' motorcycling across America and hitchhiking around much of the world. In the late sixties, he married and settled down in Syracuse, New York. He has since divided his time between working as a radio announcer, theatre critic, regional-theatre actor, TV talkshow host, award-winning journalist and college professor. Still an educator, Brode teaches film courses at Syracuse University's Newhouse School of Public Communications and serves as coordinator of the Cinema Studies program at Onondaga College, Syracuse. He is listed in the 2004 edition of *Who's Who Among American Teachers*.

Several recent releases from KINO Video International include Brode's commentaries as liner notes for their *Silent Shakespeare* DVD series. Brode has lectured on aspects of classical cinema and popular culture in places as diverse as the Hudson Valley Film Festival near Lake George, New York, and the International Literary Festival in Aspen, Colorado. Leading newspapers, including the *New York Times* and the *Washington Post*, regularly cite his opinions on the relationship of mass media to modern society. His commentaries are also included in many installments of the Bravo channel's "Profiles" series and A & E's "Biography." Popular magazines that have published his work include *Rolling Stone* and *TV Guide*. Brode's analyses have also appeared in more academic journals such as *Cineaste* and *Television Quarterly*.

Two of his original plays, *Heartbreaker* and *Somewhere in the Night*, have been professionally produced. Brode's screenplay *Midnight Blue* (filmed by the Motion Picture Corporation of America, released on home video by Orion) was hailed by one reviewer as "the best of the low-budget erotic thrillers." Upcoming projects include two volumes on Walt Disney for the University of Texas Press, Austin, to be followed by a study of western movies for that publisher. Brode will also edit a commemorative anthology of essays on *Annie Hall* for Cambridge University Press. As we go to press, he is concluding work on *Elvis Cinema*, a serious study of the Presley musicals, for McFarland.

Sweet Prince is Douglas Brode's long-awaited first novel.